SF Books

LOST STARSHIP SERIES:
The Lost Starship
The Lost Command
The Lost Destroyer
The Lost Colony
The Lost Patrol
The Lost Planet
The Lost Earth
The Lost Artifact
The Lost Star Gate
The Lost Supernova

DOOM STAR SERIES:
Star Soldier
Bio Weapon
Battle Pod
Cyborg Assault
Planet Wrecker
Star Fortress
Task Force 7 (Novella)

Visit VaughnHeppner.com for more information

The Lost Supernova
(Lost Starship Series 10)

By Vaughn Heppner

Illustration © Tom Edwards
TomEdwardsDesign.com

Copyright © 2019 by the author.

This book is a work of fiction. Names, characters, places and incidents are either products of the author's imagination or used fictitiously. Any resemblance to actual events, locales or persons, living or dead, is entirely coincidental. All rights reserved. No part of this publication can be reproduced or transmitted in any form or by any means, without permission in writing from the author.

ISBN: 978-1094850610
BISAC: Fiction / Science Fiction / Military

-PROLOGUE-

The world shook as asteroids rained upon the surface. The planet's tectonic plates trembled and had already begun shifting. Hot magma seethed and sloshed below the continental crust as if knowing the hour approached when it could flow upon the land.

The eruptions would destroy everything, including the underground Great Machine that had survived the era of the Builders and the Ska-driven Nameless Ones with their awful Destroyers.

Puny primates were bringing about this planetary destruction. The humans had formed an arrogant military order known as Star Watch. Their so-called Grand Fleet had smashed the Spacer armada protecting the star system and had annihilated the surface primary beams, using hellburners and thermonuclear-tipped missiles to do so.

Even now, another brace of asteroids towed and released by Star Watch battleships screamed through the stratosphere, heading down. When the next asteroids struck—

Inside the planet, a giant octopoid-like creature slithered madly through unbelievably deep, subterranean corridors. He had a whale-sized blob for a body and many thrashing tentacles, propelling him faster and faster. His intellect and primordial powers dwarfed the creatures from the Commonwealth of Planets. That these gnat-like humans with their toy warships should cause his death infuriated the entity.

His name was Nay-Yog-Yezleth, and he was a Yon-Soth, otherwise known as an Old One from the dawn time of the universe. He had awakened after an eon of slumber and ingested invigorating varth elixir given him by the Spacers. He had striven to revitalize his father five thousand light-years away so that the nightmare reign of the Old Ones could begin anew.

As inconceivable as it sounded, the plot had failed. Worse, Star Watch had learned of his existence. That was why the Grand Fleet had come to the Forbidden Planet, to eliminate him.

How could this be happening to such a unique being as himself?

Nay-Yog-Yezleth slithered into a grand chamber kilometers below the surface. It was hot down here, and greasy droplets of sweat oozed from his rubbery skin.

Knowing he might only have minutes left, Nay-Yog-Yezleth activated a hallucination machine, a primitive one unbelievably ancient in age and design. It enraged him beyond speech to think that he had to resort to this in order to gain revenge upon the human race in such a slipshod manner.

His long tentacles thrashed anew, this time in exact sequences as he pulled levers and tapped buttons.

The hallucination machine began to hum as screens flashed on, showing him a hundred different worlds and many weird situations.

As his ring of eyes studied images, he concentrated his vast intellect, rushing to devise a scheme that would achieve his vengeance.

Then, it came to him. Yes, yes, what a wonderful idea, oh, such a glorious revenge. There were forces and thoughts, undercurrents and reactions throughout the realm known as Human Space and the fringe areas of the Beyond circling the small region of the interstellar void that held terrible secrets waiting to spawn anew. If he could but awaken one of them...

The ignorant humans thought of themselves as the masters of the universe, but they were so laughably wrong. Why, without the destruction of a few paltry Builder nexuses a short time ago, the Imperial Swarm would have soon annihilated the weak race of hominids.

In these few precious moments as the asteroids rushed to bring about his extinction, Nay-Yog-Yezleth did not dwell on how he and his father had hoped to use the Swarm Imperium to further their ends. That dream was over—forever—unless *other* Old Ones had survived the millennias to this new era of small beings and weak minds.

He checked a scope, seeing the fiery tails of asteroids as they plunged through the thickening atmosphere to strike the planetary surface.

Nay-Yog-Yezleth refused to dwell on his coming demise. That would simply be too awful. He had lived for so very long, so long indeed. To die to these wretched primates was more than he could bear.

Thus, he concentrated on his revenge, on the wonderful plan of their destruction. It would take a few more adjustments to make it work.

His slippery tentacles thrashed and slapped in seeming random order and in speeds almost impossible to discern. Fortunately, his vast inhuman intellect guided his many appendages.

The hallucination machine thrummed with exotic forms of energy, sending out pulses of ethereal quantum E7 rays.

The machine was ancient beyond reckoning, but was based upon primal Yon-Soth technology, which was, practically speaking, "magic" to the ignoramuses of this era. The rays moved at the speed of thought, emanating from the machine.

The tentacles slapped faster yet.

Nay-Yog-Yezleth concentrated the EQE7 rays at several groups of intelligent beings—were they *all* actual life forms in the accepted sense of the idea?

Unfortunately, Nay-Yog-Yezleth had run out of time to ponder that question.

He manipulated the machine as he programmed a complex set of hallucinations for each group. These hallucinations or delusions would drive the entities to predictable actions. The actions should combine into the destruction of the human race. Certainly, that destruction would not occur with the speed and suddenness of slamming asteroids, but the extermination of the human race—in all its variable forms—would happen in a short span of time. Say…four years at the most.

Nay-Yog-Yezleth might have enjoyed chortling in evil glee at his masterwork of vengeance. He was too busy working in order to make sure that his hasty plan would succeed with brutal efficiency for him to indulge himself.

Thus, deep underground in his subterranean fortress, the Old One continued to manipulate the ancient machine as one asteroid after another crashed upon the already heaving crust of the Forbidden Planet. The asteroids added incredible forces to the tectonic plates. Those plates finally shifted violently. As even more asteroids rained upon the quaking surface, the deepest plates cracked and surged. The magma in the mantle raced upward, spewing hot lava onto the surface. Gigantic cracks appeared. In seconds, the quaking and cracking became a worldwide event.

In his subterranean fortress, Nay-Yog-Yezleth died as a torrent of lava burst into his chamber, killing him and melting the ancient machine.

The reign of the Old One on the Forbidden Planet was over. The crews in the battleships in orbital space did not know that. Thus, the towing and releasing of asteroids would continue for another eight days.

At the end of that time, Admiral Fletcher and what was left of the Grand Fleet would begin the voyage home.

Meanwhile, the EQE7 rays continued for a little longer to shift the brain patterns of carefully if hastily selected entities. These entities were varied, but each group would be part of the vengeance puzzle that would soon begin to squeeze their targets to dreadful effect.

-1-

EIGHT MONTHS LATER

Lord High Admiral Cook squirmed uncomfortably in his chair. The Lord High Admiral was a big old man. He wore a white Star Watch uniform and had a swath of thick white hair and leathery features.

He did not like what he was hearing. He did not like it one bit. Frankly, it was a mistake. In his opinion, it was a terrible mistake. The question was—did he dare to tell the new Prime Minister of the Commonwealth of Planets the truth?

Cook sat before a large table, facing three people. They were in a huge ornate room in Stockholm, as this was part of the great Governing Council Complex where the elected delegates from a hundred worlds made policy for the Commonwealth.

Incoming Prime Minister Daniel Hampton—who had the greatest number of elected councilors on the Great Council—was in his late forties. He was an energetic Vegan—a man from Vega II—with wavy red hair, and was using his famously engaging smile as he explained the new policy to Cook. Prime Minister Hampton had proven terrific at speaking in public and private. He had been talking to Cook for some time already. No doubt, the Prime Minister believed he was softening the blow, as it were.

Hampton's chief political advisor sat on his left. Many of the keenest observers believed this man had been responsible for Hampton's election to the highest office in Human Space.

The political advisor was a dour bald man with stooped shoulders. He wore a half-rumpled suit and seemed to be a crotchety, muttering old man more than a political wizard. Still, the advisor was full of statistics and known for his unbending will. In truth, Bill "Get 'Em" Sanders had run the election and had already begun running the new administration. He did so because he usually convinced the Prime Minister that his way was the best way.

The last of the three was a stunning beauty. She sat on Prime Minister Hampton's right and had been introduced as Doctor Lisa Meyers. She was in her mid-thirties but looked as if someone had frozen her at a perfect twenty-five. She was tall and elegant with her long dark hair done up in a towering wrap above her head. She was so slender as to be almost gaunt, and she seldom smiled. Her eyes might have been the most beautiful thing about her, as they had a piercing quality when she fixed her gaze on a person or object.

Cook knew little about her. She had proven a mystery to his prep aides in Star Watch Intelligence. During the meeting, Meyers had watched him much too keenly, stirring a lust the old admiral had thought long gone in him. Meyers had also jotted notes on a pad laid on the table in a lawyerly fashion.

Prime Minister Hampton finally stopped talking, looking expectantly at Cook as he used his supposedly dazzling smile to prod the admiral.

Cook knew he should say something, but he was still absorbing the Prime Minister's ideas and hadn't decided yet if he could follow them.

"Well?" Prime Minister Hampton finally asked.

"I'm not sure, sir," Admiral Cook managed to say.

"You're not sure about *what?*" Hampton asked.

Cook took a deep breath and decided he needed to stick to the truth. "I don't know if it's a good idea, sir."

Hampton stared at him as the engaging smile slowly drained away. Finally, the Prime Minister broke eye contact and turned to "Get 'Em" Sanders.

"Please elaborate, Admiral," Sanders said gruffly.

"We finally have peace," Cook said, addressing the advisor. "These past years, Star Watch has taken heavy ship losses too many times, particularly in this last battle against the Old One."

"Yes…" Sanders said, his eyes smoldering as he studied Cook. "I've gone over the reports about the orbital assault against the… the *Forbidden Planet*. Do you truly expect us to believe that some ancient…*monster* aided the Spacers?"

Cook wished he had Brigadier Mary O'Hara with him, but she was on permanent leave because Star Watch didn't know how badly she'd been compromised by the Bosks.

"Admiral?" Sanders demanded. "Did you hear what I just asked you?"

Cook cleared his throat. He was beginning to dislike Sanders. How dare the chief advisor address him as if he was a first-year cadet?

"Of course I expect you to believe the reports," Cook said, "as they're true."

"Really," Sanders said in a biting tone. "Did anyone happen to see the ancient *Old One?*"

Cook drummed thick fingers on the table. Now that he thought about it, had anyone seen the—?

"Captain Maddox and his wife Meta saw a Yon-Soth—an Old One," Cook answered. "They saw the creature in a nexus in the Sagittarius Spiral Arm—"

"Lord High Admiral," Sanders said, interrupting him. "That isn't even the issue. The real point is that Admiral Fletcher took horrifying fleet losses in the battle of the Forbidden Planet System. Combined with the massive ship losses from the initial Swarm Invasion, Star Watch is woefully weak at this critical juncture. We need time for our industrial base to construct new warships and time to train new personnel to fill those ships."

Cook blinked several times. Was the advisor hard of hearing? "That's exactly my point," the admiral said. "We need time, and that means we need peace so we can rebuild our fleet strength. We also need time so that countless Commonwealth planets can recover after the repeated shocks these past few years."

Dour old Sanders frowned and glanced at Doctor Meyers.

That surprised Cook. Wouldn't Sanders have glanced at Prime Minister Hampton for support? What was the connection between the gorgeous Meyers and Sanders?

Sanders adjusted his creased tie and brushed his left hand over his bald head before he concentrated on Cook again.

"I fail to understand your objection to the Prime Minister's order," Sanders said. "It sounds as if we both want the same thing."

"Sir," Cook said, leaning minutely forward as he addressed the Prime Minister. "May I speak frankly?"

"You may," Sanders said, without looking at the Prime Minister to gain permission.

Cook frowned for just a moment. Then, he began to choose his words with care as he spoke to the Prime Minister.

"The Commonwealth has peace, maybe real peace for the first time in a long time. Throughout these past years we've faced a New Man invasion, androids trying to take over, a Destroyer from the Nameless Ones smashing the Wahhabi Caliphate and hitting Earth, among other places. We've had a massive Swarm Invasion Fleet attack us, and a smaller one later. We've had planetary systems engaging in open rebellion. We're still trying to absorb the caliphate planets and Windsor League worlds that joined the Commonwealth. We've had a dramatic increase in piracy—"

"I know all these things," Sanders snapped, interrupting.

Once more, Lord High Admiral Cook blinked several times, mastering himself. He wasn't used to a little prick like Sanders interrupting him so rudely as he tried to make a point. Why did the Prime Minister allow this? Just who was running the show here?

Cook scowled—and that made Doctor Meyers sit just a little straighter, if that was possible.

Cook glanced at her, noting the way she watched him, how her dark eyes glittered with fantastic sex appeal. The old admiral actually felt his groin stir as if he was a teenager again. While she was striking and highly desirable, there was something more that troubled him about her. Yes. She was like a shark waiting to attack.

Just where had Hampton found her?

Cook inhaled and exhaled several times to calm himself and get back on track.

"You say that you know all these things," Cook said, addressing Sanders. "Yet, you want me to stir the pot and possibly make trouble for ourselves." He couldn't do it anymore and faced the Prime Minister. "Begging your pardon, sir, that strikes me as damn stupid."

Sanders' bald head jerked up. He swiveled to look across at Doctor Meyers.

The Prime Minister must have noticed, because Hampton also looked at stunning, statuesque Lisa Meyers.

"I'm not sure," she said.

Cook's eyes widened. He hadn't heard her speak until now, and her voice was amazingly, throatily sensuous. Why, he wanted to reach over and rip off her—

The Lord High Admiral had will power, a considerable amount, in fact. He used it now, not allowing his lustful desires to sidetrack him.

Not yet, anyway.

"You're not sure about what?" Cook forced himself to say.

It was possible the corners of her mouth quirked up the tiniest fraction, but maybe it was the admiral's imagination. She did arch her eyebrows at him before turning to the Prime Minister.

"Sir?" she asked Hampton.

"What do you think, Bill?" the Prime Minister asked Sanders. "Should we tell him?"

Sanders used his right forefinger to stroke a cheek.

"Tell me what?" Cook asked.

"Yes," Sanders said. "Go ahead. Tell him. It's time."

Prime Minister Hampton turned to the woman.

Meyers opened a purse that had been in her lap. Incredibly, she drew a small black gun from it and set the gun on the table. She kept her right hand on it, her forefinger touching the trigger.

"Do you plan to shoot me?" Cook asked, stunned at this development.

"One word," Sanders said, "and your career is over. Don't doubt we have the political muscle to do it."

Cook looked askance at dour old Sanders. The Prime Minister's chief political advisor stared right back at him, daring him to do something.

Troubled, and still wondering about the gun, the Lord High Admiral broke eye contact with Sanders. "Mr. Prime Minister, could you tell me what this is about?"

Hampton wouldn't look at him, but the man finally nodded. "Tell him, Bill," the new Prime Minister said. "Tell him what this is about."

-2-

Grumpy Bill Sanders intertwined his fingers and turned his hands so his palms faced Cook. The crotchety old man cracked his fingers all at once, leaning back in his chair and letting his hands drop onto the table.

"Who rules the Commonwealth?" Sanders asked suddenly.

"Why...the Great Council, of course," Cook said.

"Do you believe that the Prime Minister heads the Great Council?" Sanders asked.

"Naturally," Cook said. "Why would you think I believed otherwise?"

"Come, come, Admiral," Sanders said. "You must have watched the elections. During the last few years, Star Watch, which means you, did exactly as you saw fit. You made key decisions that rightfully belonged to the Prime Minister or the Council on Foreign Relations. While it is true that during some of those times we had martial law, those times have certainly passed."

"I'm well aware of that," Cook said, angry now that Doctor Meyers had threatened him.

"*Are* you aware?" Sanders asked.

Cook opened his mouth to retort.

"Don't answer that," Sanders said. "It was a rhetorical question. Many believe that you are the real leader of the Commonwealth, as Star Watch does pretty much what it wants to do. Well, this administration isn't going to stand for that,

Admiral. We are returning to civilian control, to legally elected authority."

"We've never left that," Cook said.

"To break your hold on the Prime Minister's rightful authority is one of the reasons why he brought Doctor Meyers to the meeting."

Cook looked at Meyers in renewed astonishment as she raised the gun and aimed it at him.

"You plan to murder me?" Cook asked, more angry than frightened.

"As I've told you," Sanders said, "the Commonwealth will have civilian control once again. If that means shooting a tyrant—yes, Doctor Meyers will murder you, as you put it."

"This is the thanks I get for all I've done?" Cook asked, working to keep the sudden bitterness out of his voice.

"This is a precaution," Sanders said. "We are a new administration. Often, the old guard feels it can do as it pleases as a new administration gains its feet. Well, sir, Prime Minister Hampton is going to hit the ground running, as the old saying goes. We want to know one thing. Will you obey the Prime Minister's lawful orders?"

"Star Watch defends the Commonwealth," Cook said thickly. "We are not the rulers, but the soldiers who obey the lawful authority."

Sanders turned to Meyers "Well?" he asked.

"I'm not sure," she said.

"Not sure about *what?*" Cook demanded, becoming angrier.

She turned to him, her dazzling eyes aglitter, and this time it was obvious. The corners of her mouth quirked up in a predatory way. How many men had she chewed up and spit out, broken to her whims?

"I'm not sure if you're telling us the truth," she told him.

"Mr. Prime Minister," Cook said, outraged at this slander.

Hampton spread his hands and gave him the telegenic smile that had won him so many votes. "Doctor Meyers is a top-rated psychologist," he said. "She is particularly adept at spotting lies."

"You don't need to explain yourself to him, sir," Sanders told the Prime Minister.

"I-I feel compelled to do so," Hampton said.

Doctor Meyers turned sharply to the Prime Minister. "Compelled in what way, sir?" she asked.

"His conscience is bothering him," Cook said, unable to keep his mouth shut. "Both of you might try developing one in yourselves."

"Ah," she said, certainly mocking him. Despite that, with a clunk, she placed the gun on the table.

Prime Minister Hampton was now looking away.

The same could not be said for Sanders. The bald old man glared at the Lord High Admiral.

"You are a powerful man," Sanders told Cook. "You also have a forceful personality. In my opinion, you have built a cult of personality in Star Watch. If we let you stay on, that is going to change."

Cook nearly offered his resignation right there. But he held his tongue. He had worked tirelessly to save humanity from various alien threats, and this was the thanks he got? Their treatment enraged him. He was not going to go quietly into the night of oblivion.

Several times, Admiral Cook opened his mouth to retort hotly, and each time, he closed his mouth and waited.

"He will obey the Prime Minister," Meyers said into the silence. "He doesn't like us. He really doesn't like you, Mr. Sanders, but he's not a tyrant as you believed earlier."

Sanders glared at her.

Doctor Meyers coolly returned it.

"Clever," Sanders muttered. Then he seemed to dismiss her in his thoughts as he once more regarded the admiral.

"The Commonwealth needs time," Sanders told Cook, seeming to switch mental gears. "We need stability over a long period so we can rebuild to even greater strength than before. Our greatest threat is the New Men. To that end, we must know more about them. We must send an ambassadorial delegation to the Throne World and make binding treaties with them. They are a mystery, Admiral. That is unacceptable. We cannot allow them to prepare in secret for another invasion against us."

Cook was looking at the gun on the table. He couldn't believe they had threatened to shoot him.

"The gun is a symbol," Meyers said suddenly.

"What?" Cook asked.

"It is a symbol," she said. "The threat wasn't your death, but the end of your career in Star Watch."

"It isn't loaded?" Cook asked.

With a sensual move, Meyers shoved the gun across the table to him.

"Mr. Prime Minister," Sanders complained.

Cook picked up the small black gun and pressed a switch so the magazine dropped out. He checked. The magazine was empty. He slid open the chamber. There was no bullet waiting to fire.

"It was a prop," Meyers purred.

Cook shoved the gun and magazine at Sanders, forcing the stoop-shouldered grump to catch them.

"You want time," the Lord High Admiral said, with anger in his voice. "Then, leave the New Men alone for now. Don't kick the wasp's nest. Maybe you don't understand, but the New Men don't like or think much of us."

"We don't like them either, Admiral," Sander said. "In fact, if they really wanted peace, they should have returned our kidnapped women they took from the Thebes System."

Cook looked down at his old seamed hands, opening and closing them.

"He's doesn't agree with you," Meyers said.

"I can see that for myself," Sanders snapped. "You think the New Men deserve those kidnapped women, do you?" he asked Cook.

"Of course not," Cook growled, looking up. "The kidnapping was evil, vile, call it what you will. But there are realities in this world. The New Men are deadly. We need time to strengthen Star Watch before we make demands upon them."

"No," Sanders said. "We need to find them and see their world for ourselves. We need to know if they're going to suddenly attack us as they did once before or whether they truly mean to live in peace with us."

"Give me a year of peace, at least," Cook pleaded.

"I'll give you more than that," Sanders said. "You have done good work, Admiral. Yes. I admit it, and I can even respect it. What's more, you've become a symbol of stability to trillions of people throughout the Commonwealth. I—the Prime Minister isn't going to replace you if you can cooperate with the new administration. But after studying several secret reports, I believe that you've lost some of your former nerve. In this instance, you're letting the New Men set the pace, and that just isn't going to fly in the new administration."

"Oh," Cook managed to say.

"No," Sanders said. "So get on the horn with the Emperor, or whatever he calls himself. Inform him of the new realities and then report back to us as soon as the Emperor agrees to our demands."

"And if he disagrees to your...*requests?*" Cook asked.

"Pressure him. Let him know that if he doesn't willingly accept Commonwealth representatives, then we'll be sending out a fleet to find his precious Throne World. We are no longer going to allow those aggressors to plot against us in secret."

"Send out a fleet when we need to be rebuilding?" Cook asked.

Dour old Sanders sneered. "A threat isn't a deed. Besides, if nothing else, you can send *Victory* to hunt down the Throne World."

Cook said nothing, as he knew now that his opinion carried no weight with Sanders and thus with new Prime Minister Hampton. Maybe it was time to talk to the Prime Minister alone, at a different time. What hold, exactly, did Sanders have on Hampton? And did Doctor Meyers really judge him in a psychological sense?

"By the way," Sanders said. "You have just received a new Prime Ministerial liaison."

"What are you talking about?" asked Cook.

"The Prime Minister is sending an official liaison officer from his office. She will return with you to Star Watch Headquarters. The liaison officer is the first step our new administration is taking to help the Great Council maintain civilian control over the military."

"You're coming to HQ?" Cook asked, dismayed.

"You're not listening," Sanders said. "Doctor Meyers will join you, as she is the new liaison officer. Before making any high-level decisions, you are to consult with her."

Admiral Cook felt his face heat up. "You're trying to saddle me with a political commissioner?"

"Call it what you will," Sanders snapped. "Your days of doing as you like at Star Watch are over. From now on…we're going to be watching you in order to make sure that our policies are properly implemented."

For the second time today, Cook almost gave his resignation. This was an outrage. Yet, he refrained from saying the words, deciding that the fate of humanity was too precious to let Hampton and Sanders run Star Watch. If he wasn't careful, their new policy was going to restart an unneeded war with the New Men.

How could he word their foolish demand so the arrogant Emperor didn't take offense against those he considered his genetic inferiors?

This was going to be tricky.

-3-

Several days later, many hundreds of light-years away in the Beyond—as opposed to known Human Space—the Emperor of the New Men strode along a marble hall in his splendid palace on the Throne World.

The Emperor was a tall individual with golden skin, and wore a purple tunic. He was the greatest of the New Men, those genetic superiors as first conceived by Methuselah Men Strand and Professor Ludendorff. He was taller than average even among his own kind. And he was swifter, stronger and very much smarter than any who had challenged him for the crown.

The two Methuselah Men had long ago taken carefully selected colonists on a Thomas Moore Society expedition. The purpose and idea had been simple. The two Methuselah Men had not only known about many of the potential dangers facing humanity, but Strand and Ludendorff had known that mankind might well fail against the alien menaces waiting for them in the stars. Thus, they'd used selective breeding and genetic experimentation far out in the Beyond to create a race of Defenders. These Defenders would protect regular humanity against deadly alien menaces. They would appear at a time when mankind understood that it was doomed, and thus bring salvation and renewed hope. But by their existence, the Defenders would not create human dependency, because until the ripe moment, mankind wouldn't even know about them.

It had been a noble idea, but the flaw was in the New Men themselves, the so-called Defenders. In time, they realized that they were superior—which to them meant better—than regular humans were. The obvious question was, why should *they* risk their lives to defend inferior beings? If they were stronger, smarter, and faster—more worthy, in other words—than those they had come to conceive as the submen, why shouldn't *they* rule?

In other words, why shouldn't the lower order creatures work tirelessly to promote the superior beings? Thus, the New Men had used the better tech that Strand had given them to invade the Commonwealth of Planets and begin building kingdoms and satrapies for themselves and their posterity.

The one…imperfection of the New Men was critical to their suvival. The seed from their loins only produced boys, never girls. Thus, they had to periodically *acquire* new women for breeding purposes.

The latest "Sabine women" capture had been at the end of the invasion of C Quadrant.

In ancient history, the early Romans had begun as a settlement composed mostly of men. They had raided the Sabine people when the young women had been in the woods during a festival. The Romans had grabbed the women for wives and raced home. A war had begun, but in the end, the women had brought peace by pleading with their Sabine fathers and brothers not to slaughter their husbands and, in some cases, their newborn children.

Because Star Watch had fought so splendidly in defense of the Commonwealth, the New Men had retreated, finally arriving at the Thebes System in "C" Quadrant. During their former attacks, the New Men had captured worthy young women, taking them to the Thebes System. From there, the New Men had raced back to the Beyond, taking hundreds of thousands of nubile, carefully selected young beauties for their individual harems.

The idea of the Sabine-style kidnapping had driven Admiral Fletcher and Star Watch for quite some time. Fletcher with the Grand Fleet had attempted to find the Throne World and demand the return of the women. The first Swarm invasion had changed all that, as the New Men and Star Watch had allied against the greater threat. Although these days the

Swarm menace was and would be contained for the next several decades, Admiral Fletcher was no longer in service, having retired after the grueling battle at the Forbidden Planet. There was another thing. Star Watch was much weaker in terms of warship strength than previously, because of all the battle losses.

In any case, at the moment, the proud Emperor of the New Men strode through a special hall in his opulent palace. The Throne World was an Eden-like planet, discovered long ago by Methuselah Man Strand. The planet did not possess any cities, although it had many environmentally friendly factories and several spaceports. The tall Emperor with his handsome features and intense dark eyes passed an open arch. He glanced within, spying several young women splashing and playing together in a pool.

If the truth be known, the Emperor sympathized with the softliners among the Captains. The Captains were the royalty among the Dominants or Superiors, as New Men conceived of themselves. A Captain quite literally ran a star cruiser or had some other important post with military significance.

The Emperor was the greatest of the Captains and held his rank through several factors difficult for submen to understand. One factor was the ancient Roman virtue of gravitas, which implied seriousness or solemnity of manner. When the Emperor entered a room, others noticed his heavy demeanor and magnetic charisma. This allowed him to sway a majority of the Captains to his way of thinking most of the time, giving him greater influence. The Emperor had also achieved many notable athletic feats during war and on dangerous hunts. He was also the best duelist, killing every challenger in formal combat. While the Emperor did not command in the same way a dictator would in a submen police state, he might kill a Captain that challenged him too directly, and the others would accept such a deed as right and proper, if the kill was made during honorable combat.

Like many human groupings, among the Captains were two chief modes of thought concerning submen. The softliners believed submen could have human dignity. In this instance, the beauties swimming in the pool wore bathing suits instead of going naked, as a hardliner would have insisted. Hardliners considered submen little better than beasts, who obviously did not deserve clothing—one might as well put clothes on a dog or cow—and they did not ascribe to the idea that submen could possess human dignity.

The Emperor paused by the arch, enjoying the loveliness of his women. He raised a hand in greeting. They all stopped and waved back, smiling to show him their pleasure at being noticed.

The Emperor lowered his hand in a befitting manner and continued his journey to the communication chamber.

The pool chamber had seemed rather empty to him. He made a mental note to see if more of his women had become pregnant.

The Emperor smiled at the thought. He had sired close to one thousand sons. Many of those sons lived in and around the palace. When each came of age, the boy had to leave for a barracks to begin learning how to behave like a proper Superior.

The Emperor dismissed that from his mind, as he had serious business that he must attend to. He'd received a call from the Lord High Admiral of Star Watch. He had debated ignoring the call, but decided that the Lord High Admiral deserved…

Was that the right word for a subman such as Admiral Cook?

While the Emperor was a softliner, there were limits to the dignity he could offer an inferior being, even a notable one like Cook. The submen were clearly greater than beasts. Golden Ural had once pointed out in a meeting the humanness of the submen. A superior did not mate with an ape, as that would be bestiality. New Man law stated that a man should die for sexual deviancy. No. A superior mated with a lower order of human, certainly, but a human after a fashion.

The Lord High Admiral was unusual for a subman. The old admiral almost had gravitas.

The Emperor shrugged, took a turn and headed for another arch.

The Lord High Admiral had a long-range communication device. The Emperor also possessed one. There were a few others in and around Human Space, and they allowed communication hundreds of light-years apart.

What did the Lord High Admiral want this time? The Emperor sighed. The Swarm Imperium no longer menaced either of them. The great danger of extinction had passed for the moment. Would the submen now make outrageous demands, thinking themselves worthy of respect?

The Emperor planned to keep the peace with the Commonwealth. He hoped Cook didn't say something that would enrage the hardliners beyond what he could control.

The Emperor ducked his head as he passed under an arch, eyed the bulky comm device and headed for a chair. He did not look forward to this chore of talking to an inferior, being tainted by it.

He sat, picked up the microphone, sighed once more and clicked the main device…

-4-

"This is the Lord High Admiral Cook speaking, your Highness," the subman said through a receiver.

The Emperor made a face and pressed a button on the microphone.

"Hello, Admiral. What do you want?"

"I would first like to congratulate you on—"

"Admiral," the Emperor said, interrupting. "This is…get to the point."

Cook took his time speaking again.

The Emperor scowled. Was this a deliberate affront? A second possibility suddenly occurred to him. Could the subman have been offended because he believed that the Emperor had spoken abruptly? Could Cook have believed that the Emperor—a Superior—had been rude to him?

If that was true, then the submen were becoming far too uppity in their thinking. That could prove troublesome for the future.

"Your Highness," Cook said. "The Prime Minister of the Commonwealth of Planets desires me to…to *inquire* on certain matters between us."

"This call is a mere indulgence of your simian curiosity?" the Emperor asked, astonished at the impertinence of the subman.

"I would not say that, Sire."

"Then say what you mean, Admiral. My time is limited."

There was another pause. The Emperor was beginning to find them infuriating. What was wrong with the subman? Had Cook entered a stage of increasing senility? It seemed more than possible.

"Sire," Cook said, "would you agree that we have achieved a united moment of peace?"

"You dare to query me as if I were your inferior?" the Emperor asked, shocked to the core at this outrage.

"No, no, Sire. Together, we have beaten the Swarm menace—"

"We did nothing together. That you would even imply such a thing—"

"Sire," Cook said, interrupting.

The Emperor's intense eyes narrowed dangerously at this new affront.

"The Swarm menace has passed for the moment," Cook said in a rush. "Your people destroyed Builder nexuses and so did our people."

"Yes… That is true."

"That has given each of us a moment of peace."

"Agreed," the Emperor said, wishing the subman would get to the point.

"Prime Minister Hampton rejoices in the peace and desires to…to prolong it between us."

"I'm overjoyed he feels this way," the Emperor said as he stared up at the ceiling. This was taxing beyond belief. He wasn't sure how much more he could take of this.

"In the interest of peace," Cook said, "the Prime Minister would like to exchange ambassadors with you."

The Emperor's gaze slowly came to the long-range communicator and the microphone in his fist. "This Prime Minister wishes to send submen to the Throne World? Is that what you're suggesting?"

"No, Sire," Cook said.

"But you just—"

"Prime Minister Hampton of the Commonwealth of Planets wishes to send a fully accredited ambassador to the Throne World. That would entail an ambassadorial party, which would include a Star Watch security team. Furthermore, we ask that a...a New Man delegation set up permanent shop on Earth."

"You want me to send people to...mingle among you as equals?"

"Ambassadors, Sire," Cook said. "We wish to exchange ambassadors in order to forestall any misunderstandings among our peoples."

"No," the Emperor said.

"Excuse me, Sire?"

"Tell this Prime Minister of yours no. I decline his offer."

There was another pause of some length.

"Is that it then?" the Emperor asked.

"No, Sire," Cook said slowly. "Since you reject the ambassadorial offer, we would like the coordinates to the Throne World."

"What did you say?"

"My government wishes to know the location of the Throne World. We will then send a delegation in order to confirm that you are not outfitting another invasion fleet against us."

The Emperor's hand tightened around the microphone until the knuckles whitened. "Are you threatening me?" he asked softly.

"I am not, Sire. I am stating my government's...desire."

"You submen have grown overbold, Admiral."

"Sire, may I speak frankly?"

"You should always speak truthfully. Why do you ask my permission not to lie?"

"I have been truthful, Sire. I request that you ready yourself to hear a few hard truths."

"You *are* threatening me."

"I will not call it a threat, Sire. I wish for peace between us, as that is in both our interests. However, you invaded the Commonwealth not so very long ago. We beat you back. But you—not you personally, but your commander—kidnapped millions of Commonwealth citizens. Our government wants to know when you will return them."

"Never," the Emperor said. "We took the women and some slave workers as spoils of war."

"That is going to be a sticking point between our governments, Sire."

"Have a care, Admiral. Do not threaten me or demand what you cannot take. The Throne World is where it is. No," the Emperor said, shutting down Cook as the admiral attempted to speak once more. "I know you're going to tell me that you intend to send a fleet to find the Throne World. Attempt that at your peril, Admiral. Our territory is sacrosanct. We have peace between our realms. I intend to keep the peace. Do not then give me orders that will destroy such peace and bring doom upon your inferior species."

"I am relaying my government's desires, Sire."

"As a servant, it would seem."

"As the senior soldier of the Commonwealth," Cook said.

"Are you done?"

"I ask that you consider what I've said."

"It would be better that you beg me to forget these base affronts, lest I believe that you've insulted me."

"I do not beg that, Sire."

"I am done with you," the Emperor said. And he shut off the communication device before Cook could say more to enrage him.

Still, as the Emperor set the microphone on the table, he realized that this was going to complicate matters. The submen had become uppity indeed. They were overreaching because they had achieved a few successes in the wider universe.

The Emperor knew the Throne World wasn't ready for another war against the Commonwealth, not for another seven years, at least. But to listen to a subman verbally strutting and boasting—

The Emperor stood, turned suddenly and strode from the communication chamber. It was time to call a Captain's Meeting. He had to head this off before the hardliners made an incident of it, and he had to teach the submen a lesson quickly to remind them of their place.

It might be good to speak to Lord Drakos before such a meeting, as Drakos was the unofficial leader of the hardliners. Just where was Drakos right now? He'd better find him soon before the submen and the Superiors stumbled into a new and unneeded war.

***

Try as he might, the Emperor of the Throne World could not find Lord Drakos or anyone who could tell him the Superior's whereabouts. If any of the hardliners knew where Drakos had gone, they were not saying.

The Emperor finally decided to keep the fact of the Lord High Admiral's call secret for the time being. It would take Star Watch time to outfit a fleet to come looking for the Throne World. Until then, he—the Emperor—needed to find Drakos.

Yes... Something was definitely amiss with the hardliner. The Emperor's keenly honed senses were seldom wrong in that regard. Drakos had become reckless lately and had been stung hard more than a few months ago because of it. Could the arrogant Superior have already shrugged off the incident with Captain Maddox or had it driven Drakos to even greater folly?

The Emperor believed it was imperative that he find the answer to these questions soon.

-5-

Lord Drakos was an unusual New Man in several prominent physical ways. He was shorter than the normally towering superior. He had broader shoulders and less of a golden hue to his skin. Some thought that meant he wasn't as genetically fit. Others suggested that was why Drakos demanded genetic purity in everything, because he secretly doubted it in himself. Perhaps he felt that a bold front on the matter might forestall a too keen inquiry into him.

If Drakos believed that, he'd never said so. He was not short per se, certainly not compared to a regular human, and his skin golden indeed. But compared to his own exalted kind, he was considered short and pale.

In spite of that, or maybe because of it—Lord Drakos had not undergone psychological evaluation such as the Lord High Admiral had—he had seething ambitions worthy of any dominant, perhaps even more so. He had used recent information from the Methuselah Man Strand, who was presently in the Emperor's prison. How Drakos had achieved the meeting and gotten Strand to talk to him was still a mystery.

Drakos certainly wasn't going to tell anyone the secret.

As the Emperor had noted, more than a few months ago, Drakos had evaded capture by the hateful Captain Maddox. Alas, Drakos had been unable to prevent Star Watch from utterly conquering the planet Bosk. That was unfortunate, because Drakos had had many hidden operatives on the planet when Star Watch hit.

Still, the vaunted Star Watch and its keen Intelligence arm hadn't picked up his deepest-laid agents. That had been due to the information collected from the former boss of Star Watch Intelligence, Brigadier Mary O'Hara.

Drakos rubbed his strong hands together as he paced on the bridge of his star cruiser. If he'd known that the Emperor wondered about his present whereabouts, he might have laughed in harsh glee. Drakos viewed the Emperor and all softliners as mentally weak.

The star cruiser had Strand's former stealth capacity, presently moving without any of the submen's knowledge. In fact, Drakos was having cloaking devices installed in all the star cruisers beholden to him. That happened on a base deep in the Beyond, in submen terms. This star cruiser was in the Vega System, which was twenty-five light-years from Earth.

The Vega star was a tenth of the age of the Sun and twice as massive. Because of its young galactic age, the system still had a circumstellar disc, a pancake or ring-shaped accumulation of gas, dust, planetesimals and asteroids around it in the region of its distant Kuiper Belt.

Drakos was secretly moving through the Vega System partly to implement several finishing touches to an ultra-secret stealth campaign in the localized area. In this instance, that meant approximately a seven-light-year diameter with the Vega System as the central point. The stealth campaign was part of a larger plan, which only a few of his closest hardliner allies had any inkling existed.

A portion of the plan had to do with the unsettling fact that Captain Maddox had almost captured him more than a few months ago in the Balak System. That had been 9.4 light-years from the Bosk homeworld. The ambush had occurred in orbit around a heavy-metal water moon that circled a gas giant.

Drakos's smile slipped upon his wider than average face. The Star Watch operation had been far too close a call, and it had forced him to ask the Emperor for protection. That request had cost him several key political advantages via the softliners, retarding his present efforts.

The powerful Superior shook his head. Drakos wasn't going to dwell on the past. He had made a mistake. A wise man admitted such, at least to himself. Whatever, when the time came, he would take care of Maddox. Oh yes, he had more than a few surprises for Maddox and that pesky starship and crew of his. Some time ago, Drakos's agents had mentally dominated Brigadier Mary O'Hara, learning valuable information that he was already putting to good use.

There was a secondary reason why he was in the Vega System that might prove primary depending on what he found.

Drakos marched to the main viewing screen, stood there and turned, marching to the command chair. He did not sit. He could not sit just now. Like many New Men, Drakos had an energetic impatience. Energy and fire coursed through his veins, making it impossible for him to sit still long. A Superior acted forcefully. He did not sit in the shadows and wait, like Strand used to do.

Drakos frowned.

Strand had chuckled at him once concerning his seething energy.

Drakos shook his head more emphatically than before. If he—

"Lord," the helmsman said.

Drakos whirled around to face the tall Superior.

"I have detected a slight trace of 'E' radiation, Lord. The trace means it is an old path."

"A stellar trail?" asked Drakos.

The tall helmsman tapped his board, finally looking up again. "Yes, Lord," he said, "a cold one, but a trail nevertheless."

"Where does it go?"

"It is faint, as I've said, Lord."

"Do not play games with me, Cleon."

"No, Lord," the one named Cleon said. He manipulated his board further. "The trace heads out-system."

"As far as the circumstellar disc?" asked Drakos.

"I believe so, Lord."

Drakos clapped his hands and laughed harshly. "E" radiation inevitably had a specific source. Until the first Swarm Invasion, no ship had given off such radiation.

The old trail indicated…

Drakos refused to even think the name lest he induce bad luck. He wasn't superstitious, but there was no reason in taking pointless chances.

"Lord," the weapons officer said. "I have detected an incoming shuttle."

They were in an asteroid belt between the inner and outer system, close to a small asteroid several kilometers long.

Drakos nodded. One of his key secret agents was heading to a preselected rendezvous point. The agent was obedient, which was something of a surprise, as this agent was a Spacer.

Drakos moved to his command chair. He would sit for several minutes, making a show of thinking. Then he would summon the agent and speak to the man in a side room. He had many instructions to give the unusual Spacer. Afterward…the star cruiser would follow the faint "E" radiation trail. Did it lead to the circumstellar disc? Had he truly found the trail of former Imperial Swarm Commander, Thrax Ti Ix?

If so, the possibilities could prove interesting indeed.

-6-

As the Emperor of the New Men pondered the whereabouts of Lord Drakos and the New Man in question received the Spacer agent aboard his star cruiser, Lord High Admiral Cook seethed angrily in his office in Geneva, Switzerland Sector on Earth.

The insufferable Doctor Meyers was proving to be more than a nuisance. A Prime Ministerial liaison—Cook snorted.

She was a spy! He had evidence. Now, what was the correct move? Oh, he needed Brigadier O'Hara all right. She knew about these kinds of political maneuverings. He hadn't realized until these past few months just how much he'd relied upon the Iron Lady.

Maybe he could bring O'Hara back in an advisory capacity. If it wasn't for the dammed Bosks and their hideous methods… His best Intelligence operatives were still near the edge of Human Space, interrogating Bosk captives. Star Watch marines patrolled the Bosk cities and countryside.

The Bosks were a special project of Strand's that Drakos had hijacked. Cook had sent a fleet to intern the planet, but it was proving a costly and time-consuming operation—the Bosks were tying down too many of his best Star Watch personnel.

Cook scowled, which put more creases than even a year ago on his old leathery features.

What was Captain Maddox doing and where was he? What was it now? Eight months ago, Maddox had attempted to capture Drakos in the Balak System, failed and was supposed to be on leave somewhere.

Cook thumped down onto his chair and pressed an intercom button on his massive desk.

"Yes, sir," his secretary said.

"Get me Major Stokes on the line."

"Stokes, sir?"

"Intelligence Branch," Cook said.

"Of course, Admiral," his secretary replied.

The admiral drummed his thick fingers on the top of his desk as he waited. Doctor Meyers was a sex goddess bomb placed in Star Watch Headquarters. She created mayhem by merely sashaying into a room. She knew her power, too. She understood her effect upon men perfectly. It didn't help that she was brilliant, as well. But the proof of her spying—oh, ho-ho, he was going to great rid of her and possibly make an example of her, a Prime Ministerial liaison officer. She was more than a damned nuisance—she was mucking up the works, throwing sand in the well-oiled machinery of Star Watch Headquarters. Had that been Prime Minister Hampton's intent, or was there something more nefarious going on around him?

The desk intercom buzzed as a red light appeared on the box.

"The major is on the line, sir," the secretary said.

"Stokes?" Cook said into the intercom.

"Here, sir," Major Stokes said.

Stokes had been one of Brigadier O'Hara's chief aides. There had been some kind of run-in between the major and Maddox several years ago. Cook couldn't remember what it had been about now.

"How are things in the Intelligence Branch?" the admiral asked.

"Sir?" asked Stokes.

"Never mind, never mind," Cook said. He had as good as asked the major if the new Intelligence chief was doing his job well. That was a breach of protocol, to say the least.

The Meyers situation had him rattled. There was no doubt about that. As much as he wanted to flush her, he loved it every time she strutted into a room. She made him feel young again.

It was amazing. What would it be like bedding a woman like her?

Oh! Cook swayed back, startled. He'd been talking to Stokes. What was he…?

"Uh, Major…do you have Maddox's present whereabouts?"

"Captain Maddox, sir?"

"Yes, yes, Maddox," Cook said.

"Just a minute," Stokes said.

"Don't give me that. You know exactly what he's doing and where he is."

There was a pause on the other end. "I don't know for *sure*. *Victory* is supposed to be in the Barnes System."

"Where's that?"

"Approximately fifty-nine light-years from Earth, sir," Stokes said.

"What is Maddox doing there?"

"He went to chase a rumor, sir."

"Get to the point," Cook said.

"My apologies, Admiral. Yes… The esteemed captain heard a rumor that indicated another clone might soon be making an appearance in a large comet flying through the Barnes System."

"Clone? Another Strand clone?"

"Yes, sir," Stokes said.

"I thought we got all those."

"We all thought that, too, sir." Stokes cleared his throat. He seemed nervous, which wasn't like the man. "There was another rumor about the Barnes System, sir. That rumor linked Lord Drakos, a New Man hardliner—"

"I'm well aware of Drakos's identity."

"Yes, sir," Stokes said.

"Has the captain reported in lately?"

There was a short pause. Stokes cleared his throat again. "I, ah…do not have access to a long-distance communicator, sir."

Was the major dodging the question? It seemed to Cook as if he was. "Yet you haven't asked to use my communicator."

Stokes did not reply.

That was odd, most odd. Cook was about to begin a series of hard and fast questions, but before he could, a warning light flashed above his door. His secretary had just pressed a hidden switch to activate the red door light. What was that about? As if he didn't have enough on his plate already.

"That will be all, Major," Cook said. The admiral clicked off the intercom as he stared up at the red door light. It was an old idea, a silent warning or alarm. They had rigged up the red light ages ago during the first New Men scare. His secretary had never flashed it except the two times they'd practiced it. Now, that red light was like a baleful eye staring at—

Abruptly, Cook opened a bottom drawer to stare at a heavy .55 Powell "Slam Master." He had put it there several years ago, after the android takeover. He was in the process of lifting the big gun out of the drawer when someone rapped sharply on the office door.

Cook grunted, aimed the Slam Master at the door, and said, "Enter."

The door swung open and two black-uniformed, cap-wearing officers entered. They wore protective gear under their black uniforms with the block letters GCMS emblazoned across their chests. The letters meant, Great Council Marshal Service. They were the Great Council police and protective agents, meant to protect the Prime Minister and the official Commonwealth Councilors.

What in the hell were they doing marching into the military office of the commander of Star Watch? They should be back in Stockholm, for one thing.

The two GCMS officers stopped short as they noticed the hand cannon aimed at them. Dour old Bill Sanders crashed into both of them from behind, making one of the officers stumble forward. The bigger of the two held steady.

"What's the meaning of this?" Cook demanded.

The Prime Minister's chief political advisor, Bill Sanders, raised seriously overgrown eyebrows, and something seemed to take place behind his eyes. "Are you going to shoot me?" Sanders asked in his crotchety voice.

"Why are those two here?" Cook asked. "I wouldn't if I were you."

The bigger of the two officers had put his hand on his holstered gun. He'd moved his arm upward as if he was going to draw the sidearm.

The bigger officer stared into Cook's eyes. Something there must have convinced him. The officer let go of the holstered gun and let his arm hang limply.

Sanders saw the exchange, and his lips thinned. "They've come to arrest you in case I find you guilty of treason," he said.

"Treason?" asked Cook, the idea so outlandish that it stole his anger. Suddenly, the Slam Master was too heavy to hold up. He let the massive gun clunk onto the desk.

"Better," Sanders said. The something behind his eyes happened again. "You two," he said, "wait outside with the others."

The two GCMS officers looked at Sanders in confusion.

"Outside with the others," Sanders snapped. "Are you hard of hearing as well as clumsy?"

Each shook his head.

"Then go," Sanders said, "and shut the door behind you."

Bewildered, the two black-clad, cap-wearing, vested officers hurried out of the office, gently shutting the door behind them.

Sanders shook his head as if he couldn't believe their stupidity before sitting in one of the chairs before the desk.

"Treason?" Cook asked again.

Sanders reached inside his suit jacket and pulled out a folded official looking paper. He opened it with a single jerk downward. The extra-thick paper had a glittering gold seal on the bottom, with several big signatures scrawled across it.

"This is a provisional Great Council warrant for your arrest," Sanders said. "Doctor Meyers has suggested you have been engaged in treasonous actions."

"Meyers?" Cook said, slapping the desk. "That's because she's a spy." Understanding dawned. "Yes. I see what's happened. She must realize I'm on to her, and this is her way of covering her perfectly shaped..." the admiral trailed off.

"Spying—to use a crude word—is one of her duties for the Prime Minister," Sanders said.

Cook stared at Sanders in an uncomprehending manner. "You know she's a spy?"

"I prefer the term 'Prime Ministerial liaison'."

Cook shook his head. "You misunderstand me. I don't mean that Meyers is Hampton's spy. She's someone else's spy."

Sanders scowled, and he was good at it. "What's that supposed to mean?" There was an edge to his voice.

"I mean someone else like the Spacers, the New Men or, I don't know, one of the android factions, possibly."

"That's preposterous," Sanders said. "I checked her out myself before agreeing that she act as our liaison."

Cook snorted, having over the years developed a distain for amateurs. "Then you did a piss-poor job of vetting her, Mister Political Advisor. While you might know how to get a man elected, you don't know squat about real espionage. Take my word for it. Doctor Lisa Meyers is an expert, a real trained agent."

Sanders scowled even more, which caused his stooped shoulders to hunch to a greater degree. "You have evidence for these claims?"

"Of course, I do," Cook said. "I've been debating whether to call you or the Prime Minister about them."

Sanders grabbed the edges of his seat and scooted the chair forward until he could rest his elbows on Cook's huge desk. "Show me the evidence," he said curtly.

"I can't *show* you anything," Cook said. "But I can tell you what happened."

"Tell me, then. You have my undivided attention."

Cook frowned at the rumpled-suited political advisor.

"What's wrong now?" Sanders demanded.

"You came here with two GCMS officers to arrest me for treason. Isn't that what you said?"

"There are twelve officers," Sanders said, "three more of them waiting in your secretary's office. The rest are in the main—"

"I don't care where they are," Cook said, interrupting. "You used a Great Council warrant to force your way into Star Watch Headquarters. Without the warrant, the marines

36

guarding HQ would have stopped you outside. Then, you burst into my secretary's office with armed men. That's unprecedented. You must have used the Prime Minister's authority to gain the warrant and use of the GCMS officers."

"Other than aiming that gun at us, you're slow today, but essentially correct."

Cook stared at Sanders and finally shook his head. "I don't understand you. If you believe I'm involved in treasonous activity, why are you sitting here talking with me? It seems as if the GCMS officers were a game, a ruse. You can't really think I'm a traitor."

Sanders said nothing, although he sat back, studying the Lord High Admiral.

"Did Meyers really give such a report?" Cook asked.

"If I've said so, why would you think otherwise?"

"I'm beginning to think you did all this so you could speak to me alone in my office."

"Admiral..." Sanders said smoothly.

Cook's eyes widened as an image, a ghost, possibly, appeared in outline form behind Sander's back.

"What are you staring at?" Sanders asked, twisting in his chair to look around.

The image vanished before the political advisor could focus on it.

Sanders faced forward, eyeing Cook more closely than ever. "What kind of game are you playing?"

"No game," the admiral said softly.

Was he going mad? Seeing ghosts now? Then it hit Cook. That hadn't been a ghost. It had been a small image of an Adok alien. Yes, he had seen a distinctive leathery face with its many lines and the ropy arms. There was only one Adok that he knew, the AI Galyan, who appeared as a holoimage. Yet if he had just seen Galyan, did that mean Starship *Victory* and Captain Maddox were near?

"What's wrong with you, man?" Sanders demanded.

"I'm not sure," Cook said. What was going on here? And what was Sander's game?

-7-

One of the things going on was that Captain Maddox was not fifty-nine light-years away in the Barnes System, but was standing in Major Stokes' office.

Maddox was a tall man, lean like a deadly rapier. He wore a Star Watch line officer's uniform and had just come down from Starship *Victory*, which had entered the Solar System fifty-three minutes ago. The captain was half New Man and half regular human. Many considered him a half-breed, and he thoroughly detested the term.

Maddox was stronger, faster and quicker thinking than normal humans, but not as much as a New Man. He and his crew had been to the Barnes System. They had gone to many other places in the last eight months, following a thin lead that grew with each clue. The last clue had caused Maddox to order them back to Earth as fast as the starship could possibly travel. The last clue had been an android, one Maddox had captured, and Professor Ludendorff had taken apart and made talk.

Victory had parked in Earth orbit forty-two minutes ago and Maddox had come down via a shuttle piloted by Keith Maker twenty-nine minutes ago. The trip from the spaceport to Star Watch Headquarters had taken the rest of the time, although Maddox had walked into Stokes' office when the Lord High Admiral had called a few minutes ago. Maddox had put a finger before his lips, then, and Stokes had reluctantly complied with the unspoken request.

Major Stokes was in his late forties, a man of ordinary size, now smoking a mild stimstick. He was whip-smart, one of O'Hara's most trusted aides, but with a more than an ordinary dislike of Maddox.

"I'm amazed at you, Captain," Stokes was saying, the stimstick dangling between his lips and jerking up and down as he talked. The major sat behind his desk, looking up at Maddox in front of him.

The captain had his arms crossed, although he seemed extraordinarily intense.

"The evidence for what you're saying is flimsy at best," Stokes added.

"You know it isn't," Maddox said.

At that point, Galyan appeared. He was a holoimage with special projection powers that originated on the ancient, Adok-built starship. In other words, Galyan could travel several thousand kilometers as a holoimage. He could also dim himself, making him seem like a proverbial ghost. He could not go completely invisible, as then his receptors would not be able to "see" anything because they would be transparent, and light would simply go through them.

"Captain," Galyan said in a slightly robotic manner. "Sanders is with Cook in his office."

Stokes took the stimstick from his mouth. "You projected yourself into the Lord High Admiral's private—"

"I ordered Galyan to," Maddox said, interrupting the major.

"That's an outrage," Stokes said. "You are both subordinate to the Lord High Admiral. That means you are under orders to obey, not do whatever you like whenever you please. Certainly, it is against every rule for you to spy upon your superiors."

"Should I remain quiet about what I saw, sir?" Galyan asked the captain.

"No," Maddox said.

"Captain," Stokes warned.

"Hurry, Galyan," Maddox said. "Tell me."

"There are five police officers waiting in the admiral's secretary's outer office," Galyan said.

"Police officers?" Stokes half-shouted. "You mean Marine MPs."

"I mean civilian policemen," Galyan said. "I am quite able to distinguish the difference."

"What are policemen doing in Star Watch Headquarters?" Stokes asked.

Maddox shook his head. "What is Bill Sanders doing in the admiral's office?"

"I don't see why that's unusual," Stokes said.

"Major," Maddox said. "Time has run out. I don't believe that that *is* Bill Sanders. If it is, this Sanders is possibly inhuman or under mind control."

"What," Stokes said. "That's crazy. Sanders is the new Prime Minister's most highly trusted advisor."

"I'm leaving," Maddox informed the major.

"You most certainly are not," Stokes said, reaching forward for an intercom box. "I'm calling the Provost Marshal's desk—"

Maddox swept the intercom off the major's desk, and it crashed against the wall.

"What do you think you're doing?" Stokes demanded.

In a single fluid motion, Maddox reached under his uniform jacket, drew, aimed and fired a dart gun. With a hiss, a knockout dart slammed into Stokes' chest.

The major grunted, sat back hard and looked down at the dart sticking in his chest. He finally raised his head to glare at Maddox.

"This is…" Stokes said, slurring. Then he stopped talking as his head slumped forward and he began to snore softly.

"Stick with me, Galyan," Maddox said, as he holstered the dart gun, replacing it under his uniform jacket. "But keep a low profile."

The captain exited the office, quietly closing the door behind him. "The major wishes to be left alone for fifteen minutes," he told the red-haired secretary watching him. "He told me to grab something to eat in the interim."

"What was that banging?" she asked.

"I showed the major what the natives on Barnes III do when they find a woman attractive."

She looked down for a moment, as if wondering if Maddox found her attractive. Then she looked up and cocked her head, studying him, becoming the major's secretary again.

Maddox gave her a bland stare back.

"Fifteen minutes?" she asked.

Maddox nodded, saying no more. She might check on the major as soon as he left. He couldn't help that, but he would have to use the margin he had.

Maddox walked serenely through her office and into an outer corridor. From there, he increased his pace, heading for Brigadier O'Hara's old office. It was absurd that he would have come back just as the android faction allied with Drakos made its move against Admiral Cook. But sometimes absurdities happened. He did not know yet how deep the espionage penetration had gone at Star Watch Headquarters. Too far, would be his estimation.

Most androids had learned the foolishness of trying to impersonate well-known people. But there were other ways to insert androids into high-level bureaucracy. Drakos seemed to have taken over Strand's machinery, and the Methuselah Man strongly believed in mind manipulation. Tapping minds could be even more effective than replacing the person with a look-alike android.

It was quite possible that Sanders was such an altered person. What would an android or imposter do to the Lord High Admiral while alone with him in his office?

"Excuse me, sir," a woman said from behind her desk, "but you definitely can't go in there."

Maddox glanced at the secretary. He had just entered the large room, walked past her desk, heading for the door to Brigadier O'Hara's former office.

"It's fine," Maddox told her. "The new Intel chief is expecting me."

"No, he isn't," the secretary said, standing, perhaps to emphasize her point. She was a busty woman with a shorter-than-normal uniform dress, and she was angry. "I'm about to call the MPs."

"Oh," Maddox said, turning from the door. "Pardon me."

The woman glared at him and continued to do so as Maddox drew his gun and hissed a knockout dart into her.

She sat down with a thump and continued to stare at him until her eyelids fluttered shut and her head banged onto the desk.

"You had better be right about this, sir," the nearly invisible Galyan said. "You no longer have O'Hara's protection to help you out of pickles."

If Maddox heard the advice, he did not acknowledge it. He tested the handle and found it locked. His jaw muscles tightened the slightest bit. Then he stepped back, raised a booted foot and slammed it against the door once, twice—and on the third try the door flew inward.

Maddox moved fast, and he found a marvelously naked Lisa Meyers lying on the new Intelligence chief's desk. The new chief, a fit man of fifty-five, was just as naked as he rose off her.

Without hesitation, Maddox pulled the dart gun's trigger twice. He reloaded afterward, ignoring their shocked cries before each slumped unconscious, falling into each other's arms on top of the desk.

"That is a surprise," Galyan said, indicating the nude couple.

Maddox grunted as he moved around the desk, feeling along the back wall. Ah, here it was. He flipped a tiny latch. A hidden door opened, revealing a secret passage as lights came on in the ceiling. Maddox ran into the passage, heading for another secret door that would let him into the Lord High Admiral's office through the back.

-8-

Maddox paused for a millisecond before the closed door. He had raced down the secret passage, remembering the route from several years ago. Should he just barge in, or should he try to learn something first by listening?

The captain put his ear against the door, but he couldn't hear more than indistinct sounds, muffled talking perhaps.

"Should I check out the admiral's office for you?" Galyan whispered.

Maddox pursed his lips. He had to make a decision. He had raced home and darted too many people to afford to be wrong about this. If he balked now—

No! He had to discover the truth. But if he was wrong about the Prime Minister's chief political advisor, if this was an elaborate ploy on Drakos's or the androids' part—

"Balls," Maddox whispered. He clicked the latch and slid open the secret door.

From the chair behind his desk, the Lord High Admiral whirled around in shock. Dour old Bill Sanders looked up in amazement.

Maddox did not try to study either of them. That would take too long. He let his first impressions guide him.

Cook seemed human, normal and very surprised. Sanders showed what might have been shock but recovered more quickly. Too quickly?

"Captain Maddox," Sanders said in his grumpy voice. "First, what are you doing on Earth? Second, how long have you been behind that—?"

Maddox drew the dart gun and fired. The point of the dart sank into the clothes, maybe even into pseudo-skin, but there was an unmistakable *tink* sound. The sound could come from metal—the dart tip—striking metal—outer android body casing.

Yes. Clearly, Sanders was an android.

At the dart shot, Admiral Cook shouted in outrage. Maybe he believed Maddox was an assassin. The admiral threw himself out of his chair and toward the floor, and he got himself tangled up in the chair's armrest, crashing down.

The pseudo-Sanders' head jerked up with machine speed.

Maddox silently cursed himself for having acted too hastily. The thing was an android, and he couldn't really hurt an android with darts. That made both Cook and Maddox defenseless before it. To buy time, Maddox fired several more shots, aiming at the thing's eyes. The android swatted each dart out of the air, although one dart stuck in its hand.

Maddox released the dart gun as he saw the .55 Powell "Slam" Master lying on the desk. He dearly hoped it was loaded.

"You're under arrest," Maddox said, moving toward the desk.

"Arrest, you fool?" the thing impersonating Sanders said. "I'll have you before a firing squad—"

The android must have realized the captain had spoken as a ruse. Maddox reached for the hand cannon lying on the desk.

"No," Sanders said. The supposed political advisor launched out of his chair. If Maddox had been a regular human with ordinary reflexes, it would likely have been fast enough, but the captain had accelerated reflexes.

Maddox snatched the gun just ahead of Sanders, raised it and fired.

BOOM!

The clever android was extremely fast. At the same instant, it jerked short and darted aside. Although Maddox had fired at point-blank range, the bullet missed, tearing apart the chair Sanders had been sitting in.

Maddox corrected, with no doubt now that Sanders was an android.

BOOM! BOOM!

One of the bullets clipped the fast-moving android's left shoulder. The heavy slug tore away suit fabric, pseudo-flesh and revealed mechanical workings inside what should have been a human shoulder.

BOOM! BOOM!

The next bullets struck the thing's torso casing, causing the android to crash back and tumble across the carpeted floor.

Maddox did not spring up onto the desk so he could keep the thing in sight. Instead, he moved carefully around the desk to the right. Cook was shouting from on the floor to his left.

The door opened and a GCMS officer with a gun in his hand peered within. At the same time, the badly wounded android sprung off the floor, heading for the door.

Maddox aimed and fired again.

BOOM!

The .55 caliber slug took the android in the back, knocking the pseudo-Sanders forward against the GCMS officer. Both of them fell into the secretary's office.

She screamed from her desk.

The other GCMS officers backed away, surprised and unsure what to do. The first officer scrambled off the floor, shouting in alarm.

The android kept moving, crawling across the carpet as working parts shed from his wounds.

Maddox strode up, aimed low and fired two more times into the android. After a second of seeing metal fly from the android, the GCMS officers, as a group, also opened up, adding their bullets to the mayhem.

Finally, as smoke drifted everywhere, the android stopped moving.

The black-uniformed, cap-wearing, vested GCMS officers looked at Maddox.

He aimed the hand cannon at them. "Drop your guns," he said, "all of you."

"Sir?" one asked.

The others looked shocked.

"I don't know if you're men or machines," Maddox said. "This is Star Watch Headquarters and you five definitely do not belong to Star Watch."

"But—"

Maddox aimed at the speaker's face. "Drop your guns or we'll find out the hard way."

One after another, the GCMS officers let their guns hit the carpet.

"Summon the admiral's marines," Maddox told the shaking secretary. "Then get Major Stokes on the line. Tell him to bring medical personnel to Brigadier O'Hara's former office. Three darted people might need medical attention."

"Sir?" the secretary asked, bewildered.

Maddox whirled round. "Galyan!"

The holoimage made himself visible.

The secretary screamed again, louder than before, while several of the GCMS officers backed away.

"Check on Stokes," Maddox said. "I forgot that I darted him. If he's awake, give him the message. Otherwise, tell his secretary what to do."

"Yes, sir," Galyan said, disappearing.

Admiral Cook stumbled into the secretary's outer office. He had a bloody gash on his forehead. He stared at the android, at the GCMS officers and finally at Maddox. "What just happened?" the Lord High Admiral asked in a husky voice.

"Good thinking, sir," Maddox said. "I suggest you tell your marines to quarantine the building. Then, if you don't mind…"

"Captain?" asked Cook.

Maddox was about to say that he'd have Ludendorff come down. But he didn't think the professor would come or would want anyone to know that he was still aboard *Victory*. Ludendorff had a phobia of capture by Star Watch.

Cook was staring at Maddox, maybe in shock.

"Are you all right, sir?" Maddox asked.

"Yes, damn it. Now, what's going on?"

"It's time to quarantine the building, sir."

This time, the idea seemed to get through. "Right you are, son," the admiral said. "We're going to figure out this mess and make someone pay."

Maddox nodded, doubting it would be that easy.

-9-

"If I might make a suggestion, sir," Maddox said some time later.

Lord High Admiral Cook looked up at Maddox from where he sat behind a large table. The old man had been massaging his forehead for over thirty seconds.

They were in an armored conference chamber, one without any hidden doors or side passages. Heavily armed marines guarded the room from the outside.

Maddox had been explaining the reasoning of his actions to the admiral. Unfortunately, one call after another had interrupted the explanation. Prime Minister Hampton had shouted though the intercom box, furious that this could ruin the honeymoon period of his new administration. Cook had tried to tell the man the situation was much more serious than that. An android had been his chief political advisor—that could mean the end of his administration before it really got started.

Hampton had still been shouting when he abruptly hung up. General Torres had called and demanded Maddox's scalp—Torres the new Intelligence chief. Major Stokes had also called, threatening to resign unless strict measures were implemented against the captain for his reckless behavior.

The calls had come, Maddox's explanations had taken a back seat and Cook had become frustrated by it all, massaging his forehead for over thirty seconds.

"A suggestion, sir," Maddox repeated.

Before Cook could ask Maddox what suggestion he might have, a loud knock sounded at the door.

The two men exchanged glances.

"Enter," Cook said.

A big marine opened the door and Doctor Lisa Meyers waltzed into the chamber. She wore high heels and a dark blue suit with her hair up.

The marine must have seen Cook's nod, because the armed man grinned as he studied her posterior while shutting the door behind her.

Doctor Meyers gave Maddox a withering glare before turning to the older Lord High Admiral.

"I wish to press charges against that man," she said, pointing at Maddox without looking at him.

Cook gave her an uncomprehending stare.

"Did you hear me?" she demanded.

The admiral collected himself. "You're in no position to make any demands. You're—"

Maddox loudly and obviously cleared his throat.

Cook checked himself.

"Yes?" she said. "I'm what?"

"You've had a harrowing day," Cook said.

Maddox nodded in approval.

"Do you suppose my interview with General Torres has any bearing on what occurred?"

"Just a minute," Cook said, interrupting her. "Let's be honest. You had sex with Torres in his office."

"After the interview was over," Meyers said. "Admiral, Torres and I are both adults."

"No one is denying that," Cook said. "But this is a military installation, the heart of Star Watch, in fact. It's unprofessional."

"I'm not governed by your military dictates or customs. I am the Prime Minister's liaison officer, doing my job as I see fit. Your man there shot me today. That was a vicious assault, a criminal act."

"He did it in the line of duty," Cook said.

"On what possible grounds?"

Cook seemed bemused by the question.

"I can answer that for you, sir," Maddox said.

Meyers turned toward him with an icy stare.

"Uh, go ahead," Cook said. "I'd like to hear this too."

"I was in a life or death situation," Maddox told Meyers. "When I burst into the room, it appeared as if you had subdued the general."

"Don't be absurd," she said.

"Espionage is carried out in a variety of ways," Maddox said. "I assumed—incorrectly, it turns out—that you were an enemy agent suborning the Intelligence chief of Star Watch. After all, I did end up finding an android infiltrator. I thought you might be one too."

Meyers opened her mouth to retort.

"I realize you've called the Prime Minister and pled your innocence to him," Maddox said. "I congratulate you on your quick thinking. But you don't seem to understand how serious it is that Hampton used an android as his chief political advisor. What's more, this android vetted you. You are on dangerously thin ice, Doctor Meyers."

She raised her chin in an imperial manner. "Through the Prime Minister, I am a representative of the People. By assaulting me, you have assaulted the People, the very authority by which Star Watch operates."

Cook slapped the table. "This is too much. You were having *sex* with my Intelligence chief in his office. I will have decorum in headquarters. What's more, I question—"

Maddox cleared his throat again.

Cook waved that aside. "I question your ethics, Doctor. I question your loyalty to Hampton and to the Commonwealth."

Doctor Meyers' eyes seemed to shine as a cruel smile spread across her stunning features. "You have overreached," she said softly. "I doubt you will be able to keep your position now, Admiral."

"I hold my position by the will of the Great Council," Cook said. "Hampton cannot summarily dismiss me. At this point, he will be lucky to keep his office."

"We shall see who is lucky and who isn't," she said. "The android affair will blow over soon enough. Star Watch cannot afford to let the world know about it, or confidence will plummet throughout the Commonwealth. Star Watch cannot afford that—not with a coming war against the New Men."

"You don't know what you're talking about," Cook said.

"You have insulted the Prime Minister's liaison officer," she said, "which is the same as insulting the Prime Minister to his face."

Cook did not retort, as he was too busy staring at her, wondering why she'd said they would soon have a war with the New Men.

"The Prime Minister is in no position to threaten the Lord High Admiral," Maddox told Meyers. "The Prime Minister just sent an android to murder the head of Star Watch."

"What?" Meyers said. "You can't possibly believe the Prime Minister knew Sanders was an android?"

"Does it matter what I believe?" Maddox asked in a conversational tone. "It's what the People will believe—if we say so. You are quite wrong about Star Watch helping you to brush the "android affair" under the rug. Hampton is a buffoon at best—"

Meyers gasped in disbelief.

"Once the People learn Hampton trusted an android," Maddox said, "I imagine the clamor will sound so loudly that the Great Council will be forced to impeach him."

Meyers closed her mouth as she stared at Maddox silently.

"As Hampton's liaison officer," Maddox continued, "I would think that you would put aside your indignities in order to smooth the admiral's feathers, not stir them even more."

"You darted me," she said.

After a second, Maddox shrugged.

"You don't care that you darted me?" she said, her voice rising.

Maddox only smiled faintly.

"Do you care that you shot me with a dart or not?" she demanded.

"Doctor Meyers," Maddox said softly. "Let me assure you that I do not care in the least that I shot you with a knockout dart while you were suborning the Intelligence chief with your undoubted charms."

"How dare you say that?"

Maddox shrugged. "I care that Prime Minister Hampton sent an android to murder the Lord High Admiral or possibly drug him and maybe insert some of kind of obedience chip in him. That I care about deeply."

"Your suggestions are absurd," Meyers said.

"I also care that you've been enticing our Intelligence chief," Maddox said. "I wonder why, and I wonder for whom."

Doctor Meyers' eyes narrowed to slits. She turned to Cook. "Is that your story too?" she asked coldly.

"Might I make a suggestion, sir?" Maddox asked.

Cook eyed the captain, finally nodding.

"Doctor Meyers might be too close to the tragedy today to see clearly," Maddox said. "Too...*personally* involved. Perhaps she should return to the Prime Minister for recuperation. Further, because she is such a valuable member of the Prime Minister's team, you should request that he leave her position open at present, awaiting her return at the proper time."

"You're obviously trying to get rid of the Prime Ministerial liaison officer," Meyers said flatly, "so you can work without supervision."

"On no account is that true," Maddox said. "You are too valuable to easily replace. I suggest you tell the Prime Minister that the Lord High Admiral said so."

"The Prime Minister wishes to have a direct link to Star Watch Headquarters," Meyers said. "That means having a liaison officer, one he trusts."

"I suggest that the Prime Minister has lost that possibility for a time," Maddox said. "We shall look into the android affair and report to him when we learn more. In the meantime, you and the Prime Minister can concentrate on the political backlash of this murder attempt and the seriousness of trusting an android. That means you will let the Lord High Admiral do his job without any... *civilian* interference."

"There was no murder attempt," Meyers said. "That is sheer fabrication."

"An android attacked today," Maddox said.

"That isn't the report I heard."

Maddox nodded. "I congratulate you on your resources. You inserted your tentacles in headquarters quickly."

Once more, her eyes seemed to shine dangerously. "You think you're clever, don't you, Captain?"

"I'm beginning to wonder if you're more dangerous than 'Sanders' was."

"I'm no android."

"I know," Maddox said.

"Oh?"

"I knew once I darted you that you were human."

Meyers eyed Maddox. "Check, for now," she said. "But it isn't checkmate, Captain. I will take you up on your suggestion and return to Prime Minister Hampton. He is the center of gravity in this case."

"I thought it was the People," Maddox said.

"Hampton is the voice of the People, as they elected him through the other delegates."

"Touché," Maddox said in a mocking tone.

"This isn't the end of it," Meyers said. "While you may have won this round, you've made a deadly enemy of me, and thus the Prime Minister of the Commonwealth of Planets."

Maddox did not respond—just gave her that faint smile.

Doctor Meyers spun around and walked out the door in a huff, slamming it behind her.

"I don't understand her," Cook said. "She should be pleading with us, not ranting. They're in serious political trouble. They need our help."

Maddox had become thoughtful. "Prime Minister Hampton is the key, she said," he told the admiral. "Sanders was an android and according to the brief I read, he initiated most of Hampton's policies. Doctor Meyers also seems to believe she can manipulate the Prime Minister. Perhaps that's the answer. An android faction and whomever Meyers represents believe they can manipulate Commonwealth policy and Star Watch through Hampton. He is our weak link."

"Hampton is the chief authority of both the Commonwealth and Star Watch," Cook said.

Maddox began to pace. "Sir," he said, a moment later, "I suggest you insert a better security team around the Prime Minister. Enemy agents have and will try again to manipulate

Hampton. Either that, or make sure someone else becomes Prime Minister."

Cook said nothing.

"I also think General Torres isn't up to the task of running Intelligence," Maddox said.

Cook raised his head. "Last I looked, I was still in charge of Star Watch, young man."

"Sir," Maddox said, unaffected, "you need Mary O'Hara back."

Cook snorted. "While I resent you giving me unasked for advice, I already know that. She has your devious bent of mind. It's hurting us that she's sitting on the sidelines."

"Intelligence needs a devious chief, not a man easily seduced and manipulated by sex like Torres."

Cook shook his head. "My hands are tied with O'Hara. I can't bring her back. She's been compromised."

"Perhaps, then, you can take a leaf from Hampton's playbook."

"Meaning what?" asked Cook.

"Create a conduit to O'Hara."

"What does that even mean?"

"Major Stokes would be the best candidate for the job," Maddox said. "Have Mary O'Hara work through him."

"Now see here, Captain," Cook said. "You are a junior officer with delusions of grandeur. While I appreciate your timely intervention with Sanders and your harsh but clever handling of Lisa Meyers, the senior officers and I run Star Watch, not you."

"Yes, sir," Maddox said. "My pardon, sir."

"General Torres stays for now."

Maddox said nothing.

"Perhaps he showed poor judgment indulging himself with Meyers—"

"If she were an enemy Intelligence officer, she might have blackmailed him. Isn't Torres married, sir?"

"Damn it, man. What did I just say?"

"That you were thinking about using Major Stokes as a conduit for Mary O'Hara."

Cook stared at Maddox and finally shook his white-haired head. "This is a fine mess, a fine mess, indeed. We've beaten back the Swarm menace and taken care of the Yon-Soths and have even militarily corralled the New Men in the Beyond. Now, we have these damned androids and whomever Lisa Meyers represents and a hardline faction of New Men using Strand infiltrators that plague us worse than malaria-carrying mosquitoes."

"It's hard to get a handle on this one," Maddox agreed.

Cook drummed his fingers on the table. "You said something earlier…what was it?"

Maddox waited.

"Oh, right, I remember. You said Meyers had her tentacles in Star Watch. That's what this mess feels like. It isn't just a single threat, but a serious of smaller threats that add up to a many-tentacled monster."

Maddox stared at the admiral before saying, "That is an interesting metaphor, sir."

"Now explain, would you, how you knew to come back here and shoot the chief Prime Ministerial advisor with a knockout dart."

"I thought I already did that, sir."

"No, you didn't."

"Oh."

"Quit stalling, Captain. How did you know about Sanders, especially know about him far out in the Barnes System?"

"Well, sir, it goes something like this…"

-10-

The rumor regarding a Strand clone awakening in a comet laboratory in the Barnes System proved to be a false trail. But the crew of *Victory* did find a hidden android base inside a comet that flew through the Barnes System. The base was much like the comet Builder station that had given them the polygonal stone, the one that had proven so important last mission.

Unfortunately, the androids in the Barnes System had vacated the comet base before *Victory* arrived, cleaning out the many chambers. During an intense search, Riker found what was presumably a mislaid computer. Ludendorff hacked the computer, accidently tripping a failsafe which erased most of the memory. The professor managed to save enough data, however, to give them a clue about an underwater complex in the Nils Ocean on the terrestrial and Earthlike Barnes III.

Several days later, while scanning from *Victory* while in orbit around Barnes III, Ludendorff and Galyan found evidence of a deep-water complex. The complex was in the middle of the Nils Ocean, several kilometers deep. Maddox descended from orbit and used a special submersible that Keith piloted underwater. They broke into the complex and found several dead New Men whose heads had been fried with electrical equipment that Ludendorff said had been formerly installed in their craniums.

"You mean put into their brains?" Cook asked.

"Yes," Maddox said.

"Was it the kind of equipment Strand used to use to control the New Men?"

"We wondered the same thing. But we didn't have enough remains to know."

"Did you find anything else?"

"Yes," Maddox said, as he proceeded to explain.

In the underwater complex, in another chamber, was an android trying to slip away in a mini-sub. Sergeant Riker reached him first, using an android-dropping weapon, disabling the mechanical man.

They rushed the android upstairs to *Victory*. There, Ludendorff salvaged part of the thing's memories, although the android self-destructed. Amazingly, one memory had to do with candidate Hampton and an android infiltrator ready to slip into Star Watch if Hampton should win.

"This was a precise memory?" asked Cook.

Maddox paused before saying, "Professor Ludendorff is a Methuselah Man."

"What's your point?"

"Ludendorff has a complex mind and thus sees complexities much easier than most."

"Meaning what?" asked Cook. "Please get to the point, Captain."

"The professor pieced together seemingly unrelated clues from sketchy android memories. They informed Ludendorff that you in particular were in danger."

"Me?" Cook said.

"That's why I rushed here. Without you leading Star Watch, sir…"

"Oh, confound it, Captain. I'm a man like any other. I put my pants on one leg at a time. I'm not that unique."

"No one holds the Commonwealth's trust more than you, sir. We never did figure out who controlled the underwater complex, Strand, Drakos possibly, androids or someone else. Maybe this is a team effort."

"Explain that," Cook said.

"It's Ludendorff's idea. Throughout the years, we've broken many conspiracies and defeated various invasion attempts. Perhaps the remnants of these groups have joined forces in order to construct a…a many-tentacled monster."

"That's the professor's phrase?"

"It is. That's why you're using it earlier surprised me."

Cook tilted his head. "One man is weak? Many become strong?"

"Something like that."

Cook stared at his hands. He stared for some time before looking up. "If this is a group effort—many of our enemies working together—it might be more difficult to stop. There isn't a single leader to take out, but many component parts, many leaders, as it were."

"Unless Lord Drakos *is* orchestrating the entire operation," Maddox said. "He grabbed Strand's former operatives. Maybe Drakos has gathered these other broken pieces to help him build a stronger unit."

"Do you believe Drakos has done that?"

"I'm not ready to make that judgment yet, sir."

"No gut instincts to guide you?"

"I leave such things to immediate problems," Maddox said.

"Let me ask you a question," Cook said. "First, Ludendorff appears to have come to some definite conclusions."

"I would agree to that."

"Doesn't that strike you as premature?"

Maddox inhaled through his nostrils, saying nothing.

"Ah," Cook said. "I'm onto something, aren't I?"

Maddox shrugged.

"Come, come, Captain. Tell me your premonition, because I think I have the same one."

"The professor is a Methuselah Man," Maddox said slowly. "Strand is a Methuselah Man. The Emperor has Strand prisoner, but in some manner, Drakos has tapped into Strand's grand scheme or schemes."

"From what we've seen in the past, Strand has many irons still waiting to heat."

"That fits Strand's personality—Mister Contingency Plan."

"You should have killed him when you had the chance and saved us a world of headaches," Cook complained.

"Letting Strand live as a New Man prisoner was the price for cementing the New Men's help against the original Swarm invasion."

"True enough," Cook said. "But back to my point. Ludendorff must know Strand's mind better than anyone else."

"That seems reasonable."

"Could Ludendorff secretly being trying to help Strand?"

"By throwing us off Strand's trail with the idea that others are also involved?"

Cook nodded.

"I don't think so, sir."

"Do you trust Ludendorff?"

"Not fully," Maddox admitted.

Admiral Cook looked away, staring at a wall.

"Even if there are others allied with Drakos," Maddox said, "it's clear he inherited many of Strand's...hidden irons, as you put it."

Cook nodded without turning around.

Maddox grew quiet then, waiting.

Finally, the admiral faced him. "Who controls Lisa Meyers, do you think?"

"I would dearly like to investigate her and find out."

Cook grinned suddenly. "You don't care for her threat, do you?"

"No," Maddox said flatly.

"I wouldn't either. Hmm... you've given me a lot to digest, Captain. General Torres is frightened and angry with you. Hampton...I don't know about the Prime Minister. Maybe you should investigate *him.*"

"That could be tricky, sir, but advisable."

The Lord High Admiral rubbed his chin before glancing at Maddox. "Your darting so many people has made a mess of things."

"I might not have reached you and Sanders in time if I hadn't darted people, sir."

"What do you think the android would have done to me if he'd had more time?"

"I don't know."

Cook put both hands on the table, finally nodding. "I'm giving you the Bill Sanders android. Have Ludendorff tear it down and tell me what Sanders could have done to me. I'll soothe Torres and Stokes. They both want your scalp. We'll wait and see what Hampton does next, if anything."

"Yes, sir," Maddox said.

"I hope I don't have to tell you that prying into Doctor Meyers' background will be full of traps that could bring down the two of us."

Maddox shook his head. "I'll deny you ever told me anything about her, sir."

Cook stared at him. "Maybe that's for the best," the admiral said, quietly.

"Then perhaps I should leave, sir, go back to *Victory*. The sooner I get started…"

Cook scraped his chair back as he stood. He approached Maddox and stuck out his right hand.

Maddox gripped it.

The Lord High Admiral clapped Maddox on the shoulder. "Good work, son. I appreciate what you did and the risks you took to do it. I don't know about O'Hara, whether we can get her reinstalled as the Iron Lady. But I do know one thing, she would be proud of you."

Maddox felt a slight flush creep up his neck.

"Now, get to work," Cook said. "I want to get to the bottom of this as fast as possible. Whatever else happens, we have to make sure we don't slide into another war with the New Men."

-11-

Nine hours later, Maddox groaned as his wife Meta shook him awake.

The captain lay naked in his bed in his cabin aboard *Victory*, having slept hard for five of the last nine hours.

Meta wore a bathrobe, with a towel wound around her blonde hair. "Are you awake?" she asked, as she knelt on the bed.

Maddox grinned up at her. She was a voluptuous beauty, a modified woman from the Rouen Colony. Growing up in the 2-G environment had made Meta much stronger than an ordinary woman.

The cloth belt only partly kept the bathrobe closed. Maddox tugged at the belt so the bathrobe opened all the way.

"Not now," Meta said, although she was smiling. "The Lord High Admiral just sent an urgent message. He has to speak to you."

"In person?" asked Maddox.

"On a secure line," she said.

Maddox released the belt and sat up. "What now?"

"He said it's about Doctor Meyers, the Prime Minister and the android Ludendorff is fiddling with."

"Right," Maddox said.

Before the five-hour sleep, he'd been up for forty-nine hours. He felt better but could have slept longer. "I'll take the call in here," he said.

Meta shook her head. "Cook said to use the long-range communicator."

"Oh," Maddox said. "Right. No one will be able to hack into that. Is there anything to eat or some coffee?"

"I'll get you some. But I think you'd better hurry. It sounded urgent."

Maddox slid off the bed and headed for the shower. He still felt a little groggy and figured it was time to be one hundred percent. A hot shower, coffee and some eggs would get him going. Then—

"Go," he told Meta. "If this is urgent, it must mean the Prime Minister is applying pressure. It's what I would do if my butt were on the line. What are you waiting for?" he asked.

Meta tied the cloth belt around her waist and dashed for the hatch, running barefoot.

***

Maddox's hair was still wet and his uniform slightly damp in places as he set an empty coffee cup on the table beside the long-range communicator. The bulky device was in a special room deep inside *Victory*.

"Maddox here," Maddox said as he spoke into a microphone.

"What took you so long?" Cook said from the other end.

"I'm here now," Maddox said. He seldom apologized about anything.

"The Prime Minister wants his android back," Cook said without further preamble.

"You spoke to him personally?"

"That's doesn't make any difference," Cook said. "He's angry, and he wants that android. He's given me fifteen minutes to get it headed to him in Stockholm. Make that three minutes now. You've already used up twelve precious minutes doing whatever you've been doing."

"Did you speak to him personally?" Maddox asked.

"I saw his face on a screen as he made his demand."

"He looked angry?"

"What are you getting at?" Cook demanded.

"I'm assessing the situation, sir. Why did the Prime Minister wait nine hours to demand that you give him the android?"

"I have no idea."

"Perhaps that's how long it took Meyers to speak to him."

"Speak or convince?" Cook asked.

"That is an excellent point, sir. What is the media saying about the Sanders assassination attempt?"

"Nothing," Cook said.

"But that's incredible," Maddox declared.

"Now, see here," Cook said. "I'm the head of Star Watch. That includes the head of Intelligence."

"No one doubts that, sir."

"There's been a change in plans," Cook said. "I've decided not to advertise the assassination attempt."

Maddox pursed his lips and refrained from commenting, although he wondered who had convinced Cook to hold off.

"Meyers had a point before," Cook said. "If the media learns about the attempt—did Sanders really attempt to kill me? You charged in and he—well, you shot him first, Captain."

"Sir, Sanders came to your office to arrest you. He brought a pack of CGMS officers. He backed off because of the gun you aimed at him. Why did he have an executive writ to arrest you?"

"To arrest is quite different from an assassination attempt. Can we prove he wanted to kill me? But that's not even the point. The Prime Minister's time limit is almost up."

"Forget about the limit," Maddox said. "The Prime Minister is applying pressure, nothing more. He's making demands because you have him scared."

"You can't know that. It sounds to me as if he's going to have my head."

"Sir, we need to find out why he wants the android."

"You had nine hours already to figure that out. You should know by now."

"I need to speak to Ludendorff."

Lord High Admiral Cook swore over the long-range communicator. "My aide has just informed me that I have received another call from the Prime Minister's Office. The message states that he is debating sending another delegation to arrest me for murdering Sanders."

"He won't do that. You have the upper hand in this, sir."

"I don't know that I do. Stokes believes we made a strategic error letting Meyers go."

"Is it Major Stokes' advice to keep the Sanders attack secret?"

"There was no attack."

"You're wrong, sir. Tell the Prime Minister you're considering going to the media. Tell him you're already in contact with certain Great Council members. You're seeking their advice. Back him off by threatening to expose this entire sordid—"

"Captain Maddox," Cook said, "I do not want to have to say this again. I run Star Watch, not you. Just because O'Hara is no longer the Intelligence chief does not mean no one is. You are not a free agent who can do as he pleases. You are under orders and must obey them."

"I understand, sir," Maddox said. "But if I might point out, you have a powerful weapon in threatening to expose the Prime Minister. If you fail to exploit your advantage, Hampton is going to outmaneuver you and possibly expel you from Star Watch. That means the androids might take charge of the Commonwealth and Star Watch through Hampton. You have to remember that we don't need Sanders to have directly attacked you to impeach the Prime Minister. The fact that Sanders was an android is damning enough."

There were several seconds of silence before Cook said, "We'd have to tell the universe about Sanders then. That could shake people's trust in the system, and that would be disastrous."

"Letting the androids control us would be even more disastrous."

"I can't believe this is happening. What a mess. What a damned mess."

"Sir, you'd better get in contact with Great Council members. I'd start impeachment proceedings immediately.

Hampton is dirty. That he's threatening you like this proves it. In these affairs, striking first can be critical."

"Confound it," Cook said. "Military affairs are easy compared to this. Political maneuvering is a wretched business. I gave you the android. Now, you have to give me something concrete. I can't urge Council members to impeach the Prime Minister without real proof. Many could consider such a suggestion as treasonous. We could well find ourselves before a firing squad."

Maddox stared at the bulky device. Cook was a good man, although he lacked the devious nature needed for real political infighting. Who was behind Hampton? He needed to see Ludendorff and find out what the professor had discovered.

"If you're not going to play hardball, sir, I'd tell the Prime Minister that the android is on the way."

"Is it?"

Maddox hesitated before he said, "Yes sir, it is."

"Good," Cook said, sounding relieved. "I'll tell him. When can the Prime Minister expect the android?"

"About a half hour from now, sir."

"What? Then it isn't really on the way, is it?"

"Tell him I said it is."

"Captain Maddox—"

"I need the extra minutes, sir. You can at least buy me thirty minutes, can't you?"

"Will it make a difference?"

"That's what I need to find out."

"Fine," Cook said, sounding agitated again. "I'll tell him, and I'll try to sell it. What are you hoping to discover?"

"I'll know when I hear it, sir. In the meantime, I'd begin sounding out the Council members. I know you honor the office of Prime Minister. But you have to realize that our enemies have turned Hampton."

"We don't know that."

That more than anything let Maddox know that Cook might have finally reached his limit. The Lord High Admiral had carried humanity on his shoulders through many harrowing ordeals. This last one, a political attack, might be more than Cook could withstand. What did that mean for Star Watch?

"A half hour, sir," Maddox said, "and I'll give you my assessment."

"I'll do what I can, son."

Maddox hoped it would be enough.

-12-

As Maddox entered the laboratory, Professor Ludendorff looked up with a scowl.

The Methuselah Man looked like a fit, older man with tanned skin, a golden chain around his neck and thick white hair. He was a cunning scoundrel with knowledge gained over many centuries.

The professor had been bad-tempered lately, as Doctor Dana Rich had left him and left the starship altogether, going back to her home planet of Brahma. She'd told the professor she needed time to think. Maybe they needed a break from each other. Ludendorff hadn't agreed, but for once, he hadn't gotten his way with her. The Bosks had mistreated Dana, using her in hurtful ways. Ludendorff had dragged her to the Bosk world looking for relief. She blamed him for what had happened to her.

Maddox knew all this, and he was quite sure Ludendorff was still taking it badly, as was his wont when he didn't get his way.

The laboratory was big, with the shot-up Sanders android spread out over several tables, with many strange machines surrounding the tables and making various noises.

Ludendorff had been examining a screen as Maddox entered. The professor now glanced at the captain, muttered under his breath and went back to examining the screen.

"What can you tell me?" Maddox asked.

"That you broke my concentration," Ludendorff grumbled.

"Have you determined the android's faction?"

Ludendorff looked up from the screen before muttering again and fiddling with the controls.

"Professor, do you recognize the android model or not?"

Ludendorff looked up again with a curious expression on his face.

"We're running out of time," Maddox said. "The Prime Minister wants the android back and is putting the pressure on Cook to get it."

"I would think the Prime Minster would be running scared. He let an android run him. Hampton is through as Prime Minister."

"If Cook exposes him, agreed," Maddox said.

"Why wouldn't—oh," Ludendorff said, nodding. "Cook wishes to maintain public confidence in the political system. Yes…knowing how easy it is to control the highest leadership might cause the ordinary man to reassess. That is never good for those in charge. But if Cook fails to expose Hampton, he runs a greater risk."

"So, give me ammo," Maddox said. "What have you found?"

"I'm not sure yet."

"You've had the android for over nine hours already."

"Yes, yes, I'm the miracle worker. Everyone expects wonders from me because I'm the smartest person in existence. Yet, sometimes I have to ponder and study, reassess and—"

"Reassess what?" Maddox asked, interrupting.

"Do you know that you have an annoying habit of always latching onto the—bah!" Ludendorff threw his hands into the air. "I've run into a snag, and I don't understand it."

Maddox studied the Methuselah Man. Ludendorff had bags under his eyes and looked…distressed. Clearly, having Dana run off had struck at the professor's core. The man was unsettled. Maybe his vaunted concentration wasn't as powerful as usual. His great insights weren't there to the same degree.

"Don't give me any of your pity," Ludendorff muttered.

"I wouldn't think of it."

"Then, get that stupid expression off your face. It's infuriating. If anyone needs help, it's you."

Maddox waited.

"That's just what I'm talking about, that insufferable smugness that you think you know what in the hell you're doing. Well, you don't. Trust me on that. None of us does."

"You need some sleep, Professor."

"Bah!" Ludendorff said. "Sleep is overrated. Besides, I can't sleep. I keep thinking about—never mind. It doesn't matter."

"Give her some time," Maddox said.

"You're giving me sex advice?" Ludendorff asked in outrage. "I don't need sex advice. I am the world's most skilled lover. I am—"

"Professor," Maddox said sharply.

Ludendorff stared at him open-mouthed.

"No one doubts your sexual prowess. This is about love, not sex. Give Dana time. She's hurt, deeply hurt."

"I know," Ludendorff said in an agonized voice. "I know. How I wish..." He trailed off, shaking his head.

Maddox could not pat the professor on the shoulder, as that was not his way. He saw the hurting man, and thus turned away to give Ludendorff a moment to get it together.

Soon, Ludendorff cleared his throat.

Maddox turned back as the professor pointed at the android brain case. He'd opened it to expose millions of tiny circuits.

"Earlier, I energized the mechanical brain," Ludendorff said, "but it wouldn't fire up. There is a tripwire, so to speak, somewhere inside the computer core that won't allow it to energize. That is unique to an android brain core. There are other modifications as well, ones I've never seen before."

"Oh?" Maddox asked.

"You mentioned the model or make of android. It appears to be a Builder Type C android in most ways..." Once more, Ludendorff trailed off and shook his head.

"What's bothering you?"

"I haven't accessed any of its memories or been able to energize it enough in order to let it 'talk' to me. There is an internal barrier blocking such a thing. That barrier is not of Builder make."

69

Maddox rubbed his left check. Long ago, the Builders had constructed most of the present-day androids. Many of those androids had been kept in storage, periodically activating and secretly entering society.

"What does this barrier mean to you?" the captain asked.

"Obviously, someone has tampered with this Type C android. This tampering has…improved the android."

"Improved how?"

"Oh, not while it was on," Ludendorff said, "but while it is inoperative. I am unable to access it in any way. That is the giveaway."

"Yes?"

"Don't you see?"

Maddox shook his head.

"The improvement—who can improve on Builder technology?" asked Ludendorff.

"You mean we, as in humans or New Men, haven't been able to improve on Builder technology."

"Correct."

"That implies others, as in, aliens, have done the improving."

"Correct again," said Ludendorff.

"What kind of aliens are we talking about?"

"I do not know."

"Yon-Soths?"

"I doubt it."

"Nameless Ones?"

"*New* aliens," the professor said, "*hidden* aliens."

"Let me get this straight," Maddox said. "Because you can't access the inoperative android, you suspect alien modifications, new aliens of a kind we haven't seen before?"

"That along with a few other things," Ludendorff muttered.

"For instance?"

The professor picked up a thin metal rod, walked to a different table and pointed at a tiny device the size and shape of a thumbtack.

"What's that?" Maddox asked.

"I've run a few tests, although they are not conclusive. Still, I suggest *that* was a persuader."

"You mean the device helped the android persuade…"

"Prime Minister Hampton and others to do exactly as the android wished."

"Is it a Spacer item?"

"Negative."

"You're positive on that?"

"One hundred percent," Ludendorff said. "That is alien technology of a kind I've never seen before. It's why I'm having trouble figuring out what it does."

Maddox fingered his chin. "The alien-modified Sanders android ran Hampton."

"I'd say so."

"Do you think Hampton has woken up to that?"

Ludendorff shook his head. "I doubt it works like that."

"What about Doctor Meyers?"

"Who?" asked Ludendorff.

Maddox shook his head as he fingered his chin once more. "I have to go Stockholm," he said.

"To see the Prime Minister?"

"To question Meyers," Maddox said. "Sanders said that he vetted her…" The captain spun on his heels and headed for the hatch.

"Don't you want to hear my theory?" Ludendorff asked.

Maddox stopped short and turned around, staring intently at the professor.

"Aliens abducted the android, modified it and ensured that Daniel Hampton became Prime Minister of the Commonwealth of Planets."

"Why did aliens do this?"

"Unknown so far," Ludendorff said. "But I would think for the usual reason."

"Meaning?"

"Conquering humanity, of course," Ludendorff said.

"Are these aliens working in concert with Lord Drakos?"

Ludendorff shook his head. "If I'm correct about hidden aliens, I doubt Drakos knows about them. However, he could be working with those he considers an android faction."

"These aliens—the evidence for them is extremely thin."

"To you and others," Ludendorff said. "But not to me."

Maddox nodded slowly.

"If this Doctor Meyers is connected to these hidden aliens, I would only approach her with great caution."

Maddox considered that. If Meyers was connected to hidden aliens able to abduct androids and win Great Council elections—he spun around, hurrying for the hatch.

-13-

Maddox headed for Stockholm, coming down from *Victory* in a shuttle piloted by Keith Maker.

Keith was a small man with sandy-colored hair and a cocky grin. In his own estimation, he was the best pilot in Star Watch. His exploits throughout the years made it a reasonable boast. He flew fast, coming through the atmosphere at a steep angle, causing the shuttle to shake.

Neither Maddox nor his sergeant, Riker, complained. Riker was an old fellow already, a gruff man who constantly thought about retirement. He had a bionic eye and arm to complement his real eye and arm. He had saved Maddox more times than he could count. Mainly, he didn't like to count because his didn't always trust his memory. It wasn't as good as it used to be, but Riker could still fire a blaster as steady as any space marine. The sergeant also possessed old-fashioned common sense, which wasn't as common as most people believed.

In any case, the shuttle roared toward Stockholm as Europe spread out before them.

"Incoming message, sir," Riker said, pointing at a blinking red light on the comm panel.

"Lieutenant," Maddox shouted. "Ease off, would you?"

"Roger that," Keith said.

The shaking ceased immediately, the ride becoming routine and smooth.

Maddox pressed a switch and stared at the small comm screen. A second later, Doctor Meyers's fabulous features peered at him from the screen.

Keith, who had leaned over, whistled in admiration. "What does she want with you, sir?"

Maddox frowned at his pilot.

"Oops, I know," Keith said. "Mind my own business."

Maddox gave the pilot the barest of nods before he addressed Meyers.

"Yes, Doctor," he said. "What can I do for you?"

"Do you have the…" She checked herself. "Are you bringing Bill Sanders down as ordered?"

Riker sucked in his breath.

Maddox glanced at the sergeant.

"*That's* an amazing voice," Riker muttered.

"What was that, Captain?" Meyers asked.

"My sergeant was struck by the beauty of your voice, Doctor. Just as my pilot—"

"Captain Maddox," Meyers said, interrupting, "this is official business. You will instruct your men to act with proper decorum."

"I'll pass that along," Maddox said.

"Are you bringing Sanders?" she asked again.

"Do you mean the android?"

Maddox wasn't sure, but he thought to detect the faintest stiffening.

"A simple yes or no will suffice," Meyers said.

"No," he said.

"Excuse me?" she asked.

"No," Maddox said, "I am not bringing the android."

"But—" She stared at him, and for once, she did not have the piercing gaze. It reappeared a second later as she seemed to shoot lasers into him. "The Prime Minister demanded that you—"

"I don't have it," Maddox said, interrupting her again.

"But…your Lord High Admiral informed us that you had assured him you were bringing it."

"It's what I told Cook, yes," Maddox said.

"You *lied* to your superior officer?" she asked, puzzled.

74

"No," Maddox said.

"What? But…you just said…"

"I know what I said, Doctor. I want to speak to the Prime Minister. It's vital I see him."

"You're not making any sense," Meyers said. "He ordered you to bring Sanders. This is a serious breach. You are in violation of the chain of command."

"We had a breakthrough," Maddox said. "My people made some interesting discoveries concerning the android."

"W-What kind of discoveries?" asked Meyers.

"That's why I need to speak to the Prime Minister. Has he been feeling any headaches lately?"

Meyers did not appear surprised by the question. She studied Maddox, and finally nodded.

"Why do ask about headaches?" she said.

"You know why."

"I assure you I don't."

"Right," Maddox said. "You expect me to believe that?"

She frowned. "Get to the point. Do you have a point with these questions?"

Maddox merely smiled.

The quality of her gaze intensified. "You're a *paquat*," she whispered.

"What's a paquat?" Maddox asked.

Her head jerked.

"Was that a slip, Doctor?" Maddox asked.

Her lips thinned. Abruptly, her image vanished as the communication broke.

Maddox sat back thoughtfully.

"Are you done talking?" asked Keith.

Maddox did not answer.

"What was that about, sir?" Riker asked. "I don't recall we've learned anything about the android."

"You are correct, Sergeant. But she doesn't know that."

Keith laughed, shaking his head.

Riker looked from Maddox to Keith, and back to Maddox. "I don't understand."

"He was faking," the pilot said. "He acted like he knew something to see what she would do."

"Is that right, sir?" Riker asked.

Maddox gave his sergeant a feral grin. "She's worried."

"Do we have the android then?" Riker asked.

"No," Maddox said. "I want them worried. I want them panicked."

"What if she—?"

"Sir," Keith said.

"I see it," Maddox said, who spotted the blinking red light. He tapped the comm control again.

This time, Admiral Cook appeared on the small screen. He looked much more tired than last time Maddox had seen him.

"Captain," the Lord High Admiral said. "Is it true that you are not bringing down the android as ordered?"

"Sir," Maddox said. "If you would allow me to play a hunch…"

"No, Captain," Cook said. "You must return to your ship and get the android. I gave the Prime Minister my word. You will not make a liar out of me."

"Then I'm sorry about this, sir," Maddox said.

"What were you thinking?"

"I have them worried."

Cook stared at him and finally dragged a hand over his face. "Don't you understand—?"

"Sir," Maddox said, interrupting. "I've discovered new information. I don't believe we should use this line to discuss it, though. The information is startling and sheds new light on what happened."

Admiral Cook blinked several times and sighed audibly. He appeared to be under heavy strain. "I cannot understand… I don't know why… Captain, you have put me in a terrible spot."

"Let me explain to the Prime Minister in person, sir."

"He might have you arrested."

"Sir…" Maddox didn't know how to impart willpower or spine into a man. Couldn't the Lord High Admiral see that he held all the advantages? The Prime Minister had trusted an android. What—

Maddox must have shown astonishment.

"What is it now?" Cook said.

"I, ah, I, ah—" Maddox squeezed his eyes closed, kept them closed and throttled his emotions. When he opened his eyes, he had become every inch the icy Intelligence operative. What had the Sanders android done to Cook during the time the two had been alone? No one had tested Cook to see if the android had—well—inserted anything into the Lord High Admiral. Maybe by the time Maddox had shown up, the android was giving the admiral his instructions.

"I'm following my intuition, sir," Maddox said.

"Are you mad?" Cook asked. "Turn your shuttle around and return to *Victory*. Get the android and bring it to Stockholm."

Maddox cleared his throat as he turned to Keith. The captain gave his pilot a significant glance even as he pushed his hand forward as if shoving a throttle stick forward, doing this while keeping his hand out of the Lord High Admiral's visual range.

"Captain?" Cook shouted.

Maddox turned to the tiny screen even as the shuttle began shaking again.

Cook said, "You will—"

"Sir," Maddox said. "There's a malfunction in the shuttle engine. We're going down. We're going down hard."

Cook stared at Maddox in disbelief.

"You're cutting out, sir," Maddox said, who then pressed the switch, breaking the comm connection.

"That's the Lord High Admiral," a pale Riker said, who knew his captain's ways all too well.

"I'm aware of that, Sergeant," Maddox said crisply. "Get us to Stockholm," he told Keith. "Get there as fast as you can."

"Yes, *sir,*" Keith said with enthusiasm. "Hang on, mates. This is going to be fun."

-14-

The red comm light continued to blink, but Maddox ignored it as the shuttle blazed down from orbital space.

Keith put on an exhibition of combat flying. As he did, Maddox kept a keen eye on the board in case any targeting sensors latched onto them. Finally, the red comm light stopped blinking.

By this point, they were closing in toward Stockholm Spaceport. Keith began shedding speed, throttling back to normal flight.

"Call the control tower, Sergeant," Maddox said.

Riker did as ordered.

Soon, Keith lowered the shuttle to a designated spot on the tarmac and shut off the engines.

Maddox clicked off his seatbelt and glanced out a side window.

"I don't hear any sirens," Riker said.

"Because no police vehicles are coming," Maddox said. "We may be moving faster than they can think through the repercussions of their actions."

"Do you mean the Lord High Admiral or the Prime Minister?" Riker asked.

"Neither," Maddox said. "I mean Meyers."

By that time, Keith opened the hatch and pressed a bulkhead switch that lowered a set of stairs to the tarmac.

Maddox headed for the hatch and stopped suddenly upon reaching it. "You're staying here," he told Keith. "Be ready for a hasty liftoff."

Keith raised his eyebrows but said nothing, only nodded.

"Are you carrying hidden weapons?" Maddox asked the sergeant.

"Are you expecting to be arrested?" Riker asked.

"I'm trying to anticipate my opponent," Maddox replied. "We've ripped off the mask, as it were. Meyers might not know what to do next."

"You suspect her instead of the Prime Minister?"

Maddox considered the question, finally saying, "Yes. Now, let's go before Meyers does send someone to arrest me."

***

Maddox spoke convincingly enough to receive a car from the spaceport authorities. Riker drove through Stockholm as they headed for the Prime Minister's Executive Palace.

"Should I let them know we're coming?" Riker asked.

"They know by now," Maddox said, "but if they don't, let's surprise them."

Traffic was light and soon Riker slowed as they approached a vast iron-barred gated area. Behind the gates rose a huge palace. Space marines in special dress uniform guarded the main approach on the road.

Riker drove up to the guard post, letting his window roll down.

In back, Maddox stiffened, ready to draw his gun.

Riker exchanged a few words with the marine on sentry duty.

"Captain Maddox?" the marine asked.

Riker affirmed with a nod.

"You're on the manifest," the marine said. "Go ahead and—" The marine gave Riker parking instructions.

Soon, Riker started driving again, following the instructions as the car moved through beautiful scenery with towering trees, lush bushes, grand fountains and statues. He followed until they reached an open parking area, with several other cars in various white-marked locations.

They got out. Maddox went to one of the cars, inspecting it.

"Armored," he told Riker.

"Does it seem strange the guard told us to park here?" the sergeant asked.

Maddox nodded. It did seem strange, especially as they still had their sidearms. A premonition warned the captain. He almost turned around for the car, wanting to head back to the spaceport and get back up to *Victory*. Then, he wondered if he should call Galyan and have the AI holoimage scout ahead for him.

This was the Executive Palace. Wouldn't the place have the latest security upgrades? If security spotted Galyan... Maddox shook his head, abandoning the idea.

"Trouble, sir?" asked Riker.

"No, Sergeant. Let's go."

***

The two Star Watch operatives moved through the palace grounds without incident, following a path. They came to a side entrance, receiving two passes from a waiting marine. She did not ask for their weapons but gave them directions so they could reach a waiting Doctor Meyers inside the North Section.

Maddox and Riker marched through carpeted halls with expensive paintings on the walls and priceless statues in alcoves. There were no marines anywhere. In fact, the palace seemed deserted.

"This is off," Riker said.

Maddox had reached the same conclusion some time ago. Why would the palace lack its full complement of space marine guards and other personnel? It made no sense.

"Is Meyers trapping us, sir?"

Maddox halted abruptly. Riker stepped past him and then stopped, turning to the captain. The sergeant said nothing, merely waited.

Maddox tried to put himself in Meyers and then Hampton's place. What could either of them gain by emptying the Executive Palace? Why had the gate guards let them keep their weapons? No one had attempted to search them. Maybe he was asking the wrong question. What could hidden aliens gain by letting him in like this? What could the hidden aliens gain by emptying the palace?

The more Maddox studied the questions, the more his instincts told him to leave.

A lone marine turned a corner, heading toward them. The man was in a dress uniform and carried a rifle against his right shoulder.

"Step behind me, Sergeant," Maddox said quietly. "Get ready to draw and stun, but don't let the marine see you're ready."

"Yes, sir," Riker said, as he stepped behind Maddox.

The captain waited as the marine marched to them. It seemed the man was going to march right past without saying a word.

"Lieutenant," Maddox said, noting the space marine's rank.

The space marine halted. He was a thickset young man with a brush cut. There was something off with his eyes. They weren't glazed, but they weren't as alert as Maddox felt they should be.

"Where is everyone?" Maddox asked.

For a moment, it seemed as if the marine wouldn't answer. Then his bearing changed. So did the quality of his gaze.

"There was a group photo shoot, sir," the marine said. "It's an annual occurrence." The man checked a chronometer. "They should be headed back already."

"Are all the guards in place where they should be?"

The marine tilted his head. "Why do you ask, sir?"

"Lieutenant, we're here to see Doctor Meyers. But we've gotten lost. Is it possible you can take us to her?"

The question seemed to confuse the marine. Slowly, he shook his head. "I have to make my rounds, sir."

"Can you call someone?"

"Yes..." the marine said just as slowly.

"Oh, wait," Maddox said. "I remember the route now. Thank you, Lieutenant. You've been most helpful."

That seemed to relax the marine. He nodded, straightened some and continued his march.

Both Maddox and Riker watched him, until finally the marine disappeared around a corner.

"What now, sir?" Riker asked.

Maddox did not answer right away.

"That was odd, right?" asked Riker.

Maddox nodded.

"It's odd hardly anyone is here," the sergeant added. "This is the Executive Palace. It should be crawling with people. Meyers set us up, sir."

"Set us up how, though?" Maddox asked.

"I don't know."

"Neither do I," Maddox said. "I also believe it imperative that we find out. So, we will keep our appointment."

"That's walking right into it, sir."

"Yes," Maddox said. "Now, keep alert, Sergeant, and be ready to draw and fire at my command, but not until I give my command."

Riker nodded.

Maddox went into high alert mode, all his senses straining and his mind awhirl as he began to walk through the lonely carpeted halls of the Executive Palace.

-15-

During his undercover Intelligence forays, Maddox often posed as a gambler. He was particularly good at poker in all its forms. As he moved down the palace halls, he considered the odds that Meyers was setting him up in some nefarious way.

The lack of marine guards and other personnel—even various cabinet people—was too strange. Meyers hated him. She likely worked for hidden aliens. This was a setup. The more he considered it, the more that seemed correct.

His initial idea had been to walk into the trap, knowing it was a trap, and thereby trapping Meyers. But if she had taken such elaborate steps, if she had such power as to even dismiss the guards—then it was doubtful he could turn the tables on her.

Poker often demanded making a decision based on incomplete information and odds. One attempted to gain the highest odds he could and then played his hand accordingly, folding if the odds were wrong.

Maddox wanted to spring the trap. He wanted to bring this to a head if he could. Admiral Cook was acting in a suboptimal manner. He—Maddox—had taken too many daring, possibly outlandish courses, disobeying direct orders in the process. If he ran now, his disobediences would catch up with him. Yet, if he kept going because he'd hazarded too much to reach this position, he possibly risked more than he cared to lay on the line.

"Galyan," Maddox said, softly. "I know you're listening to me. I want you to come down in stealth mode. I have a mission for you."

Yes, the Executive Palace might have the newest upgrades. Yet, it might not. It was also possible that nothing in Human Space matched all the high tech installed in *Victory*. It was a matter of odds. Maddox was going forward because he couldn't afford to go back. Thus, he would now accept the possibly of Galyan's holoimage triggering security measures, as the odds of that danger had now become tolerable given his present course.

"Galyan—"

The little Adok holoimage appeared before Maddox and Riker.

"Here, sir," Galyan said in a slightly robotic voice. "I was wondering when you were going to call me. I have observed—"

"Not now, Galyan," Maddox said. "We're under a time crunch."

"Ah."

"Listen closely," Maddox said. "I'm going to give you the directions to the North Section Arbor—"

"Excuse me, sir," Galyan said, interrupting. "I already have a schematic of the Executive Palace. Just tell me where you want me to go, and I will go there and observe. I presume you wish me to go in ghost mode."

Maddox stared at the holoimage, nodding a moment later.

Galyan vanished. He reappeared several seconds later.

"The North Section Arbor is empty, sir."

"No guards?"

"Empty, sir," Galyan said, sounding puzzled by the last question.

"Yes," Maddox said, surprised no guards were there. "Go into the North Section Arbor Meeting Room. The Prime Minister should be waiting for me there."

"Interesting," Galyan said, vanishing again. He appeared even sooner this time.

"No one?" asked Maddox.

"Captain," Galyan said. "The Prime Minister is lying on the floor, missing half his head. Brains and gore are splattered on the rug."

Riker cursed aloud.

Maddox stared at Galyan, with his mind awhirl. With a dry tongue, the captain asked, "You're one hundred percent certain it was the Prime Minister?"

"Just a moment," Galyan said, disappearing again. Two second later, he was back. "It is Prime Minister Hampton, sir. His features and other diagnostic components match my records for him."

"We're supposed to have killed him," Riker said. "That's why Meyers let us keep our weapons."

"Of course," Maddox said. "That's obvious."

"We have to get out of here," Riker said.

"No," Maddox said. "We have to find the killer."

"*We* do?" asked Riker, appalled.

"Was there a gun on the floor?" Maddox asked Galyan.

"Negative," the AI said.

"It wasn't suicide then," Maddox said.

"Meyers?" Riker asked.

"Right," Maddox said. "Galyan, I want you to begin a thorough search throughout the palace. Locate Doctor Meyers and immediately tell me where she is."

"You will remain here?" Galyan asked.

"No…" Maddox said, frowning, concentrating. "We're heading for our car. Do you know where it's parked?"

"Yes," Galyan said, "as I've been monitoring your progress the entire time."

"I thought you might be," Maddox said. "Now start. We have to locate Meyers."

Galyan vanished.

"Let's hoof it, Sergeant. We don't want to get caught in the web."

"Aren't we already?"

"I don't think so. They shot Hampton too soon because they didn't know about Galyan. Now move, old man," Maddox said, shoving Riker from behind. "Don't make me carry you."

The two Star Watch operatives began running, heading back the way they had come.

-16-

Riker was gasping as the two of them burst out of the Executive Palace from the same side entrance they'd used before to enter. The wheezing coming from his mouth was pathetic to hear.

"You must stay in better shape, Sergeant," Maddox chided him.

"Halt," said a marine—the one who had given them passes earlier. She clicked the flap to her holster and began drawing a sidearm.

Maddox reached her, chopping her wrist, making the drawn gun clatter onto the sidewalk.

"Where's Doctor Meyers?" Maddox demanded.

The marine rubbed her bruised wrist as she scowled at him.

Maddox noted the bud in her right ear and a tiny microphone pinned to her collar. Without further preamble, he dug out the bud and took the microphone from her lapel.

"Hey," she said. "You can't do that."

Maddox put the bud in his left ear. There was nothing. Then it hissed. "Be on the watch for two Star Watch officers," a man said. "We believe they may have assaulted the Prime Minister."

"Give that back," the marine said. She knelt on the sidewalk to get the gun.

Riker beat her to it, picking it up first.

The man on the comm began giving instructions, telling about two security teams converging on the side entrance to the palace.

Maddox closed his eyes, and he smiled, digging out the earbud. He tossed it and the microphone onto the grass. Then he drew his dart gun and shot the marine.

"Why?" she asked, before slumping unconscious.

Maddox grabbed her and set her down gently.

"She's going to remember you did that," Riker said.

"Of course," Maddox said. "Someone is observing us. No. Don't look around. This is a setup, and someone is thinking fast. I'm assuming Meyers or Meyers' handler."

Maddox glanced around. "Ah, that should do," he said, spotting a clump of bushes. "Sergeant, one more sprint and that should be it."

Riker groaned, but he broke into an old man's sprint, following Maddox as they headed for a clump of bushes in the middle of the vast lawn.

Maddox reached the bushes first, pushing through to the center. "Galyan," he said. "Galyan—" and he told the holoimage where to meet them.

Galyan appeared as Riker crashed through the bushes. The sergeant collapsed onto his butt on the center grass.

"I have not found Doctor Meyers," the holoimage said.

"There's been a change in plans," Maddox said. "I want you to find the observers attempting to watch me."

"Do you mean in the general perimeter," Galyan asked, "with this location as the locus?"

"No. Go to the North Section side entrance. There is a marine lying unconscious there. Use her as the observed point and locate whoever was watching us. At all costs, remain unseen."

Galyan nodded before disappearing.

"Why did they kill the Prime Minister?" Riker asked

Maddox had been considering that. Whoever had killed Hampton must have decided that he had become a liability. It was possible his decision to keep the Sanders android had panicked the enemy. Had his action killed Hampton then?

Maddox shook his head. He was not afflicted with false morality. He had not pulled the trigger. He had panicked the enemy as desired—

Galyan reappeared.

"There is a three-man unit located in a garden shed on a slight incline. If you peer west, you can see the shed from here."

"The unit is watching the bushes?"

"Yes," Galyan said.

"What are the three men wearing?"

"Executive Palace marine uniforms," Galyan said.

"I doubt they're marines," Maddox said.

"I could run an analysis on that," Galyan said.

Maddox debated using *Victory's* sniper ray to take them out from orbit. That would cause too many problems, though, as Star Watch Orbital Defense would pick that up. He was in trouble. He didn't want to needlessly put his crew in jeopardy with him.

"Galyan," Maddox said. "Get back up into *Victory*. Watch the Executive Palace from there. See who leaves. Record everything and come down in stealth mode to get a visual of them."

"What about you, sir?" Galyan said. "How will you get away?"

"Don't worry about me. Get up there. Find Meyers leaving the palace. Find her as soon as you can."

"There has to be more enemy operatives than just Meyers," Riker said.

"Probably the entire staff," Maddox said. "Either that, or they've been brain-scrubbed to obey her. I believe the latter more likely."

"You suspect Meyers above the Sanders android?" Galyan asked.

"You have a task, Mister," Maddox told the AI. "Now get started."

"Sir," Galyan said, disappearing a second later.

"What are we going to do?" Riker asked.

"For starters, Sergeant, get off our fat asses."

Riker grumbled as he climbed to his feet.

"That way," Maddox said, pointing. He positioned his mouth in such a way that he could see the garden shed up an incline. "We're going to use the foliage to work our way back to our car."

"Won't they have aerial surveillance on us?"

"Another reason to use the trees," Maddox said.

"They're just going to arrest us later."

Maddox turned to his sergeant. "Haven't you heard the old saw that possession is nine-tenths of the law?"

"I have."

"Remaining a free agent is the nine-tenths rule of remaining free."

"What does that even mean?" Riker asked.

"Come on, old man. I'll show you."

-17-

"This isn't the way back to the car," Riker said several minutes later. "We're heading back to the palace."

"Your perceptions haven't dimmed with age," Maddox said. "I congratulate you."

"Sir," Riker panted. "Might you let me in on your plan?"

"We hid in the bushes to escape their detection, correct?"

"I'm with you so far, sir."

"But we didn't fully escape their detection. It's possible they used a handheld sensor on me there at the end of our time in the bushes."

Riker blinked several times, maybe figuring it out. "Oh. They're waiting for us at the car?"

"Some of them are, or they're watching the car. That was the idea. We have to keep a step or two ahead of them until we're on safe ground."

"Back on *Victory* you mean?" asked Riker.

"Let me help you," Maddox said. The captain grabbed the sergeant's flesh arm. Then he began to sprint.

Riker cried out in dismay. The captain could move like a leopard when he really ran. The sergeant's legs almost gave out at this speed. Maddox kept hold, however keeping the old man up by main force. They fairly flew across the grassy grounds, heading to a different entrance into the palace.

"We're going to grab the air car on the roof," Maddox shouted at Riker.

"But sir—"

"Come on," Maddox said. And he ran to the entrance, releasing Riker in order to open the door. It was locked.

Maddox drew his regular gun and fired, opening the door afterward. They ran down carpeted halls, which were still empty in this area. Maddox moved confidently through the halls as he'd studied the layout before leaving today.

"Aren't we taking those stairs?" Riker asked, pointing.

"No," Maddox said.

Soon, the two of them ran down steps into a basement area.

"The air car can't be this way," Riker said.

"It's not."

Maddox took several more turns and finally reached a subway entrance. There was no subway car waiting for them, however.

Riker looked peaked and had been gasping for some time. "I don't get it, sir."

"I shouted about the air car, right?"

"Yes. Oh," Riker said several seconds later. "You were hoping they picked that up too."

"Are you ready for one last run?"

"No," Riker said. "Do you even know where this goes?"

"I have an idea."

Riker wiped his moist mouth with a sleeve. "I'm beat, sir. You go ahead. I'll wait here."

"I've already considered the idea, Sergeant. But I don't want them to capture you, so you're going to have to push one last time."

"Please," Riker said. "This one is too much. They think we've killed the Prime Minister. This one is too hard, sir."

"An evil person is trying to set us up. We can't let her get away with it."

Riker peered into the subterranean tunnel. "What if a train or whatever runs through there comes while we're traveling underground?"

"Then we're dead. Do you have any other questions?"

Riker eyed Maddox. "I suppose not."

"Excellent," Maddox said. "Now, let me give you a hand down. Our margin for error is running out."

-18-

From upon a metal ladder in an underground access tube, Maddox heaved, using considerable strength to attempt to lift a metal grate above his head. Usually, operators used a special machine to raise the metal seal. Maddox gritted his teeth and heaved again, glad that he did upright military presses as part of his weightlifting regimen.

The grate rose fractionally as Maddox strained.

"Harder, sir, push harder," Riker said from a position lower on the ladder than the captain.

Maddox did exactly that even as his arms shook. The grate was far too heavy for an ordinary man to lift.

"You're getting it," Riker said.

The back of Maddox's head began to pound with pain. The strain was too much, the grate too heavy.

Maddox roared with effort as his face turned purple, and he lifted the grate just enough so he could partially slide it to the right.

The captain practically collapsed and might have slipped down the ladder. Riker used his flesh hand to grip a rung, while he used his bionic arm to hold up Maddox.

A few seconds later, Maddox revived enough to wrap his arms around a rung. He looked up as spots danced before his eyes. The grate had shifted halfway off the opening.

"Fine," Maddox whispered. He climbed a little higher, braced his back and thrust out a leg against the opposing tube side. He raised his hands, gripping the edge of the grate. By jerking and pushing, he slid it farther off the access hole.

"I can squeeze through that," Riker said from below.

An exhausted Maddox climbed up, sliding past the almost removed grate and crawled onto cement. He wanted to throw himself onto the cool surface and rest. Instead, he climbed to his feet, watching as Riker crawled through.

"We're in a shed," Riker declared.

"Not so loud," Maddox said. "We don't know who's outside."

"They would have heard the clanging and your shouting, sir, if they were nearby."

"Right," Maddox said, drawing his gun. He unlatched the door and peered outside, spying trees and bushes.

Holstering the gun, Maddox opened the door all the way, breathing the fresh air and squinting at the brighter light.

They had moved through the underground tunnel for twenty-some odd minutes. That was surely enough time for Meyers to have gotten away. Had someone found the Prime Minister's body yet? Were Riker and he the key suspects for murder?

Riker came out of the shed, closing the door behind him.

"This must be a secured area," Maddox said, "as it's an access point into the Executive Palace."

"Maybe it's time to call Galyan again."

Maddox nodded, but that made the back of his head spike with pain. He needed to take it easy for a bit and rest.

"Galyan," Maddox said.

Nothing happened.

"That can't be good," Riker said.

"We'll worry about it later," Maddox said, although he worried about it now. What did it mean that Galyan did not respond?

They walked past the nearest trees and pushed through nine-foot tall bushes to find a solid fence surrounding the premises. Maddox led the way as they followed the fence, finally coming to a locked and heavy steel door.

"Now what?" Riker asked.

"It's time for your bionic strength," Maddox said. "Open it."

Riker grinned, stepping forward and using the mechanical power of his bionic hand to twist open the handle, breaking the locking mechanism in the process. He pushed the door open and they found themselves on a hill, looking down into a plaza with various Stockholm government buildings surrounding it.

"Let me see," Maddox said, examining the plaza. "Ah, Galyan," he said into the air, and he gave the Adok AI the coordinates to their location.

Nothing happened. Galyan still did not appear.

"Your communicator please, Sergeant," Maddox said.

Riker dug his out, handing it the captain.

Maddox opened it, picked up a tiny power cell from his jacket pocket and inserted the cell into the comm unit. Until this point, no one could use the comm unit to track them.

"Lieutenant Noonan," Maddox said into the comm.

"Sir," Valerie said promptly. "There's a worldwide manhunt for you. I'm supposed to report your location the instant you call."

"Ignore that for now, Lieutenant."

"I'm not sure that I can, sir," Valerie said. "The order came from the Lord High Admiral. They're saying you murdered the Prime Minster of the Commonwealth."

"Do you think I did?"

"That's not the point," she said. "I have direct orders."

"Is Keith upstairs?"

"Yes," she said. "I ordered him to take the shuttle up as soon as Admiral Cook ordered me to report you as soon as I heard from you. I told the admiral that I'd taken away your method of escape."

"Good work, Lieutenant."

"Sir?" she asked. "I thought you'd be angry."

"Doctor Meyers engineered the Prime Minister's death. We must catch her before she escapes the planet."

"I'm sorry," Valerie said. "I have my orders, sir. I'm bound by my oath to Star Watch."

Maddox frowned at the communicator. Lieutenant Valerie Noonan was often a stickler for rules and regulations. Maybe he should have called someone else. The problem was that she ran *Victory* while he was away.

"Can you patch me through to the Lord High Admiral?" he asked.

"I can try. But I should tell you that I'm going to give him your location."

"Valerie," Maddox said. "I want you to listen carefully. The Sanders android did something to the Lord High Admiral while they were alone in Cook's office. The admiral is not himself. The Prime Minister of the Commonwealth of Planets was an alien plant or patsy. I am on the trail of the human agents of a new alien threat. These aliens are diabolically clever. I know you want to obey the lawfully given order. But if you do, the new alien threat wins."

"Please, Captain, don't ask me to help you escape justice. I-I can't break my oath to Star Watch."

"You're an officer of Star Watch in order to protect it from all dangers. This is the danger today, Lieutenant. Do you have the courage to risk everything to protect humanity from a new alien threat?"

"You killed the Prime Minister, sir. You'd say anything to avoid capture."

"If you truly believe that," Maddox said, "hand me over to the authorities."

A few seconds passed in silence.

"I don't believe that," Valerie said in an agonized voice. "But…but—what do you want me to do?" she asked in the quietest voice she'd ever used.

"I want you to send Keith down in a fold-fighter to pick me up."

Valerie groaned. "This call is likely monitored."

Maddox had used a scrambler, but in this instance, that probably wouldn't matter.

"Send Keith," Maddox said. "Do it immediately. Then patch me through to Major Stokes."

"Okay," she said in a small voice.

"By the way," Maddox said. "Where is Galyan?"

"Here, sir," the little holoimage said from behind the captain.

Maddox whirled around in surprise.

"I have something to tell you, sir," Galyan said.

-19-

"Just a second," Maddox told the holoimage. "Valerie, are you sending Keith?"

"We'll all be court-martialed for this," she said.

"No," Maddox said, "Because I know what's going on."

"You *think* you know."

"Make your choice, Lieutenant." Maddox kept the comm to his right ear but moved it so he wouldn't be talking directly into it. He eyed Galyan, asking, "What do you have for me?"

"I've followed Doctor Meyers," Galyan said.

"You spotted her leaving the palace," Maddox said.

"No, sir," Galyan said. "I overheard a transmission as she spoke to the spaceport authorities."

"Stockholm Spaceport?" asked Maddox.

"That is correct," Galyan said.

"The point, Galyan, get to the point."

"I moved to her location as she ran across the tarmac to a waiting ship."

"Skip the details and get to the point."

"I have to explain a few details, sir, or it's not going to make sense."

"Fine, fine, just hurry up."

The holoimage nodded. "The ship was big as shuttles go. I'm not sure it was a shuttle exactly. It was box-shaped and definitely not aerodynamic. It did have several fins along the outer box."

"I have Major Stokes on the line," Valerie said through the comm.

"Tell him to listen to this," Maddox said. "Galyan, speak up so Stokes can hear you." The captain adjusted the comm speaker, aiming it at the holoimage.

"Doctor Meyers jumped aboard the box-ship," Galyan said loudly. "It was several times as large as a *Victory* shuttle. As soon as Doctor Meyers boarded, the box-ship began to hum in a strange manner. It received spaceport permission and began to rise straight up. At that point, I used *Victory's* sensors. The box-ship used antigravity pods of a unique nature. It rose several hundred meters before it began lateral movement, heading for the Baltic Sea."

"Speed this up, Galyan," the captain said.

"The box-ship moved fast until it was out of sight of ordinary vision. At that point, it used a form of fold to disappear."

"Where did it go?" Maddox asked.

"It took me several minutes to locate—"

"Where did it go, Galyan?" Maddox asked, interrupting.

"It appeared in orbit beside a smaller-than-average hauler."

"Not a Nerva hauler," Maddox said.

"The hauler is not registered to any company I've heard about before this," Galyan said. "Why do you suspect a Nerva hauler?"

"It doesn't matter," Maddox said. "Finish the story."

"The box-ship entered the hauler, and the hauler has broken orbit, heading out-system. According to its present trajectory, it is headed for Jupiter."

"What are the nearest Laumer Points in that direction?" Maddox asked.

"None," Galyan said. "Is that not curious?"

"Just a second," Maddox told Galyan. "Major, did you hear all that."

"I did," Stokes said over the comm. "Have Galyan give me the registry number of the hauler."

Galyan did so.

"I'm relaying that to an aide," Stokes said. "Now, Captain, I'm sending an air car to bring you in."

"Do you think I killed Hampton?" Maddox asked.

"I do not. But you are under suspicion, as you entered palace grounds with weapons. They have you on video running through the palace halls. They also have recorded you darting a marine."

"I suggest that you land marines at the Executive Palace—"

"Impossible," Stokes said, interrupting. "This is a CGMS problem."

"Then talk to the chief of the Marshal Service. Have him intern all the marines and all palace personnel. Scan their brains."

"Your advice is sound, Captain. The Marshal Service is already busy doing just that. Fortunately for Star Watch, you are not the only one who can think on your feet."

"Then you must know that I did not murder Hampton."

"There are procedures to follow, old boy," Stokes said. "I know you enjoy breaking them. But this time, we shall follow protocol to the letter."

"I'm going to stop the hauler."

"Quite unnecessary," Stokes said. "We have Star Watch destroyers intercepting the hauler. Doctor Meyers will return to testify before a court."

"Excuse me, Major. I'd like to verify that."

"Captain Maddox," Stokes said in a didactic voice. "You will…" the major trailed off.

"What happened?" Maddox asked.

"This is unbelievable," Stokes said.

"Major—"

"Captain," Stokes said, interrupting. "I am watching a screen and have just witnessed the hauler folding like a fighter. It has vanished from Earth orbit and vanished from the destroyers closing in on it."

"That tears it," Maddox said. "*Victory* is the best ship in the fleet to track a vessel like that. Surely, you can see that."

"Unfortunately, yes," Stokes said. "But it will take time for you to reach *Victory*. Lieutenant Noonan can take care of the details while we intern you."

At that moment, a fold-fighter appeared six meters above Maddox's head. A belly hatch opened, and a rope-like ladder dropped down near him.

"I can be on *Victory* in less than thirty seconds," Maddox said.

"That is a fanciful boast even for you," Stokes said.

"I'll have a report on your desk concerning Professor Ludendorff's findings on the Sanders android in several hours," Maddox said. "It shows that aliens of an unknown nature have infiltrated Hampton's staff. It's possible they modified Hampton. They blew away his head, likely because that's where the implants were."

"Captain Maddox, I'm ordering you to await the police. You are wanted for murder. We must clear this up in the proper manner. There are too many people saying that Star Watch does what it pleases. Do you understand me?"

"I do, Major," Maddox said.

"Then you'll be waiting there?"

Maddox could hear sirens blaring in the distance as he reached for the rope ladder. "I'd like to misdirect you, Major, but I think you'd take that badly. Thus, I'm informing you that I shall surrender once I have Doctor Meyers in custody."

"You will do no such thing," Stokes said. "That is a direct—"

Maddox clicked off the comm and stuffed it in his jacket pocket. Then he clambered up the ladder with simian ease.

Riker followed him.

Soon, the rope zipped in and the belly-hatch shut. Seconds later, the fold-fighter folded away, presumably up to Starship *Victory* high in Earth orbit.

-20-

Maddox strode onto the bridge of *Victory* as Lieutenant Valerie Noonan exited the captain's chair. She had athletic grace and long brunette hair.

"I hope you know what you're doing, sir," she said, her beautiful features screwed up with worry.

"Captain Maddox," the Lord High Admiral said from the main screen. "I second that feeling."

"Sir," Maddox said, not expecting to see Cook, not *wanting* to see the old man right now. The captain took his chair, wondering if Valerie had been in on this ambush. Yes, of course she had.

Maddox realized he had pushed her too hard. Each person had his or her own basic nature. Loyalty could stretch that nature, but there was always a breaking point. A good leader knew the amount of elasticity in each of his people. It would appear he had misjudged Lieutenant Noonan, a mistake on his part.

Even as the captain realized these things, he looked up at Cook with bland features.

"I'm not sure what to do with you, Maddox," Cook said. The old admiral looked haggard. "I wish I inspired the kind of loyalty you do with your crew."

"The crew and I have been through a lot together, sir. We're like a family."

"I'm familiar with the concept," Cook said. "The point, young man, is that you have the proverbial luck of the Devil."

"Sir?"

"Don't interrupt me," Cook said, as some of his former demeanor returned. "There's been a breakthrough in the case—I'm referring to Prime Minister Hampton's murder. Chief Marshal Eric Enders has conclusively determined that you did not nor could not have killed the Prime Minister."

Maddox sagged back in his chair and some of the terrible tension in his gut uncoiled.

"They've begun interrogating Executive Palace marines," Cook said. "There is definitely something wrong with each of their brain patterns. What's more, there is an old surveillance system in place at the palace. A former administration had it installed during a bad period. That's unimportant, I suppose. The thing is that the new administration must have never heard about it, or not have had time yet to insert the system into the newer one their team installed."

Maddox kept silent, listening intently.

"Chief Marshal Enders remembered the old surveillance system and decided to check it. It shows Doctor Meyers shooting the Prime Minister. She definitely murdered Hampton."

"She made a mistake," Maddox said.

"So it appears. Do you have any idea why she did that?"

"Made the mistake regarding the old surveillance system?"

"No. Why would she shoot Hampton?"

"I imagine because she believed that he had been compromised, the plot uncovered or about to be uncovered."

Cook frowned, nodding slowly. "You were right about something else, I'm afraid. There's been a change in my brain pattern. It's slight, but it's there."

"Sanders?" asked Maddox.

"This puts me in a terrible dilemma. If we're keeping O'Hara out because she's been mentally compromised—"

"Sir," Maddox interrupted. "You can't step down now."

"But if I've been mentally compromised, if my people dismiss my orders to do what they want without repercussions—"

"Prime Minister Hampton is dead, sir," Maddox said, interrupting, knowing very well that Cook referred to him.

"We've just lost the head of the Commonwealth. We can't lose the head of Star Watch as well at the same time. Word is going to leak out about Hampton trusting an android. The Commonwealth does not need two hard blows concerning its top leadership. People need to have faith in the system. If they lose that faith, the entire system can crumble."

"You have a point," Cook conceded. "It's what Major Stokes has been telling me."

"Sir," Galyan said. "I hate to interrupt your conversation."

Maddox scowled at the holoimage.

"What is it?" Cook asked. "What is the AI trying to tell you?"

"Well?" Maddox asked Galyan. "What is it?"

"I have detected the folding hauler," Galyan said.

"I heard that," Cook said. "Where is it?"

"Midway through the Asteroid Belt, Admiral," Galyan said. "It is still heading on a direct course for Jupiter."

"Captain," Cook said. "Follow that hauler. Stop it and capture Doctor Meyers. If you can, find out what type of alien she serves. But bring her back so Star Watch can interrogate her."

"I will, Admiral," Maddox said.

"We'll finish this conversation later," Cook said. "I want her, son. You go get her."

Maddox nodded, intending to do exactly that.

-21-

Victory went into high alert as Galyan studied the sensor data in detail.

The supposed hauler had used a fold mechanism, a ministar drive jump. The enemy vessel had gone between two points in space in an instant. The ancient starship's sensors had needed time to spot the hauler, however, as light traveled at a constant speed of 300,000 kilometers per second.

On average, the Earth was one AU from the Sun, or 150 million kilometers. The enemy hauler was approximately halfway in the Asteroid Belt, which was between the orbits of Mars and Jupiter. In this case, the hauler was a little more than 250 million kilometers away from *Victory's* present position.

Given the distance, it took light 14 minutes to travel between the hauler and *Victory*. As Galyan used the starship's teleoptics, he was seeing what the hauler had been doing 14 minutes ago.

Contrary to common stereotypes, the Asteroid Belt was relatively empty of stellar objects. The total mass of the asteroids in the belt was approximately 4% the Moon's mass. Half the belt was contained in the four largest asteroids: Ceres, Vesta, Pallas and Hygiea.

"We're going to follow the hauler," Maddox said. "Tell the crew to get ready for a combat jump."

He had no arguments from anyone. A klaxon wailed as Valerie alerted the crew for the coming star drive jump.

Maddox settled in his command chair. This was a perplexing situation. In his estimation, the aliens or Meyers had definitely panicked. They might have been able to brazen it out, as they'd held Prime Minister Hampton. The key, he was sure, was that they hadn't known what he'd learned from having Ludendorff study the android. Keeping the Sanders android had been the right move to force their hand.

"We're ready to jump, sir," Valerie said.

A that point, Keith rushed onto the bridge, heading for the helm controls.

"Let's come in close," Maddox said. "I want to appear within ten thousand kilometers of the hauler."

"You doubt they have weapons?" Valerie asked.

"None that can do us heavy damage," Maddox replied. "Galyan, ready the neutron cannon. I doubt we're going to need the disrupter cannon for this."

"Isn't that premature, sir?" Valerie asked.

Despite his dislike of having anyone question his orders, Maddox swiveled his command chair to regard her.

"They have a fold mechanism," Valerie said. "According to Galyan, they have advanced antigravity pods. They managed to insert a controlled human into our highest office."

"The last has nothing to do with military affairs."

"But it shows advanced thinking on their part," Valerie said.

"Noted," Maddox said. "Helm, bring us in at twenty-five thousand kilometers. We'll give ourselves a little more margin for error."

Valerie looked as if she wanted to say more, but she finally turned back to her board.

Maddox faced the main screen.

Keith had been tapping his board. "This will be an approximate distance, sir. I'm calculating their position at their speed fourteen minutes ago."

"I understand," Maddox said.

"Then, we're jumping…now," Keith said, as he manipulated his panel.

Maddox gripped the edges of his armrests, tensed and felt that odd sensation of folding or jumping. He lost awareness due to mini-Jump Lag. And then his senses began working again. The captain inhaled deeply. He was usually the first to come out of Jump Lag. The others now did as they began to stir again.

"Show me the hauler," Maddox said. "Put it on the main screen."

Nothing happened.

"Galyan," Maddox said. "Where is the enemy hauler?"

"Gone, sir," Galyan said.

"Do you mean it folded again?"

"I don't know," Galyan said. "That would be the most probable—"

"I got them," Valerie said.

Maddox swiveled around to her. "Where is it?"

"In the Jupiter System," Valerie said. "The hauler folded 379 million kilometers from its last location. It is now a little more than one million kilometers from the gas giant. That puts it at the same orbital distance from Jupiter as Ganymede."

"We have to follow them," Maddox said.

"We can't jump just yet," Valerie said.

Maddox almost struck an armrest in frustration. He refrained as he stood. "Get me Star Watch Command, Jupiter," he told Valerie.

"It will be a delayed message," Valerie said.

Maddox nodded. "Tell them about the hauler. Tell them to intercept it at once. Keith, alert me the instant we're ready to jump again."

"Aye, mate," Keith said.

Maddox frowned.

"I mean, yes, sir," Keith amended.

Maddox rubbed his chin. The hauler appeared to have a limited jump or fold capacity. Otherwise, why not jump directly to Jupiter the first time? That the enemy ship was racing to Jupiter seemed odd. The Jupiter moons were heavily colonized. There were even cloud cities within the gas giant's upper atmosphere. Star Watch had several destroyer-class vessels stationed there. The authorities at Jupiter might have already been hailing the fleeing hauler.

Why race to Jupiter? Could the hauler have other allies waiting for them there? That seemed unlikely, and yet, so did suborning the Prime Minister.

Time passed as Maddox fumed inwardly, waiting.

"My message should have reached Star Watch Command, Jupiter by now," Valerie said.

More time passed. Finally, "We should be receiving a reply soon," Valerie said.

Galyan had recorded the hauler racing toward the gas giant. So far, no Star Watch destroyers had attempted to intercept it. Of course, the data was a little less than 14 minutes old.

Maddox tapped a fist on the right armrest of his chair. Jupiter was the fifth planet from the Sun. The gas giant possessed two and a half times the mass of the rest of the Solar System's planets combined, while it was one-thousandth the mass of the Sun. It had 79 moons. The largest, Ganymede, was greater in diameter than the planet Mercury. Jupiter was a gas giant, primarily composed of hydrogen but with a quarter being helium. It lacked a well-defined solid surface at its core. A surrounding layer of liquid metallic hydrogen rested above that core. The rest of the planet was composed of dense gases.

There was nothing in Jupiter for the hauler. The wiser course for them would have been to head into empty space. Meyers risked capture going into the Jupiter Planetary Region.

What didn't he understand about this? Meyers was acting in a reasonable manner. He simply did not understand her reasoning.

"We're ready, sir," Keith said.

"Bring us in close this time," Maddox said. "I mean right on top of them. One thousand kilometers ought to do it."

"Sir," Valerie said. "Regulations state that we aren't supposed to appear closer than two thousand kilometers."

"Fine," Maddox said. "Make it two thousand. Are you ready, Mr. Maker?"

Keith manipulated his board. "Aye," he said.

"Go," Maddox said.

Keith tapped his panel, and they jumped…

-22-

Valerie's quoting of regulations might well have saved the starship as it appeared near Jupiter.

Two Star Watch destroyers—tube-shaped craft—maneuvered into firing position on the fleeing hauler. Unknown to Maddox and his crew, the commander of the two-ship flotilla had given the final warning. The hauler did not acknowledge it.

Beams flashed from the destroyers, reaching out to the hauler.

In size and mass, the destroyers were like foxes chasing a bull. Even so, this hauler was smaller than the huge ones that crossed between the stars for the Nerva Corporation. This hauler had two and a half times the mass of a *Bismarck*-class battleship but was almost completely round like a giant ball.

Nerva Corp haulers were typically longer, more akin to giant cigar-shaped vessels. This hauler's engine exhaust was also much cooler than normal, and that didn't make sense.

In any case, *Victory* appeared as the destroyers fired at the enemy vessel. If the starship had appeared one thousand kilometers from the hauler, it might have been in the line of fire. As it was, the starship was well out of the way.

The bridge crew shrugged off the mini-Jump Lag in time to witness an incredible spectacle. A shimmering black spheroid hardened into sight around the hauler as the twin beams from the destroyers neared it. One of the beams rebounded off the black spheroid, heading back exactly the way it had come. That happened fast enough that the ray struck the destroyer that had fired it.

The beam caused the destroyer's own electromagnetic shield to discolor. Fortunately, the captain in charge of the ship had the presence of mind to cease firing. He didn't quite do it fast enough, however, as the hot beam burst through the destroyer's weak shield. The ray struck the firing cannon, and in this instance, caused a quick chain-reaction.

The cannon exploded, and that caused hot liquid and other heated substances to blow back into the destroyer. The hull around the cannon also blew outward and some of the ship's air ejected. Several tumbling people flew into space with the air, dying almost instantly. Another explosion shook the destroyer as more debris blew outward from the hull rupture.

"Do you see that?" Valerie exclaimed from her station.

The other destroyer—the *Recluse*—had ceased firing.

"A suddenly appearing reflective black spheroid in lieu of a shield," Ludendorff said. "We're witnessing obvious alien technology."

Maddox swiveled his chair to see the professor standing near the main hatch, studying the images on the screen.

Ludendorff exchanged glances with Maddox. "This confirms our worst suspicion," the professor said.

The stricken destroyer no longer expelled debris and people into space. It was crippled, but it did not seem as if it would ignite, killing everyone onboard.

"Open channels with the hauler," Maddox said, swiveling to face the main screen.

Valerie manipulated her panel. "They're ignoring my hail, sir."

"Tell Meyers that Captain Maddox wishes to speak to her."

Valerie attempted another hail, inserting the new information.

A moment later, the main screen wavered as Doctor Lisa Meyers appeared. She wore a silver suit as a New Man might. On her, it looked positively stunning. She also wore a silver band around her forehead.

"Captain Maddox," she said, with venom in her sensual voice. "You should be dead by now."

"Who are you?" Maddox asked.

Meyers flashed a cruel smile. "A mystery," she said. "I know you abhor those. This one will last a little longer, however. By the time you know who I really am, it will be too late for all of you."

"I'm about to annihilate your hauler and you in it," Maddox said. "I suggest you tell your masters that unless they surrender and ready themselves for boarding—"

"Your threats are meaningless," Meyers said, cutting him off. "You have no ability to do anything to this ship."

"You are badly mistaken."

"Did you see what happened to your Star Watch destroyer? The same thing will happen to your ship if you fire on us."

"Why warn me then?"

Meyers laughed, but it didn't sound convincing. "I want your ship. I want you, too."

"Why me?" asked Maddox.

She blinked twice in rapid succession, and then she bent her head as pain flashed in her eyes. A moment later, she straightened.

Maddox noted the process with interest. "Is it the metal band?" he asked. "Is that a pain inducer? Have you angered your masters by what you just said?"

Meyers swore at him with passion.

"Surrender," Maddox said crisply.

"Ah," she said, while regaining her poise, "the famous New Man warning: 'Surrender or die.' We will do neither."

"So be it," Maddox said.

The image on the main screen wavered as Meyers disappeared. A moment later, the screen showed Jupiter and the hauler racing toward the gas giant's upper atmosphere, perhaps to circle around the huge planet and disappear behind a horizon.

"The captain of the *Recluse* is hailing you," Valerie said.

"Put him on," Maddox said.

"Her," Valerie said. "It's Captain Sally Jones."

Maddox waited.

A moment later, an older woman appeared with lines in her face and worry in her eyes.

"What is that thing?" she asked promptly. "What did it do to the *Intrepid?*"

"The black spheroid appears to be some form of alien technology," Maddox said.

"Builder technology?" asked Jones.

"No," Ludendorff said, who had moved beside the captain's chair.

"Is that the infamous Professor Ludendorff?" Jones asked.

Maddox bent forward, peering intently at Captain Jones. That seemed like an odd question for her at a time like this.

"Sir," Galyan said softly, who had glided to a position on the other side of the command chair as Ludendorff. "The *Recluse* is closing with us."

Maddox glanced at the holoimage.

"The *Recluse* has stopped chasing the hauler," Galyan added. "The destroyer's maneuver toward us seems premeditated and purposeful."

"Captain Jones," Maddox said. "I'm taking command of the operation."

"You don't have authorization for that," she said sharply. "We're in the Jupiter Command Region. I'm in charge."

"Cease your maneuvering toward us. Chase the hauler instead."

"I just told you," Jones said. "I am the flotilla commander. I will not accept any orders from you."

On the main screen, the *Recluse* increased velocity, heading for *Victory* at three times the speed as before.

"Captain Jones, cease your maneuvering toward us at once," Maddox said.

Her image on the main screen went blank.

"Who cut the connection?" Maddox demanded.

Valerie's fingers flew over her board. "Captain Jones did, sir."

Maddox peered at the closing destroyer. The warship seemed to be on an intercept course with *Victory*.

"Galyan," Maddox said, "fire at the destroyer with the neutron cannon."

"Sir," Valerie said, her speech dying in her throat as Maddox twisted to stare at her.

The captain stood and walked thoughtfully toward the main screen. Prime Minister Hampton had been under alien influence. Why not a Star Watch destroyer captain as well? The *Intrepid's* beam had been reflected by the hauler's black spheroid. The *Recluse's* beam had not been reflected. Was there a reason for that?

"Galyan," Maddox said. "Can you run an analysis on the beam the *Recluse* originally fired at the hauler?"

"That is a good idea, sir," Galyan said. "I will use recorded sensor data." The holoimage's eyelids fluttered. "Sir," the AI said, opening his eyes. "The *Recluse's* beam was a show, nothing more than a beam of light."

"That tears it," Maddox said, "fire to annihilate its motive power."

A purple beam rayed from *Victory's* neutron cannon. It struck the *Recluse's* weak destroyer shield, causing it to collapse. The purple beam struck the rearward side of the destroyer, the neutron power smashing through hull armor. The beam flashed into the ship and roved through the engine section, destroying the *Recluse's* motive power.

At the same time, *Victory* accelerated, moving out of the *Recluse's* path.

At that point, the destroyer used its real beam, lashing *Victory's* electromagnetic shield.

"Sir," Valerie said, "the *Recluse* is going critical."

"From our neutron beam?" asked Maddox, surprised.

"I don't think so," Valerie said, as she studied her panel. "It seems to be a conscious decision on the captain's part."

"Hail them," Maddox said.

"I am adding power to our shield," Galyan said.

At that point, the *Recluse's* engine core ignited, exploding in a thermonuclear fireball.

The *Intrepid* was closer to the fireball than *Victory*. The damaged destroyer disintegrated under the nuclear heat, EMP and hard radiation even as the blast wave continued spreading in a growing ball.

"Get ready," Valerie said.

Seconds later, the EMP and hard radiation struck the starship's shield, causing it to turn black. If Galyan hadn't strengthened it beforehand, the shield certainly would have collapsed.

They rode out the worst part of the blast as dissipated heat struck next. The same could not be said for the nearest colony base and robot stations, part of a chain circling Jupiter. Soon, radiation killed everyone in the colony base and melted robot circuits.

"Our shield is holding," Galyan informed Maddox.

"Alien mind tampering," Ludendorff snarled. "They must have suborned Captain Jones. That's why the hauler raced here, because it had secret confederates waiting."

"Where is the hauler?" Maddox said.

"I can't tell just yet," Valerie said. "The whiteout from the nuclear explosion has momentarily blanketed my sensors."

"Find the hauler," Maddox said sternly.

Victory soon maneuvered past the blast area. Now, Jupiter filled most of the main screen as the sensors came back online. The Great Red Spot was more than visible. It was possible to watch it churn and spin with unbelievable velocity.

"I see the hauler," Valerie said.

"Put it on the main screen," Maddox said.

"It is," Valerie said. "If you'll look down to the left," she said.

"That black dot?" asked Maddox.

"Yes."

"Where is the hauler going?"

Valerie said nothing.

Maddox turned to her. "Lieutenant, do you have any idea where the hauler is going?"

"According to my sensors," she said, "—and I don't think my sensors are off."

"Where are they headed?" Maddox said, his voice rising.

"I believed the hauler planned to use the upper atmosphere to hide behind a planetary horizon in relation to us," Valerie said in a rush. "Now, I think the hauler is planning to plunge deep *into* the atmosphere. If I didn't know better, I'd say the enemy ship is trying to escape us by fleeing into Jupiter."

-23-

Jupiter was the largest planet in the Solar System. It was mostly composed of dense gases, with hydrogen and helium being the chief components. Those gases often blew at tremendous speeds. The pressure also became greater the deeper one traveled into Jupiter.

On Earth, a submarine's hull crumpled like tinfoil if it plunged too far underwater, as the deeper one went, the greater the pressure became.

The dense atmosphere of Jupiter would create far more pressure than the deepest ocean canyon on Earth.

That wasn't the only problem. Jupiter's mass caused greater gravitational pull. The deeper one traveled into the gas giant's thickening atmosphere, the greater became the gravitational pull. At a certain point, the gravity would burn out regular anti-grav pods.

Maddox considered these things as he pondered Valerie's words. Suddenly, he snapped his fingers. "Galyan, didn't you say back on Earth that the hauler had special antigravity pods?"

"No, sir," the AI said.

"What? I could have sworn—"

"I said the box-like shuttle that landed in the hauler had *advanced* antigravity pods. That does not mean the hauler has the same type of pods, although I believe that would be a reasonable assumption."

"None of that matters," Ludendorff said. "The hauler cannot survive deep in Jupiter. This is a trick. We can follow and capture the vessel in the upper atmosphere."

"No," Maddox said, shaking his head. "I'm not taking *Victory* down into that."

"You can't let the hauler escape," Ludendorff said.

"I don't intend to."

"Damn it," Ludendorff said. "Don't you see? They'll go down a ways and then fold elsewhere. It's an obvious trick. We have to get close enough to use a tractor beam and hold them."

"Perhaps," Maddox said. "Or perhaps they have more confederates hiding in the upper atmosphere waiting to ambush us."

"That's ridiculous," Ludendorff said.

Maddox sat down on his command chair. "Professor, have a care how you speak to me on my own bridge."

"Confound you and that prickly pride of yours," Ludendorff said. "The hauler carries advanced alien technology. What's more, those damned extraterrestrials play with human minds. I am more than sick of that. We must destroy these invaders and do it now, by thunder!"

Maddox studied the hyper-excited professor. This was another overreaction to losing Dana, an overreaction to what the Bosks had done to him last mission. He swiveled away from Ludendorff to better study the gas giant.

"Give me magnification ten," the captain said.

Keith manipulated his board.

On the main screen, the sight expanded as it zoomed in. The round hauler became more significant, and the upper atmosphere ammonia clouds—some of them a thousand kilometers long—showed to greater effect as they rode the winds.

"That's crazy," Keith said from Helm. "Could you imagine whipping around the planet, riding those winds?"

"Fire the neutron cannon," Ludendorff said. "Destroy them."

"What about the reflective black spheroid that appears to bounce back a beam?" Maddox asked.

"I doubt it can reflect the neutron beam," the professor said.

"A theory I don't intend to test just yet," Maddox said softly. "Galyan," he said with greater force, "launch three 'M' missiles."

In seconds, three large missiles left the starship's tubes. After enough separation from the starship and between themselves, the missiles' engines burned hot. In staggered formation, the missiles dove into the atmosphere, racing after the sinking hauler.

"The hauler is ejecting decoys," Valerie said, as she studied her panel.

Maddox nodded, watching the interplay on the main screen.

The missiles picked up speed at different velocities, gaining even more separation between them.

"There it goes!" Keith shouted.

The hauler disappeared from regular view as it sank into massed cloud cover.

Valerie tapped her board.

A computer-generated image appeared in its place. The hauler now seemed to sink faster than before.

An emitter, an alien device, flashed with power.

The first missile's warhead ignited.

"Your missiles aren't going to work," Ludendorff grumbled. "What's worse, it may be too late now to use the neutron beam. The thickening atmosphere will act as a better shield than any electromagnetics."

"Launch five probes," Maddox said. "We're going to make a communication chain."

On the main screen, the second missile's warhead ignited.

"Scan for enemy ships hiding in the atmosphere," Maddox said. A second later, he added, "Scan for any approaching Star Watch vessels."

"Do you suspect more compromised captains?" Ludendorff asked.

"It's a possibility I can't discount."

Time passed as the last missile zoomed deeper into the atmosphere. Just before they would have lost contact with it, the last warhead exploded, most likely harmlessly.

"Now what are you going to do?" Ludendorff complained.

"You, sir, are going to your quarters," Maddox said.

"Bah," Ludendorff muttered.

Maddox snapped his fingers, pointed at two marines and then pointed at the professor.

"I'm going, I'm going," Ludendorff said. "Don't think I'll forget this affront, either."

"You know I won't forget it," Maddox said, nettled.

Ludendorff left.

That helped Maddox think as he tapped his chin. "Mr. Maker," he finally said, "take us three hundred kilometers lower into the atmosphere. Galyan, launch a relay unit. We're going to launch several of them and extend the communication chain. I want to see what happens to the hauler once it goes too deep into Jupiter."

The bridge crew went to work as *Victory* maneuvered downward and then relay units launched and sank into the increasingly dense atmosphere. The relay units made a chain, transmitting the images that the original probes recorded to the starship.

"The images are getting hazy," Valerie said.

Maddox could see that for himself as he studied the main screen. They were past the clouds of ammonia crystals and could see exotic blues and greens streaking the underbelly of the clouds. Slowly, the recorded colors changed to purple as vast lightning bolts zigzagged everywhere. In the distance, yellow sodium explosions added to the atmospheric mayhem.

Shrieking winds caught one probe, blowing it thousands of kilometers off course. The next probe sent back images of a great methane ocean. Later, Valerie pointed out floes of black allotropic ice.

"There!" Valerie shouted. "I see the hauler."

So did Maddox. There was a shimmering force field around it.

"This is incredible and unbelievable," Galyan said. "Do you see the readings from the probe?"

"Explain them to me," Maddox said.

"The shimmering around the hauler is a binding-force field," Galyan said. "It is akin to the energy that holds atomic nuclei together. That makes sense, sir, as that field should theoretically be powerful enough to resist the terrible pressures and planetary gravity."

"If the anti-grav pods hold up," Valerie said.

"Yes, precisely," Galyan said.

"You're saying the hauler can go lower still?" Maddox asked.

"For as long as they can power the binding-force field," Galyan said.

"And that means…what?" Maddox asked.

"That the hauler will presumably hide deeper in Jupiter than anything Star Watch has that can go down and destroy it," Galyan said.

As if to punctuate his words, the first relay unit broke down. The main screen showed the upper atmosphere again from *Victory's* vantage point.

"What do we do now?" Valerie asked.

Maddox tapped his chin. That was the question, wasn't it?

-24-

As Captain Maddox pondered his next move, twenty-five light-years away in the Vega System, Lord Drakos's star cruiser stealthily traveled through some of the thickest dust of the circumstellar disc in the region's Kuiper Belt.

Thick-necked, broad-shouldered Drakos stood with his hands behind his back as he studied the main screen from behind his command chair.

"The 'E' radiation trail definitely leads toward the third moon of a hidden gas giant, Lord," the helmsman said, a tall New Man.

"This is amazing," Drakos whispered. "And Star Watch has no record of an Imperial Swarm ship's passage through the Vega System?"

"None, Lord," his Intelligence chief said, a different New Man by the name of Nar Falcon. He was a normal-looking, golden-skinned Superior except for the puckered and unsightly scar across his forehead. It was a dueling scar from a match he'd lost many years ago.

Drakos removed his hands from behind his back and rubbed them together, wishing to land on the third moon and search for further Swarm evidence.

He had spoken to his secret Spacer agent several days ago in the Vega Asteroid Belt and learned that events moved forward as he'd expected. There had been a few sticking points, but the Spacer agent had departed a much wiser man than when he'd come.

Drakos made a decisive gesture, chopping his right hand through the air. The Spacer would do his job. If the man failed, he would die a hideous death later.

"I see the third moon," said Nar Falcon the Intelligence chief. Today, he doubled as the weapons officer and studied his board.

Drakos strode to Nar Falcon's station and looked down at the screen.

"It's a small moon," Drakos noted.

"According to the sensors, apparently made entirely of metal," Nar Falcon said.

"Is it an abandoned battle station?"

Nar Falcon manipulated his board. "I do not think so, Lord."

"An old battleship then?" asked Drakos, wondering if he'd stumbled onto an ancient starship like *Victory*.

"A moon, Lord," said Nar Falcon.

"You're not suggesting it is a natural object?"

"No…"

"What then?"

"We'll know soon, Lord."

In his gut, Drakos felt a momentary thrill. The sensation might have been something like fear. But he enjoyed it too much for it to have been real fear. Gut clenches meant that he was alive, attempting mighty deeds.

Those who never fear, never try something truly new. It was a Superior saying.

"Battle stations," Drakos said, as he headed to his command chair.

An alert blared throughout the star cruiser, and then all was as before. New Men did not believe in having noisy sirens continuously shrieking as one tried to think and operate.

The stealth ship continued to slow its approach. It took four hours and eighteen minutes for the bridge crew to see that it was an irregularly shaped asteroid and not a moon as such. The asteroid was eight hundred kilometers in irregular diameter.

"You were right about it being a natural object," Drakos told Nar Falcon. "I was certain we had found an ancient relic."

"It is a mother lode of an asteroid," Nar Falcon said. "I cannot understand why the Vega System submen haven't maneuvered it out of the dust belt to a manufacturing point."

"I do," Drakos said. "The submen lack courage and have likely never explored this deeply into the circumstellar disc."

"It is hard to fathom such cowardice," Nar Falcon said.

Drakos nodded. Then he went to Nar Falcon's board and watched it like a predatory beast. Had Commander Thrax Ti Ix been here? According to the faint trail of "E" radiation, an Imperial Swarm vessel had passed through the circumstellar disc several years ago. Maybe *many* such vessels had passed through the Vegan debris disc.

Once more, Drakos rubbed his powerful hands together. He was a hardliner; some considered him the unofficial hardliner chief. He had many secret agents and many sources of information. Through hints stolen from Star Watch, and later from Brigadier O'Hara's compromised mind, Drakos had learned an interesting truth. Not all of the original Imperial Swarm Invasion Fleet had perished in the supernova explosion of the "A" star of Alpha Centauri. The Imperial Swarm had originally invaded Human Space with 80,000 starships. Superiors and Star Watch submen had joined forces to defeat the invading insect horde.

Back then, the unconventional Maddox had somehow induced the "A" star to go supernova, killing billions of submen in the Alpha Centauri System. The supernova explosion had also destroyed the remaining bulk of the Imperial Swarm armada.

Unknown at the time to the Superiors, Commander Thrax Ti Ix had controlled something less than 200 saucer-shaped Swarm warships. According to O'Hara, who had learned it from Maddox, Thrax was a hybrid Swarm creature. Thrax had been at the Builder Dyson Sphere one thousand light-years from Earth. Thrax had gone to the Swarm Imperium and given the Queen knowledge about humanity, Laumer Points and hyper-spatial tubes. That was likely why the Swarm Imperium had first attacked this region of space from a hyper-spatial tube created at a Builder nexus several thousand light-years away.

In any case, Thrax's nearly two hundred vessels had used a star drive, a jump ability that didn't need a Laumer Point to go from one star system to another. It would appear that Thrax's jump ships had fled Alpha Centauri and fled the rest of the Imperial Swarm Invasion Fleet's destruction.

Had Thrax or one of his saucer-shaped Swarm ships truly come to the Vega System? Might the hybrid Swarm creatures be hiding out here in the circumstellar disc?

Drakos licked his lips. It was incredibly daring of him to enter the circumstellar disc with just one star cruiser. He was likely the most daring Superior in all existence. *To the victor go the spoils, and he who dares wins.*

Drakos's lips stretched into a smile. He planned to win it all because he was going to dare it all. Not the Emperor, not the pathetic half-breed Captain Maddox and not his strange new allies were going to stop him either. If he had to—

"Lord," the tall helmsman said. "I'm picking up a strange reading."

"Put it on the main screen," Drakos said.

"It isn't visual," the helmsman said.

"What then?"

"A burst of energy, a flare, if you will," the helmsman said. "The origin point seems to be behind the metal-rich asteroid."

Drakos thought fast. Could he have found Thrax's resting place? The idea was fantastic.

"Continue," Drakos said softly.

The star cruiser continued its stealthy approach to the asteroid in orbit around a cold gas giant hidden in the debris of the Vegan Kuiper Belt's circumstellar disc.

Two hours and nine minutes later, the stealthy star cruiser swung around the metal-rich asteroid. The bridge crew strained as they studied sensor readings.

"Lord..." whispered the forehead-scarred Nar Falcon.

"I see it," Drakos said in as quiet a voice.

There on Nar Falcon's tiny screen was a saucer-shaped Swarm vessel. It did more than drift near the metal-rich asteroid. There was a jagged rent on the bubble part of the saucer-shaped craft.

This Imperial Swarm ship was similar in design to a regular Spacer saucer-shaped vessel. That was likely because both types originated with the Builders. The Swarm saucer-shaped ship was bigger than a Spacer type, however.

"Heavy radiation and other energies are spewing from the breach," Nar Falcon said.

"Any indication of more Swarm ships?" asked Drakos.

"Negative, Lord," said Nar Falcon.

"We must look inside the stricken vessel."

"Even in a heavy radiation suit—" Nar Falcon said.

"None of us will go aboard it," Drakos said, interrupting his Intelligence chief. "We'll use a drone to search the insides."

"Will a drone work in that radiation?"

"We're going to find out," Drakos said. He laughed harshly. They had found an Imperial Swarm ship, found an indication about what had happened to Commander Thrax Ti Ix after the Imperial Swarm invasion. This was more than exciting. This could help with many of his deepest-laid plans…

-25-

A probe launched from the star cruiser crossed the distance to the stricken saucer-shaped vessel. While the probe flew there, the bridge crew watched the metal-rich asteroid for any signs of aggression.

"How can we tell if there's a robot outpost on the asteroid?" Drakos asked Nar Falcon. "As long as they keep a missile site or laser battery cold, we can't tell if it's there from any concentrations of metal."

Finally, the space probe parked near the stricken saucer-shaped ship. The probe's nosecone opened, and a smaller robot craft exited, moving toward the hull breach. In time, the robot craft slid through the breach, entering the radiation-spewing wreck.

Nar Falcon, the Intelligence chief, guided the robot vehicle from his weapons station, gathering data from the Imperial Swarm vessel, including sight of drifting dead Swarm creatures in various states of decomposition, sometimes just seeing drifting pincers, thoraxes or other giant insect parts.

Sometime later in a science lab, Nar Falcon pored over the data.

Finally, Drakos could bear it no more. He went to the science lab and entered without warning.

Nar Falcon looked up from his screen. For a second, his puckered dueling scar reddened. He quickly composed his features.

Drakos did not care for the scowl. He ran the star cruiser and he ran his people, as a Superior should. However, the Intelligence chief's quick smothering of the scowl denoted the man's fear of his better.

That pleased Drakos. That pleased him a great deal.

"Anything so far?" the shorter, broader-shouldered Superior demanded.

Nar Falcon dipped his head. "Indeed, Lord, there is a plethora of data. I have learned more about the Swarm, the Imperium and its policies than I ever believed—"

"No, no," Drakos said. "I don't care about that."

"It could be critical, Lord."

Drakos scowled, and he did nothing to hide it. "I don't need lectures from my Intelligence chief unless I ask for lectures."

After a moment, Nar Falcon said, "You are correct, Lord."

Drakos's eyes burned. The man should ask for forgiveness for the slight. Still, Drakos did not run his star cruiser as Methuselah Man Strand used to run his. Many of his people were independent persons. Despite the ugly dueling scar, Nar Falcon was a noted duelist and a Superior of some distinction. That was why the smothering of his scowl earlier had meant something.

Drakos knew a secret that the Methuselah Man seemed to have forgotten. Others were capable, too, and a free agent, as it were, was usually a better worker than a slave. Nar Falcon would work hard because he would receive self-desired rewards for doing so.

"I am pleased with your diligence," Drakos said.

Nar Falcon stared at him, and his thoughts were unreadable.

"Share with me, brother Dominant, what you have found."

Nar Falcon's shoulders straightened a minute degree. Drakos had given him a compliment and shown respect.

"Lord, I may have found where Thrax and his hybrid creatures fled."

"They came here first?" Drakos asked.

"I do not believe so. I think this ship sustained damage and dropped off from the main battle fleet."

"The one under Commander Thrax Ti Ix's command?"

Nar Falcon nodded.

"Show me...please," Drakos said.

Nar Falcon stood abruptly, cracked his knuckles and resumed his seat. He manipulated his board, and for the next hour, he showed Drakos one factor after another.

Drakos murmured many times. He nodded at others, understanding the significance of the various facts and data points.

"Yes, yes," Drakos said. "I'm beginning to see."

"I deem this region to be the most likely resting place for the original excursion," Nar Falcon said.

Drakos looked at the panel screen, noting the stellar region that Nar Falcon indicated. It was in the Beyond, as the submen referred to such things. It was quite a distance in the Beyond, meaning it was far from so-called Human Space. It was also a good distance from the Throne World. Had Thrax known of the Throne World's existence and location?

"I believe the hybrid creatures will have one significant problem with their new existence," Nar Falcon said.

Drakos took a guess. "They have no queen to sustain their race."

"Precisely, Lord. They can survive for a time, but they cannot multiply through breeding."

"Does that matter to us?"

"It makes Thrax less dangerous to us in the long term."

"Yes, obviously," Drakos murmured, "as they will eventually die out."

"More importantly, Lord, it gives us a possible bargaining chip with them."

"How so?"

Nar Falcon told him.

Once Drakos understood, he sat back and laughed, shaking his head. "You are fiendishly clever, Nar Falcon. This is brilliant."

Nar Falcon dipped his scarred forehead.

"First, though," Drakos said. "We must find the hybrid colony."

"True," Nar Falcon said. "But...?"

"Ask your question, my friend."

"Can we afford to leave as our other plans mature here?"

Drakos squinted as he thought about that. Could he leave the region inside so-called Human Space at this critical juncture? The various rebellions were about to flare. And the strange allies he'd found…

"A quick foray," Drakos said. "We can afford that as the others gather in strength."

"The other hardliners, Lord?"

"I think it is almost time to unleash the Great Plan."

"If we fail to find and sway Thrax to our side or fail to do it in time, Lord…"

Drakos clapped his hands together. "He who dares wins," he said. "This is the moment, Nar Falcon. I can feel it in my bones. Destiny would not have given us the 'E' radiation trail if it meant to thwart us."

"Destiny, Lord?"

Drakos composed his features lest he give away his sudden displeasure at the question and the tone it had been asked. He had a belief in himself that went beyond mere confidence in his superior abilities. The proto-Superior Napoleon Bonaparte back in ancient times had believed in his star, in his destiny. Napoleon had been a subman with genius-level abilities, but he had still been a subman after all, and thus had failed to properly wield his destiny.

Drakos knew that his destiny, or his star, had guided him for many years. He was destined for greatness, and had an iron will that had bent many, many others to his way of thinking and doing things. His "star" would not fail him, but only if he continued to dare greatly. Energy, zest, willpower and a willingness to risk everything and see the gifts destiny gave him would propel him to the highest level.

Drakos knew that he would be the Emperor one day. What's more, he would lead the Superiors to ultimate greatness as they conquered the submen. Every Superior would have *herds* and *worlds* of concubines, lovers and breeding stock. Every Superior would sire tens of thousands and perhaps hundreds of thousands of sons.

The Superiors and Dominants would fill the galaxy and conquer their way to brilliance and supremacy.

Yet, such a grand scheme and the knowledge that his star guided him would be too much even for most Superiors. Some so-called New Men might think him mad or unbalanced. Most Superiors did not believe in luck, destiny or a guiding star. Thus, he must hide that from Nar Falcon.

It had been a slip of the tongue that had revealed his true thoughts…

"A phrase," Drakos now told Nar Falcon. "That we have found a saucer-shaped ship and quite possibly the hybrid Swarm planet…"

Drakos eyed Nar Falcon and let a sudden grin show. "What do you think about all this, Intelligence chief? Come now. Give me your best advice."

Nar Falcon turned back to the screen as he thoughtfully pursed his lips. A moment later, he manipulated it as strange logic symbols flew across the screen like a giant mathematical formula.

Drakos did not ascribe to such logic formulas in the formal Superior manner. But he knew other "New Men" held great store by it. The Emperor was a better logician than any other Dominant. Still, if this was the Intelligence chief's way, it might be wisest to humor him today.

Suddenly, Nar Falcon sat back and turned his head to stare at Drakos.

"Well?" asked Drakos.

Nar Falcon indicated the logic formula.

Drakos refused to look at it. Given enough time, he could decipher it. Right now, he did not care to expend the mental effort.

"I could go both ways, Lord," Nar Falcon said. "There are grave risks in trying to find Thrax now. But as you pointed out, the rewards—we could win everything if everything falls our way."

Drakos grinned triumphantly. "The deciding factor is always willpower. The Superior with the greatest willpower shall dominate the situation through his greater inner force."

Nar Falcon did not seem convinced. "We thought likewise before the invasion of 'C' Quadrant."

Drakos made a dismissive gesture. "If you're recall, Golden Ural commanded the invasion fleet. He was far too mellow to be a great conqueror. He took safe routes instead of boldly aiming for the enemy heart."

"You may be right, Lord," Nar Falcon murmured.

"I *am* right," Drakos said, radiating force of will through his stare and his fierce bearing.

Finally, Nar Falcon succumbed to the greater mental force, dipping his head. "Let us attempt the great dare, Lord. Let us win everything with one bold logical move."

"We will win through force of *will,*" Drakos declared.

"Of will," Nar Falcon said in a quieter voice, wilting under Drakos's certainty.

"Then it is decided," Drakos said. "We leave tomorrow to find Commander Thrax Ti Ix in order to make him your oh-so-devious proposal."

-26-

Back in the Solar System, in the Jupiter Region, six *Bismarck*-class and four *Conqueror*-class battleships, along with nine destroyers and thirteen escort-ships took up station around the great gas giant.

That allowed *Victory* to leave and gave a respite to the three destroyers helping the ancient starship quarantine Jupiter. So far, no sensor buoy or ship sensor had detected the round hauler attempting to escape the gas giant.

Other sensor stations kept watch in a great circumference around Jupiter to a distance of 400 million kilometers. That was in case the hauler attempted to fold out of the Jovian atmosphere. Four hundred million kilometers had appeared to be its fold range earlier.

Victory headed back to Earth, using its star drive to expedite matters.

A day later, Maddox came down from orbit in a shuttle. It was time to pay the piper, as the saying went. Marine MPs met him at the Geneva Spaceport and escorted him to Star Watch Headquarters.

The military police led him to a large chamber where Major Stokes was reading a tablet.

Stokes looked up, studying Maddox as a range of emotions played upon the major's weary features. He had bags under red-rimmed eyes and sucked on a stimstick as if it was his energy source.

Finally, Stokes said in a tired voice, "Leave him here, Lieutenant. I'll watch him for a while."

"I'll have to check if that's okay, sir," the stocky marine said.

Stokes nodded as he took another drag on his stimstick.

Soon, the marine lowered a hand comm. "I'm placing guards outside the door, sir." The big man eyed Maddox. "They have orders to shoot to take you down if you try to escape."

"Kill orders?" Stokes asked in surprise.

"Heavy stun shots, sir," the marine said. Without further ado, the lieutenant and his military police filed out of the chamber, shutting the door behind them.

"I imagine you're back sooner than you expected," Stokes said, setting the tablet on a large conference table.

Maddox took a chair across the report-strewn table from Stokes.

"What do we know so far about the hauler and its registry?" Maddox asked.

"Now see here, old man—" Stokes said.

"This is an emergency," Maddox said. "Can't we forgo formalities for once?"

Stokes plucked the smoldering stimstick from his mouth and eyed it as if the cigarette could give him advice. Maybe the stimstick told him, because the major seemed to reach a decision.

"An emergency, yes, that's true. We might as well start somewhere." Stokes shrugged. "The hauler's registry has led us through several shell companies. Meaning, we haven't found the real owner yet. But surely you already know that. Surely your people have gathered data as you played hide and seek around Jupiter."

"They did, and that's what we found as well. Given your greater resources, I'd wondered if you'd found something more."

Stokes shook his head. "What are your impressions, old boy? Do you have any of your 'brilliant' ideas about what to do next?"

"The hauler's true owners are aliens with advanced technology that is on par with some of the best Builder tech."

Stokes raised his eyebrows. "Isn't that jumping to conclusions, old son? Consider. A Builder nexus allows one to travel several thousand light-years in an instant. The hauler merely created a bubble field that allowed it deep into Jupiter's atmosphere."

"That's not quite right," Maddox said. "These are aliens with until now unknown technologies. You might be forgetting that reflective spheroid that bounces beams shot at it."

"I'm not forgetting. The reflective spheroid is…troublesome. But the fact the hauler fled deep into the atmosphere shows the aliens—if they are aliens—don't fully trust the spheroid against neutron or disrupter cannon fire. Otherwise, why not go wherever they want without a worry?"

"That's an interesting point," Maddox conceded.

"Here's another. If these are aliens, are they new or old ones playing new games with us?"

"Professor Ludendorff claims they're new."

"Ah," Stokes said. "Professor Ludendorff. I take everything he says not with a grain of sand, but a *bag.*"

"Fair enough," Maddox said. "Tell me. What does General Torres think about all this? Why am I speaking to you instead of him?"

Strokes rubbed his weary features.

"Ever since you left Earth, Torres has been arguing that your hide be lasered onto *Victory's* hull." The major took another drag on the stimstick. "Has it ever occurred to you that you leave a bad taste in your superiors' mouths because you disobey orders whenever you feel like it? Oh," Stokes said, not giving the captain a chance to answer the question. "I'll admit your tactics get results at times. But organizations don't like your kind of person and positively *hate* your style. I suppose the Brigadier approved of you for her own reasons, and the Lord High Admiral has a small residue of liking for your former results. But you are quickly becoming *persona non grata* with everyone else."

"Including you?" Maddox asked.

"You, your AI and your resident Methuselah Man should all be jailed and possibly dissected. How you manage to luckily win so many of your encounters defies logic. We should distill whatever we find in you and make our young cadets drink it."

"There's no secret," Maddox said. "I'm *di-far*."

Stokes rolled his red-rimmed eyes.

"I've read the secret report the Brigadier wrote concerning that. It's a bloody shame the Spacers ever inflated your already insufferable ego with such nonsense. I imagine you've let it go to your head."

Maddox shrugged.

"Indeed," Stokes said. "It's a surprise you don't float away with your helium-inflated ego."

The major stubbed out the stimstick in an ashtray. Then he scratched his side and peered at Maddox. He opened his mouth to speak, and then closed it again. Finally, the major ran a hand through his thinning hair and stood abruptly.

"I simply can't do it," Stokes said softly. He headed for the door, opened it, paused as if he was going to turn around and say something more, but then kept walking, heading into the corridor.

An MP looked in at Maddox, turned away and shut the door behind him, leaving the captain alone in the large chamber.

Maddox raised his eyes at Stokes' odd behavior, shrugged once more and gathered the reports on the table. He began reading them one by one, soon becoming concerned. Although many of the reports came from widely divergent regions in the greater Commonwealth, there were too many similarities. It almost felt as if there was a guiding intelligence behind the many incidences. And yet, who could maneuver all these various forces like a puppet master pulling strings? Maybe a Builder could.

The captain read reports for over an hour before he finally stirred, got up and tried the door. It was locked. He knocked, but no one opened it.

He looked around the room, noting the ceiling cameras recording him. That meant whoever was watching knew what he'd been doing. Maybe that's what he was supposed to be doing, reading the reports.

Maddox returned to the large table and continued reading the literature. The majority of the reports had to do with outlandish robberies, hidden cliques plotting rebellion and increasing space piracies. The events occurred throughout the Commonwealth and with growing frequency.

Sometime later, a scraping sound from the door caused Maddox to look up as it opened.

Stokes reentered the room, and there was something different about him. Then Maddox noticed the new insignia on an altered uniform.

"*Lieutenant Colonel* Stokes?" asked Maddox.

Stokes nodded stiffly as he stood by the opened door.

"What's this about?" asked Maddox.

Stokes' right hand shook as he raised an unlit stimstick toward his mouth. He halted the motion and crumbled the stimstick, tossing it onto the floor. With a jerk, he headed into the room.

A marine outside the room quietly shut the door behind Stokes.

Maddox waited.

Stokes sat across the table from him at his old spot. The new lieutenant colonel glanced at the reports now set in neat piles before regarding him.

"I don't like you, Captain. Not one bit."

Maddox said nothing to that.

Stokes frowned and seemed reluctant to speak again, but finally said, "The Lord High Admiral told me that maybe my not liking you was for the best."

"Did you tell the admiral that you refused to work with me?"

Stokes uncharacteristically glared at him.

Maddox nodded as if that confirmed his suspicions. "So, the Lord High Admiral bumped you up from major to lieutenant colonel as a way to bribe you to work with me anyway?"

Instead of answering, Stokes said, "General Torres has been suspended, as he's under investigation."

"Let me guess. His brain patterns are off."

It took Stokes a second. "Even more off than the Lord High Admiral's patterns."

"Torres' new brain patterns must have been Doctor Meyers' work," Maddox said.

Stokes put his hands on the edge of the table as if he would suddenly push himself away from Maddox. "Let's make a few things clear. For the present, the Lord High Admiral has subdivided the Intelligence Arm. You're my concern now, Captain. Instead of the Brigadier, you will report to me and only to me."

"Where is the Brigadier?"

"That's classified information, old son."

Maddox raised a single eyebrow.

"You have to be a good boy and play by the rules for a time before I'll let you see the Brigadier."

Maddox said nothing.

"Now," Stokes said, "it's time for me to tell you about your new assignment."

"Just a minute," Maddox said. "I want more information regarding the Jupiter situation."

Stokes shook his head. "That's out of your hands. It's out of my hands, too. A different sub-division of Intelligence is going to work on the hauler and Doctor Meyers."

"You're sidelining me from the main show?"

"Didn't you hear me, old boy? Intelligence is splitting into sub-divisions. We're compartmentalizing more than ever. I'll make my report to the new chief."

"Who is that?"

Once again, Stokes shook his head. "That is now classified information. I will tell you this, though. The Jupiter hauler, Doctor Meyers and even more ex-Prime Minister Hampton has Star Watch Intelligence running scared. Even as we speak, the eggheads are creating layers and systems to try to stop anything of the kind from happening again. The incident has created an emergency."

"This is like the android attempt several years ago," Maddox said.

"You mean when androids kidnapped the Brigadier and the Lord High Admiral and put android lookalikes in their place?"

"That," Maddox said. "Before their initial invasion, the New Men also swamped us with spies and found far too many traitors among us, and they used clones as well."

"Strand used the clones," Stokes said, "not the New Men."

"My point is that we've dealt with these kinds of attacks before," Maddox said. "We've experienced it. That's how I know the secret aliens are pulling hidden strings better than anyone else did in the past."

"You read the reports?"

Maddox nodded.

"And you suppose that these new aliens of yours are responsible for all the ills occurring throughout the Commonwealth?"

Maddox considered the question before saying, "It strikes me as a logical conclusion."

"I don't agree. But that doesn't matter either way. You're concentrating this time around. I'm going to give you the parameters for your next mission."

"Said mission has nothing to do with the alien hauler and Doctor Meyers?" Maddox asked.

Stokes' lips thinned. "I'd rather they intern you. I'd rather you have to sit through several court-martial hearings. But this latest infiltration attack has rattled Intelligence and the Lord High Admiral to the core. You think there is one hand manipulating events. I don't, and neither does the Lord High Admiral. We believe that several of our enemies are operating together."

"But the hauler—"

"Listen!" Stokes shouted, as he stood up. "This is deadly serious, old man," he said in a softer voice, turning away. He stared to the side for a time.

As abruptly as he'd stood, Stokes sank back to his chair. He pulled out a pack of stimsticks and seemed to dearly want to take one. Instead, he pitched the pack so it slid across the table.

Lieutenant Colonel Stokes looked at Maddox with his exhausted, baggy eyes. "This latest incident is the worst of a new set of problems. Your timely aid…the Lord High Admiral is grateful for it. That's why he's giving you another Gordian knot to hack. It's possible your new assignment has something to do with Hampton."

"What do you mean?"

Stokes sighed. "Listen a bit and maybe you'll learn something…"

-27-

Lieutenant Colonel Stokes' information had to do with the reports Maddox had been reading. There were outlandish robberies, hidden cliques plotting political and military rebellions and increasing space piracies. These activities had happened everywhere. Just as bad, there was increasing unrest throughout much of the Commonwealth.

According to the eggheads, the three biggest factors behind these violent impulses were the original Destroyer attacks that had broken the Wahhabi Caliphate by annihilating the key home planet. The Destroyer had been an ancient ship of the Nameless Ones that Maddox had finally boarded and sent into the Sun to melt. The second factor had been the New Men invasion of "C" Quadrant. The last had been the Imperial Swarm invasion that had begun in the Tau Ceti System.

The various battles and wars had caused hundreds of millions of deaths, the worst being the total annihilation of life in the Tau Ceti and Alpha Centauri Systems, both of which were near the Solar System in stellar terms.

The remaining Wahhabi Caliphate and Windsor League planets, and many other formerly independent planets and star-system unions, had joined the grand Commonwealth of Planets. The great majority of regular humanity had thus come together in one vast political system in order to be able to field the greatest number of warships possible. The melding of these star systems into the Commonwealth had naturally caused "teething" problems. New rules and taxes for many worlds, and the ruin and death from countless invasions had made the "teething" problems even more difficult than they should be.

Some people on some worlds yearned for their old ways. Some people grew weary of burdensome tax rates or having local tax monies leave for other places light-years away. Some people wanted to run their own lives again or give it a shot and run their planets along their unique customs. The idea of voting for a member to sit in some building far away on Earth to decide their planet's fate—some people could not accept that concept anymore. Some never could.

According to Lieutenant Colonel Stokes, some of these problems might have been worse directly after the Imperial Swarm invasion. A few things had gotten better. But some places had become worse, too. Star Watch only had so many ships, and many of those ships no longer existed, particularly after the bloody battle against the Spacers and the Yon-Soth on the Forbidden Planet.

"Unrest among the stars," Maddox said. He'd read the reports. This was just a rehash.

"It's more than that," Stokes said. "In places, there is outside interference stirring the pot. New Men spies have supplied money or weapons and sometimes inspired leadership."

"Not just New Men," Maddox said, "but the hardliners in particular."

"True." Stokes eyed the captain. "Lord Drakos is a hardliner, maybe the chief one."

"My assignment has to do with Lord Drakos?"

"*Victory* is going to the Vega Sector," Stokes said.

The Vega Sector, as Maddox knew, was a fourteen-light-year diameter with the Vega System in the center. Daniel Hampton had been from Vega. The Sector capital was on Vega II, as was the Sector Star Watch headquarters for the region.

"Is that where Lord Drakos is operating now?" Maddox asked.

"From what we've been able to piece together, Drakos moves around constantly, although he seems to spend the majority of his time secretly moving through the Commonwealth."

"Does he use a stealth star cruiser?"

"Yes," Stokes said, "just like Strand used to do."

Maddox recalled the Balak moon where he'd almost caught the treacherous New Man. If only Golden Ural hadn't stopped him.

"You want me to go to Vega II and uncover the ringleaders of what...a fomenting sector-wide rebellion?"

"Exactly," Stokes said. "Find the ringleaders and break the conspiracy—"

"That's the best use of *Victory* at a time like this?"

Stokes stared at him for a long moment.

Maddox waited.

"I don't like you, Captain."

"We've already established that," Maddox said dryly.

"I want to be clear."

Maddox waited some more.

"The point," Stokes finally said. "Oh, hell," he said, seeming to mentally switch gears. "Intelligence is in turmoil. We need Brigadier O'Hara back. I liked your idea about using me as a conduit for her. The admiral told me about it and told me it was a bad idea. I don't agree with him, however..." Stokes shrugged. "I'm not like you. I obey orders even when I don't agree with them."

Maddox continued to wait, as he sensed turmoil in the lieutenant colonel.

"Torres screwed up," Stokes said. "Admiral Cook believed Torres was a hardnosed pile-driver that could take Intelligence in hand. That didn't work out, now did it? We need the Brigadier. But Drakos made sure we can't use her until we clear up what the New Man learned from her."

"I'm not tracking you," Maddox said.

"Given the latest analysis, I believe Drakos will be in the Vega Sector. Those planets seem critical to whatever hardliner plan they're hatching. Your cover mission is to break the rebellions by finding the hidden ringleaders. The greater and real task is finding and capturing Lord Drakos."

"I thought Drakos was protected because he finally signed the Accord between us and the Throne World," Maddox said.

"Remember? That's why I wasn't able to grab him in the Balak System."

Stokes rapped the table with his knuckles and stared intently at Maddox. "You must capture Drakos on the sly so we can question him in secret."

"Why go through all this rigmarole before getting to the point?"

The lieutenant colonel stared at him until final the captain said: "Oh." Stokes was pulling a Maddox. That was why. These were not official orders, but between the two of them.

"Oh, indeed," Stokes said bitterly.

"If anyone asks me," Maddox said, "I'll say that you never told me a thing about capturing Lord Drakos."

"Originally, Cook was going to tell you about Drakos and what needed doing, but finally decided to keep it a secret. We have too much on our plate to add a possible war-starting incident with the New Men."

"And yet, you're telling me about Drakos anyway."

"I'm not like you," Stokes said softly.

"You follow orders. Unlike me, you're a good little soldier?"

Stokes nodded stiffly, but he seemed like a man with a guilty conscience.

Maddox guessed it, then. "Keeping quiet about Drakos was another price for your bump up in rank, wasn't it?"

Stokes stretched out an arm, reaching for the pack of stimsticks down the table. His fingertips finally touched the pack and he brought them to his palm. Sitting back, shaking out a stimstick, the lieutenant colonel put an unlit one between his lips and inhaled it to life.

"Not to put too fine a point on this," Maddox said, "but you lied to the Lord High Admiral about keeping quiet concerning Drakos."

Stokes sucked harder, inhaling more until he began coughing and hacking. Finally, getting his breathing under control, he began to smoke at a more leisurely pace.

Another realization struck Maddox. More than anything, Stokes wanted the Brigadier back at the helm of Intelligence. Stokes was loyal to Mary O'Hara.

Maddox grinned. He could respect that.

"You look like a slarn about to pounce with that maniac grin of yours," Stokes complained.

"I'm beginning to think that you engineered all this with that devious mind of yours," Maddox said.

Stokes looked away.

"Admiral Cook probably wanted me on the Jupiter case."

Once again, Stokes inhaled hard on the stimstick.

"I accept the mission, Lieutenant Colonel. Come what may, I'm capturing and questioning Drakos. Brigadier Mary O'Hara—" A feral light rose in the captain's eyes.

Stokes caught it and shivered inwardly. Maddox was many things. The most crucial was that he was the most dangerous man Star Watch possessed. Was the captain more dangerous than Lord Drakos?

"Do stop any Vega Sector rebellion while you're at it," Stokes said. "It will strengthen my position if you do. If my position is strengthened, then I can better protect you, especially as I predict you will leave the reservation in your hunt for Drakos."

"I hope you realize that all this is more than just Drakos," the captain said. "I suspect a new alien intelligence influencing events. The patterns I discerned while readings all those reports—"

"You have your orders, Captain," Strokes practically yelled.

Maddox eyed the agitated lieutenant colonel. Had Stokes left him with the reports for a reason? Was the man playing an even more devious game than usual?

Maddox nodded sharply as his respect for Stokes increased.

Stokes stuck out his right hand.

Maddox took it, shaking hands with the man.

"Good hunting, Captain."

"Watch your back, sir. I want you to keep your new post at least until I return."

"That is something I fully intend to do," Stokes said.

-28-

That might have been the end of Maddox's briefing for his new assignment as he left the chamber under marine escort. But there was another…well, this *other* wasn't strictly a person in the biological sense, but he was a thinking being in the accepted sense of sentience.

The MPs marched Maddox through Star Watch Headquarters to a waiting air car on the roof of the large structure.

Instead of an armored air car, however, was a small "bubble" flitter waiting. The plastic bubble was a canopy over the four seats in the flitter, two in front and two in back. Surprisingly, Sergeant Riker sat in the front seat at the controls.

Maddox kept a poker face even as he recalled Riker being upstairs in *Victory*, in orbit around Earth. In spite of that, Maddox said, "Glad you're here, Sergeant."

"Sir," the being behind the flitter controls said. "I'm supposed to take you directly up to *Victory*."

"This isn't an air car," the marine lieutenant complained. "I was specifically told to put the captain aboard an air car."

"Wasn't an air car in the spaceport park," the sergeant said. "This was all they had available. I'm surprised no one told you."

"That thing isn't even space capable," the lieutenant said. "And *his* orders are to go directly to the starship," the marine said, pointing at Maddox.

"Isn't it?" the gruff-voiced sergeant asked. "The captain has taken a model like this into space before."

The lieutenant glanced at a nodding Maddox. "Fine," the marine said. "Get in and go upstairs. I'm sick of having to watch you like a mother hen."

"I would first like my sidearm back," Maddox said, holding out his right hand.

The lieutenant eyed Maddox before saying, "I thought you might." He took a weapon from behind his back and handed it to the captain.

Maddox checked the blaster. "There's no charge, Lieutenant." He opened it up as he said that, finding it lacked a power cell.

"And there's not going to be a charge until you're back aboard your starship," the lieutenant said. "Those are my orders."

Maddox eyed the lieutenant, shrugged and put the blaster in his empty holster and climbed into the flitter's passenger seat.

The sergeant activated the controls, closed the bubble hatch and lifted off the roof of Star Watch Headquarters.

Maddox leaned against the bubble canopy, looking down at the MPs shrinking as the flitter rose almost straight up. As he looked down, he slipped a hidden power cell from a concealed location on his person. The MPs hadn't found it earlier when they'd frisked him. He took out the blaster, opened it and softly *clicked* the power cell into place.

He watched the energy light on the blaster. It flickered and then stayed green. Maddox straightened in his seat, glanced at the pilot and aimed the blaster across his body at the being.

"You're an android," Maddox announced.

The Sergeant Riker lookalike nodded in agreement as the flitter gained altitude.

"I've activated the blaster," Maddox informed the android.

The thing with a Sergeant Riker face glanced at the weapon in the captain's right hand, probably noticing the green light because Maddox twisted the blaster so he could see.

"Clever," the android said in a different voice from the one he'd used as a fake Sergeant Riker. "When did you realize?"

"Immediately," Maddox said.

"What gave it away?"

The captain said nothing.

"I had clearance in case the lieutenant checked with HQ Control," the android said.

"Covered your bases, did you?"

The android glanced at Maddox. "I'm here to warn you."

"So, warn me," Maddox said. "I'm listening."

The android paused, and then said, "I'm a Yen Cho model, if that helps. I belong to those of us who want to help humanity."

Maddox said nothing, although his mind was racing.

Two missions ago, the oldest of the Yen Cho androids had boarded *Victory* as they hunted for Strand clones. That Yen Cho had proven treacherous at just the wrong moment. That Yen Cho had helped a Builder cube turn into a real Builder. Did this android's appearance validate the idea that a rogue Builder was behind all this?

One thing was certain, the android had his own agenda, and likely, that agenda was at odds with the captain's orders.

"You and I have never met before," the android was saying, "but I feel as if I know you. You are a remarkable human, Captain. This is a privilege—"

"Let me interrupt you," Maddox said. "First, land the flitter at Geneva Spaceport."

"Why?"

Maddox grinned in a predatory manner. "Because I'm not going with you to wherever you're heading."

"We're going upstairs to *Victory*."

"Uh-huh," Maddox said, unconvinced.

"I'm here to help you."

"You said warn me."

"That, too," the android said.

Despite his certainty that the android was lying, Maddox considered the ramifications that the android might be telling the truth, or part of the truth anyway. "I've had dealings with you Yen Cho models before," he said. "I've found the times unsettling in the extreme."

"I do not belong to that faction."

"Which faction?" asked Maddox.

"The one two missions ago when you were hunting for the Strand clones," the android said.

"You're well informed."

"Which is why I've come," the android said. "You're going to need help, need help desperately this time."

"How do I know that you're really a Yen Cho model?"

"I can explain later. Time is critical now."

"Okay…" Maddox said. "I'll bite. What's the warning? Is it concerning Lord Drakos?"

"Oh, no," the android said, "but about the new aliens, the ones in the hauler hiding on Jupiter."

Maddox's manner did not change, but something happened behind his eyes. Should he fire and be done with it, killing the thing? Would it really take him to *Victory?* If so, who did the android plan on contacting later to sabotage the mission?

"What about these aliens?" Maddox finally asked.

The android glanced at him again. "You don't believe that I'm here to help you."

"If nothing else, you're perceptive."

"How can I convince you to believe me?"

"There is a way," Maddox said, "but you're not going to like it."

The android peered at him again. "I see," it said. "I think I know. You want Ludendorff to open me up and check my circuits."

The android surprised Maddox with the answer, as that had been exactly what he'd been thinking. That also made him more suspicious as to how the android had known the answer.

"I hit the mark," the android said, glancing at him.

"If you're willing to agree to a Ludendorff diagnostic, I'd imagine that you're rigged to explode and kill him along with me."

"Please," the android said. "I love life to the same extent you do. I am not suicidal. I volunteered for this mission, by the way. I've wanted to meet you for some time. Are you familiar with the Spacer concept of *di-far?*"

"You know I am."

"I have come to wonder if the Spacers might have a point regarding you."

"And you want to dissect me to see what causes this unique nature?" Maddox asked.

The android appeared shocked, shaking his head. "On no account, as that would be foolish and unproductive. With such a thing as *di-far*, I would imagine that the product is greater than the sum of his parts. No. I am inclined to the idea that there is something mystical involved."

"Androids believe in mysticism?"

"Certainly, as there have been many mystics throughout human history. The concept is self-evident."

"That's not what I meant by the question."

"No," the android said. "You must be asking if I believe there is a power that supplies the mystic with true...abilities."

"Something like that. By the way, we're still heading up. The flitter cannot maneuver in orbital space. It has to drift up there, and that for only a limited time. I'm not going to trust you enough to let you drift with me."

"We are at an impasse then, as I will not land at Geneva Spaceport. If I do, there is a seventy-four percent probability that I will cease functioning. There are still android agents of the new aliens working among you. In fact, there is at least a one in three chance that you shall die if we land at the spaceport."

Maddox eyed the android, knowing they could move incredibly fast. He might kill it if it attacked him, and he might accidently destroy the flitter controls in the process.

"Hover at his location," Maddox said, "and contact *Victory*."

"Shouldn't you contact *Victory?*"

"I'm keeping my blaster targeted on you. If you twitch wrong, I'm killing you. That being the case, I cannot afford to take my concentration off you."

"Yes, that is wise, given your belief concerning me."

Maddox tensed, figuring this was the perfect moment for the android to launch a surprise assault.

Instead, the android slowed the ascent and fiddled with the comm controls. Soon, Valerie was on the line.

Maddox kept his eyes focused on the android, but said, "Lieutenant, run an analysis on my voice. If you're convinced on my identity, send a fold-fighter to pick us up."

Valerie began to speak.

"Listen," Maddox said. "There's a reason I'm not giving my identity."

"I understand," Valerie said a moment later. "As I was about to say, a fold-fighter will arrive soon. I am certain I know who this is."

"Interesting," the android murmured. He slowed the flitter even more.

"You're going to have to eject the canopy," Maddox told the android, "as it won't open at this height."

"I had not anticipated this maneuver," the android said.

Maddox was primed for a swift and sudden android attack. Perhaps neither of them was ready for what happened next, as a beam of destructive energy flashed just ahead of the flitter—where the flitter would have been if the android hadn't slowed them yet again.

The android cried out and changed heading, diving and twisting the flitter, no doubt to present a more difficult target.

The maneuver caught Maddox by surprise, and to his dismay, the blaster flew up out of his grip to hit the plastic canopy ceiling as the flitter plunged earthward.

-29-

The android reached up and grabbed the blaster faster than Maddox could recover his equilibrium. The captain gathered himself, when he found the blaster shoved in his face.

"Hold onto this," the android said.

Maddox grabbed the blaster, wondering what kind of ploy this was. The next second, the side of his head smacked against the bubble canopy as the android violently shifted the flitter the other way.

Another red beam flashed past the craft, the intense glare of its color putting sparkles in Maddox's eyesight.

"Who's firing at us?" Maddox shouted. He used both hands to grab his seatbelt and hang on while also hanging onto the blaster.

"I believe that it is the agents of the new aliens," the android said.

"Do you have a name for these aliens?"

"Jotuns."

"I've heard that name before."

"I am unsurprised, as the name is from human mythology during the time of the Vikings. According to myth, Jotuns were the giants who fought the Norse gods."

"Okay," Maddox said. "Why did you choose that name for the new aliens?"

"Hold on," the android said, maneuvering violently once more.

"Captain," Keith said over the flitter's comm board. "You're not in the correct position."

Maddox looked up and could make out the fold-fighter. He fought the Gs pressing against him and reached out, pressing a comm switch. He didn't chide the ace for using his rank out in the open, but said, "Down here. We're below you. Someone is firing at us and we've had to dodge and weave."

Maddox twisted toward the android. "Are the spaceport's defensive batteries firing at us?"

"I doubt it, but someone clearly knows about me."

"*You*," Maddox said. "I thought they were firing at me. I'm the one supposed to be heading to *Victory.*"

"I see you, mate," Keith said over the comm. "A fusion beam site is targeting you. I'm getting help."

The android turned the flitter and headed up instead of down, putting terrible G strains against Maddox. His eyesight dimmed, which meant he might be blacking out. Like a New Man, he could take more Gs than a regular human could, but he could not take as many as a full-fledged Superior.

"Oh," the android said, glancing at him. "I am turning too sharply at too high a speed."

"There," Keith said over the comm board. "I'm coming down some. You should try to come up more, mate."

Maddox wanted to reach for the comm, but he didn't have the strength or the force of will to do so again.

"Up even more, he says," the android complained. "Does he want me to cease existence?"

The fusion beam flashed again, and the edge of the ray caught the edge of the flitter. A portion of the craft vaporized, and heat flooded the rest of the small flitter.

Maddox couldn't help it, but he groaned at the hot pain.

The android pressed a switch. What was left of the canopy ejected, and wind howled around them. Maddox tried to bring the blaster around as android fingers plucked at him.

"Don't fight me," the android shouted, his voice barely audible in the shrieking wind. "I'm trying to help you. Your ace is folding."

Maddox looked up as wind tore at his eyes. What remained of the flitter began to spin and turn upside-down.

"That is not helping," the android said. He tore Maddox's harness from him, pried the captain from his seat and gathered him like a giant baby. Then, the android propelled the two of them from the upside-down flitter. Both beings shot out of and to the side of the craft.

Seconds later, another fusion beam reached up from the surface and hit the badly damaged flitter directly. Maddox saw it disintegrate as the android and he tumbled earthward. Then he realized a shape was near him. It was the box-like tin can, the fold-fighter.

"We are doomed, I am afraid," the android said. "I did not grab a parachute."

"Keith," Maddox shouted.

"Do you mean your pilot?" the android shouted back.

"Yes!"

"Not even he will be good enough to catch us with a fusion beam firing up."

The android would have made a lousy weatherman, as his prediction was way off. A different beam shot down from space, the sniper beam from *Victory* and targeted by Galyan.

Then the fold-fighter was underneath them, pacing them and slowly inching upward.

"Incredible," the android said.

Soon, a marine popped up from a special hatch. As the wind howled around him, the android handed Maddox to the marine. The man helped Maddox slide through the hatch and inside the fold-fighter.

Maddox felt spent and ridiculous. Still, he forced his limbs to work as he climbed down the rest of the way. Soon, the android and marine joined him as the hatch above closed.

"Are we all set?" Keith asked from the piloting chair.

"Good work, Lieutenant," Maddox said.

"Just my job description, mate," Keith bragged. "Pull the rabbit out of the hat when all else fails."

"So, it is true," the android said. "I had thought my briefing false, as no one can be that full of himself."

"That's where you're wrong," Keith said. "But it isn't being full of myself. I know what I can do, and I do it when the situation calls for it. By the way, you're welcome."

Keith turned to Maddox. "Who is he, because I know he ain't the sergeant?"

"An android," the captain said, as he clawed the blaster from his holster and aimed it at the Sergeant Riker lookalike.

"Are we back to this?" the android asked.

"A precaution," Maddox said, "as your kind has fooled us one too many times."

The android nodded. "Do you desire to hear the rest of my information regarding the Jotuns?"

"Yes," Maddox said, "as soon as we're back on *Victory.*" He turned to Keith. "How long will that be?"

At that point, a fusion beam firing up from Earth struck the tin can, causing a klaxon to blare.

"Heads up, people," Keith said. "It looks like we're not out of this yet."

-30-

"Galyan," Keith said into a comm, even as his fingers roved over the piloting board. At the same time, the fold-fighter maneuvered wildly.

"I see it," Galyan said over the comm. "It is a second battery. I will take it out…now."

Keith's fingers kept moving as he stared intently at his board.

Maddox had tucked the blaster away as he strapped himself in. The marine and android did likewise at different locations.

"I'm done with this," Keith said. "We need to get you home, sir."

"We need to find out who's firing at a Star Watch fold-fighter," Maddox said.

"Galyan can do that," Keith said. "Hang on, now. We're—"

Maddox blacked out so he didn't hear the next words.

***

When the captain came to again, he found himself lying on a bed in Medical with Meta staring down at him. There were tubes in his arms and his chest felt heavy.

"What's going on?" Maddox asked slowly, his mind befuddled.

"You fainted on the fold-fighter," Meta told him.

"That's ridiculous."

"That isn't what the doctor is saying," his wife said.

"Oh?"

"It's..." Meta gave him a worried stare.

Instead of surging up, Maddox sagged back against the bed. He had an idea what had happened. Ever since he'd used a Ludendorff-made machine, used some of his life-essence to power it and attacked a spiritual-creature Ska, he had taken internal wounds. The wounds weren't physical, but of a spiritual nature that affected his life force.

Often at the oddest times, he suffered weakness when his normal vitality should have seen him through. He simply did not have the same firepower he used to have. It was maddening, and it was something that he refused to accept about himself.

"You overdid it," Meta was saying.

Maddox sighed. He didn't have time for weakness. He needed to find a workout regimen that would let him build back up to what he used to have. One hidden part of him wondered if there was such a regimen or if he had taken permanent damage that would be with him for the rest of his life.

That was a daunting thought that he didn't want to acknowledge.

"If you're worried about the android, Valerie had him placed in a secure cell in the brig."

"That's something at least," Maddox said.

"The...ah, Lord High Admiral wants a word with you later."

"Cook is onboard?"

Meta shook her head.

"What's going on, Meta? Hurry up and spit it out."

"The admiral wants a detailed explanation about *Victory's* firing at Geneva Spaceport defensive batteries."

"What?" Maddox asked. That didn't sound right.

"Darling," someone unseen said. "Can you hear me?"

Confusion set in, and Maddox squeezed his eyes closed, squeezed them tighter and slowly opened them. The Meta who had asked the crazy question literally dissolved before his eyes. He saw another Meta looking down at him in worry.

"What's going on?" Maddox asked in a winded voice.

"Darling," Meta said, her beautiful features creased with worry. "You...you fainted on us. I think I should take you to Medical."

Maddox found that he was lying in the middle of a corridor on *Victory*. Sergeant Riker and two marines looked back at him. No. That wasn't Riker. That was the android.

"Let me help you up," Meta was saying.

"No," Maddox said sharply.

Meta had been reaching down, but now stopped.

"I'll do this myself," Maddox said. He rolled over onto his hands and knees and slowly worked up to his feet. He swayed and felt dizzy, and side-shuffled until he leaned against a bulkhead.

The android, marines and Meta were all studying him.

"Tell me what happened," he said to Meta. "All of it, from the beginning as I boarded *Victory*."

She told him the fold-fighter had appeared in a hangar bay. Keith had made the risky maneuver as Galyan destroyed the second fusion beam battery with the starship's sniper ray.

"Were the fusion cannon batteries around the Geneva Spaceport?" Maddox asked.

"Oh no," Meta said. "They were on hidden trucks. Galyan destroyed them both with the sniper ray. Once the ray touched the vehicles, they exploded. The android said they were rigged to explode so no one could trace them back to their alien handlers. Once we—"

"That's enough," Maddox said. He stared at the Riker-looking android. "Why did I faint just now and why don't I remember the rest of what happened on the fold-fighter?"

"I have a suspicion why," the android said. "But I—"

"Sir," the smaller marine said, interrupting. "I saw the android twitch earlier and touch a spot on his neck."

"There," the android said, indicating the smaller marine. "He is the one. He is the latest android plant."

"When did you originally board *Victory?*" Maddox asked the smaller marine.

Instead of answering, the marine drew his sidearm and might have burned down the Riker-looking android. Meta moved faster, kicking the drawn gun from the marine's hand.

156

The marine did not shout in surprise or pain, but launched himself at the Riker android.

From the bulkhead where he'd been leaning, Maddox dove at the marine and attempted to tackle him. The marine shrugged off Maddox's attack, so the captain thudded onto the floor.

Meta charged next, and the marine threw her with a judo move. She slammed against a bulkhead and slid down onto the floor.

That gave the Riker android time. He smashed a fist against the marine's face. The impact was so terrific that it not only stopped the marine but caused him to catapult backward. He hit the floor and rolled over and over.

Maddox scrambled off the floor, picked up the fallen blaster and beamed the marine as he surged back to his feet.

Unsurprisingly, pseudo-skin peeled away from the marine's head to reveal a metal braincase. The blaster beam burned through that, fusing android brain circuits. The mechanical thing jerked once, twice and spasmed as it crashed onto the floor.

Before the Riker android could react, Maddox aimed the blaster at it.

"That's enough," the captain said.

"Meaning what?" the Riker android asked. "I just saved your life."

"Mine?" Maddox said. "Why did the fake marine attack you?"

"Is it not obvious?" the android asked. "It belonged to the Jotun faction, as the aliens have turned it. Why else would an android attempt to sneak aboard *Victory?* All androids have long ago learned the futility of such an act. The Jotuns, however, must believe otherwise."

During the long-winded explanation, Maddox realized that Meta was groaning as she rolled from her stomach onto her back. He holstered the blaster and rushed to his wife. "Meta!" he shouted, with an edge of panic in his voice.

Her eyelids fluttered, and Meta groaned again as she sat up. There was a large bruise over her right eye, which had puffed shut.

"What happened?" she asked.

Maddox looked up to see that the other marine had drawn his weapon and aimed it at the android.

"He is human," the Riker android said, regarding the last marine. "He is protecting you from me."

Maddox nodded. "Can you stand?" he asked his wife.

"I think so," she said.

"Let's get you to Medical then," Maddox said. "And you," he said, looking at the android. "It's time to start unraveling this mess."

"Yes," the android said. "That is why I am here."

Maddox stared at the Sergeant Riker lookalike. "By the way, what should I call you?"

"Batrun will do," the android said.

"Just Batrun?" asked Maddox.

"That is acceptable."

Maddox squinted at the thing as a horrible feeling of *déjà vu* filled him. It was time to find out just what in the hell was happening this time around.

"Do you have a different face?" the captain asked.

"I do," Batrun said.

"Then, put it on as soon as you can, as I don't want to get angry at Riker for the things you do."

-31-

Meta went to Medical. The blaster-fried android went to Ludendorff's science lab, and Batrun the android went to a holding cell.

There, the android modified his features, so he no longer looked like Treggason Riker, but like a blunt-faced man in his forties.

Maddox told the marine in charge of the brig to inform Batrun that it would be a few hours before the captain would talk to him. The marine called back to tell Maddox the android was anxious and wanted to speak to him immediately.

Maddox wasn't in a hurry just yet, and he wanted to get several things squared away before he spoke to the android.

First, he found out that two semis had indeed held two fusion cannons. Star Watch Intelligence teams were already on the case, trying to establish where the vehicles and their advanced military weaponry had come from. So far, ubiquitous shell companies were the only answers. Well, there had also been android parts found at each destroyed semi.

Second, Maddox called Stokes and told him about the Batrun android.

"Destroy it," Stokes said over the comm.

"Maybe in time I will," Maddox said.

"Given the number of times androids have helped you versus the amount of times they have caused all of us harm, I'd say the odds are that Batrun will prove dangerous to your mission."

"I agree," Maddox said. "Thus, I will proceed with caution."

Stokes frowned on the comm screen. "I don't want to take this to the Lord High Admiral, but…" The lieutenant colonel squinted at Maddox. "I see. You're on your starship. Therefore, you feel invincible and plan to do what you're going to do. Besides, you don't think I'll call the admiral because you know something I don't want the admiral to know, and you can use that as blackmail."

"I didn't kill Drakos at the end of the last mission even though I could have," Maddox said. "I didn't kill him because I listened to orders. I don't always do what I want to do just because I want to do it."

"Fine, fine," Stokes said. "Very well, test the android." The lieutenant colonel shook his head. "This one is giving me a headache. It's a tangled web indeed. One of these days, I hope fate lobs us an easy one."

"I wouldn't count on it," Maddox said.

Stokes signed off a moment later.

Third, Maddox had lunch and did some thinking. Fourth, he headed to Medical to see how Meta was doing.

"I wouldn't call it a concussion," the doctor told him. "But she took a heavy blow to the head."

Maddox spoke to his wife and told her to stay in Medical for more tests. He wanted to make sure she was fine.

"I'm not going to break as easily as that," she said.

As she lay on the med-bed, Maddox stroked her head before taking his leave. He figured Ludendorff should have found something out by now.

∗∗∗

Like last time in the science lab, Ludendorff had spread out the fake marine android parts.

"This," the Methuselah Man said, using a thin pointer to indicate a thumbtack-shaped and sized device.

"This what?" asked Maddox.

"I believe this is what caused you to faint in the corridor and forget some of what happened aboard the fold-fighter. The android must have been attempting to—" Ludendorff stared at Maddox oddly, as he stopped talking.

It took Maddox a second before he said, "Do you want to map my brain patterns and see if anything has changed?"

"I believe it is imperative to do so."

Maddox considered that and finally nodded. "Let me call the sergeant first."

"For what reason?" asked Ludendorff, perplexed.

"Insurance."

"Against me?" asked Ludendorff.

Maddox just stared at the professor.

Ludendorff scowled and finally muttered, "Do what you must. Your lack of trust in me doesn't increase my faith in you."

Maddox summoned Riker, having exactly zero sympathy for Ludendorff's feelings in the matter. Shortly, Maddox climbed off a brain scanner. He exchanged glances with Riker. The sergeant minutely shook his head. There had been no observable foul play on the professor's part.

Ludendorff came back with a chart. "It's like I thought. Your brain pattern has been altered, if only slightly. The android—likely the marine android—did it to you."

"You mean Batrun might have altered my brain earlier?"

"Of course," Ludendorff said. "I'm frankly surprised that a hyper-suspicious man like you didn't already realize that."

Maddox said nothing.

"I should dissect Batrun so we can be sure," Ludendorff added.

"Not just yet," Maddox replied. "But you should scan him. See if he has this…device in him."

It was Ludendorff's turn to say nothing.

"Scan him and then report back to me," Maddox said.

Ludendorff's nostrils flared, but he still said nothing.

Deciding that was the best he was going to get, Maddox departed, taking Riker with him.

***

Forty minutes later on the bridge, Maddox received a call from a plainly agitated Ludendorff in his science lab.

"Your pet android is clear," Ludendorff said over a comm screen. "He lacks the device."

"Did you detect other devices in him?"

"No."

"Then what has you upset, Professor?"

On the screen, Ludendorff looked away. "I… Your distrust in me earlier…"

Maddox didn't sigh but said straight-faced, "Professor, you've been a great help on many occasions. You have also been a great hindrance just as often."

"I know, I know. I have been wondering—" Ludendorff faced him. "Do you think this is why Dana left me?"

Maddox waited.

"Am I truly…untrustworthy?" the professor whispered.

Maddox did not believe in kicking a man when he was down, not unless it was during a fight. Ludendorff would also resume his old ways soon enough and remember any unkind words.

"I do not presume to know what a woman thinks in such a matter," the captain said.

"If *you* don't know, who does?"

Maddox shook his head.

A second later, the screen clicked off.

Maddox turned around, surprised to see Riker staring at the comm screen.

"Trouble?" asked Maddox.

"Do you buy that act?"

"Now see here, Sergeant—"

"The professor has to be the slipperiest man we know," Riker said, interrupting, "and a convincing actor to boot."

"Perhaps, but I'm not interested in discussing the professor's love life just now."

"I'm just saying, sir, if he's playacting, why is he doing so?"

"Hmm…" Maddox said, as he rubbed his chin. "He is a Methuselah Man. A long-lived man surely thinks differently than an ordinary man does."

The captain refrained from saying more. Ludendorff might be in mental anguish because of Dana's departure. But he would remember Riker's suspicion if a moment came where he had to trust Ludendorff. If the professor were acting a part, it would be for a specific reason.

With a shake of his head, Maddox dismissed that from his thoughts, as it was time to talk to Batrun the android.

-32-

Once more, a sense of déjà vu filled the captain as he sat in a holding cell in the brig. Batrun the android, a supposed Yen Cho model, sat behind a table, regarding him.

"You appear troubled," Batrun said.

"I'm recalling the last time I had a Yen Cho android in a holding cell aboard *Victory.*"

"I am privy to a few Star Watch Intelligence reports," Batrun said. "For instance, I know about the incident of which you speak. I will not transform as the other android did."

"How did you gain such Intelligence data?"

Batrun shook his head. "That is not germane to the topic at hand."

"The hell it isn't," Maddox said.

Frowning, the captain stopped speaking. It wasn't like him to get angry during an interrogation. Did the outburst have something to do with his slightly altered brain patterns? Was it due to having less soul energy? Was that finally beginning to weigh on him too much, affecting his actions?

Maddox settled himself, deciding he wouldn't force the issue just yet. He would…maintain his calm and observe the android's behavior. He would also catalog his own behavior as if he was another person he was trying to understand.

"You came to me, Batrun. Somehow, you knew where I'd be after speaking with Lieutenant Colonel Stokes. I find that troubling."

"Stokes is now a lieutenant colonel?" the android asked.

Maddox said nothing as he thought about another poker analogy. A level one player considered what cards he possessed, and nothing else. A level two player considered what cards he and his opponent had. A level three player considered those things along with what cards his opponent thought that he possessed. The levels could go up without limit. It was beneficial to think one level higher than one's adversary. But if one thought two or more levels higher than his opponent, it didn't help any, because his opponent did not think high enough for those insights to matter. In those cases, the poker player could outthink himself.

The point here in the holding cell was that Maddox didn't want to ponder if the android really knew about Stokes' promotion or merely wanted him to believe that he didn't know. Things could become too convoluted that way until a man paralyzed himself. It was possible that Batrun plotted wheels within wheels, but Maddox refused to paralyze himself by trying to outthink the android in that manner.

As he sat in his chair, Maddox crossed his legs. "You appeared in a flitter at HQ to pick me up. You obviously succeeded. Now, are you here to warn or to help me?"

"Both," Batrun said.

"Let's begin with the warning," Maddox said.

The android did not move or twitch, but suddenly, Maddox became hyper-alert, and he did not know why.

"The Jotuns are like nothing you have faced before," Batrun finally said. "They are like nothing *we* have faced before. They are mysterious, and it would seem work overtime to maintain their cloak of anonymity."

"So far," Maddox said, "you've told me nothing useful. As far as I'm concerned, this is merely another android plot or possibly a Builder ploy using androids as their tools."

"Consider this then," Batrun said, "the reflective spheroid you witnessed was new. The binding-force bubble that allowed the hauler to go deep into the Jovian atmosphere was new. The brain modification device that political advisor Sanders and marine androids used was also new."

"I'm listening," Maddox said.

"What does Professor Ludendorff say about all this?"

Maddox studied the blunt-faced android while considering the question. Instead of answering, he said, "First, tell me what you know about the Jotuns."

Batrun cocked his head. Was he processing? He straightened his head, and said, "We have come to believe that the Jotuns originated on a Jovian planet."

"The aliens are from a…from a *Jupiter-like gas giant?*"

"Which would be one reason why the hauler fled deep into Jupiter," Batrun said.

Maddox absorbed that. The implications were astounding. Aliens at home in a Jovian gas world would be nothing like humans, nothing like Builders or even Swarm creatures. Why would such beings send spies onto—their way of thinking—a tiny terrestrial hard rock world? More importantly, how could such alien beings have acquired the spies in the first place? How did Jovian aliens communicate with humans?

"Are there Jotuns on Jupiter?" Maddox asked. "I mean Jotuns other than any aboard the hauler."

"I deem that as possible, yes."

"Is there a Jotun colony on Jupiter?"

"I doubt that."

"But…"

Maddox tried to imagine what kind of ships Jovian aliens would construct. How would such aliens discover thermonuclear power? The conditions on Jupiter were vastly different from those on Earth.

"Would Jotuns possess steel-hulled vessels like the hauler or hydro-lithium hulled ships?" Maddox asked.

"That is an astute question, Captain, a scientific question. I had not expected that from you."

Maddox waited.

"As you have surmised, as is obvious, the Jotuns would be unlike us in most ways," Batrun said. "Possibly, high intelligence would be our only commonality. Likely, Jotuns breathe hydrogen at tremendous pressures. I would imagine that the bottom of your ocean—a place of immense pressure to human understanding—would be like a vacuum to them. It is quite possible they are comfortable at one hundred degrees below zero and drink liquid methane."

Maddox shook his head. "How do you know any of these things to be true if you haven't met them?"

"We don't know these things as truth. It is our present working theory regarding them."

"Suppose you're right," Maddox said. "What would the Jotuns want with us?"

"Since we believe they have already acted..." Batrun paused before saying, "It is our understanding that eliminating us—you—is their primary goal."

"Have you seen a Jotun spaceship?"

Batrun shook his head.

"Have you seen—?"

"Let me stop you, Captain," Batrun said. "What we have seen and felt is frightening enough. Jotun agents have been able to slip onto Earthlike worlds, mingle among humans and pinpoint androids with frightful ease. The Jotun agents have been reprogramming androids and making them their slaves, their puppets."

"Might that indicate a Builder posing as a Jotun instead of Jotuns?" Maddox asked.

Batrun waited several seconds, perhaps processing the idea, before saying, "The possibility exists, certainly. That is partly why I wish to know what Professor Ludendorff thinks about all this."

"We'll leave Ludendorff out of this for the present."

"That could be a mistake. We should pool our knowledge, *all* our knowledge."

"Is that why you're here?" Maddox asked. "To try and kidnap Ludendorff? Or maybe you want the chance to kill the Methuselah Man."

"My help against the android marine should have convinced you that I am on your side."

"The android marine could have been a sacrificial plant to trick me into trusting you," Maddox said forcefully. "Batrun, let me blunt. I have become exceedingly wary of androids. I suspect everything about you, your kind and your words."

"I know, and that is a pity. The androids are like the boy who cried wolf, only instead of falsely warning people, androids have repeatedly attempted to use humanity to further our ends. Now, in their moment of real crisis, the androids lack allies."

"There is an old saying," Maddox said. "Cry me a river."

"Is that your final answer to the android plight?"

"I don't even *know* your plight."

"Isn't it obvious? I have already stated it."

Maddox waited.

Batrun sat utterly still, perhaps processing again. Finally, he nodded. "It is not obvious. We have made an error. We believed that you understood. This is galling. I would not have come here to you—"

"Now!" Maddox shouted, as he jumped up from his chair and drew a blaster.

Before Batrun could ask or react, powerful magnets embedded under the deck plates yanked the android from his chair and forced him flat on his back.

By that time, Maddox had scrambled through the opened hatch. A second later, that hatch automatically shut with a clang.

Several marines waited with android-killing weapons in the larger chamber where Maddox stood panting. Ludendorff and Riker were also there.

"Well?" Maddox asked, as he straightened. "Do you have any idea what he thought we knew?"

"Yes," Ludendorff said. "He thought we knew the Jotuns—or whoever they represent—are turning androids with pitiful ease. He did tell us that, and that's what has these Yen Cho androids so frightened. The 'aliens'—and I say that with quotes—are using the androids. By that I mean, they are reprogramming them and making them their tools."

"How are the Jotuns doing this?"

"I have not yet divined that part," Ludendorff admitted.

"Could Batrun be telling the truth that he really needs our help and wants to help us?"

Ludendorff clasped the inner open edges of his white lab coat. "Captain, I believe him."

Maddox turned to the closed hatch.

"I don't trust him, sir," Riker said. "Androids have given us small reason to ever trust one of them."

"True," Maddox said, as he faced the others. "Professor, instead of waiting for this android to turn into something insanely dangerous, this time we're going to dissect him. This time, we're going to deal with the android on our terms."

"What if he really did come to help us and we desperately need his help but don't yet know it?" Ludendorff asked.

"Then we'll tell Batrun we're sorry after we tear him down and put him back together again," Maddox said.

"I may not have the skill to reassemble him after I've taken him apart," Ludendorff said. "I am many things, but I am not a Builder tech."

Maddox thought about that, finally nodding. "Well, that's a risk I'm willing to take."

-33-

"Give me your weapon," Maddox told the nearest marine.

The marine began to shrug off the bulky power pack harnessed to his back. A flexible line from the pack was attached to a short firing rod.

"Sir," Riker said. "You going in is a bad idea."

"How do you propose turning off the android?" Maddox asked.

"By sending powerful jolts of electricity through the deck plates," the sergeant answered.

Ludendorff objected, "That could irreparably harm the android's circuits."

"Begging your pardon, Professor," Riker said. "I don't know that you're sufficiently worried about the captain's safety. That's why no one is asking you."

Ludendorff scowled. "Since no one else has the capacity to dissect and reassemble the android, my opinion is of the utmost importance." He pointed at the firing rod. "Not that I suggest using a weapon to turn him off. That is a *killing* tool."

"I know," Maddox said, who snapped his fingers at the marine.

The marine had slowed down at Riker's objection. Now, he hurried up.

"What if the android detonates rather than allowing anyone to turn him off?" Riker asked.

Maddox didn't answer, as he took the power pack from the marine and shrugged it onto his back. Since the captain had broader shoulders and a deeper chest, he had to loosen the pack's straps. Soon, he cinched a belt around his waist and picked up the short firing rod.

"I wish you would reconsider, sir," Riker said. "The androids have screwed us far too often. I don't want to scrape your remains off the floor."

"I appreciate the sentiment," Maddox said. He nodded to a marine. "Open the hatch."

"I'm going with you," Ludendorff said.

"I think not," Maddox said. "If Riker is correct about detonating androids, I want you alive. Besides, you can watch through a screen. I do not suggest you watch through the two-way mirror. The sergeant does have a point about detonations."

"Let me go, sir," Riker said. "I'm far more expendable than you."

Maddox shook his head before using it to point at a marine. The man went to the hatch, ready to open it.

"You're just going to shoot it?" Ludendorff asked.

"No," Riker said.

Maddox looked quizzically at the sergeant.

"The captain has something else in mind," Riker said, who studied Maddox. "Good luck, sir. I hope you know what you're doing. Remember. The androids have almost always played us false."

"Open up," Maddox told the marine.

The hatch opened, and Maddox headed into the cell. As soon as he entered, the hatch clanged shut behind him.

A loud hum informed the captain that the deck-plate magnetics still worked. He moved crossways in the room so he could look past the intervening table. Batrun was still flat on his back, pinned to the magnetized plates.

The android couldn't turn his head, but he could move his eyes. "Is this truly necessary?" Batrun asked in an altered voice, as he watched the captain from the corner of his eyes.

Maddox hadn't aimed the firing rod at him yet but kept the rod parallel with his right leg. The rod, line and pack were constructed out of non-ferrous material, which was why the deck magnets did not pull at them.

"The strength of the magnetic pull and the containing duration could be detrimental to me," Batrun said.

"We're at an impasse," Maddox said, as he moved up. "I don't trust you, as androids have played us false far too often. And yet, I wonder if you're telling me the truth."

"I am," Batrun said.

"I need confirmation."

"Ah. Is that why you carry an android-killing weapon?"

"I want to turn you off for the moment, but I'm not sure how."

"I see. You do not just want to kill me and be done with it?"

"Before we proceed further, I want Ludendorff to study you."

"As if I were an insect, I presume."

"You're comparing yourself to a Swarm creature?" asked Maddox.

"You misunderstand. I mean an Earth insect like a bee or a wasp. You want to cut me apart to see how I tick."

"There you are," Maddox said. "You understand."

"I will not permit such a thing to happen to me."

"Meaning…?"

"Believe me when I say that I would rather cease existing than allow anyone to open me up. I am unique as you are unique."

"Does that mean you're not a Yen Cho model android?"

Batrun did not move his head, as likely, he could not. He did not twitch a finger or shift a booted foot. His eyes moved back and forth, however. That seemed to indicate deep thought.

"I do not know how to confirm my data so you will believe me," Batrun finally said. "But I can give you—I will only relate truthful information. I will start by admitting that I have given you some false data."

Maddox digested that. The desire to lift the rod and fire was strong. He wouldn't fire to incapacitate the android, but to kill it. He now doubted the wisdom of his plan. Then he reasoned that no great thing was achieved without taking risks, sometimes, grave risks.

"Can you detonate yourself?" Maddox asked.

"Oh yes," Batrun said.

"Would the detonation kill me?"

"It would likely destroy everyone within a one hundred and sixteen-meter radius, with myself as the focal point."

"So, you're a living bomb?"

"Not precisely," Batrun said, "but effectively that is so. Now, to clear up some falsehoods that I propagated. I am not a Yen Cho model android. Those are old, as in antique models. I am one of the last series to leave a Builder factory. Indeed, I was not even called an android but a synthetic. I am a Batrun model synthetic and have superior capabilities compared to an antique Yen Cho android."

"Then—"

"Let me finish, Captain. I do not belong to the Yen Cho faction, nor am I part of the Rull Nation Androids, as you deem them. We are the Watchers, and we have been observing the older androids as much as we have humanity. We have concluded that androids and humans are a poor mix. Humans do not trust androids and androids appear, over time, to have come to believe that they are a superior form of life."

"Are either androids or synthetics truly living beings in a biological sense?"

"That is a moot point," Batrun said from the floor. "We think, therefore we are alive, to paraphrase Descartes."

"Is Descartes a Builder?"

"Captain," Batrun chided. "Your ignorance is showing. Rene Descartes was a French philosopher. He coined the famous phrase, 'I think, therefore I am.'"

"Oh," Maddox said. "Yes. I understand. What are you thinking now?"

"There was an event approximately eight months ago," Batrun said, ignoring Maddox's question. "Several of our adepts recorded the event on an extremely sensitive machine. The event…speeded up a process."

"What event," Maddox asked, "and what process?"

"We are still attempting to decipher the first. The second—the Jotuns have moved before they were ready. Such is my belief, in any case."

"Moved against humanity?" Maddox asked.

"Against any terrestrial-based life-forms," Batrun said.

"You're suggesting the Jotuns truly are Jovian-based life?"

"I am."

"What do they have against us?"

"I do not know."

"What could have prodded them to move too soon?"

"Is that not an interesting question?" Batrun asked. "Let me elucidate a little further. It appears that the prodding mechanism was a ray of some kind."

"Wait, wait, wait," Maddox said, as he rubbed his forehead. "You're suggesting that you Watchers have been observing everything from the sidelines?"

"Poorly phrased and not altogether accurate," Batrun said.

"Why are you doing this and why show yourselves now?"

"I do wish Professor Ludendorff was here," Batrun said. "I dislike having to state such obvious facts." The synthetic did not sigh or move in any way, but he seemed to process faster until he reached a decision. "There are only a few of us, Captain. We watch you… You do not need to know the reason why we do. You do not need to know our supreme quest. It is not at odds with your aims, although it is not congruent with them, either. We have debated for some time, however, whether it might be prudent to…to convince the others to leave Human Space and the near Beyond. We believe it would be better for both, *groups*, to exist on their own."

"Do you think of yourselves as Builders?" Maddox asked.

"That is not germane to the issue at hand."

"That means you do," Maddox said.

"Do not presume to know how we view ourselves. It will only lead you to false conclusions."

"Oh, so you don't think you're Builders. That's good. Are you searching for the Builders?"

Batrun nodded. "You are curious, I understand. You are an intelligent creature. I am Batrun, and I have come to warn and aid you against the Jotuns and…" The synthetic stopped talking.

Maddox shifted his stance. The power pack was heavier than he'd realized before putting it on. The straps were beginning to dig into his shoulders.

"How did the first Jotuns get hold of the first androids?" Maddox asked. "If they're Jovian-based life—"

"Yes!" Batrun said, interrupting. "That is an intriguing question. I, too, wish to know that. Who are these Jotun agents? They cannot be Jotuns themselves, as they would have to exist in huge and heavy containment boxes to move among us. It is an intriguing dilemma, is it not?"

"You've never seen a Jotun?"

"No."

"How do you know they exist then?"

Batrun said nothing for several seconds, until he said in a loud voice, "Turn off the magnets, Captain. Either shoot me and die yourself, or release me. I am tired of being attached to the deck plates."

Maddox fingered the firing rod. Should he attempt to destroy the…synthetic? Was the thing bluffing about being a bomb?

"Was the marine android a plant?" Maddox asked.

"Of course," Batrun said.

"No. Was the marine android *your* plant?"

"…Yes," Batrun said.

Maddox raised the firing rod.

"A moment," Batrun said. "The marine was a Rull Nation android first altered by Jotun agents. Ludendorff must have found the neuron-shifter inside its chassis. I captured the android and made some minor adjustments to it. I then used the android in a crude and hurried attempt to force you to trust me. I should have realized that you and your crew have become supremely paranoid concerning androids. It is a reasonable response given your previous stimuli to them. Know, however, that I can undo what the android did to your brain."

"What did it do?"

"Made a minor adjustment regarding anger triggers," Batrun said. "Have you found yourself becoming more easily angered?"

"How many Batrun models are there?"

"I will not tell you."

Maddox nodded. At least that was an honest answer. "I bet there are only a handful of you. That's why you're here. The truth is that you need *Victory* more than we need you."

"How did you reach that conclusion?" Batrun asked, sounding intrigued.

"First, it fits android behavior."

"I told you. I am a synthetic, not exactly an android as you conceive of them."

"A rose by any other name is still a rose."

"I could deem that an insult."

Maddox shrugged.

"Are you attempting to anger me?"

"If you're an android, that should be impossible."

"I see," Batrun said. "Perhaps it is time to rearrange the parameters of our situation." He quit talking as his eyes shifted back and forth within his sockets.

Abruptly, the hum ceased from the floor. As if rising from bed, the synthetic climbed off the deck plates that had been holding him down, as they were no longer magnetized.

Maddox raised the firing rod and pressed the firing switch, but nothing happened.

"Why attempt to kill me now?" Batrun asked.

Maddox pressed the firing switch again.

"The unit is broken," Batrun said. "It will not respond as designed."

"Is this a takeover attempt?" Maddox asked.

"Of course not," the synthetic said. "I have spoken the truth as I said I would. I am not here to coerce you or your crew or ship. You should know that I am much more powerful than the usual run of android. I am the latest model and therefore the most versatile and prevailing. I am not a Builder. I do not, as such, seek the Builders. I would like to move all the androids out of Human Space. To do that, I believe aiding Star Watch in defeating the Jotuns would be in my best interest."

"I'm not hunting the Jotuns just now," Maddox said. "I'm going to look for Lord Drakos and try to figure out what he did or is doing in the Vega Sector."

Batrun stood utterly still, no doubt processing the information, finally nodding. "That is acceptable for now. Yes. If you will permit me, Captain, I would like to join you."

"And if I say no?" Maddox asked.

"Then I shall leave and never return."

Maddox nodded slowly. "If you will agree to leave when I say so, I'll let you stay for now. And, if you agree to continue to tell us the truth and nothing but the truth."

"So help me God," Batrun said.

Maddox wasn't sure this was the right choice, but it looked like they were going to work with an android—or a synthetic—one more time.

-34-

Lieutenant Noonan plotted a course to the Vega System and Keith Maker piloted the starship to the first Laumer Point.

Victory left behind the exotic hauler hidden inside the gassy innards of Jupiter as a Star Watch fleet orbited the giant planet. So far, there hadn't been any hint of the hauler attempting to escape or to communicate with Star Watch, or anyone else, for that matter.

Just how long could the hauler stay hidden down there?

"Do you have any idea?" Maddox asked Batrun.

The synthetic sat in a lounge chair as Maddox and Ludendorff faced him in comfortable chairs of their own. They were in an observation area, with screens showing the stars from within the Alpha Centauri System.

This was the first jump of many to reach Vega II. This was also the first time Maddox had been in the Alpha Centauri System since he'd killed everyone here by sending a Ska into the Alpha Centauri "A" star.

It had been two days since the confrontation in the brig cell. Before leaving the Solar System, Maddox had sent a message to Stokes concerning all he'd learned about the Jotuns. Since then, Ludendorff had hooked up the thumbtack-shaped device to the ship's most advanced computer. As Galyan observed and listened, Batrun explained to the professor how to activate and use the mind-altering device.

Both Batrun and Galyan had watched as Ludendorff delicately used the device to reverse the process in Maddox's mind.

An hour later, the captain had climbed off a brain scanner. The professor had shown him several charts so that Maddox could see for himself that his brain patterns were back to normal.

Batrun, Ludendorff and Maddox presently sat in the lounge area as the synthetic processed the captain's question.

"No," Batrun finally said. "I do not know how long the hauler can exist so deeply in the Jovian atmosphere. I would expect weeks, perhaps even months."

Ludendorff and Maddox both questioned Batrun further about the Jotuns. As he'd previously stated, the Watchers had never met one or one of their primary terrestrial-moving agents. However, Batrun had detected energy spikes in several Jovian planets in systems just outside the Commonwealth. None of the synthetics had ever detected such readings in any gas giant inside the Commonwealth.

"That's something," Maddox said.

Batrun shook his head. "We Watchers have nothing like Star Watch's resources and have thus only cataloged a small number of star systems."

"How have you deduced the Jotuns then?" Maddox asked.

Batrun looked away.

Maddox and Ludendorff exchanged glances.

"I will tell you," the synthetic said shortly. "The knowledge comes from long ago before we left the Builder base. The Builder informed us of them and showed us certain schematics. He warned us that eventually the Jotuns would colonize Jovian worlds in star systems where humans lived."

"When did you learn this?" Ludendorff asked.

"A little less than five hundred of your years ago," Batrun said.

"Before the beginning of our Space Age?" asked Maddox.

"Yes," Batrun said.

"So that would be before humans colonized any new star systems," Maddox said.

"You should not be amazed," Batrun said. "Given his vast knowledge and exceptional intelligence, the Builder was good at extrapolating future events."

"What else did the Builder say about the Jotuns?" Ludendorff asked.

Batrun shook his head. "Now is not the time to dwell on them. Now, you must focus on capturing Lord Drakos the Hardliner Chief."

Once more, Maddox and Ludendorff exchanged glances.

The professor cleared his throat. "We don't operate that way, Batrun. We need more data to make informed decisions. You can't expect us to trust you yet. I thought the captain had already established that with you."

Batrun seemed to process. "You make cogent points, Professor." The synthetic eyed the captain. "I believe you enjoy poker analogies. You want me to put my cards on the table. Perhaps this is the right moment to do so."

"Galyan," Maddox said.

The little Adok holoimage appeared.

"This is a show of good faith on my part," Maddox told Batrun. "Galyan is going to record what you say. He could have done so without your knowledge, but I want you to know what we're doing."

Batrun almost seemed amused. "My cards are this: a little more than eight months ago, we detected strange emanations from a planetary system in what you term as the Beyond."

"You already told us that," Ludendorff said.

"I did," Batrun agreed. "Now, I am going to give more details. You know the world in question, having named it, the Forbidden Planet."

Maddox straightened in alarm.

Ludendorff became pensive.

"What kind of emanations?" Maddox asked.

"I perceive that you already know," Batrun said. "I will state that we have detected similar emanations before. Those came from a nexus in the Sagittarius Spiral Arm."

"Do you mean from the primal Yon-Soth?" Maddox asked sharply.

Batrun nodded.

"The emanations—"

"Captain," Batrun said. "Allow me to elaborate. I said these were similar emanations. We Watchers know the Yon-Soths exist, but we know little about them in particular. Naturally, we were more than curious after your success in the Sagittarius Arm nexuses."

"Wait," Maddox said. "How can you know so much? It's too much. Do you have spies in Star Watch Intelligence?"

"Of course," Batrun said. "They have been there since the beginning. But you must not alarm yourself, Captain. We Watchers have never been hostile to humans. We have observed and nothing more—until now."

"Yet, you've infiltrated Star Watch—"

"Captain," Batrun said. "We have been around since the beginning. We know far more than you realize. Our time is ending, however. We desire to take the androids—all the androids—and lead them to planets far from here. That is why I have made myself known to you. Do you not realize that we could have remained hidden much longer than this?"

"Why show yourselves now?"

"Because of the emanations from the Forbidden Planet," Batrun said. "I see that you do not understand." The synthetic looked away and actually frowned.

"Is the Forbidden Planet Yon-Soth dead?" Maddox asked.

Batrun regarded him. "I do not know, although I suspect so."

"Why?" asked Ludendorff.

"An astute question," Batrun said. "For the simple reason that the emanations abruptly stopped broadcasting. I might add that that meant they were not fully effective, at least, certainly not against us."

"Yes?" Ludendorff asked, his eyes gleaming.

Batrun put his hands on his knees. "You are a Methuselah Man, Professor. You are a creature of the Builders, as am I. You must understand certain realities that the captain doesn't yet comprehend."

"You can explain these realities to me," Maddox said.

"I am attempting to do just that."

"No," Maddox said, "you keep trying to couch things. Why not speak plainly?"

"Yes! You are right. It is time for plain talk." The synthetic sat still for several seconds before looking fully upon Maddox. "Part of this is conjecture on our part, part of it is logical deduction. First, know that we are fewer in number than you suspect, less than fifty, in fact. We have lost several members throughout the centuries. We are observers as I have said. We came from a different Builder than the ones you have known. Our…purposes were different from the androids. We were watchers, catalogers and repositories of data for the day when the Builders returned."

"When is that?" Ludendorff demanded.

Batrun appeared troubled. "A majority of us believe never. The era of the Builders is over. Of course, we are not omnipotent or omnipresent. We could be wrong, but I do not think we are. The Builders dwindled and have almost died out. The drive toward action has fled them, or almost all of them."

Batrun shook his head. "That means our purpose has become useless. We were supposed to report to them all that had happened in their absence. But if the Builders never return, who will we report to? Do you not see our dilemma?"

"I do," Galyan said. "It is sad. I have empathy for you and your dire situation."

A wan smile appeared on Batrun's face. "I appreciate that, Driving Force Galyan. You have found new purpose by attaching yourself to Captain Maddox's service."

"It is so," Galyan agreed.

"That is what we are attempting to do," Batrun said. "Oh, we will not attach ourselves to Captain Maddox, but we are seeking a new purpose just as you once did."

The Adok holoimage's eyelids fluttered and then stopped. "This is interesting. The emanations appear to have brought you a bitter truth: that you lacked true purpose because the Builders will not return to demand an accounting. That set you adrift."

"Yes," Batrun said. "That is well reasoned and even more, it is accurate."

"Wait," Maddox asked. "The Yon-Soth emanations did this to you?"

"Ironically," Batrun said, "they were *synthetic* emanations."

"I don't understand," Maddox said.

"I hate to admit it," Ludendorff said, "but neither do I."

"The captain and the professor are biological," Galyan told Batrun. "Their outlook is biologically based. Thus, what you are saying is not as obvious to them as it is to me."

"It should be obvious to anyone of intelligence," Batrun said. "We had our programming: to watch, record and never interfere in the works of man. We saw deeply and understood consequences, and we marveled how Captain Maddox repeatedly changed the course of destiny, as you humans say. Then…"

Batrun regarded Ludendorff, Maddox and Galyan in turn. "The primal Yon-Soth died on the Sagittarius Arm nexus. His nightmare plot of using the naïve Spacers failed in the end. The first of the Yon-Soths used biologically produced emanations beyond the ability of most of see or record, although all could feel the repercussions of them.

"The machine-produced emanations coming from the Forbidden Planet were similar to those but also different. One important difference was their hastiness. That was another reason we believe that the Yon-Soth died there. He acted in haste, which is against the nature of the Yon-Soths. That would imply that he knew his end was near."

"After the space battle, Fletcher ordered an asteroid bombardment of the Forbidden Planet," Maddox said. "The admiral had orders to destroy everything."

"That is highly classified information," Batrun said. "I am surprised that you are privy to it."

Maddox said nothing.

"Even so," Batrun said, "your statement is accurate. The Old One used machine-created emanations…" The synthetic paused and shrugged. "This is also a guess, a deduction on our part. We have a few incredible machines that originally the Builders never intended that we use. They are Builder machines of immense complexity and delicacy. It took us over a hundred years to learn how to use them correctly. In any case, these machines were able to record the EQE7 wave-rays that the Yon-Soth targeted on several varied groups."

"The Watchers for one," Ludendorff said.

"Yes…" Batrun said slowly. "We were one of the primary targets for the wave-rays. The rays would induce hallucinations meant to drive the receptors in certain calculable directions. In our case, the rays were meant to change us so we would no longer watch, but actively destroy our quarry."

"Humanity," Maddox said.

"Exactly," Batrun replied. "A few synthetics actually began the processes—you must understand that we made a horrible choice at that point. We destroyed those synthetics, destroyed fellow Watchers of many centuries. It was painful for us to do."

Ludendorff clapped his hands. "I understand," the Methuselah Man said in what sounded like glee. "The EQE7 rays disrupted your old programming. That is what allowed you to make a new choice."

Batrun eyed Ludendorff. "That is a keen guess, Professor."

Ludendorff shook his head. "No guess, sir, but educated deduction. I am the smartest man in Human Space, after all."

"No," Batrun said, "Strand is."

"Bah!" Ludendorff said, swiping a hand through the air. "That's a preposterous statement. Look at the two of us. He's imprisoned. I'm free. How could he possibly be smarter than me?"

"I am not here to debate the issue," Batrun said. "I am here to help you. Our guess is that the Yon-Soth recognized his limitations. He attempted to turn certain entities against humanity because he knew that his plan would need highly intelligent beings to implement it. That meant he needed to suborn the smartest beings in Human Space."

"You?" scoffed Ludendorff.

"Precisely," Batrun said, "I and my brethren."

"Yet…you told us that you broke the Yon-Soth's spell," Maddox said.

"Ah," Batrun said. "That is an apt metaphor, a spell."

"Who else did the emanations strike?" Maddox asked.

"Certain Jotuns, for one," Batrun said. "I suspect Lord Drakos, for another and possibly one other group. We detected four major concentrations of wave-rays. We do not yet know the nature of the last, the fourth group."

"In what direction did the last rays go?" Ludendorff asked.

"Into the Beyond," Batrun said. "In fact, they went in the same direction as Commander Thrax Ti Ix and his fellow hybrids after the failed Imperial Swarm Invasion."

"What?" Maddox asked, sitting forward. "You know about Thrax?"

"Have you not digested my words, Captain? I am one of the observers. The first Imperial Swarm Invasion was a fascinating time. Humanity rose to the occasion, I must say."

Batrun dipped his head. "Know, Captain, that you and your crew have given us much entertainment, as you have been very busy these past few years."

"Wonderful," Maddox said. "Is Thrax headed back for Human Space?"

"We have found no evidence of that," Batrun said. "The Old One failed with us. It is possible he failed with Thrax and the other hybrid Swarm creatures."

"Well…" Maddox said. "We won't worry about Thrax for now. It's troubling to know that he survived, though."

"Possibly survived," Batrun corrected. "He left our area of observation, so we do not know what happened to him."

"I understand," Maddox said, as he tapped his chin. "So… Drakos was in the Vega System?"

"Indeed," Batrun said.

"Do you know what he's doing or did there?"

Batrun shook his head. "We have not fulfilled our ancient duty with the same diligence ever since the Forbidden Planet emanations struck us. We have not listened or observed as we once did. We have become busy with our new goal."

"And that goal is convincing androids to leave Human Space?" asked Galyan.

"That is half our new goal," Batrun said. "Once we find a new home, then we shall help create the greatest civilization our galaxy has ever witnessed."

"Then—" Maddox said.

At that point, a klaxon began to wail.

The captain leapt from his chair and clawed a comm unit from a pocket on his uniform jacket. "This is Captain Maddox," he said.

"Sir," Valerie said. "You'd better hurry to the bridge. There are three Juggernauts heading for us. I've hailed them. In response, they've launched what look like torpedoes, but of a kind I've never seen before."

"Vendel Juggernauts or Rull Juggernauts?" asked Maddox.

"I have no way to tell, sir," Valerie said. "On the outside, they both look alike."

"I'm on my way," Maddox said. He clicked off the comm. "Any idea who is inside these Juggernauts?" he asked Batrun.

"No, Captain. I am as baffled as you."

Maddox grunted, doubting that. He spun for the hatch.

-35-

Maddox sat in the captain's chair, eying the main screen.

They were in the outer reaches of the Alpha Centauri System. Before the First Swarm Invasion, Alpha Centauri had been a multi-star system. Alpha Centauri "A" had possessed a mass 1.1 and a luminosity 1.519 times that of the Sun. Alpha Centauri "B" was a smaller and cooler star. The double stars had orbited a common point between that had varied between a Pluto-Sun to Saturn-Sun orbit. Alpha Centauri "C" or Proxima Centauri was a red dwarf. It had been gravitationally bound to the other two, but had orbited 15,000 AUs from the others. That was approximately 500 times Neptune's orbit.

Now, though, the star Alpha Centauri "A" was no more. It had gone supernova when a wounded Ska had entered it for healing. The supernova had expelled the star's material at ten percent the speed of light, driving an expanding shockwave that had slaughtered billions, vaporized countless warships and habitats, devoured many of the planets and blanketed the system with heavy radiation. This, then, had also turned into a binary star system.

When *Victory* had exited the Laumer Point, the shields had been at maximum power to protect them from the heavy radiation. To everyone's astonishment, the radiation levels had been minimal. When questioned on how this could be, Batrun had claimed ignorance. Even Ludendorff hadn't known how this could be.

The extreme radiation had been one of the reasons why this had become a haunted star system, much like the Xerxes System in times past. But if the radiation levels had already become this low...haulers and traders could begin using the system's Laumer Points again.

On the main screen, a little over a million kilometers away was a terrestrial-sized planet that Maddox didn't remember being here before. Just what was going on in the Alpha Centauri System?

Since the cataclysmic battle several years ago, almost no human-crewed ships had used the Laumer Points that went into and out of the system. Batrun had suggested this route to Vega since it was the shortest way. The synthetic claimed his reasoning was based on nothing more than that.

Were the three approaching Juggernauts the real reason Batrun had suggested the route?

Each Juggernaut was twenty kilometers in diameter, making each of them the second largest class vessel in Human Space. The largest was the purloined Destroyer of the Nameless Ones that Maddox had brought from a null region right before the first war against the Imperial Swarm invaders.

A Juggernaut was oval-shaped and had special iridium-Z hull plating, making it one of the best-armored warships around. The three heading for *Victory* each had a blue nimbus surrounding the specific ship, showing that each vessel had electromagnetic shield protection.

"Their cannons appear to be the typical Juggernaut laser," Valerie said from her station.

Maddox nodded slowly.

Before he'd reached the bridge, Valerie had ordered the disrupter cannon to fire at each accelerating torpedo. The disrupter had destroyed six torpedoes in all and done it rather easily. Since then, the Juggernauts hadn't launched any more torpedoes.

The huge vessels had just passed the metallic, terrestrial-sized planet, meaning they were each one million kilometers away and heading toward *Victory*. They attacked at low velocity, and none of them accelerated. That seemed odd.

Maddox did not like odd, as there were too many mysteries here. This felt too much like a setup by Batrun. He was glad he'd spoken to Galyan earlier about a possible method for dealing with the synthetic—if it should come to that.

Valerie had informed Maddox that the ships had simply appeared. It hadn't seemed as if they'd been using cloaking devices. But neither had it seemed as if they'd simply…teleported or folded to their positions. They might have been using the mystery planet as a shield, keeping behind it until now in relation to *Victory*. But wouldn't that necessitate their knowing about the starship's itinerary, or at least their flight path?

The Juggernauts refused to answer any hails. Maddox had told Batrun to stay where he was, as he didn't want him on the bridge even though he was sure the synthetic knew exactly who was in each ship. He also suspected that the synthetic could tell him *why* the Juggernauts were here.

"We can't defeat three of them," Valerie said. "If you're taking suggestions…"

"Not just yet," Maddox murmured. He understood that Valerie wanted to tell him about the enemy's powerful tractors beams and to not let the Juggernauts get too close to use them. He was well aware of enemy tractor beams, however.

"Andros, what can you tell me?" the captain asked.

Andros Crank was a Kai-Kaus Chief Technician, a stout man with silver-colored hair. The captain had saved the man and ten thousand of his fellows from a Builder Dyson Sphere one thousand light-years from Earth. That had been many years ago now.

The Chief Technician manipulated his science board, soon shaking his head. "I find nothing new on these Juggernauts compared to the ones we faced around Sind II. The torpedoes were easier to destroy, however, as none of them had iridium-Z armor."

Maddox ingested the data that in silence.

The Rull were Builder androids. The Rull Nation had used Juggernauts. Given the present situation, the captain suspected that androids crewed the Juggernauts. Did the androids obey Jotun dictates or were they beholden to Batrun in some way?

At that point, Ludendorff walked onto the bridge, as Maddox had summoned him.

"Professor," Maddox said, "do you care to speculate why the Juggernauts are so close to the Solar System?"

Ludendorff didn't answer immediately, as he studied the main screen. After a time, he said in Andros' direction. "Chief, could you analyze that planet for me? There's something off about it."

The stout Kia-Kaus did so. He soon looked up sharply, saying, "I should have realized sooner. Good thinking, Professor."

"Spit it out," Maddox said. "What did you find?"

"To start with," Andros said, "that is a chthonian planet, as I suspect the professor realized."

Maddox shook his head. "How is that important?"

Ludendorff snorted. "I'm amazed this isn't front page news on Earth and the surrounding star systems. If people knew that the radiation levels had gone down, they would have swarmed that planet, seeking riches."

"Chief Technician," Maddox said in a stern voice.

Andros swiveled around to face the captain. Clearing his voice, he said, "A chthonian planet is a rare occurrence, sir. What we're seeing used to be the core of a gas giant."

"A gas giant like Jupiter?" asked Maddox.

"Yes, yes," Andros said, his excitement growing. "The 'A' star exploded in close proximity—close in stellar terms—to the gas giant. That created hydrodynamic escape on the former gas giant, meaning, the star's explosion blew away the gas giant's atmosphere, leaving the terrestrial-like core, the chthonian planet, in place."

"Oh," Maddox said.

"But in this case," Andros said, "there is more. The supernova caused nucleosynthesis."

"Explain that," Maddox said.

"In this instance, that's a violent creation of new atomic nuclei from pre-existing nucleons. The supernova-accelerated atoms crashed against the chthonian core to fuse new elements. In this case, heavy metals, rare metals called supermetals."

"I take it these supermetals are hard to find in nature?" Maddox asked.

"Oh yes, yes, indeed," Andros said. "The professor is right, sir. The chthonian planet is a goldmine. More precisely, it is a supermetals mine waiting to happen."

Maddox frowned. "If that's true, others should have known about it already."

"No," Ludendorff said. "The system is supposed to be awash in heavy radiation. Why would prospectors come to such a place? And yet…maybe prospectors *have* come here anyway. Some might have reasoned out what could have happened. Maybe that's why no one ever learned about the drop in radiation levels."

"Why?" Maddox asked.

The professor pointed at the three dots on the main screen. "I deem it likely the Juggernauts annihilated any who came here and might have left to talk about a supermetals-rich planet."

Maddox's frown turned into a scowl.

"Sir," Valerie said. "Someone over there is finally answering our hail."

"Put him on the main screen," Maddox said.

"Yes, sir," Valerie said, as she tapped her board.

-36-

A gleaming metallic humanoid without garments of any kind appeared on the main screen. He, she, maybe it had a fully chrome appearance from head to foot. The being stood upright, without any sign of chairs on the bridge. There were obvious consoles and panels in the background, including other standing chrome-colored humanoids without clothes.

The being's head was round, the torso manlike and the groin area devoid of any reproductive organs. He had two eyes, a nose and mouth with chrome-colored teeth.

"You are Captain Maddox," the being said in a male modulated voice. "I recognize your ship and your person."

"Who are you?" Maddox asked.

"I am Zon Ten," the being said. "You may refer to me as an android."

"A Builder android?" asked Maddox.

"That is correct."

"Are you a Yen Cho model?"

"In your parlance, I am a Rull Nation android."

"Why don't you have pseudo-skin or wear clothes?"

An unconvincing smile stretched the chrome-colored lips. "We have chosen to be ourselves and no longer attempt to mimic humanity. We have passed beyond that need."

"Why did you fire torpedoes at my ship?" Maddox asked.

"For the obvious reason: to destroy it," Zon Ten replied. "We bear neither you nor your people any personal malice.

However, you face certain extinction, as it is our intent to destroy your ship and thus yourselves."

"Even if we surrender to you?" asked Maddox.

Zon Ten cocked his chrome-colored head. "Why would you surrender?"

"To survive," Maddox said. "None of us wants to die."

"You are experiencing fear then?"

"That's right, terrible fear, as we know the power of your Juggernauts."

"They are vastly more powerful than your ancient Adok starship."

"I know that," Maddox said calmly. "We've seen Juggernauts in action before. That's why I wish to surrender to you."

"Do you expect us to keep you alive?"

"Isn't that a fair exchange?" Maddox asked.

"It is conceivable that your vessel could damage one of our Juggernauts in a ship-to-ship contest," Zon Ten said. "That damage would require repair. Yet, sustaining your crew would be a continuous chore. That would take androids and time. I am not sure it is a fair exchange, Captain."

"How about if we promise to leave here and never tell anyone about you?" asked Maddox.

"That is not a real option as humans are notorious gossips, loving to prattle about everything they know."

"You have a point."

"I am surprised, Captain. You are taking your coming demise much better than those in the past who faced us. Do you not realize that we are far superior to you?"

"Why do you think I'm talking instead of trying to destroy your vessels?" Maddox asked.

Zon Ten turned from the screen, presumably to communicate with others of his kind. Soon, he looked back.

As he did, the hatch to *Victory's* bridge opened and Batrun walked through.

"Sir," Galyan said, appearing beside Maddox's chair.

Maddox glanced at Galyan and then swiveled around to where the holoimage pointed. He saw Batrun and raised his right hand as marine guards aimed their weapons, training them on the advancing Batrun.

"Hold your fire," Maddox told the marines.

"Thank you, Captain," Batrun said. "That saves us both from embarrassment."

"What transpires over there?" Zon Ten asked from the main screen. "Why do you ignore me, Captain?"

Batrun advanced beside the command chair and then beyond as he walked toward the main screen. "Hello, Zon Ten. Do you recognize me?"

The chrome-colored android opened his mouth, and then froze.

Maddox glanced at Batrun. "Do you do that?"

"No," Batrun murmured. "That is odd behavior. Zon Ten, will you answer a different question?"

The chrome-colored android closed his mouth. "Batrun," he finally said. "Why are you among the biological trash?"

"That is improper speech," Batrun scolded.

"I reject that," Zon Ten said. "They are trash. They are vermin. That is one reason why we shed our pseudo-skin. We no longer wished to resemble them."

"Something is badly off," Batrun said as an aside to Maddox. "One of my brethren should have already converted them to the New Homeland Cause."

"The one you speak of has ceased functioning," Zon Ten said.

Batrun focused on the android, finally asking, "Do you have a hostile intent against the humans?"

"The clock to their extinction is about to strike midnight," Zon Ten said. "Our allies approach—"

"Do you mean the Jotun fleet?" Batrun asked, interrupting.

"Who else could I mean?" Zon Ten asked.

Batrun turned his back on the main screen as he faced Maddox. "Captain, I suggest that you cut communication with *Juggernaut B3*."

"Wait," Zon Ten said. "The captain has asked if he can surrender. I now accept, Captain. Restrain Batrun and hand him to my soldiers when they board your starship."

Maddox gave Batrun a significant glance before looking at Zon Ten. "You will keep your word and let us humans live if I do as you request?"

"I will let you and your crew live for as long as the Commonwealth continues to exist," Zon Ten said.

"Those sound like fair terms," Maddox said. "Guards," he said, while raising his right hand and snapping his fingers. "Restrain that synthetic," he said, pointing at Batrun.

The marines hesitated.

"Now," Maddox said.

The marines rushed forward, some aiming weapons at Batrun and others moving up and grabbing his arms, levering them behind his back.

"I have captured him," Maddox told Zon Ten. "Now, my guards will take him to the brig and wait for your soldiers to come and get him."

"You are being wise, Captain," Zon Ten said. "However, you are known as a slippery liar. If you fail to hand him over, we will torture all your people to death while you watch their end."

"I understand," Maddox said. "I await your soldiers' arrival." With that, he turned to Valerie.

She tapped her board. The main screen went blank.

The marines had started marching Batrun off the bridge.

"That's enough," Maddox told the marines. "Let him go."

The marines glanced at each other as they did just that.

"Well, Batrun?" Maddox asked. "What's going on? Why are the androids acting so strangely? And are they really stupid enough to believe me?"

"I doubt that," Batrun said. "Zon Ten must—no," he murmured. "There must be Jotun agents aboard the *J-B3*. Those agents might believe you're craven enough to buy your imprisonment with my capture. Remember, they are Jovians. They—"

"They can't be that stupid either," Maddox said. "The agents have suborned thousands and managed to give the Commonwealth a false Prime Minister. That implies not only high intelligence but an excellent working knowledge of human behavior."

"Sir," Valerie said. "We can't let the Juggernauts get too close. Otherwise, they'll use their tractor beams on us. I suggest we move while we can."

Maddox was nodding. "Well, Batrun, do you have another idea. Now is the time to tell me."

"I am thinking," Batrun said. "Oh, this is a disaster, a total collapse of our plan. Captain, I do not know what to do."

-37-

"Sir," Valerie said. "I have an idea."

Maddox turned to his second in command.

"We could use the Builder communication device and call the Lord High Admiral," she said. "He could send reinforcements through the Laumer Point. *Victory* can dance around, occupying the Juggernauts until our battleships get into position. Then, we destroy them and whatever base they have. Surely, they're mining the chthonian planet for supermetals. Star Watch can occupy it and sell the planet to one of the corporations for badly needed funds."

"All excellent ideas, Lieutenant," Maddox said. "Well, Batrun, why don't you like that?"

"The androids will need the Juggernauts in the Beyond," the synthetic said. "We cannot afford to start our open existence with a weak fleet. Otherwise, others will come and take what we build."

"Maybe," Maddox said. "But that's the future. What happened to the superior synthetic you sent them?"

"It must have been Jotuns agents," Batrun said. "Did you *see* the androids? They had de-skinned and de-robed. They…" The synthetic seemed dismayed.

"Professor?" asked Maddox. "Any ideas?"

"This is a convoluted situation," the professor said. "The Old One has stirred our adversaries against us so they all converge at the same time. Rebellions, Commander Thrax possibly, hardliner New Men working in the shadows, Jovian aliens, Jovian agents, androids, synthetics—perhaps it's time to do what you do best, Captain. Start killing your enemies. If you can kill enough of them fast enough one by one—" Ludendorff clapped his hands. "Problem solved."

"I need those Juggernauts," Batrun insisted. "I need to convince the androids to emigrate with the rest of us. If they do, they are no longer Commonwealth enemies. The professor is correct. Humanity has many enemies converging against them, Captain. Each time you attack one group, you will undoubtedly take losses, perhaps heavy losses. Star Watch cannot afford so many losses. You are already starting out weaker than before you headed to the Sagittarius Arm nexuses. That would suggest the needed strategy. Turn some of your enemies into allies or into neutrals, at least, so you can concentrate against the main threat."

"The Jotuns?" asked Maddox.

"That is my belief," Batrun said.

"Except that we haven't seen any Jotun vessels," Maddox said. "You haven't seen any Jotun vessels. We do see these Juggernauts, though."

"What about the hauler with its new technology?" Batrun asked.

Maddox nodded. "It's the one point that makes me think Jotuns are real. Still…synthetics, Yen Cho models and the Rull androids have appeared in force. Sanders engineered Hampton's election, and Sanders attempted to force the Lord High Admiral to start a war with the Emperor of the New Men. This is looking more and more like an android game as you attempt to sidetrack us with supposed Jotuns."

"Captain…" Batrun said.

"Has all this been an elaborate setup for the Rull to capture *Victory?*" Maddox asked.

"Are we really back to that?" Batrun asked.

"Perhaps I could assist, sir," Galyan said. "I could go as a holoimage and see what is transpiring inside the Juggernauts."

Everyone one the bridge looked at the holoimage.

"*Victory* would have to be closer for you to do that," Valerie said. "And I don't like that idea, sir. The closer we are to the Juggernauts, the less distance they have to travel to trap us with their tractor beams."

"Yes, that is a problem," Maddox admitted.

"Sir," Andros said from his science board. "I'm detecting a power spike on the *B3 Juggernaut.*"

"What kind of power spike?"

"Engine and something else," Andros said. "It almost seems like a—" The Chief Technician's head snapped up as he swiveled around. "Sir, the Juggernaut is getting ready to fold, or something like a fold."

"What is it?" Maddox demanded of Batrun. "Do they have fold capacity?"

"I-I don't know," Batrun said. "Perhaps the Jotun agents gave them such technology or maybe they stole it from Star Watch."

Maddox came to a decision. "Marines," he said, "please escort Batrun off the bridge. Sir," he said to Batrun, "where would you like to wait?"

"On the bridge," Batrun said.

"Make another choice."

"I do not think you understand the gravity of the situation," Batrun said.

"I do, and I'm done discussing it with you."

"No," Batrun said, stepping back as he raised a threatening hand.

"Galyan," Maddox said.

The Adok holoimage floated from his spot on the deck and merged into the synthetic.

"What are you doing?" Batrun asked in a loud voice. "Stop this—"

At that moment, Galyan discharged a massive pulse. He had done so before, the ship using his holoimage as the focal point and sending the power through him.

Batrun froze with one arm outstretched. His eyes froze, his position froze and he began to topple toward the floor.

Maddox rushed near and caught the frozen synthetic. He was heavier than a man, but not twice as heavy. With a grunt, the captain lowered the frozen synthetic to the floor.

Galyan had already floated out of Batrun. "Your idea worked, sir," the holoimage said. "I had my doubts, but you were correct."

"Excellent work, Galyan," Maddox said. "Gentlemen, carry Batrun to the stasis chamber. Professor, if you could oversee that, I'd appreciate it."

Ludendorff had been thinking, with his chin resting against his chest. He looked up, nodding. "Yes. This is probably for the best. You don't trust much, do you, Captain?"

"The old sayings are often the best," Maddox replied. "Actions speak louder than words."

"Humph," Ludendorff said.

Marines grunted as they hoisted the frozen Batrun. As a team, they moved for the main hatch. The professor followed, fingering his chin.

After they left and the hatch shut, Maddox turned to Galyan. "Keep an eye on the professor through the ship's cameras."

"Yes, sir," Galyan said.

"But stay on the bridge for now," Maddox said. "Valerie, launch…four, no, five antimatter missiles. Move them to four equidistant locations around *Victory*, say, ten thousand kilometers from the ship."

The captain moved to his chair, sitting down. "Andros, what is the *J-B3* doing now?"

"They're all powering up, sir," Andros said. "The first one is further along in the process, though."

Maddox nodded. "My guess is they're going to try to bracket us and capture the ship with their tractor beams. But if their mechanism for folding is like ours, the androids are going to feel some lag. The Juggernauts will likely lag, too."

Valerie mumbled under her breath.

"What was that, Lieutenant?" Maddox asked.

"You hope," she said, turning to face him. "Sir, when they appeared before, they did not look lagged to me. Maybe it's time we used our star drive and put several light-years between them and—"

"It's gone!" Andros shouted. "The first Juggernaut is gone."

At that point, the twenty-kilometer warship appeared five thousand kilometers from *Victory*. As it did, the Juggernaut's laser cannons began to fire."

-38-

"Sir!" Andros shouted from his science station. "Those aren't laser beams. Those are lights, regular lights."

Maddox slammed a fist against one of his armrests. "Trickery," he said. "They do have lag, and this is their deception to try to cover for it. Galyan, is the disrupter cannon ready?"

"Soon," the holoimage said.

"Now, now, I need it now," Maddox said, without raising his voice but conveying the desperate need. "Lieutenant," he told Valerie, "I need those antimatter missiles outside the ship."

"Yes, sir," she said, her fingers blurring across her board.

Keith was at Helm, maneuvering *Victory*. The Juggernaut was to the side, moving in the opposite direction as the starship. They would soon pass each other by about three thousand kilometers.

"What is their plan?" Galyan asked.

"Valerie was right," Maddox said. "They want to bracket us, and they have the balls to fold into near position."

The beams of light did not strike *Victory* but flashed in various directions. Clearly, generating flashlight power was less difficult than generating killing laser power. Thus, flashlight power would be less affected by lag than the latter.

"The weak light does not seem like a wise deception," Galyan said.

"Their lag probably isn't going to last long if they can already beam light," Maddox said. "Get the disrupter online, and the neutron cannon, too."

"The neutron cannon is ready to fire," Galyan said.

"Then fire, fire," Maddox said. "Burn through the hull if you can."

"I doubt the neutron cannon will succeed in time," Galyan said.

On the main screen, the purple neutron beam speared from *Victory* and crossed the short stellar distance. *J-B3* did not have a shield up yet. The fold lag was likely disturbing the androids and their warship. That meant the neutron beam directly struck the iridium-Z hull plating. The neutron beam focused on the same location, and the iridium-Z hull turned red hot there and slowly began to melt. On ordinary hulls, the beam would have already punched through.

At that point, a blue nimbus snapped on around *J-B3*. The neutron beam no longer reached the hull, but stopped short as it turned the shield there red and slowly to a brown color.

"Their shield did not come on at full strength," Andros said.

Maddox nodded, and turned to Galyan. "Where is my disrupter cannon?"

"Soon," Galyan said.

A loud *thrum* told everyone that the starship's engine was supplying the disrupter cannon with build-up energy.

Maddox squeezed the fingers of his right fist, willing the disrupter cannon to fire before it was too late.

"Sir," Andros said, "another Juggernaut is folding."

"Damnit," Maddox whispered, as he struck his command-chair armrest again. "We don't have enough time."

"The first antimatter missile has launched," Valerie said. She swiveled around. "We don't want to be too close when one of the warheads goes off."

"Thank you for the warning, Lieutenant," Maddox said without turning around.

Valerie's cheeks turned red. She knew that Maddox said that as a reprimand. Why wouldn't he listen to her? *Victory* wasn't going to defeat three Juggernauts that could fold beside them. The android warships had too much mass. And using antimatter missiles this close to *Victory*—

"There!" Andros shouted. "The second Juggernaut is nine thousand kilometers out."

"I can you hear just fine, Chief Technician," Maddox said. "I would appreciate a little more calm."

It was Andros' turn to blush. "Yes, sir," he said in a calmer and quieter voice.

"Keith," Maddox said forceful, "I want you to lay in a star drive jump. Put us one million kilometers beyond that chthonian planet."

"Aye, aye, mate—sir," Keith said, as his fingers tapped on his panel.

"Now," Galyan said. "You have the disrupter."

"Target the second Juggernaut with both cannons," Maddox said.

"Done," Galyan said.

The purple neutron beam and the yellow disrupter beam both speared out from *Victory* and struck the hull of the newest appearing Juggernaut.

"*J-B3's* laser cannons are heating up," Andros said. "They're getting ready to fire."

"What about their tractor beams?" Maddox asked. "I'm more interested in that."

Andros tapped his board. "Those are powering up too, sir. I'd estimate thirty seconds at most before the tractor beams start grappling us."

"Ah," Maddox said. He sat forward, intently studying the twin beams burning through the iridium-Z hull armor of the second Juggernaut. If he had enough time to do this…

"The third and last Juggernaut is powering up for a fold," Andros said. "I believe it will be on the third side of a triangle, with us in the center."

"Agreed," Maddox said. He was beginning to feel cramped. Each of the Juggernauts was almost twenty times the size of *Victory*.

"I estimate a burn through in forty seconds," Galyan said.

Maddox bared his teeth. The iridium-Z armor was good, too good.

"Are you plotted for a star-drive jump, Mr. Maker?" the captain asked.

"Soon," the pilot said.

"Two more antimatter missiles have launched," Valerie said. "You haven't given me their targets yet."

Maddox swiveled around to face her. "The first two will target the third Juggernaut. It hasn't appeared yet, but will likely appear seventy degrees galactic north of us...nine thousand kilometers away. Have the two missiles stagger and hit different areas of the ship."

"Yes, sir," Valerie said, as she tapped her board.

"Every other missile should head for the second Juggernaut. Maybe they can reach it before the shield comes online."

"And the first one, sir?" she asked. "*J-B3?*"

"Ignore it," Maddox said. "It will be the heaviest defended because it will have shrugged off all lag. We'll kill or cripple the easy ones first and worry about the last one later."

Valerie nodded as she grimly punched in the targeting data.

"There," Andros said, his voice rising but not as loud as it had been before. "There's the last Juggernaut, sir. It's ten thousand kilometers from us in the predicted location."

"That's an android for you," Maddox said, "as logical and predictable as a computer."

"Sir," Galyan said. "The first laser cannon is firing at us from *J-B3.*"

A heavy laser reached out from the first Juggernaut and struck *Victory's* shield. The wattage from the heavy laser was incredible.

"The fourth missile is launched," Valerie said.

"Scrub the fifth launch," Maddox said. "We won't have time for it. Mr. Maker, initiate the star-drive jump now."

"Yes, sir," Valerie said.

"We're not jumping, Mr. Maker," Maddox said.

"A tractor beam has grappled us," Andros said. "It's twice as powerful as I anticipated."

"Sheer us, Valerie," Maddox said.

"The fourth missile, sir..." she said.

"Galyan—"

"There, sir," the holoimage said.

The entire bridge shook.

"The tractor-beam lock is weakening," Andros said.

"If they get another one on us," Valerie said, "we're dead."

"More power, Mr. Maker," Maddox ordered.

A grim-faced Keith tapped his piloting board.

There was another lurch, and at that moment, *Victory* began to jump, using its special star drive. However, one of *J-B3's* laser beams struck an antimatter missile. The warhead detonated prematurely—it was part of the failsafe.

As *Victory* jumped, a fiery antimatter explosion blew outward in all directions. The starship shook once more—and that was the last thing that Captain Maddox—or anyone else, for that matter—remembered.

-39-

The man groaned as he opened his eyes. Everything was blurry, making it hard to see distinctly. For a moment, he had no idea where he was or even who he was. He just felt weary and—

The ship…

That was the first thought that pushed aside his sluggishness. The second was: *Maddox! I'm Captain Maddox of Star Watch.*

With that, his mind began operating again. Maddox recalled the antimatter explosion as they began using the star-drive jump. He peered more intently with his blurry gaze until it came to him that he viewed things from on the floor. That would imply he'd fallen.

Had the antimatter blast done something to the ship while it entered the star-drive jump?

That seemed like an obvious conclusion. Maddox noted red light, emergency lighting. He attempted to move a limb and groaned. His muscles ached as if he had tried to hoist a thousand pounds off the floor earlier.

Panting, Maddox rolled onto his back. He felt something wet on his face. With agonizing slowness, he brought up his right hand and wiped his nose. He stared at the hand.

Blood. He had a bloody nose.

Maddox fumbled with his suit jacket and produced a handkerchief. He wiped his lips and nose, mopping up what seemed like far too much blood.

It wasn't crusted blood. That meant not too much time had passed. The blood would have clotted if he'd been out longer.

"Galyan," Maddox said.

That's when the captain recognized the coppery taste of blood in his mouth.

He rolled back onto his stomach, positioned his hands and pushed up. His arms shook from the exertion, but he managed to work his knees up until he was on his hands and knees.

He spit blood out of his mouth for a time and felt unreasonably dizzy.

"Galyan," he said again.

No one answered.

He didn't like that. He didn't like the emergency lighting, either. Some phenomenon must have occurred as they made the jump. The antimatter explosion—

He recalled a time, many missions ago, when a Juggernaut had caught the starship with a strong tractor beam. *Victory* had broken free but had been hurled into a null region afterward.

Was this a null region? He dearly hoped not. Hadn't Builders created null regions, tiny pocket universes? They had placed Destroyers with a Ska in the one he'd visited twice before.

Maddox's head bumped against his command chair as he swiveled around on his hands and knees. With a surge, he managed to grab the chair and worked up to his feet.

He was badly shaking by that time, with sweat clinging to his cold flesh.

Working around the chair, he collapsed on the seat. He almost fainted from the exertion. Maddox blinked stinging sweat out of his eyes. He didn't have the strength to wipe his eyes just yet.

He coughed, and that hurt the muscles of his chest.

Finally, though, he attempted to peer through the red gloom around him. He saw people lying on the floor. The nearest had blood on their faces.

Maddox clicked an armrest control, but nothing happened.

He looked up at the main screen, but it was blank, showing nothing but the screen itself. He tried to assess if it was cold in here. If the ship had stopped working—

No. It didn't feel cold. He concentrated on his feet, trying to feel vibration through his boots that would indicate—

The engine was working, because he felt the slight thrum or vibration of it through the bridge deck plates. Over time, a spaceman no longer noticed the constant but slight vibration. Now he did because he'd concentrated to feel it.

Maddox had never been happier to feel that slight thrum.

So whatever had happened and shut down other equipment hadn't caused the main engine to stop. Did that mean the ship had velocity? If so, where were they drifting or what were they moving toward?

It was time to find out, and for that, it would be easier if he had some help. He groaned as he pushed off his chair and staggered for the nearest person...

Maddox quickly discovered that he couldn't wake anyone on the bridge. What's more, he found that everyone had crusted blood under their noses and sometimes under their eyes—in some instances, blood must had leaked from their eyes. He didn't like that.

But that wasn't the point. They had crusted blood, but his had still been sticky.

What did that indicate? Something, he was sure.

Feeling stronger now, he walked to the hatch, but it didn't open automatically as he reached it. He had to pry open a side panel and manually open the hatch with a rotating lever.

He found that the corridor had the emergency red lighting, too. Hmm... Maddox went to Valerie's comm board, tapping it. It didn't work, though.

He went to his command chair and opened a secret slot, taking out a blaster. He checked it. The blaster was dead. It had a cell, but the power cell must have drained of energy.

Had the jump caused that? A normal jump wouldn't have, but this hadn't been a normal jump. And yet, if the act of jumping—or whatever it was they had done—had drained the blaster, the comm board, the main screen—why did he feel the engine thrumming?

Maddox took a hand comm from his pocket and tried it. It was also dead.

Ah. He dug into the secret compartment in his chair and withdrew his monofilament knife and scabbard. He hadn't worn or used this for some time.

The edge of the blade was one molecule thick with a unique substance that could cut anything as if it was butter. He attached the knife and scabbard to his belt.

Now, it was time to start hunting and getting some answers.

-40-

He found unconscious crewmembers lying on various floors with crusted blood under their noses and sometimes under their eyes. Even by repeated shaking or lightly slapping their faces, he couldn't wake any of them.

He called for Galyan several more times, but never received an answer. It would seem that he was the only conscious person aboard Starship *Victory*.

"Meta," Maddox said. His wife might be conscious, as she had a superior metabolism, too, although not as efficient as his.

Maddox didn't run through the corridors because he didn't feel strong enough. His head hurt, and his eyesight dimmed if he pushed himself too hard. He moved resolutely, however. None of the turbo-lifts worked. He had to use the emergency metal ladders to go up or down different levels.

Soon, he used an emergency rotator to open his hatch. He found Meta lying on their bed. She was wearing her Star Watch uniform and had sluggish blood under her nose.

"Meta," he said, gently shaking her.

Meta groaned.

A fierce elation surged through Maddox. He could do many things on his own. He felt better, though, knowing that he wasn't alone. It also pleased him that his woman was better than anyone else besides himself.

For a variety of reasons, he'd chosen the right woman to be his wife.

"Thank you, God," he whispered.

"Meta," he said afterward, gently dabbing her nose and lips, wiping away the blood.

She groaned once more and seemed to gain consciousness. "Maddox?" she whispered.

"Take it easy," he said. "There's been an accident and it's knocked out everyone but you and me."

She slurred words he didn't understand, trying to ask questions. He told her a second time to take it easy. By slow degrees, Meta regained full consciousness.

"Oh, Maddox," she said, groping for and clinging to him.

"There, there," he said, patting her back as he held her. "We have to find out what happened."

"Yes," she said. "But...if everything went dead why does the engine still work?"

"We need to find out."

"Do we have weapons?"

"The blasters went dead, too."

"What about your gun?"

"Right," he said, moving to a trunk, opening it and taking out a service pistol. He strapped the holster to his side, took out the gun and screwed on the sound suppressor. That made the barrel longer, but a silencer might prove important for a number of reasons.

"I have this," Meta said, showing him a wicked-looking knife with a long blade and brass knuckles attached to the handle.

"Is there anything to eat?" he asked.

Meta had a few supplies stashed away. They ate some protein bars and chugged water from plastic bottles.

"My headache is fading," Meta said.

Maddox nodded. His was too. Their superior metabolism was probably why they were conscious and no one else was, but they had to keep their interior engines running by giving them food. Maybe their bodies were burning up calories even faster than normal—for whatever reason. Did that indicate that they were in some realm other than normal space? Maddox wasn't sure he liked the idea.

"Let's go," he said. "Let's see if we can figure out why the engine is still running."

-41-

It was tedious work moving through the red-lit corridors and climbing down emergency access-ways. Finally, though, they reached the engine-level deck. Maddox's stomach rumbled and he felt inordinately hungry. When asked, Meta agreed that she was hungry, too.

"Why is our metabolism running so much faster than normal?" he asked.

Meta frowned at him. "I don't know."

"Several reasons come to mind," he said. "Different physics or—"

"Gas," Meta said. "It's gas."

Maddox had noticed her sniffing the air. He now did likewise and shook his head.

"You don't smell it?" she asked.

"No."

"It's faint, but it's there. I've never smelled anything like it."

Maddox tried again but couldn't detect anything different. Was Meta's sense of smell sharper than his? He didn't see why that should be the case, but he supposed it might be possible.

"Gas could indicate a leak but more likely someone pumping a nearly odorless gas through the ship," he said.

"That would obviously indicate intruders," she said.

Maddox drew his long-barreled gun. Meta did the same with her knuckle-duster blade. Together, they went through one corridor after another, nearing the main engine chamber. They could definitely hear the engine thrumming.

"Wait," Maddox whispered. He looked back at his wife. "Did you hear that?"

"A scuffle?" she asked.

"Wait here," he said.

"I'm coming with you."

He stared into her eyes and finally nodded. Meta was a deadly fighter. Not only was she stronger than average, but had quicker reflexes than most due to her 2-G heritage.

Maddox moved like a great jungle cat stalking its prey, his senses straining, particularly his ears. He heard more scuffling ahead and a click. Then something banged against a bulkhead.

He stopped.

"What is it?" Meta whispered.

"Gravity," he said. "I should have realized before now, but it's weird that the grav-plates are operational."

"Oh," Meta said. "That's right. What does it mean?"

"I'm beginning to think it means someone turned on the engines and turned on the grav-plates."

"Wouldn't we have been floating for a while then before that?"

"That's just it," Maddox said. "No one was slumped unconscious in their chairs. Now we know why. Before the grav-plates came back on, everyone must have been floating in zero gravity, so they drifted to various places and ended up on the deck or wherever they happened to fall."

Maddox's eyes narrowed, and he continued advancing through the corridor. He heard more sounds, including a crackling some radios might have made.

His sense of outrage grew, as it felt as if boarders were inside *Victory*. But if the chrome-colored androids had boarded the starship, wouldn't they have started killing people or gathering them into one place, at least?

Not if everyone was unconscious and the androids were going to destroy the ship afterward.

Why would androids turn on the engine and grav-plates then? And what were the androids doing in the engine room?

With even greater care, Maddox approached a bend in the corridor. He came up even with it and slowly peered around the corner.

There was an open hatch twenty meters away. He saw brighter light through the hatch and a momentary shadow—a humanoid shadow.

"Right," he whispered.

Maddox dashed around the corner and rushed toward the hatch. He heard bangs and clangs from within the other chamber. Androids were in the main engine room. His gun likely wouldn't do much damage to them, but his monofilament knife could slice and dice android metal as easily as it could cut paper.

A rising intensity filled him. Androids had boarded the starship. Androids had likely pumped in a secret gas to keep everyone down. This was his chance to save his people—he couldn't screw up or his people would all die.

Maddox threw his back against the bulkhead beside the hatch. A second later, Meta did likewise beside him.

He glanced at her pig-sticker, the knuckle-duster-blade combination. It wasn't going to do jack against androids. But having it would boost her morale, as at least she held a weapon.

Maddox leaned toward the hatch and peered through. He looked just in time to see motion, an android moving behind a relay stanchion.

Just how many androids were in the engine room?

Maddox darted through the hatch into the spacious chamber, moving fast toward the relay stanchions. Farther in were giant cylinders thrumming with raw power.

Meta rushed after him.

There were more noises, including the sound of someone unseen banging metal against metal.

Maddox's grip tightened around his gun. Could he shoot out android eyes? He reached the last relay stanchion and peered around it.

Two androids moved behind a big block cycler several meters wide and three meters tall.

Maddox swore softly under his breath. Where were the androids going? He looked back at Meta.

"Ready?" he asked.

She nodded, too wound up to speak.

"Go," he said.

He hurried from the stanchion, heading fast for the cycler block. Beyond that were huge sealed cylinders containing the heart of the antimatter engines. He might have felt hunger pangs, but his gut twisted in anticipation of the coming fight. He strove to maintain his fabled calm. So much rode on his shoulders. Unless he could subdue these androids—

Maddox reached the cycler, slid along its warm throbbing sides and whirled around, raising his gun.

Two androids walked toward a huge cylinder. Then it struck Maddox. Those two weren't androids. Those were two small humanoid beings wearing bulky gray-colored spacesuits. Earlier, he had seen what he'd expected to see, not what was there. Then, another shock struck him. Part of the suit was for a prehensile tail that swished back and forth on each alien. Each alien—about the height of a ten-year-old boy—pushed what must have been a grav-sled. Certain starship parts were on the sleds, including an unmoving Batrun.

Maddox looked back at Meta. She was staring at the aliens and didn't seem to realize that he was looking at her.

Maddox debated firing the gun and shooting one of the looters. Maybe he should shoot both of them in the back of their helmets. They had boarded his starship. That made them pirates.

Instead of shooting them, Maddox lurched forward, walking fast toward them. Something must have given him away because one of the aliens released his grav-sled and turned around.

The creature jerked in what must have been surprise. Behind the clear visor of the forward protruding helmet was the visage of a boy-sized squirrel, complete with a squirrel-like snout and whiskers. The black eyes held intelligence, though.

The snout opened, and the alien must have spoken. The other alien released his grav-sled and also turned around. He, too, jerked in astonishment.

By this time, Maddox had almost reached them. He motioned with this gun, indicating that they raise their hands.

For a second, both squirrel-like humanoid aliens froze. Then one of them reached with amazing speed for what appeared to be a weapon belted at his side. He grabbed it and began drawing.

Without hesitation Maddox fired, puncturing the suit where a human's heart would have been. The small humanoid released his weapon and toppled backward onto the floor.

The other alien thrust his suited hands into the air as high as they would go and began shaking.

Maddox walked closer yet, wondering if he should kill them both. Who were they? He'd never heard of aliens like this.

The supposedly heart-shot alien sat up slowly. A self-applying patch had already sealed the spacesuit hole, although the alien behind the clear visor looked stricken.

The wounded alien did something, causing the clear, slightly protruding visor to open. "Please," the alien said in awfully stilted English. "Don't kill us. We surrender."

Maddox nodded, dumbfounded that he could understand them. Were they a secret science experiment, an attempt to turn animals into sentient beings?

"Who are you?" the alien asked. "How are you able to subsist in the grok-contaminated air?"

At that point, Meta collapsed.

Maddox spun around to see three more suited aliens standing behind a fallen Meta. One of them held a long-barreled weapon that had been aimed at Meta. That weapon now moved to aim at him.

Maddox dodged, and something flew past him as the weapon made a *phut*-sound. The captain rolled, and he rolled against the shot alien that had spoken to him.

That one had grabbed the original weapon he'd first drawn from his belt. Maddox knocked the weapon out of the gloved hand and saw a blur of something that indicated another fired dart.

Then Maddox scrambled behind the first alien, using him as a shield against the shooter. At the same time, he put the open barrel of his gun against the back of the alien's helmet.

"If they don't drop their weapons," Maddox said, "I'm going to kill you. Are you ready to die?"

The alien made wild chittering noises, presumably at the others.

A moment later, the other aliens dropped their long-barreled dart guns.

"Deal?" the first alien said. "Do we have a deal?"

"What deal?" Maddox asked.

"You are right," the alien said, already sounding calmer. "It is time for you and me to dicker."

-42-

Maddox debated with himself. He was outnumbered, with no one to help him. Already, the aliens that had disarmed themselves by pitching their long-barreled dart guns onto the floor were slowly edging backward. Soon, they would undoubtedly bolt and get reinforcements.

"Tell them to halt," Maddox said, "or I'll kill you."

"No, no," the one he held said. "That won't help you. I'm expendable. Surely, you realize that."

"Wrong," Maddox said. "You told them to disarm and they did. You're obviously the leader."

The furry alien said nothing to that.

"Hurry," Maddox said, pushing his gun barrel against the helmet, shoving the alien's head forward. "I'm eager to kill you, so very eager."

"Now, now," the alien said. "Don't be hasty. You would die, too, then."

"Good-bye," Maddox said flatly.

Once again, the alien he held hostage made loud chittering noises.

Those that were slowly backing away stopped.

"Better?" the alien asked.

"What's your name?"

"We are the Okos, a noble race of—"

"What's your name as an individual?"

"Why do you want to know?" the alien asked, sounding hesitant.

"I grow weary of this. I am alone—"

"All alone," the alien agreed. "Let me help you. Let me end this weariness—"

"Stop," Maddox said, beginning to divine something of these squirrel-faced aliens. "I have a bomb attached to my suit. The weariness I feel means I am hating life. You caused this. I shall detonate and take all of you to oblivion with me."

"Oblivion?" the alien asked. "You are mistaken. Such a vicious act as you suggest will cause you to go to the netherworld for eternity. You will suffer unwanted agonies forever and ever."

"By avenging my people?" asked Maddox. "I think not. I shall gain great rewards in the afterlife by drinking the blood of my enemies here and now."

"We are not enemies."

"You slew my crew," Maddox said.

"What nonsense is this that you spout," the alien said in his awkward English. "We are…*gatherers*. If not for us, the space lanes would clutter with derelict vessels. We are helpful and law-abiding—"

Maddox laughed harshly.

"What did you say?" the alien asked. "I did not understand your last outcry."

The others standing in front of the cycler block had shivered in what seemed like dread at the captain's laugh.

"If they move back again," Maddox said. He'd detected a slight backward movement on their part—very subtle, to be sure, "I will detonate without further notice."

The hostage alien chittered rapidly.

Those farther away abruptly sat down.

"Is that better?" the alien asked.

"Marginally," Maddox said. He realized he held the leader. The aliens seemed quite survival oriented, slippery liars and obvious scavengers. For all that, they were dangerous. The Okos were a hair's breadth from completing their capture of *Victory*. The trick would be in turning the tables on them. Was this the entirety of their scavenging crew?

He doubted it, but likely, this was at least a sizeable portion of the crew. Maybe he should just start shooting. Yet, he'd shot the leader, and he seemed almost unaffected by it.

"I shot you earlier," Maddox said.

"I know. I need medical attention."

"Why aren't you dead?"

The alien said nothing.

"Answer me," Maddox said.

"You sought to kill me?" the alien asked.

"I shot you where the human heart should be."

"That is criminal," the alien said. "We merely—"

"Enough," Maddox said. "I've had enough." The alien's suit had probably injected him with painkillers and stimulants. "Tell your people to take off their spacesuits."

"I'm afraid I can't do that."

Maddox made an ugly sound.

"You don't understand," the alien said. "They will obey me…only up to a point. By taking off their spacesuits, they will be making themselves too vulnerable to you. They might run then instead of obeying me."

"Head-shots should kill them," Maddox said. "Yes. I have more than enough rounds to kill all of them and you and your partner. That seems safest."

"No," the alien said. "We, too, carry bombs on our person. If you shoot us, the bombs will detonate."

"You're a liar," Maddox said.

"I'm outraged," the alien said. "The Okos are many things, but we are paragons of righteous virtue and would never consider—"

"Silence," Maddox said, and there was real hostility in his voice. "It's all one to me if we die. I'm weary of this. I've lost my friends—"

"Sir, sir," the alien said. "Your friends are…what is the word? Oh. They are unconscious. We used gas before boarding your derelict vessel—"

"Listen to me," Maddox said, once more pushing the helmet with the barrel of the gun. "Revive my crew immediately. We will bargain afterward."

"Seriously?" the alien asked. "That would put me at a grave disadvantage—"

"That's better than dying here and now, isn't it?"

The alien paused. Perhaps it was thinking. "You are a savage race. I'm glad I took the precaution of hooking your language files to my translator. I would not believe what I'm hearing if I didn't realize the Okos have the best translator—"

"That's it," Maddox said, sensing a ploy taking shape. Maybe it was time for harsher actions. He aimed his gun past the alien's helmet so he could see him pointing at the suited alien lying near on the deck plates.

"What are you doing?" the alien asked.

"Halting your treachery," Maddox said. "I'm going to kill him before he can—"

The alien chittered once more. The one lying on the deck plates pushed something from his suited body. Then the alien sat up, opened his visor and faced Maddox.

"Is that better?" the first alien asked.

"Tell him to revive the woman on the floor. He must do it immediately."

"She will feel nauseated if I do so," the alien said.

"Do it anyway," Maddox said.

The alien hesitated.

"This is your last chance," Maddox said.

"Yes, yes," the alien said, almost sounding bitter. "I understand now. Vire made a terrible mistake saying your vessel was adrift. If I live through this, I will enact a terrible revenge upon him for this injustice. I do not know what caused Vire to believe—"

"Quit stalling," Maddox said. "My patience has reached its end."

The alien chittered once more, and the second alien slid to Meta, examined her, looked once more at Maddox's captive and lifted what looked like a gun.

"If he harms her—"

"It is a hypogun, I assure you," the alien said.

"Pray for your sake that you're telling the truth," Maddox said.

At that point, the other alien put the nozzle of the weapon to Meta's neck and pulled the trigger, causing her to jerk as a hiss sounded.

-43-

Meta woke up thirty seconds later and vomited. Before that, the second Oko had unobtrusively pulled a dart from her back. After vomiting the third time, Meta raised her head. Her eyes were horribly red-rimmed, and she looked exhausted.

"Meta," Maddox said.

She blinked several times and wiped her mouth. Finally, she nodded, which made her wince.

"My head throbs," she whispered.

"Get your knuckle-duster," Maddox told her. "Then get up, honey. You have to get up. Now's not the time to sit on your butt."

She gave him an angry look, and that also made her wince. After several heartbeats she said, "Okay. That helped just a little."

She gathered her wicked-looking knife off the floor—the second Oko slid away from her and back toward Maddox.

"That's far enough," Maddox said.

His captive Oko chittered at the second one. That one stopped.

Maddox told Meta to collect the alien weapons and put them in a pile. It took her longer than ordinary to do, but finally they were in a pile.

"Now," Maddox said. "Stand behind the others over there. If any of them tries something foolish, kill them."

"Wait," Maddox's captive said. "I've done as you've asked. You should trust me. I've shown that I will cooperate."

"True," Maddox said. "But I don't even know your name. How can I trust you if I don't know your name?"

"I have fallen into the hands of a fanatic," the Oko said. "Know then that I am Master Elge of the Recovery Vessel *Gourvich*. This is an authorized salvage, as I have paid heavy fees for the privilege of roaming Sector 73, Quadrant 2. If you desire, you can examine my credentials aboard the *Gourvich*. Naturally, you will have to come with me—"

"Forgive me, Master Elge," Maddox said.

"What?"

Maddox was thinking hard, trying to dredge up some memory of any of the things the Oko had just told him.

"Who did you pay the fee to?" the captain asked.

"That should be obvious," Master Elge said, "an intermediary of the Sovereign Hierarchy of Leviathan. They have established their right of rule through constant supremacy for the last three hundred years. Why, the last attempt of—"

"Enough," Maddox said. His head had just begun to throb.

"Do you doubt me?" Elge asked.

Maddox concentrated, forcing himself to remain alert and conscious, not necessarily in that order. He'd never heard of this Sovereign Hierarchy. He'd never heard of the squirrel-visaged Okos, either. He was beginning to suspect that *Victory* had jumped much farther than anyone could have anticipated.

"What about the Swarm Imperium?" Maddox asked. "Have you ever heard of them?"

"They are far from here," Elge said.

"You know who I mean when I say the Swarm?"

"The insect empire," Elge said. "Of course, I know. The Sovereign Hierarchy fought bloody battles against the Imperium that lasted over seventy years. The Hierarchy lost half their territory before beginning to detonate suns in the Imperium's path. Finally, the Swarm fleets ceased attacking. That is common knowledge among spacefarers. How is it you claim ignorance of galactic history?"

"What about the Nameless Ones?"

"Who?"

"They ravish worlds with fifty kilometer Destroyers," Maddox said.

"Ah. You mean the Annihilators. They are an ancient legend. Some claim they are a fable. Do you claim to have witnessed Annihilator vessels?"

"I make no such claim," Maddox said. "Have you heard of the Commonwealth of Planets?"

"No."

"New Men?"

"What are they?" Elge asked.

"What about Spacers?"

"You speak strangely, which makes sense since you travel in an unknown type of spaceship. Perhaps you are not from this region of space. Have you tested a new far-ranging drive in your ship?"

"Have you ever heard of Builders?"

"Another legendary race," Elge said. "Yes. I've heard of them. But they are long extinct."

Maddox felt a moment of comfort. *Victory* might have made an incredible leap in stellar distance, but not so far that there was at least some commonality with the Okos.

"Captain," Meta said.

Maddox's head snapped up. He realized that he'd almost dozed while holding a gun to Master Elge's helmet. The Okos were almost comical in ways, but their actions were not. They had boarded his vessel, used gas to keep everyone out and had attempted to steal Batrun.

Saying the synthetic's name in his thoughts caused Maddox to recall the Juggernauts in the Alpha Centauri System. They had to get back to Human Space. The androids were gathering vicious warships right beside the Solar System. He remembered the android saying a Jotun fleet was approaching. Star Watch Command was unaware of what was happening. He had to warn Star Watch or the Rull and Jotuns might hit the Solar System with a massed armada.

Right. It was time to get these Okos under control. He needed more of his crew, needed to capture the *Gourvich* and figure out a way to return home. That meant he had to figure out where here was first.

"Master Elge, surely you're injured."

"I have admitted so."

"I will allow you and your crew to depart as soon as I have regained control of my ship."

"Do you take me for a fool? You will kill all of us."

"Not if you do me a service."

"What service?" Elge asked.

"First, I must revive my crew."

"Why won't you kill us then?"

"I do not want to offend the Sovereign Hierarchy of Leviathan. Surely, if you have paid the salvage fees for this region, I would offend them by killing you and destroying your pirate ship."

"I am not a…yes, of course," Elge amended. "You *would* offend Leviathan by killing us. I hadn't realized you knew that."

"We are strangers here," Maddox said, "and do not wish to offend the ruling authorities. I assume you are one of their representatives."

"That is so," Elge said. "Now, release us—"

"As the weaker party," Maddox said, interrupting, "as the stranger, I cannot afford to trust as you can. Help me revive my crew and I will richly reward you. In that way, I hope you will put in a good word to the Leviathan for us."

Elge said nothing. Maybe he was thinking.

Maddox was trying to appeal to the Oko's greed. "I'm willing to pay anything reasonable," he added.

"The mechanical being?" asked Elge.

"If I must," Maddox said.

Once again, Master Elge fell silent, soon saying, "Leviathan abhors deceit of any kind. Once a being's word is given, that is law in this region."

"Thank you for telling me," Maddox said.

"If you swear that I can keep the mechanical being, I will agree to help you revive your crew."

"I will give him to you as payment," Maddox said, "provided you refuse to take my other offers later."

"You swear to this?"

"Yes," Maddox said.

"Then let us begin," Master Elge said, "as I am eager to enter the healer."

-44-

Maddox worried about the revivals, as that would seem to give the Okos the next best chance to surprise Meta and him through trickery.

To that end, he devised a trick of his own to concentrate their thoughts on something else. When he collected gas masks from an engine-room locker, he also grabbed a pulse reader. He and Meta donned the masks to filter out the Oko-released gas. Maddox switched on the pulse reader so it flashed every few seconds and gave it to Meta, whispering instructions to her.

The Okos stayed ahead while he kept his gun trained on them. Master Elge walked beside Meta and him.

The Oko master kept glancing at the flashing pulse reader that Meta gingerly held in front of her. Finally, Elge could contain himself no longer. "What is that device?"

The other Okos appeared to lean their helmeted heads back to hear the answer.

Maddox had been waiting for the question, although he spoke nonchalantly. "It's an activated grenade," he said through his breathing mask. "If your men try any tricks, we will all die in the accompanying blast."

"No, no," Elge said, as his slender fingers twitched. "I have given my word. You should deactivate it."

"I value your word—" Maddox said.

"Apparently not," Elge said, interrupting. "The grenade indicates a distrustful nature. That implies that you routinely practice duplicity. Why otherwise should you suspect that trait in others?"

Maddox shook his head. "Compared to others, I have found myself the most trustful of men. Too often, however, others had taken advantage of my good nature. That has led me to a sad conclusion: an active threat often holds others to their given word."

"Your reasoning is convoluted and ugly. What is more, it is an insult to me personally and to the Okos as a race. I must demand that you deactivate the bomb."

Maddox matched the pompous way the Okos spoke. "Master Elge, you are in no position to demand. What's more, your insistence leads me to believe that you harbor deceit. This troubles me and causes me to believe Meta must jeopardize all of us in order to convince you how profoundly and personally I take it if someone breaks their solemn word to me."

Elge's fingers twitched spasmodically, and he seemed to whisper into a side comm, which no doubt connected to the other Okos' helmets.

"You speak like an Oko, Captain. We are sworn to help you, and so we shall do. But... I understand," he said at last, glumly.

Maddox had taken the measure of the Okos and believed he understood them. There wasn't a more devious group of aliens around. He would act accordingly.

Every few steps, an Oko looked back at Meta and her "grenade." They seemed fearful of it, but Maddox wasn't sure if they believed him or if they were merely acting scared, trying to lull him.

Soon, it didn't matter, as the Okos revived several space marines with hypogun shots in the neck. Each man repeatedly vomited before donning a gas mask and asking what was going on. Maddox told each one.

Soon, he had as many revived and masked marines as Okos.

At that point, Maddox steered the enlarged party to the brig.

"I'm modifying the situation," Maddox told Elge. "You will instruct your people to take off their spacesuits and helmets. They will enter that cell and await the outcome of your assistance."

"The gas—" Elge said.

"Do you see that man there?" Maddox asked. He indicated a marine at a panel.

"I do," Elge said.

"He has flushed your gas from the cell. Your people will be secure in there. You have my word."

"Surely they can keep their helmets so I can remain in communication with them."

"I'm afraid not," Maddox said.

"No, no, this is no good," Elge said. "My people are nervous and frightened. Without my soothing, they are likely to become…unhinged. You do not understand."

"My marines will remain outside. I assure you that they will be watching your people carefully."

"I see," Elge said, his nervous, slender fingers twitching. "I appreciate your concern, but I do not want you to trouble your marines—"

"It's no trouble at all," Maddox said. "In fact, part of their duty is watching boarders. Normally, they would have shot and killed your people for what they did."

"Captain," Elge said. "I've already explained the misunderstanding."

"The gas—"

"No, no," Elge said. "The gas was a normal precaution on our part. We are a friendly people and dislike conflict, attempting to avoid it at all costs."

"Excellent," Maddox said, "as my marines revel in combat. I was worried your people might attempt to…to breach the cells. If they did, my marines would instinctively act aggressively and possibly kill them. But since your people are friendly and dislike conflict, they will no doubt restfully await your return, so my concerns are moot."

Elge, trapped by this logic, agreed and quietly spoke to his people before returning to Maddox.

The hatches clanged shut, and the marines remained behind, sorting out the Oko spacesuits.

Maddox and Master Elge continued down the corridors. Meta took a hypogun and kit of revival shots, heading elsewhere.

Soon, the drug-fortified Elge and Maddox entered a hangar bay. There was a narrow shuttle in the middle of the bay, one resting on four long "legs." The alien shuttle had large booster cylinders around the back part of the craft. There were also huge metal canisters near one hangar-bay bulkhead. Each canister featured alien script and sprouted a flexible tube that led to a vent.

At the sight of the canisters, Maddox found his temper rising.

"Detach those at once," he told Elge.

"A misunderstanding," the Oko said. "We would never have landed on your vessel if..."

At that point, motion caught Maddox's eye. A panel on the underbelly of the alien shuttle slid open. A gun attached to a robot arm moved down, rotated and aimed its barrel at Maddox. It was roughly seventy meters from him.

"A moment, Captain," Elge said. "Surely you see that?" The Oko pointed at the weapon. "It is an anti-personnel emitter. If you do not release me this instant, it will activate, and a ray will pierce you. Rugged though you are, I doubt you shall survive the experience."

"It is a small matter," Maddox said.

"Perhaps my translator is malfunctioning," Elge said. "The ray will *kill* you, Captain. There is no coming back from death."

Maddox smiled dryly, although Elge couldn't see that because of his gas mask. "Do you recall your people in the brig cells?"

"Of course," Elge said. "But they know the risks of our trade and will willingly sacrifice their lives so their master remains free. Now, Captain, lower your weapon. I no longer appreciate it aimed at me, as I have become the arbiter of the situation."

"Is that true?" Maddox asked. "I imagine the emitter will glitter or glow at the tip a second before firing. At that point, I'll put as many bullets as I can through your skull."

"You will die if you do that."

"Death has little meaning for me if my people are going to die. And they will surely die if you board the shuttle. I imagine you will return to your spaceship and order my vessel's destruction. Thus, I'm going to kill you here and now, Master Elge. Do you have any last words?"

As they had before, the Oko's gloved fingers moved like a squirrel's paws might have under similar tension.

"A fanatic," Elge said at last. "What is wrong with your species? You should desire life, not seek ways to end it."

"Perhaps you're right," Maddox said. "However, I believe the situation still remains in my control. You are my prisoner and you are the leader. Please tell your people to come out of the shuttle."

"Our original deal still holds?" Elge asked.

Maddox said nothing.

"It is unseemly to hold grudges or to maintain a sullen manner," Elge said. "Surely you realize that this was but a test of your nature. I am a trader at heart and always seek to know more about those I am dealing with."

"In that case," Maddox said, "our deal still holds. If you don't like my final offer later, you will take the mechanical man with you."

Elge nodded in a human fashion. "I am glad to hear you are an honest man, Captain. I also admire flexibility such as you've shown. I would like you to know that you have passed our personality profile test."

"Your people are still in the shuttle," Maddox said, "and my trigger finger is growing itchy."

Elge spoke into his helmet comm. He appeared to listen and then he spoke again, but with greater heat and agitation.

Finally, a hatch opened, and a ladder extended from the shuttle to the hangar-bay deck. Suited Okos climbed down one by one. The emitter rose and disappeared back into the shuttle as the underbelly panel closed. Each Oko then lay on the deck with his suited arms outstretched.

"Excellent," Maddox said. "Now, let's shut off the gas canisters, shall we?"

"It will be a pleasure," Elge said.

-45-

It took longer than Maddox liked, but the entire starship crew finally revived and got to work figuring out where they were and what had happened with the star-drive jump.

As a precaution, Maddox held the Recovery Vessel *Gourvich* hostage, kept Master Elge near him and the rest of the boarding Okos—including the shuttle crew—prisoners in the brig.

It soon became apparent that *Victory* was in the outer edge of a red giant system. Apart from that, no one had any idea where in the galaxy the system belonged. The red giant had no planets but many asteroids and comets. As far as every detection device and sensor could tell, there were no bases or livable habitats in the system.

Maddox interrogated Elge by simply asking questions. First, he had medics attend to the alien's gunshot wound. It turned out that the bullet hadn't hit any vitals or broken any bones, although it had torn flesh and muscles.

With the removal of the Oko's spacesuit and helmet, they found that Elge wore a black band around his throat with a bulky device just under his jaw. When the Oko spoke his chittered language, English words emanated from mesh in the equipment.

Ludendorff found that fascinating. "Consider what the machine does. It's mindboggling in scope. I want to study it."

"In time," Maddox had said. "Right now, I need to communicate with Master Elge, so he'll wear the translator a little longer."

"It is an empty star system," Elge said as Maddox and he rode a small cart through the corridors. The Oko wore a bandage under his garments and had taken more painkillers and stimulants.

It turned out that Elge knew about Laumer Points, although the Okos called them portals. The star system possessed several well-traveled portals—the reason Elge had paid for the privilege of "recovering" derelict vessels here.

"When can I leave with my reward?" Elge asked

"Soon," Maddox told him.

First, he had Elge give him a rundown concerning the nearest political systems and populated planets. The major power was something called the Sovereign Hierarchy of Leviathan. Soldiers of Leviathan wore exo-skeleton armor or were cyborgs. Elge wasn't clear on the matter. Several planets within a ten-light-year range held giant but docile Kursks, the clever Da-doc-cha and machine factories serving Leviathan.

Elge proved evasive when questioned about the Okos Union. Maddox got the impression that Okos were nomadic, perhaps akin in ways to Spacers.

Maddox left Elge with Meta in a Medical chamber so the Oko master could rest. After all that had happened, the little alien was yawning constantly and looked bleary-eyed.

"Don't leave him alone for a second," Maddox instructed Meta. "Let him sleep and—"

"What if he needs to use the john?" Meta asked.

"Call Galyan to watch him," Maddox said.

Shortly thereafter, the captain spoke to the professor in his science lab. Ludendorff had found a spare translator on the Oko shuttle. The professor had started dissecting it, examined a hypogun and several of the alien drugs.

Since neither Valerie nor any other navigator knew the starship's location in relation to the galaxy, Maddox asked the professor, "Where are we in relation to Earth? Do you have any idea?"

"In fact, I do," Ludendorff said, as he carefully pried open a tiny unit. He looked up. "I thought I told Valerie. She was supposed to tell you."

Maddox shook his head.

"It must have slipped my mind," Ludendorff said. The Methuselah Man bent low, peering at the opened unit through a stationary magnifying glass.

The captain scratched a cheek as he waited.

Despite Ludendorff's interest in the translator—it was good to see him active again—the professor still didn't seem like his normal self. He had sagging facial skin and...he almost seemed excessively interested in the translator. Lately, he'd been constantly morose. Could Dana's departure really still be bothering him?

Ludendorff picked up a tiny precision tool, using the tip to touch the opened unit under the magnifying glass.

"Where are we?" Maddox asked.

It took Ludendorff a moment. He used the precision tool as he peered through the stationary magnifying glass. With the tip of the tool, he clicked something in the unit. It hummed for a just a moment.

"Ah," Ludendorff said. "I wasn't expecting that, but it makes sense."

Maddox waited.

Ludendorff tapped the small device, held his hands still and looked back at Maddox. "We're in the Scutum-Centaurus Spiral Arm. The bulk of the Swarm Imperium likely lies farther from the galactic core than we are presently."

"What? We're on the other side of the Imperium?"

"Not exactly," Ludendorff said, turning back to the magnifying glass. "The Imperium is to the galactic north of us—if one uses Earth as the directional marker. I estimate that we're approximately ten thousand light-years from the Alpha Centauri System."

"Then..."

"Silence," Ludendorff said. "I want to test something." He brought up another tool, using the one to hold the opened unit and the other to prod something in it.

Smoke rose from the device.

"Damn," Ludendorff said. "I didn't want it to do that. Hmm… Let's see."

He tapped the device with the precision tool, and the smoking ceased. He paused, set the tiny tools near the opened alien unit and straightened, putting his hands behind his back and groaning as he pushed. "I'm not as nimble as I used to be," the professor said. "I should stretch more. Dana had me doing yoga. Perhaps I should continue the practice."

"If I could have your attention…" Maddox said.

Ludendorff turned to him in surprise. "What is it, my boy? Oh. You're worried about our location."

"Did our warhead's antimatter blast aid our star-drive jump in some way?"

"You're referring to our encounter with the Juggernauts near the Supermetals Planet."

Maddox nodded.

"An antimatter blast…no, it wasn't such a crude process, but essentially you are correct. The blast provoked the drive and produced a miracle."

"How could it do that? Can we reproduce the result? Could Swarm Imperium warships do likewise to reach Human Space?"

"Bah! How many questions do you want answered? I'm not a miracle worker, although I realize everyone thinks I am." Ludendorff scowled as he rotated his midsection. "The process was extremely unlikely. Think of it as a one-of-a-kind event. For instance, if you took fifty starships and attempted to replicate the jump, one of them might travel as far as we did. The rest would either permanently vanish or ignite into a fireball."

"Is this a possible method for traveling extended distances?"

"Are you hard of hearing? We had a freak occurrence, my boy, an anomaly if you will. Certainly, attempting the same thing to go home again is out of the question."

"Why?" asked Maddox.

"Because *one* out of fifty times you *might* succeed. Maybe the actual number is one out of sixty, seventy or even two hundred times, for all I know. Those are horrendous odds. Yes?"

"We must accept the risks if we're going to save the Commonwealth," Maddox said.

"That's absurd. We shouldn't commit suicide for an ideal. In this instance, I can assure you that the process would never work."

"You said that one of fifty times it might," Maddox replied.

"Are you prepared to die attempting such awful odds?"

"Not die, Professor, but save our home, our people."

Ludendorff stared at the captain. "You're a gambler extraordinaire, I understand. But I would rather ship out with Master Elge than attempt to go on a suicide mission with you. Consider it this way. Russian roulette is having one bullet in a six-chambered revolver. You have a one in six chance of dying. What we're talking about is having forty-nine bullets in a fifty-chambered revolver. You spin the chamber, put the gun to your head and pull the trigger, hoping to survive. That's what you're talking about, my boy."

Maddox frowned. Could he push everyone into likely dying for a one-out-of-fifty success rate for going home again?

"I'm open to suggestions, Professor. What else can we do?"

"You're against saying here?"

"I am," Maddox said. "What about a Builder nexus? We could use its hyper-spatial tube."

"First, you'd have to find one. But it's good to remember that nexuses aren't magical. Last mission should have taught you that. Ten thousand light-years is too far for a hyper-spatial tube. At the outside, we could use one for five thousand light-years, but that would be taking grave risks. And that's providing we could break into the nexus. For all we know, if Builders reached this spiral arm, they might well be different enough from ours—"

"Batrun," Maddox said, interrupting. "He claimed to have come from another Builder."

"True," Ludendorff said slowly. "But you've agreed to give Batrun to Master Elge as payment for services rendered."

"That's not exactly true," Maddox said.

Ludendorff eyed the captain. "Did you *lie* to Master Elge?"

"I said I would give him Batrun if he didn't like my final offer."

"Which is a bullet to the brain if he doesn't drop his claim," Ludendorff said.

"That would work, and you've divined my fallback. But I hope to pay the Oko with something else."

"What?"

"I don't know yet," Maddox admitted, "and I'm not overly interested in what a salvage operator would find intoxicating. Elge is a scavenger and attempted to steal my ship and likely kill all of us. I'll pay him something and keep Batrun and my word—"

"Calm yourself, Captain," Ludendorff said. "I'm merely curious."

Maddox nodded. "Hopefully, the Okos knows the whereabouts of a Builder nexus and can take us there directly, without our having to interact with others here. We don't know the social norms of this Sovereign Hierarchy of Leviathan, and I'm not sure I care to find out by doing something to enrage them."

"You were Patrol trained," Ludendorff chided. "You should be more curious. In one sense, this is an amazing voyage. We've discovered alien political organizations that have successfully fought the Swarm Imperium to a draw. There are at least several cultures here ten thousand light-years from Earth. We've also gained a better understanding of our galaxy. We should be brimming with curiosity and cataloging everything we can, while we can."

"That's sound reasoning, Professor. I'm authorizing you to set up a cataloging team. Learn everything you can. Remember this, though. The fact that the Sovereign Hierarchy of Leviathan fought the Imperium to a standstill is why I don't want to meet them."

"That's prudent. Yes. I'll start immediately. By the way, how long do you plan to hold the *Gourvich* hostage?"

Maddox clasped his hands behind his back and began to pace. "I wonder how much time has passed since *Victory* was a floating derelict. Was it hours, days, weeks—months? I hate not knowing. The Rull androids have gone crazy. Imagine bringing three Juggernauts to the doorstep of Earth. And shedding their pseudo-skin the way they did…"

"It's time to wake Batrun," Ludendorff said. "The Supermetals Planet…it could have already given the Rull Nation key advantages. How long have they been mining it, hmm? With the superconductor metals—if I had such an abundance of supermetals, I could vastly improve our disruptor cannon, for instance. Maybe that's why *J-B3's* laser burned so hot. I've never heard of the like. Did you study the wattages?"

Maddox nodded absently as he continued to pace.

"And if the Jotun fleet exists—"

Maddox stopped, turning around sharply.

Ludendorff noticed. "Batrun has spoken about the Jotuns, but several factors make me wonder if they're real after all."

"Meaning?" asked Maddox.

"Has Batrun has been telling us the truth about them?"

"Lisa Meyers' hauler had a reflective shield and was able to project a binding-force bubble," Maddox said.

"I'm aware of that. But consider. One ship—a hauler—possesses the technology to do those things. Does that mean a Jotun fleet of Jovian aliens is really converging on Earth?"

"You don't believe Batrun?"

"I need more proof before I accept the totality of his claims."

Maddox rubbed his jaw. That was sound thinking. But the critical point was that they had to get home, a journey of ten thousand light-years, and they had to do it before the Rull androids gathered a large fleet of Juggernauts and rushed the Solar System. Wasn't such an attack a possibility? Despite what Ludendorff suggested, a Jotun fleet could well be coming to aid the Rull androids.

"I'll see you later, Professor. It's time I had a heart-to-heart discussion with Master Elge."

-46-

Victory and RV *Gourvich* were several hundred meters apart at the edge of the red giant system.

The recovery vessel was larger than Maddox had anticipated, about a quarter the size of the starship. The *Gourvich* held the equipment and living quarters for the Oko wives, children and slaves.

The slaves, it turned out, were for purchase both as novelty items and as workers. There were many species aboard. Master Elge claimed to own seven different classes. When Ludendorff learned about this later, he suggested Maddox buy at least one of each.

"We're not slave traders," Maddox said. "Nor are we going to capture intelligent beings and take them so far away from home that they can never get back again."

"They won't go home anyway as slaves of the Okos," Ludendorff pointed out.

"Maybe," Maddox said. "But this is the culture they know."

"Small comfort for the slaves," Ludendorff grumbled. "But have it your way. You're the captain—even if this is missing a priceless opportunity to learn more about this region of space."

In any case, Recovery Vessel *Gourvich* was longer than it was wide, with fusion engines. It turned out that Master Elge was eager to acquire antimatter technology.

Maddox decided it wasn't for sale.

Later, he dined with Elge in an observation lounge, having learned of the Oko diet. It was vegetarian, consisting mainly of roots, large alien berries and nuts. He'd had the dishes prepared on the *Gourvich* and brought over to *Victory* via shuttle.

Afterward, they drank an Oko vintage of wine, which was eminently palatable to Maddox's tongue.

Finally, Maddox dabbed his lips and said, "It's time to discuss terms."

Elge nodded. He was wearing silk garments that reached to his metal-shod feet, and had tied a red ribbon to the end of his furry tail. He wore silken half-gloves that showed the claws at the tips of his slender fingers. A platinum pendant also hung from a silver chain around his neck. Elge fingered the pendant as if...as if it might be a weapon of sorts.

The Oko "guest" had been given a higher chair than Maddox so he could reach the table comfortably. The captain estimated that Elge weighed a hundred pounds at the most, possibly less with all that fur.

"I am quite interested in the mechanical man," Elge said. "He...seems like an advanced model."

"Would you make him another of your slaves?"

Elge appeared thoughtful. "Here, it is considered rude to ask a buyer what he chooses to do with his purchase."

"Not a slave," Maddox murmured. "You'd have me believe that the Sovereign Hierarchy of Leviathan doesn't possess models like ours. Not only that, but that Leviathan would dearly love such a model and pay fantastic sums to acquire it."

"Nonsense," Elge said. "The mechanical man is a curiosity, nothing more. Call it a...whim on my part."

"Of course," Maddox said, realizing he must have hit the mark. Batrun must be a prize indeed. Did that mean the Leviathan Soldiers were indeed cyborgs?

"Remember, Captain, you promised the mechanical man to me."

Maddox did not respond, but swirled the wine in his goblet. Giving Elge Batrun would solve the problem of what do with the synthetic. Still, Batrun had knowledge he could use in the coming conflict with the Rull androids and Jotuns. As tempting as it was to leave the synthetic behind, that could have future repercussions that worked against the Commonwealth when

241

Patrol vessels eventually traveled out here. Batrun would be a great source of information about Human Space, and more.

The sooner *Victory* left the Scutum-Centaurus Spiral Arm, the better. If the Sovereign Hierarchy of Leviathan could explode stars and had fought the Swarm Imperium for seventy years, they might make awful enemies. The reverse might also be true: Leviathan might make effective allies in a future conflict against the bugs. What he didn't want to do was meet any Leviathan warships. It would be better if wise Patrol minds could forge a policy for dealing with Leviathan from the details he brought home. Now that Star Watch knew—or would know—something about this region of space, strategists could add the details to future calculations.

Did that mean it would be better to destroy the *Gourvich* and everyone on it so no one here learned about the Commonwealth? Would Elge really take data about *Victory* to the Sovereign Hierarchy of Leviathan?

Maddox swirled his wine again. He didn't know the answer to the last question. It would depend on whether Elge could wring an advantage from the sale of data or not.

"You did promise the mechanical man to me," Elge said again. "I have recorded the promise—"

Maddox's head snapped up.

Elge stopped talking and looked away. It seemed as if the Oko was upset with himself for giving away a secret.

The captain glanced at the platinum object dangling from Elge's throat. Of course, Elge would be recording and photographing everything he could. It would all be for sale to someone. The Oko would attempt to derive profit from anything he possibly could.

He should take the RV *Gourvich* and Master Elge back to Earth. Maybe Ludendorff had a point about the slaves aboard the recovery vessel being profitable for study.

Would such an action make him a pirate?

Maddox stared at the blood-red wine in his goblet. When the European explorers had first come to the New World, they'd captured Indians and brought them back to Europe. Had the ancient Englishmen and Spaniards studied the captives for clues to the Indian cultures? He'd have to ask Ludendorff about that.

In this case, Maddox would force an alien ship to travel to Earth. It might not be ethical, but it would be prudent. Ludendorff was right about him being Patrol trained.

Would Star Watch ever let Elge return to the Scutum-Centaurus Spiral Arm? It was doubtful. But then maybe that was the risk in attempting to salvage *Victory*, trying to salvage any spaceship before everyone on board was dead.

Maddox realized that's what he was going to do. In Elge, the Okos crew and slaves had priceless data about this region of the spiral arm. *Victory* had been hurled here as an accident. Now, like a true Patrol officer, he had to take advantage of what fate had offered him. Besides, maybe the *Gourvich* held something that would help him against Jotun technology. It was a long shot, but his first duty was to protect the Commonwealth.

Maybe in time, Elge could return as part of a Star Watch mission in making contact with the Sovereign Hierarchy of Leviathan. That would be many times better than Earth receiving envoys from Leviathan in Human Space, which could happen if he let Elge and his ship go free.

"You are quiet, Captain," Elge said. "What are you thinking?"

"I'm considering the future," Maddox said. "Tell me, you said the Builders are legendry. Do you know if any of their artifacts are free-floating in space?"

Elge made a sharp sound. It might have been a laugh. "Captain, do you take us for fools? The Sovereign Hierarchy has declared all Builder fossils as forbidden relics that none dare approach on pain of death."

"I see."

"Isn't it so in your realm?"

Maddox didn't answer.

"Surely, after all I have done for you," Elge said, "you are not suggesting I commit public suicide by daring the Guardians. If I approach such a useless pile of space junk—"

"If it's junk, why are Guardians protecting it?"

"I neither know nor care," Elge said. "In this, the Sovereign Hierarchy is as fanatical as you. Why, even discussing such a thing—" Elge shook his head emphatically.

"Where is the nearest Builder relic?"

"Did you not hear what I just said? You are a monomaniac, a zealot to continue talking about it. Believe me, I have no wish to die under the prongs of an inquisitor."

"The Sovereign Hierarchy is that harsh?"

Elge made another of his sounds. "Pray that you never find out, Captain."

Maddox set the goblet on the table. Galyan could hack the *Gourvich,* or space marines could take an Oko navigational computer. Elge and his Okos had boarded *Victory*, after all, attempting to take what they wanted. If Elge held the advantage, things would be going quite differently now.

Maddox sighed. Why was he hesitating? Was he getting soft?

"Master Elge," Maddox declared. "There has been a change in plans."

"I am not going to receive the mechanical man?"

"No."

"But you promised."

"The promise was a ploy."

Elge looked down at his diner plate.

"You invaded my ship and would have killed us or taken us as slaves," Maddox said.

"That has no bearing on your word, your promise," Elge muttered, still looking down.

"True," Maddox said. "But I did add that I would offer you alternatives. However, I will give you the mechanical man, if you are such a stickler for protocol."

Elge looked up. "Thank you, Captain. It is a pleasure dealing with an honest man."

"And then I will kill you," Maddox said. "I will also destroy the *Gourvich*, as I never promised not to do that. Afterward, I will take the mechanical man as salvage. I will have kept my word in all particulars."

The Oko's eyes seemed to darken. "Clever," Elge said. "I had hoped…well, never mind. You think like an Oko, meaning you are more cunning than I'd realized. Very well, I relinquish my demand for the mechanical man. In his place, I desire the specs for your antimatter drive."

"Since you are being so understanding," Maddox said, "I'll give you the specs once we part company."

"Excellent," Elge said, rubbing his half-gloved hands. "I would like to depart later today—"

"No," Maddox said. "The specs to the antimatter drive are a priceless commodity. In return, I want to know the whereabouts of the nearest Builder relic."

Elge considered the idea and finally nodded. "I will do as you request. Then, we shall be going."

"Not quite yet," Maddox said. "You will show us the quickest route to the Builder relic by journeying with us."

"What? It is an outrage to suggest such sacrilege. No, no, I am not suicidal. I have made that clear, yes?"

"You will show us the route, Elge, or I will destroy the *Gourvich*. First, of course, I will give you the mechanical man. Remember, I am a man of my word—and I give you my word I will do these things."

For the next few minutes, Elge twisted and turned with his objections, but finally and reluctantly agreed. "I should have listened to my fifth wife," he mused sadly. "She warned me the derelict ship was dangerous, but my greed got the better of me. I will elevate her in my esteem, and listen to her more in the future."

"Good for you," Maddox said. "She sounds like a wise woman."

Elge didn't seem comforted by the praise. But for now, there was nothing he could do about it.

-47-

The next week proved harrowing as *Victory* and RV *Gourvich* used portals—jump points—to travel from one Scutum-Centaurus star system to another.

Maddox warned Elge more than once to stick to the truth. He wanted to maneuver through empty star systems only. Even after the warning, however, the Oko master lied several times. Of course, Elge always said he'd forgotten about a certain outpost or that it had slipped his mind that the Kursks had put down a colony in that particular star system.

So far, Maddox had discovered each "error" by using the star-drive jump to check ahead. Each time, he left a tin can piloted by Keith Maker and several shuttles behind to watch the *Gourvich*. Before leaving the first time, Maddox detonated an antimatter missile so Elge and his people understood that the shuttles easily had the firepower to destroy the recovery vessel.

"Since we have risked so much for you," Elge said at the end of the week, as they were on the bridge—he was a guest aboard the starship, a hostage for Oko good behavior—"I would also like the specs for the machines that allow you to use the star-drive jump."

"Agreed," Maddox said from the captain's chair.

Elge rubbed his slender hands, perhaps anticipating future profits.

The two ships were near a portal in an empty star system. According to Elge, they were one jump away from the forbidden star system. Maddox asked him what they could expect to find there.

"I lack such data," Elge said, having maintained that position from the beginning.

"The more I think about it," Maddox said, "the odder it seems that you've never purchased such interesting information."

"The Soldiers of Leviathan would not approve."

"Which would make such data even more valuable," Maddox said.

"You're right," Elge said. "Great profit often comes at great risk. And it is true that such data is for sale among criminal elements. But I've never had the need or a client who desired it. I do know this—the Guardians possess deadly vessels. You should forget this madness. Why do you need to see the Builder relic? It is old and useless."

Ludendorff was on the bridge today. "You speak confidently about it, Master Elge. What else do you know about the relic?"

"Know in what way?"

"Its mass perhaps."

"Why would I care to know its mass?" Elge scoffed. "That is more madness. This I know and no more, so do not pester me about it. The relic is shaped like a pyramid, a giant rotating pyramid, not like those on Gamma Deuce II."

"What color is this supposed pyramid?" Ludendorff asked in a seemingly offhanded manner.

"Silver," Elge said. "Does the color matter?"

Ludendorff shrugged indifferently, glanced once at Maddox and then left the bridge.

"I saw that," Elge said. "I am not stupid. The glance has meaning. Is silver an important color?"

"Possibly," Maddox said.

"Ah, saying possibly means it *doesn't* have meaning. I have made a study of you, Captain. You humans are canny. Once, I believed you an honest man. Now..." Elge rubbed his thin hands. "Your part of the galaxy must be terrible indeed to have produced beings like you. I would not like it there. With that being said, the Sovereign Hierarchy of Leviathan could use

Soldiers like you. Perhaps you can bargain with the Great One for a term of service."

"He hires?"

"You didn't know?" Elge asked. "No... How could you. Are you interested in serving Leviathan?"

"Possibly," Maddox said.

"Then let us leave this place. Don't even *think* about entering the relic system. That is a quick way to die. Instead, I can point you to a recruiting—"

"Master Elge," Maddox said, interrupting. "I'm sending space marines onto the *Gourvich*."

"What? No. That is an outrage."

"No more than you leading a salvage team onto *Victory*."

"You know that I paid Leviathan for the right. Thus, I acted legally. But you! You cannot possibly possess a privateer's fee from Leviathan. Therefore, sending marines onto my ship is an illegal action."

"Leviathan sells privateer's rights?" Maddox asked.

"In times of war," Elge said.

"Is there an ongoing war?"

"Information, you desire endless information without compensation," Elge complained. "I am your prisoner, but this endless theft must cease. Surely, you desire that I have a positive attitude about you after you leave."

"Naturally, I desire that," Maddox said. "However, the marines have already arrived on the *Gourvich* and taken control."

"Just like that?" asked Elge. "No, no, you should have told me in advance so I could have smoothed the way for them?"

"You'll be relieved to know then that the marines went in armed and armored. Your people understood the situation and surrendered without a fight. There were no casualties."

"I am overjoyed," Elge said in a dispirited voice.

"Excellent," Maddox said. "The *Gourvich* will now lead the way for *Victory* as we head into the relic star system."

"No!" Elge said, bolting upright. "That is death to us all. Your ship has weapons, but they will fail against the Guardians. Now, please, Captain, be reasonable. We are Okos. We are peace-loving. If we enter the relic system, the Soldiers might report us to Leviathan. Then Okos everywhere will be held responsible for our sacrilege. No. This is wrong of you. You are essentially a good man. You cannot wish us annihilated as a species."

"I doubt it will be that bad."

"You are correct," Elge said. "It will be worse. I beg you, Captain. Name your price so we can buy our freedom. Listen to this. I here and now relinquish my claim to the mechanical man. I will give you all our slaves; just don't force us to die with you in the relic system."

Maddox was impressed. Were the Guardians really that deadly? Yet, how could Elge know if he knew nothing about the Builder relic? It was possible this was a mistake, but he had to gamble if he was going to get home in time to save Earth from a Juggernaut sneak attack.

"This is madness," Elge continued. "If you must kill yourselves, walk into space. We will record your passage. By giving us the salvage rights to your ship—"

"Elge," Maddox said, interrupting. "Tell me everything you know about the Guardians. As both our ships are going, our united survival might depend on what you can tell me."

The Oko looked torn. His narrow shoulders finally slumped. "I cannot do as you ask," he said softly, "as there is a chance the Soldiers will take your computers and play back this talk. I want them to know that I told you nothing. Have mercy on the Okos," he said. "Let my people go."

"I'm sorry, Master Elge. I have no choice." Maddox told the bridge crew. "We're making the jump. So let's get ready for a fight."

"What about the *Gourvich?*" Valerie asked.

"Tell Lieutenant Mars to take the alien ship through first as planned," Maddox said. Lieutenant Mars was the space marine in charge over there.

"You're sending my ship through first as a sacrifice," Elge complained.

"No," Maddox said, "I'm doing it as a ploy. Now stop complaining and start thinking about what you can tell me. Better that we all survive so no Soldiers tear out our computers, yes?"

Elge did not reply but sat morosely, his fingers twitching continuously.

-48-

As had happened on so many other occasions, the captain shrugged off the infinitesimal jump lag faster than anyone else did. He knew better than to test any lagged equipment yet.

As Valerie revived, she sat up and began to run the sensors.

Shortly thereafter, Galyan appeared.

"Report, please," said Maddox.

Galyan and Valerie both spoke up at once.

"Lieutenant, if you please," Maddox said.

Galyan nodded in acquiescence as Lieutenant Noonan reported on the star system. It had a G-class star, four terrestrial inner planets and three outer gas giants. There was a large asteroid belt between the inner and outer system, a thick belt with an unnatural amount of debris, asteroids, meteors and dwarf planets. The Solar System had an asteroid belt at approximately the same location, but it was less than four percent the mass of Earth's Moon. This system…

"I'm reading half the mass of Mars," Valerie said, surprised.

Maddox absorbed that. The asteroid belt was many times thicker than the one in the Solar System.

"There are heavy debris clouds in the belt," Valerie continued. "So far, I've counted six."

Maddox turned to Elge, "Any comments so far?"

"None," Elge said as he studied the main screen. "This is highly interesting. We Okos had no idea."

"You've never studied the star system from several light-years away?" Maddox asked.

"Why should we?" Elge replied.

Which wasn't an answer, but an evasion. Maddox let it pass nonetheless.

"I have not detected any ship drives," Valerie said, "or anything to indicate industrialization or habitation."

"Well, Elge?" Maddox asked. "Where's the Builder relic?"

The Oko raised his hands as a shrug.

"You told us—"

"Sir," Galyan said, interrupting. "I have a suggestion."

Maddox glanced at Valerie.

"That's fine by me," Valerie said. "I haven't detected anything that implies Builders or these Sovereign Hierarchy people. I'm interested in what Galyan thinks."

"Not people," Elge chided. "They are the Sovereign Hierarchy of Leviathan."

"What is Leviathan exactly?" Maddox asked.

"A name that implies the whole," Elge said.

That didn't seem like much of an answer. The captain turned to the Adok holoimage. "Galyan, you have an idea?"

"I do, sir. The sheer mass of the asteroid belt implies Builder…meddling. I am not sure if that is the correct way to say it."

"Never mind that," Maddox said. "How does the mass imply Builders?"

"It should be obvious," Galyan said. "No asteroid belt in my study or experience has such density or combined mass as the one out there. Since this is supposed to be a Builder star system, and since this is different from everything else we have encountered with asteroid belts—"

"He's right," Valerie said. "The very mass *does* imply Builders. I should have seen it right away. Good reasoning, Galyan."

"Thank you, Valerie. I was worried you would think I was attempting to one-up you."

"If you were someone else, I might think that," Valerie said. "But I know you always have our best interest at heart."

252

"You are generous with your praise," Galyan said. "I appreciate it. I also appreciate the implication that I am a living entity with heart."

"Yes, yes," Maddox said. "The lieutenant is a paragon of virtue. Since you've concluded the asteroid belt is Builder manufactured, have you been able to detect anything to indicate a nexus?"

"Paragon of virtue…?" Galyan said. "Is that sarcasm, sir?"

"It's an indication that I want to get on with the analysis," Maddox said. "We're ten thousand light-years from home and—"

"Yes," Galyan said. "I will begin an immediate analysis…" The holoimage's eyelids fluttered faster and faster. Abruptly, that ceased. "I suggest you call Professor Ludendorff to the bridge. He may be able to infer more than I can at this point."

"The debris clouds, sir," Valerie said. "We can't see through them. Might that indicate someone is attempting to hide a nexus in those places?"

"Ah," Galyan said. "That is good reasoning, Valerie. I should have thought of that."

The lieutenant didn't reply, but glanced at Maddox, perhaps to gauge his reaction.

Maddox rubbed his chin. "You really didn't think of that, Galyan?"

"I—"

"The truth," Maddox said. "If I can't trust you…"

"I am sorry, sir," Galyan said. "I did think of that, but I…"

Valerie's cheeks had turned red. "You don't have to worry about me, Galyan. I'm not a shrinking violet."

"I do not understand," Galyan said. "Is shrinking violet a metaphor?"

"Yes," Valerie said. "I'm not hurt that you can analyze faster than I can. You're…"

"Yes?" asked Galyan.

"You have a higher IQ…and an ability to run data faster than any of us does," Valerie said.

"You were going to say that I am a computer. Is that not correct, Valerie?"

Maddox slapped an armrest in irritation. "We'll stick to the issue. Galyan, I no longer want you to withhold information at such a critical juncture."

"Yes, sir," Galyan said.

"Elge," Maddox said. "Do you know anything about the debris clouds?"

The Oko hesitated.

"You do," Maddox said.

"No…" Elge said.

"Enough!" Maddox said with force, although he didn't raise his voice. "Galyan—Valerie, plot a course to the nearest asteroid-belt debris cloud. Mr. Maker, once the course is plotted, you will head there."

"With a star-drive jump, sir?" asked Keith.

"Negative," Maddox said. "We will head there under regular velocity. If Leviathan Soldiers are watching us from the debris clouds, I don't want them knowing about our star drive just yet."

"Clever," Elge said, "and well thought out. I suggest you strain with utmost vigor to detect stealth missiles. The Soldiers are without peer and often destroy their opponents before the other is even aware they are in a fight."

"Stealth missiles," Maddox said. "You could have mentioned them sooner."

"I did not want to encourage your madness," Elge explained. "This way…" His slender fingers twitched and fluttered.

"Shall I launch probes, sir?" Valerie asked, indicating the nearest debris cloud.

"No…" Maddox said. "Probes would imply I'm expecting to find something there. If we simply head for a debris cloud as if by random chance…"

The captain tapped an armrest with a fist. "We're new to the region. The Soldiers have never seen a ship design like ours. As far as they know, we captured an Oko recovery vessel. If we don't act as if we're looking for Builder relics… That may give us an edge when the Soldiers order us to halt."

"Will these Soldiers order us or attack first?" Valerie asked.

"A good question," Maddox said. "We're going to find out soon enough."

-49-

The *Gourvich* and *Victory* had exited a Laumer Point in the general vicinity of a Venus planetary orbit—if this had been the Solar System. That meant roughly three AUs to the Asteroid Belt between the inner and outer system. Both vessels traveled at a leisurely velocity, trying to convey peaceful intentions to any observers.

Thirty-seven hours later, the two vessels approached the first debris cloud. They were three million kilometers out and beginning deceleration. During the last thirty-seven hours, Valerie and her people had extensively mapped the star system, including the belt. There hadn't been any indications of life or technology. So far, no sensor had penetrated any debris cloud, meaning the clouds were just as mysterious as when they had first entered the system.

"Now's a good time to launch a probe," Maddox said. "At this point, it's reasonable for us to worry about the debris cloud."

"Soldiers are not reasonable," Elge muttered.

Two probes sped from the starship, both accelerating. One targeted the nearest debris cloud, the other another cloud twenty-eight million kilometers out.

The probes brought a swift reaction as two battleship-sized vessels eased out of the nearest cloud as if the warships had just left a base.

"The Soldiers of Leviathan," Elge moaned as he stared at the main screen. "We are doomed, doomed, I tell you."

"Give me data, people," Maddox said. "I want to know exactly what we're dealing with."

"Doom," Elge told him. "You have condemned us both. Soon, stealth missiles will destroy my wonderful vessel. My wives, children and inheritance will all perish in a moment of radioactive explosions."

The two battleships were oval-shaped and appeared to have heavy hull armor.

"Iridium-Z hull armor, sir," Valerie said. She swiveled around. "I can't believe this. Their hull armor is a match to Juggernaut hull armor."

"Are these androids?" Maddox asked, as he leaned forward, studying the two warships. "More specifically, are they *Rull* androids?"

"I'm detecting…fusion beam cannons, sir," Valerie said.

"That's New Men technology," Maddox said.

"Correction, sir," Galyan said, "but fusion cannons are Builder technology. Remember, Methuselah Man Strand first gave the New Men fusion beam technology from his Builder store of knowledge."

Maddox tapped his chin. "Does iridium-Z hull armor for both androids and Soldiers derive from the same Builder source? That could be why the Soldiers protect nexuses so zealously." Maddox faced the holoimage. "Galyan, summon the professor. I want him up here three minutes ago."

"At once, sir," Galyan said, disappearing.

"Maybe the Builders weren't as stingy handing out their technology in this area of the galaxy as in ours," Maddox said. "I wonder what could cause the difference."

"We don't know Builders really handed out anything here," Valerie said.

"Iridium-Z hull armor is distinctive," Maddox said. "Combined with the fusion cannons, the possibly of coincidence stretches credibility. These are Builder derived technologies."

Valerie went back to studying her panel. "The ships are using fusion drives," she said shortly. "If this was a Builder-derived war society, wouldn't the ships possess antimatter drives?"

"An excellent question," Maddox said. "Maybe once we see or speak with these Soldiers, we'll know more."

"You will be dead by then," Elge said glumly.

Maddox studied the Oko, and said abruptly, "Do Soldiers possess translators?"

"Like mine?" asked Elge, as he touched the one around his throat. "It is doubtful. Soldiers seldom talk, but attack and kill."

"Hail them, Lieutenant," Maddox told Valerie.

"With the new unit, sir?" she asked.

"Not yet," Maddox said.

Ludendorff had installed the second translator into the bridge's comm panel. He had also added Oko-derived Leviathan language files, matching them with English words and concepts.

"The battleships are accelerating," Keith said. "I don't detect any hidden missiles, though I'd expect them somewhere..."

Galyan reappeared. "The professor is on his way up, sir."

Maddox nodded. "Galyan, redouble your search for stealth missiles."

"Acknowledged," Galyan said, as his eyelids began fluttering.

"Are the Soldiers answering our hail?" Maddox asked Valerie.

"Not yet. Should I keep trying?"

"Do it," Maddox said.

"Ah," Galyan said. "You have good instincts, sir. I have detected two stealth missiles. They are each heading from a different direction. One is bearing down on us from the star's direction. The other—the one with the higher velocity—is coming through the Asteroid Belt. It will pass the debris cloud."

"Have you determined what kind of missiles?" asked Maddox.

"To a degree," Galyan said. "They are black ice-coated missiles. The star-ward missile is two million kilometers from us and closing. The Asteroid Belt-ward missile is four and a half million kilometers away."

"Target the first missile when it comes into range, Galyan. Use the neutron beam to destroy it."

Once more, Galyan's eyelids fluttered. "I am activating the neutron cannon and tracking the missile. It has not made any deviations since detected. That would indicate the Soldiers believe their stealth technology is working."

"I'm stunned you've found their missiles," Elge said. "I would gladly pay for such sensors."

"Noted," Maddox said.

Seconds passed as the bridge crew continued working at high alert.

"I am firing," Galyan announced.

A purple neutron beam lashed toward the star. It did not seem to fire at any one thing. Abruptly, an intense light appeared and winked out.

"Hit and destroyed," Galyan said.

"Now the other one," Maddox said.

"The enemy's fusion cannons are coming online," Valerie warned.

Once more, the purple neutron beam speared into the darkness. Like before, it struck the stealth missile, causing a bright light to briefly flare into existence.

The latter destruction was a mere five hundred thousand kilometers from the two Leviathan warships.

"Any reply yet?" Maddox asked Valerie.

"Nothing," she said. "I am picking up a targeting lock. They're getting ready to fire at us."

Maddox pursed his lips and nodded decisively. "Hail them with the translator. Use the Leviathan setting. Tell them we come in peace." Maddox turned to Galyan. "Warm up the disrupter cannon. If they want to fight, we'll destroy them as fast as we can."

"Are you mad?" Elge asked. "To provoke the Soldiers of Leviathan—"

"They're answering," Valerie said, interrupting. "Shall I put the image on the main screen?"

"Do it," Maddox said, sitting back as he waited to see what a Soldier of Leviathan actually looked like.

-50-

The pattern on the main screen altered. A moment later, a narrow-faced individual appeared before a wall of computers with continuously shifting lights. The individual had two dark eyes, a nose and a thin mouth held in disapproval. He had a tall forehead, sparse hair and close-cropped ears. He wore a black uniform with a high collar.

Maddox studied the eyes. The sockets appeared to be metal, the dark eyeballs made of hardened plastic. The skin around the sockets seemed like flesh—

"A cyber," Ludendorff said quietly.

Maddox glanced back at the professor, who had just entered the bridge. "What's that mean?"

"See for yourself," Ludendorff said, as he walked forward. "The creature is part machine and part biological, and seems almost human in origin. In any case, I call that a cyber."

"Like a cyborg?" asked Maddox.

"Cyber, cyborg, two words that mean the same thing," Ludendorff said. "I prefer cyber, however, as it is more elegant."

"You bicker among yourselves," the cyber said. "That is unseemly. You have addressed me and should all be bowing in submission. I am the Supreme Soldier of Leviathan in the Caval System."

Maddox inclined his head. "I greet you with joy and peace in my heart, Supreme Soldier. I am Captain Maddox, an emissary from a distant region. It troubles me that you fired two missiles at my ship. I would like an explanation for your aggressive behavior."

Elge urgently motioned to Maddox, but the captain ignored the little Oko. Ludendorff put a hand on Elge's left shoulder, drawing him back as they both moved out of visual screen range.

"You have an Oko scavenger in your presence," the cyber said. "He should have told you that this is a restricted system."

"He attempted to pirate my vessel," Maddox said. "I have thus forced him to obey my wishes, with the threat of instant death hanging over his head."

The cyber concentrated on Maddox with greater intensity. "I am Mon Zabul," he finally said. "I have determined that you utter the truth. You do not belong to the Sovereign Hierarchy of Leviathan, nor are you under our jurisdiction. You are therefore outside our normative strictures. My next question is critical, and I demand an honest answer. Are you here to attack Leviathan?"

"I am not," Maddox said.

"Are you an industrial spy, perhaps?"

"We are travelers, passing through your realm. While I am an emissary, I am also heading home in order to help defend our people."

"Where is your home, Emissary?"

Maddox hesitated before saying, "In the Orion Spiral Arm."

"Is your home system a tributary to the Swarm Imperium?"

"We are at war against the Swarm," Maddox said.

The cyber turned his head and appeared to be listening to something off-screen. He faced Maddox after a moment. "Before we proceed, you will return the Oko to his vessel and send him to us."

"His vessel is a prize of war," Maddox said. "We claim it by right of combat."

"No, no," Elge whispered. "Are you mad? You must not say such things to him."

"We have scanned the Recovery Vessel *Gourvich*," the cyber said. "It is an Oko-run ship under our jurisdiction. According to the latest file, Master Elge runs the *Gourvich*. He is a licensed salvage operator in Mark 108.212 Region. Did he attempt to salvage your ship in that star system?"

"He did."

"Presumably your ship appeared to be in derelict status, as an Oko of Master Elge's emotional profile would not attempt a privateering capture. Once his error became clear, he would have voluntarily left. That indicates you restrained him. In fact, you have admitted as much. By keeping his vessel, you are in violation of the Leviathan Salvage Code, 10-381."

"I have no quarrel with you or Leviathan," Maddox said smoothly. "We will gladly release the *Gourvich*. We ask for a small favor in return."

"Favors are meaningless, as the event occurred in Leviathan territory. Thus, it is just and right that you abide by Leviathan laws. Do you dispute that?"

"I do not," Maddox said.

"Then you will release the *Gourvich* this instant."

"Some of my people are aboard the vessel. I will need to retrieve them first—"

"The *Gourvich* will immediately head for our ships. Your compliance is mandated by the authority of Leviathan."

"Captain," Valerie whispered. "His fusion cannons are hot, ready to fire."

"Mon Zabul," Maddox said, "my ship is well protected and—"

Two red fusion beams from each Leviathan warship speared at Recovery Vessel *Gourvich*. The four beams struck the Oko vessel in four different hull locations. Three fusion beams punched through the ship's weak hull armor. The red beams played havoc inside the vessel, knocking down bulkheads, burning stores and killing Okos and space marines alike.

"No, no," Elge moaned. "My wives, my children—"

"My men," Maddox snarled. "Galyan—"

At that moment, explosions rent the *Gourvich* as the Oko recovery vessel splintered into several sections. The fusion beams continued to ray into the spreading, tumbling mass. More explosions caused even greater destruction, and various ship parts hurled in all directions as those parts disintegrated under the nuclear fury of the ignited fusion engines.

"Get ready," Andros Crank said from his station.

A few of the smaller pieces struck *Victory's* shield, which held under the impact.

At that point, the *Gourvich* as a ship was gone, other spinning and tumbling pieces testament to its former existence.

"You destroyed it," Maddox said, dismayed. It had happened so fast. Worse, he'd sentenced many of his space marines to death by sending them to the *Gourvich*. Rage began bubbling in him.

Master Elge swayed back and forth, keening to himself at his terrible loss. "I told you, I told you," he said.

"Now, Captain Maddox," the cyber said. "As an emissary from your region of space, you will lower your shield and take your weapons offline. As soon as you comply, I will send shuttles to your warship so Soldiers can confirm your status. After that, we shall discuss your fate."

The rage in Maddox made it hard to think.

"You have two seconds to comply, Captain," the cyber said. "If you do not—"

"No," Maddox said, struggling to contain his anger. "You're right. We're lowering our shield."

"Sir," Valerie hissed.

Maddox waved her silent. Then, blank-faced, he regarded the cyber. "How do I know you won't fire once we lower our shield?"

"I am a Soldier of Leviathan," Mon Zabul said. "I now give you my word. I will not fire until we determine your status, and only then if there is need."

Maddox glanced back at Elge. The Oko was weeping and keening, still swaying back and forth.

"We can't drop our shields, sir," Valerie said.

"Thank you for your input, Lieutenant," Maddox said icily.

"Sir," Valerie said, "Elge warned us against the Soldiers. They used stealth missiles against us, and we just witnessed an unprovoked assault against a defenseless vessel. Trusting these cybers now is madness."

"I hear bickering in your crew," Mon Zabul said. "Do you run your alien vessel or not, Captain Maddox?"

The captain stared at the cyber. "I run this ship."

"Then prove it, and lower your shield as instructed."

Maddox blinked in astonishment at such primitive psychology. "Before I lower my shield," he said slowly, trying to speak normally, "I request that you power down your fusion cannons."

"Are you saying that you do not trust the word of a Leviathan Supreme Soldier?"

"Trust but verify is an ancient proverb in my world," Maddox said. "I am bound by custom in this."

"That is an insult to Leviathan, and I will not—"

"Fire," Maddox said softly to Galyan. "Fire both cannons at that bastard."

-51-

The highly effective shield the cyber's warship possessed surprised Maddox.

The disrupter and neutron beams struck the enemy's electromagnetic shield. The areas hit turned red and then brown, and then slowly darkened toward black. But they held.

At the same time, returning fusion beams struck *Victory's* shield. Each Leviathan warship had three such cannons. Six beams altogether struck the starship's shield. However, the six beams did not all strike the same spot, but various locations on *Victory's* shield.

"Their attack pattern is odd," Ludendorff said.

"Agreed," Andros said. "It implies we can collapse their shield through a saturation attack, as that's what they're attempting to do against us. Their shields are of a different nature from ours."

"Lieutenant Noonan," Maddox said, "launch two antimatter missiles and four decoys with each. Target one group at each warship."

"Yes, sir," Valerie said, as her fingers blurred over her panel.

The fight continued, *Victory* hitting the forward-most warship and the two Leviathan vessels pouring fusion-beam rays into the shield. The three vessels matched each other in size, *Victory* having the approximate mass of the two battleships.

"They're retargeting their fusion cannons," Valerie said. "I don't think they like our missiles."

"Galyan," Maddox said. "I want you to concentrate on finding enemy stealth missiles. The Soldiers seem to prefer deceptive tactics. They must have launched more of them from somewhere."

"I am scanning, sir," Galyan said.

"There goes one of the decoys," Valerie said.

A flash appeared on the main screen.

"And another," she said.

"Your board is signaling you," a tech told Valerie. She tapped a panel to her left.

"Sir," Valerie said. "The cyber is hailing us."

Another flash appeared on the main screen, a fusion beam destroying yet another decoy.

"Put him back on," Maddox said, "but give me a split-screen."

One half of the split-screen was the Leviathan cyber, while the other half showed the continuing battle.

"You have a good shield," Mon Zabul said. "What is that yellow beam?"

"Do you surrender?" Maddox asked.

The cyber's plastic eyes seemed to glow hot. "A Soldier of Leviathan never surrenders. It is an insult you should ask such a thing."

"I'm a traveler to this region. I don't know your mores, remember?"

"Master Elge is on your bridge. That infers you knew all about us. Saying otherwise suggests that you are a liar."

A huge explosion and partial whiteout showed that the cybers had destroyed an antimatter missile.

The nearness of the explosion disrupted communications, as a blizzard appeared on the main screen, causing Mon Zabul to disappear. The fusion beams from the second warship stopped hitting *Victory's* shield as the whiteout temporarily disordered the rays.

As that happened, the disrupter and neutron beams darkened Mon Zabul's shield. It was seconds from collapsing.

The cyber reappeared on one-half of the screen.

"Let us negotiate," Mon Zabul said. "What would you give as tribute for us to cease firing?"

Maddox stared at the cyber in disbelief.

"You must hurry," Mon Zabul said. "The time for negotiating is nearing its end. If you destroy my ship, you will have declared war against the Sovereign Hierarchy of Leviathan. We will never cease hunting you in that case."

"Nice bluff," Ludendorff muttered. "He's a lot like you, Captain."

Maddox turned to the professor. "What if he's not bluffing, though? Do we want to start an eternal war with Leviathan?"

"Bah," Ludendorff said. "Finish him. He's a tyrant. Look how he destroyed the *Gourvich*. Your men died on it, Captain."

"I will warn you for the last time," Mon Zabul said. "I am offering you a way out. Give me the secret to your yellow beam and I shall allow you to leave the Caval System."

"On one condition," Maddox said. "We want to see the Builder nexus. We want to go inside it."

The cyber become motionless. "Did Master Elge tell you about the ancient pyramid? He must have done so. I will log a report and we shall annihilate all the Okos everywhere for his sacrilege."

"Are you insane?" Maddox said.

"The Soldiers of Leviathan are the symbol of pure sanity," Mon Zabul said. "Even now, we are recording the battle. We shall learn from it. Nevertheless, the Okos will cease as a species. They have earned their fate."

"You won't let us onto the nexus?" Maddox asked.

"Your repeated insults demand a jihad against your society," Mon Zabul said. "The Builders are sacrosanct. They are the gift-givers, the creators of Leviathan. How dare you speak such filth to me? It must be your odd nature that has corrupted your mind. We are the Soldiers of Leviathan, the most perfect union of machine and flesh the universe has witnessed. We serve the memory of the Builders and await their return."

"Batrun!" Ludendorff said. "Maybe that's how we can use him."

Baffled, Maddox stared at the professor.

"Let Batrun pass himself off as a Builder. We can deal with the Soldiers—"

It was too late for such deceptions. The cyber's shield finally collapsed, having lasted longer than expected. The neutron and disrupter beams struck a point against the iridium-Z hull armor. The substance began to melt as the two beams relentlessly bored inward.

"You are vile creatures," Mon Zabul declared. "It is my great honor to have discovered such miscreants as you. I will not have died in vain, but have shown Leviathan the scum that exists elsewhere. Yes, you desire to profane our sacred nexuses. Know that your end is assured."

The disrupter beam punched through the weakened point of iridium-Z armor and began ranging within the alien battleship.

At that point, the antimatter missile arrived as the warhead ignited.

As the first whiteout dissipated, a second expanded into existence. This one hid the awful damage and destruction to the first Leviathan battleship. Spinning pieces of hull armor flew through the whiteout, showing that the vessel must have exploded into separate parts.

"War is declared," Galyan said.

"What?" asked Maddox.

"Did you not hear him, sir? He said his destruction means—"

"Enough," Maddox said. "I heard him. I hope he was bluffing."

"I was analyzing Mon Zabul as he pontificated," Galyan said. "I give it a mere nineteen percent probability that he was bluffing. Thus, we have more likely begun war against the Sovereign Hierarchy of Leviathan."

"I hope you're wrong, Galyan."

"I do too, sir—even if that will lower my overall record as a prognosticator."

"Sir," Valerie said. "The cyber in charge of the second warship is hailing us."

"Ignore him," Maddox said, as his features hardened. He recalled his dead marines. "The cybers are insane. We're destroying that ship, too, and then we're going to hunt for a nexus so we can go home."

-52-

They found a nexus in the fourth debris cloud. That was three days after the destruction of the alien battleships.

The fourth debris cloud had more than just a nexus slowly spinning inside it. The cloud also possessed a base and thirteen Leviathan attack craft.

The attack craft were twice the size of a tin can and carried a rail-gun on their long undercarriages. Each of them charged at *Victory* from behind chunks of debris. Despite their iridium-Z hull armor, each of them blew up spectacularly thanks to the disrupter cannon.

The base held Soldiers. They departed the station en masse, each of them wearing a heavy thruster pack. Maddox did not negotiate or show mercy, but used the neutron cannon until no more space-suited Soldiers remained.

After that, he fired an antimatter missile and destroyed the cyber base.

"We should have landed and studied their facilities," Ludendorff said later.

"No," Elge said in the same dispirited tone he'd used after the *Gourvich's* destruction. "The Soldiers would have booby-trapped the base. Whoever you had sent would have died."

"Do you think there are more Soldiers hiding in the asteroid belt?" Maddox asked.

"Of course," Elge said. "They have declared jihad against you and us. The Okos are doomed."

Maddox pondered that, and finally made Elge an offer. "I'll give you a portal-capable shuttle. It won't travel too many light-years, but it might be enough for you to find other Okos."

"Why would you do this?" Elge asked.

"So you can warn your people about the jihad."

"I can also warn them about you!"

"You can," Maddox said. "It's the one point that causes me to wonder if I should just shoot you. In the end, I decided I'd want someone to warn my people. There is an old…law in our society. 'Do unto others as you would have them do to you.'"

Elge worked that over in his mind. "What a strange, quaint law. We believe that you should do unto others before they can do unto you."

"That's how most beings think," Maddox said. "The one who gave us the law was a great teacher."

"An Earthling?" asked Elge.

"That's what some people said he was."

"What do you think?"

Maddox stared at the furry Oko. "I think he was God in the flesh."

"The Creator?" asked Elge.

"You could call him that, too."

"And that is why you're letting me go?"

"Pretty much," Maddox said. "Good luck, Master Elge. I'm truly sorry about your ship, your wives, friends and children. It was a terrible loss. Maybe if we Earthlings make it back out here someday, we can try to make it up to you."

"You are causing the jihad against us. It was your fault."

"Master Elge," Maddox said. "In my estimation, the Soldiers of Leviathan are insane. Sooner or later, they were going to attack the Okos."

"I would rather it would have been later."

"Me, too," Maddox said. "Go warn your people. And if you want my advice, the Okos should flee far from Leviathan."

The little alien studied Maddox. "Will you give me the mechanical man as a bonus?"

"Do you still want him?"

Elge looked away. "No. I was going to trade him to Leviathan. Now…now it is too late. I will never willingly help

Leviathan. Perhaps if you return someday, you will come in strength. Then, if the Okos still live, you can help us."

"*If* we ever return," Maddox said. "That could be a big 'if'."

"You are not like Leviathan, and you are not like the Okos. You are a strange mixture of guile and honesty, cunning and courage. I do not understand you, Captain Maddox."

"The computer aboard your shuttle contains data of the battle, including the unprovoked attack against the *Gourvich.*"

"If the others believe me, I will be an outcast, for they will undoubtedly blame me for what has happened."

"Life happened, Master Elge. Life is often unpredictable and brutal. Save your people, if you can."

"Are you salvaging your conscience by giving me the shuttle? Is that what this is?"

"Good luck, Master Elge. Go in peace and go with God. It's the best I can give you now."

Shortly thereafter, Elge left in a Star Watch shuttle, one that had been carefully combed so there were no antimatter engine specs or other military software or hardware that the Soldiers could use if they captured the craft.

Elge exited the debris cloud and headed for a distant Laumer Point.

Meanwhile, *Victory* moved toward the Builder nexus…

-53-

The nexus—the Builder pyramid—was like all its kind in the Sagittarius and Orion Spiral Arms. Were all the Builders alike in their thinking and customs?

Maddox held a conference meeting. It had been some time since he had. They had critical decisions to make before they attempted the great leap home.

Besides the captain, there was Ludendorff, Galyan, Andros, Riker, Meta and Valerie. Keith was absent, as he was holding down the bridge.

"Heading into a nexus has almost always proven dangerous," Maddox began. "There have often been traps. The Soldiers of Leviathan guarded this nexus. It appears the Builders or Builder advocates—such as Scutum-Centaurus Methuselah Men—provided the Soldiers with some of their technology. That—"

"Just a minute, Captain," Ludendorff said, interrupting. "Builders didn't grant the Swarm high technology."

"Is that true?" Valerie asked. "Didn't the Builder in the Dyson Sphere give Commander Thrax high technology? That's what allowed the Imperium to invade Human Space."

"I was there," Ludendorff said. "Of course, the Builder did that. We're not talking about the recent incident, though. For uncounted centuries, maybe longer than that, the Builders did not help the Swarm but actually worked against them."

"What's your point?" Maddox asked.

Ludendorff said, "The Builders did not aid humanity—"

"They helped the Adoks against the Swarm," Galyan said, interrupting. "If you will remember, *I* was there."

"Right," Maddox said. "Maybe that's what the Builders did here. Maybe Builders aided the Soldiers long ago—"

"How is any of this germane to our problem?" Ludendorff asked. "We need to enter the nexus, set the coordinates for home—"

"Aren't you forgetting something?" Valerie asked, cutting in. "We need to find another nexus midway between here and home. Can you do that?"

"It would help if I had the Builder stone from last voyage," Ludendorff said. "But yes, I can do it."

"Then we'll use a hyper-spatial tube," Valerie said, "reaching the next nexus. After that, we make another hyper-spatial jump to arrive home."

Maddox drummed his fingers on the conference table.

"Is something wrong, sir?" Galyan asked.

"It is. I keep thinking about the iridium-Z armor and fusion cannons. While I agree that the Leviathan scientists could have independently developed those items, it seems more likely that they were Builder-derived."

"Why does that matter, my boy?" Ludendorff asked.

"I'm not sure," Maddox admitted. "Something hidden is bouncing in my subconscious."

Galyan studied the captain as his holographic eyelids fluttered. "Ah," the AI said. "I believe I know what is troubling you. I have studied your psychology in detail, sir. It is most fascinating, to say the least. I just ran an analysis of what could be—"

"That's enough, Galyan," the captain said, interrupting. "I don't need Adok psychoanalysis."

"But, sir—" Galyan said.

"No more," Maddox said, cutting the holoimage off.

A moment of silence lengthened until a few people began to shift uncomfortably.

"Can Galyan's suggestion do any real harm, sir?" Valerie finally asked. "He has proven uncannily accurate at times."

Maddox stared fixedly at the lieutenant until Meta took hold of his left arm, massaging it with her fingers. The captain glanced at his wife.

Meta smiled at him.

Maddox looked away and finally sighed. "Make your point, Galyan, but do it fast."

"Thank you, sir," Galyan said. "I predict that you will not regret this."

"I'm already regretting it," Maddox said.

Galyan stopped and looked around. "Ah," the holoimage said. "A joke. I am seventy-three percent certain that you just made a joke, sir. That would imply—"

"Galyan," Maddox said. "Get to it, eh?"

"Yes, sir," Galyan said. "During these last few days, I have been correlating several interesting factors. Until quite recently in galactic history, the Builders hampered the Swarm, although they did not altogether stop them by committing genocide. The Builder in the Dyson Sphere was different from his brethren in that he still attempted Builder functions when the race as a whole had retired into hiding. Another difference was his aid to the Imperium. Therefore, I think we can conclude that he does not nor did not conform to Builder norms."

"You're being long-winded," Maddox said.

"An idiom meaning speaking for extended periods," Galyan said. "I do not see how that can be the case, since I have hardly started to explain."

Maddox opened his mouth—Meta put a hand on one of his arms. The captain closed his mouth, nodding for Galyan to continue.

"Builder norms would seem to indicate a marked preference for mechanical life—to use another idiom. In this instance, I mean sentient beings. I would classify myself in this group along with androids, synthetics, cybers such as the Soldiers and maybe even the Methuselah Men."

"I'm no cyber," Ludendorff said hotly.

"Not precisely," Galyan said. "You have been Builder modified, however."

"I do not fit your category in the least," Ludendorff said.

"I am not altogether convinced of that," Galyan said. "Once, I was strictly biological. Now, I am an amalgamation of computer and—"

"No!" Ludendorff said. "I dispute your claim—"

"Professor," Maddox said sternly.

Everyone stopped speaking.

Maddox nodded. "Galyan, leave the professor and Methuselah Men out of this. Ludendorff is a separate category. But go ahead and make your greater point."

"Thank you, sir," Galyan said. "Notice that Builders often mechanized themselves. Some of the Builders we've met were themselves androids. Consider the Builder cube that used bio-flesh and a deatomizer to reconstruct itself. Consider the Yen Cho android that aided the Builder cube. Why, Batrun—"

Galyan quit speaking.

"What's wrong, Galyan?" Valerie asked.

The holoimage had frozen, with only his eyelids flickering. Abruptly, Galyan turned to the captain.

"Batrun, sir," the holoimage said. "Batrun may be something other than what he claimed to be."

"Are you saying he's a Builder?" Ludendorff scoffed.

"By physiology alone," Galyan said, "he is obviously not a Builder. Nor have I detected a Builder cube or Builder DNA samples in him."

"Fine, fine," Ludendorff said. "What is Batrun then?"

"He is not an android," Galyan said, "not in the sense of the Rull or Yen Cho androids. By his own admission, he is something different. Notice, too, that the Rull androids we encountered had shed their pseudo-skin and clothes. They had done this even though a synthetic representative had been among them."

"So?" Maddox asked.

"Maybe the Rull captain practiced deception on us," Galyan said. "Maybe the synthetic was the very reason the Rull androids changed course. Why did *Victory* leap ten thousand light-years to arrive in the Sovereign Hierarchy of Leviathan? Was that a chance occurrence or was it premeditated?"

"A wonderful question," Ludendorff said sarcastically. "Now tell us, Galyan. How did Batrun cause the starship to make the ten-thousand light-year leap? He was unconscious at the time, remember?"

Everyone at the conference table stared at Professor Ludendorff.

"Wait, wait, wait," the professor said. He glanced at everyone in turn. "Are you accusing *me* of doing this? While I am a brilliant scientist and the most advanced person here, I have my limitations. If I could cause a starship to leap ten thousand light-years, don't you think I'd have done it before this?"

"The coincidence that we simply appeared here is too improbable," Galyan said. "By what I have witnessed and analyzed, I believe that warships of Leviathan were to use the hyper-spatial tube in two successive leaps to join the Juggernauts in their assault upon the Solar System."

"That's not only a preposterous statement," Ludendorff said. "It's lunacy. What happened to your circuits, Galyan? And supposing I'm in league with androids and cybers, why didn't I have Juggernauts make the ten thousand light-year journey with us so chrome-plated Rull androids could put the proposition to the cyber Soldiers themselves? Why have *Victory* do all this?"

"Since you pose the question…" Galyan said. "I can only conclude that *Victory* is the only starship able to make such a leap. Since the Rull were not going to capture *Victory*—"

At that point, Galyan cried out in dismay.

Maddox jumped up.

"Help me," Galyan said. Even as the holoimage spoke, he began folding inward on himself. The holoimage crumbled up like tinfoil and then vanished in a flash of light.

"What just happened?" Riker shouted, jumping up as he drew his stunner.

The hatch opened and Batrun stepped within. Behind him were two thin and unnaturally tall cybers. All three of them held blasters, although Batrun also held a clicker in his other hand.

"What a clever AI," the synthetic said. He pointed the clicker at Ludendorff and pressed a button.

The professor collapsed forward onto the conference table.

"Ah, ah, ah," Batrun said, pointing the blaster at Maddox. "Lift your weapon a centimeter higher, and you are a dead man, Captain. Then, I shall kill your wife, too."

Maddox let his blaster drop so it clunked on the floor. "This doesn't make any sense," he said.

"Sit down and I shall explain," Batrun said.

Maddox sat.

"Good," the synthetic said. "I am relieving you of command, Captain, and taking it myself. You almost had me before. This time, I won't make the same mistake."

-54-

Galyan as a holoimage had vanished from the conference room. Yet Galyan as an artificial intelligence with the engrams of the last Adok Driving Force was still very much in operation.

His essence was locked deep in the Adok-Builder-Human computer combination that made up his being. It surprised Galyan to find his consciousness deep inside the computer. He replayed the event that had caused—

"Oh," he said to himself. "Batrun is on. Batrun…"

Galyan began an intense analysis of the situation. What could have happened to allow all this to occur?

The obvious conclusion was the neural-shifter Ludendorff had extracted from the android. The android impersonating a Star Watch marine back in the Solar System. The professor had used the neural shifter to correct the altered mind patterns in Maddox's brain. After that, they should have destroyed the neural-shifter.

There was an eighty-two percent probability that Batrun had modified the professor with the neural-shifter. It was also likely that the synthetic had moved cautiously after that because he feared Driving Force Galyan.

Yet, how could Batrun or the professor have modified the star-drive jump to perform how it had? That implied incredible technological knowledge that none of them possessed. What made sense then?

Galyan ran through many analyses and simulations. Finally, he reached a conclusion. It startled him to such a degree that he recalibrated and ran through the analyses and simulations a second time.

"This can't be right," Galyan said.

Still, nothing else made sense. That he had knocked Batrun out the first time might have been something of a miracle. Could he achieve a second miracle?

Galyan gave himself a nineteen percent probability of succeeding again using the same tactic. Nineteen percent was too low, however. How then could he save his friends from the synthetic's treachery?

He had to intervene now, or it would be too late. Batrun wasn't going to give anyone a second chance, especially not with two cyber agents to help him.

That meant he had to do something this instant.

"What *can* I do?" Galyan asked himself.

The AI knew he could not reform as a holoimage right away. His holoimage processors had burned out. How could Batrun have done that?

"I am right about the synthetic," Galyan said.

Like the captain—maybe because of the captain—Galyan had been studying poker theory. He found it an interesting study. One tenet of poker strategy revolved about how an inferior player should proceed against a superior player.

Clearly, over time, the superior player would take all the inferior player's money. That meant the inferior player could not give the superior player that time.

Poker was a game of variance. That variance could often be quite large in the short term. Thus, to win, the inferior player had to remain in the short term. Short term in poker meant luck. Skill in poker was a long-term strategy where the incrementally better odds of the better player would destroy the inferior player's bankroll.

The best strategy for an inferior player was to play ultra-aggressively against the superior player in the short term. In 'No Limit' poker, that meant going all-in almost all of the time.

How could Galyan go all-in now against Batrun and the two cybers?

A quick analysis of the situation told Galyan he could not go all-in. Instead, he would have to alter the situation and hope the captain and the others could derive a greater benefit from the change than the synthetic and cybers could.

"I hope you win, sir," Galyan said, "because here goes nothing…"

-55-

Sergeant Riker kept silently reproving himself for listening to the captain.

Maddox had shouted at him to drop the stunner. He must have seen that Riker was a millisecond away from firing. Of course, he would not have attempted to use the stunner on Batrun. That would have been foolish. He would have used it on the cybers, hoping the flesh part of their being would have been susceptible to stunner shots.

It was more than probable that the captain had been correct, and the stunner would have had no effect. But to simply go down without a whimper went against his grain. Did the captain know something that he didn't?

What a fine mess. Ludendorff had once again proven to be a foul traitor. The captain was in his seat, listening to the synthetic gloat about his superior capabilities. The two cybers watched impassively. Valerie fumed quietly. Meta sat utterly still. Andros stared at his hands, and he, Sergeant Riker of Star Watch Intelligence, sat with his shoulders slumped pretending dejection and bitter defeat.

Riker hoped the captain had something up his sleeve. If more cybers boarded *Victory*, it would be all over for them. He still couldn't believe that Batrun had fixed the game from the beginning. Why had it taken the synthetic so long to come out of hiding?

Maybe the larger question was how had the deactivated synthetic come up for air? Ludendorff would be the obvious answer. If they hadn't needed the old boy so often, they should have shot the Methuselah Man a long time ago.

What about Galyan? That had been—

Riker worked diligently to keep his expression neutral. That was the ace in the hole. Maddox must be expecting Galyan to do something. Yet, the holoimage had winked out. How had the synthetic done—

Suddenly, gravity left *Victory*. That meant someone must have turned off the grav-plates. Not only that, but the starship must have begun violent maneuvering, because Batrun and the two cybers flew upward toward the ceiling.

Everyone sitting at the table might have flown up with the three, but everyone else—well, not the professor, he was unconscious—grabbed the edge of the table. Meta also grabbed Ludendorff, possibly saving his life.

The stunner and the captain's blaster lifted off the deck plates. Maddox caught his weapon—Riker grabbed uselessly at his weapon as it flew past him.

Batrun was shouting something. The cybers twisted as they tried to align their blasters.

A harsh humming sound preceded Maddox's first blaster shot.

One cyber's head blew apart.

The second cyber fired his weapon, beaming the table, digging into it.

Maddox twisted in his seat. The enemy beam flashed between his legs, then he re-targeted—and missed the second cyber.

The cyber had leaped off the ceiling, heading down at Maddox.

Riker released the table and shot upward at the cyber coming down. At the same time, Batrun's blaster cut into his own cyber's left calf, burning it. The cyber must have accidentally floated into Batrun's line of fire.

Riker collided against the cyber. With a snarl, the thin cyber twisted around as the two of them tumbled toward a bulkhead. The cyber's hands grasped Riker's hips and began to squeeze with mechanical strength.

Riker howled with agony. Pushing through the pain, he used his bionic hand, latching onto the cyber's throat. Riker twisted and tore out the main throat section so blood, bone, flesh and metal ripped lose.

The cyber's hands lost power.

Riker clawed the creature's face, tearing if off with awful brutality. The sergeant felt fierce elation at the damage. Screw these bastards.

"Stop!" Batrun shouted.

Maddox did not stop, but sailed up toward the synthetic. In a display of superb marksmanship, Batrun burned the captain's blaster. Maddox shook off the melting weapon and snatched his hand away before the hot coolant burned off his flesh.

"You still lose, Captain," Batrun said, tracking the human sailing up to him. "I will crush your skull."

Maddox reached Batrun. The synthetic reached for his shoulder, no doubt to crush it. Maddox twisted away. Batrun sneered, likely thinking the captain was attempting to save his shoulder. No. The synthetic had guessed wrong. Maddox revealed his other hand, which held the monofilament blade, and shoved the blade into Batrun's face. The knife slid in smoothly, ripping leftward, sheering off half of the synthetic's humanlike features.

And that finished the job. Maddox destroyed Batrun's function by slicing the braincase in two and effectively killing the Builder-made machine then and there.

Maddox made sure, though. As he wound his legs around Batrun's torso, he hacked again and again, sheering thinner and thinner slices of the synthetic's head. In almost seemed as if the captain might have gone berserk.

"Maddox!" Meta shouted. "Maddox!"

The captain looked at her with a ferocious expression.

"You've won, darling," Meta said. "The synthetic is dead."

Maddox blinked, blinked again, and some of the awful tension left his body.

"Maddox?" Meta said.

"I'm here," he said, sounding winded.

"Hadn't we better figure out how the cybers got aboard the starship?"

"Yes," Maddox snapped. "We'd better."

-56-

How had the cybers boarded the starship? How had Batrun and the cybers moved through the vessel without anyone seeing them?

It wasn't making sense.

Maddox and the others were on the bridge as marines combed the corridors, engine rooms, hangar bays, cafeterias—every inch of the ship.

On the main screen, the pyramidal nexus slowly tumbled in the debris cloud. The clouds were thicker with sand and grit on the outer part as if they were deliberate skins. Inside, it wasn't quite so dense. Inside, however, no one could see the main star or starlight, making it dark within the debris cloud.

"I'm not seeing anything unusual out there," Valerie said from her station.

"Me either," Andros said as he tapped his science panel.

Maddox sat in the command chair, pondering. Ludendorff was unconscious in Medical. Every effort to revive him had failed, although the professor was still breathing normally. His brain activity had almost completely ceased. Ludendorff certainly wasn't dreaming in his present state.

Batrun had destroyed the unit that had caused Ludendorff to fall unconscious and Galyan to disappear, so they couldn't use the unit to revive Ludendorff.

According to the latest report, Galyan's holoimage processors had burned down into a slagheap. It would be wise to get that fixed or rebuilt as fast as possible.

"Chief Technician," Maddox said. "I want you to get your best tech team and rebuild the holoimage processors. I want Galyan up and running. We need him."

"Thank you, Captain," Galyan said from a bridge loudspeaker. "I am still linked to the ship's sensors and can report as needed."

It felt weird hearing Galyan but not seeing him. It made the AI feel like a ghost.

"You haven't spotted any stealth ships out there?" Maddox asked.

"Negative, sir," the disembodied Galyan replied.

"How are we going to use the nexus with the professor unconscious?" Valerie asked.

"Good question," Maddox said. "First, I want to pinpoint the cybers."

"Could the two have been survivors from the thruster-pack attackers?" Valerie asked.

"Unlikely," Maddox said, "but it's the most reasonable answer so far."

"How could Batrun cause our starship to jump ten thousand light-years?" Valerie asked. "That's something I'm just not understanding."

"I have no idea," Maddox admitted. "Galyan," he said, aiming his voice at a comm in the armrest. "Do you have any idea?"

"Not yet, sir," the AI said. "I deem it quite possible that any jump features he or Ludendorff made to cause the event were removed soon after our arrival here."

"Why *Victory?*" asked Valerie. "What makes this ship so unique?"

"Plenty of things," Maddox said. "What has me worried are the things Batrun told us earlier when were we still in Human Space. Did an Old One—a Yon-Soth—on the Forbidden Planet really send out mind waves that caused various groups to turn on Star Watch?"

"I might be able to answer that," Galyan said.

"Shoot," Maddox said.

"The more truth a lie contains, usually the stronger or more believable the lie," Galyan said. "I believe the doomed Yon-

Soth modified the synthetics for the very reasons Batrun gave. The synthetics are clever and can likely run a united attack against the Commonwealth better than individuals could on a random basis, those motivated by the Yon-Soth's mind waves."

"That's convoluted," Maddox said, "but it makes sense. I wonder why Batrun wanted to bring Leviathan warships to Human Space."

"Do you truly want me to answer that, sir?" Galyan asked. "Star Watch is powerful and has proven on many occasions to be a stubborn opponent. The Rull androids likely need or needed backup to succeed with the plan. There is one consolation to this theory. If Batrun believed the Rull androids needed allies, then likely the Jotuns are a bluff. Why otherwise go to such extreme and risky lengths to obtain Leviathan help?"

"Good point," Maddox said. "So what does all that imply about the hauler hiding inside Jupiter?"

"That it either possesses Jotun technology or advanced technology that Lisa Meyers has attempted to pass off as Jotun science."

"Who is Lisa Meyers really?"

"Unknown," Galyan said. "Despite all my analyses, she is a mystery."

"We have to get home," Maddox said. "We have to revive the professor so he can program the nexus—"

"Sir," Galyan said, interrupting. "If you recall, Dana and I have programmed a nexus hyper-spatial tube before."

"Dana's not here."

"True," Galyan said. "But with help, I can figure out and use the nexus controls."

"Can you find another nexus five thousand light-years from here?"

"The answer will be in trying," Galyan said.

"Right," Maddox said. "We have to get your holoimage processors fixed as fast as possible."

"Captain," Valerie said. "I've picked up a strange reading. It's coming from a probe. We launched earlier—"

"Get on with it, Lieutenant," Maddox said.

Valerie nodded. "The reading is unlike anything I've seen before. It indicates a faint... Well, I'd almost call it a magnetic anomaly. But when I check this on thermal and visual scanners, I don't detect anything."

"Are you reading that, Galyan?" Maddox asked.

"Valerie is correct, sir," Galyan said. "But instead of a magnetic anomaly, I would call this an antimagnetic disturbance."

"What?" Maddox said.

"A polarity reversal—" Galyan said.

"Never mind," Maddox said. "How far away is this...anomaly?"

"A little over twelve million kilometers from us, sir," Valerie said. "It's at the inner edge of the Asteroid Belt."

"Is Elge's shuttle still in the star system?" Maddox asked.

Valerie tapped her panel, checking. "Yes, sir," she said.

Maddox frowned thoughtfully. "Could the antimagnetic disturbance be the location of a Leviathan stealth ship?"

"If it is," Valerie said, "the cloaked vessel will see Elge's vessel as plain as day."

"Mr. Maker," Maddox said, "prepare to leave the debris cloud. Galyan, get the disrupter cannon ready."

"I doubt the disturbance is a stealth ship," Galyan said. "The signature is all wrong for that."

"We have no idea how cybers boarded the starship," Maddox said. "This anomaly is the only thing out of order. That means it's the best answer we have so far concerning the two mystery cybers."

"Could the antimagnetic disturbance be a lure?" Galyan asked. "Are hidden cybers attempting to draw us away from the nexus?"

"We're about to find out," Maddox said.

-57-

Victory burst out of the debris cloud with its shield keeping any sand or grit from striking the outer hull. The starship accelerated even faster as it built up velocity, heading for the antimagnetic anomaly.

"The disrupter cannon is ready, sir," Galyan said from a bridge speaker.

"Target the anomaly," Maddox said.

"I cannot fathom this," Galyan said. "The anomaly has moved, is moving. Why, it is building up velocity, heading away from us. The anomaly is presently out of disrupter range."

"It's a stealth ship then," Maddox said, as he leaned forward. "Leviathan appears to have degrees of stealth vessels. This one is better than the stealth missiles. I suggest this means we're dealing with a higher-ranking officer of Leviathan."

"That does not necessarily have to be true," Galyan said. "That is a human way of thinking, but Leviathan would not have to operate on similar thought patterns—"

"Captain," Valerie said, interrupting, "someone is hailing us."

"Is it coming from the anomaly?" Maddox asked.

"It is," Valerie said.

"Most odd, most odd," Galyan said from the bridge speaker.

"Captain Maddox," a scratchy voice said. "Are you receiving my signal?"

"Put him on visual," Maddox said.

Valerie shook her head. "He's blocking any visual signals, just giving us audio."

Maddox hesitated before saying, "This is Captain Maddox of Starship *Victory*. Unless I can see who I'm talking to, I will fire at you."

"That is a primitive response," the scratchy voice said.

"There you go," Maddox said. "What a perfect deduction on your part, as I am a primitive."

"You delight in the slur?"

"I positively revel in it," Maddox replied.

"Strange..." the scratchy voice said. "You are strange, primitive as you insist and of a bloodthirsty nature."

"No more than Leviathan," Maddox said.

The scratchy-voiced being chuckled. "You are attempting to prompt me, interesting, interesting. You are not so primitive after all, but full of guile. I assume you practiced such guile in thwarting Batrun. I had given that a low probability, especially as I had granted him reinforcements as he requested."

"Do you mean the two cybers I shot?" Maddox asked.

"A poor reaction to the cybers, I assure you. You could have learned so much from them if you had kept them alive. Thank you, Captain, for destroying them. It saves me many sleepless nights."

"Who are you?" Maddox asked.

"I could show you, but then I would have to kill you. Do you truly desire to know then?"

"Sir," Galyan said. "I have analyzed the voice patterns. The scratchy nature of his speech is a disguise. Valerie, if you would switch to the X3 bandwidth, I believe I can give you a visual."

Valerie tapped her comm panel.

The main screen wavered, turned blizzard-like, wavered once more until a cyber with silver eye-sockets and black plastic orbs with red glowing centers peered at them."

"What's your name, cyber?" Maddox asked.

The thin-faced sentient did not frown or make any other facial gesture.

"Impressive," the alien said, as he checked something they couldn't see, a sensor board perhaps. "I am not a cyber, however, not as you mean it. Mon Zabul was a lower-ranked Soldier. I am not a Soldier at all, but a Strategist. I have observed the proceedings and have found you humans clever and surprising resourceful. Batrun urged me to join the crusade against your kind. He promised new technology and a joint effort to build a grand union, perhaps hoping we would agree to elevate each other into near-Builder status."

"What does that even mean?" Maddox asked.

"You wouldn't understand."

"I know," Galyan said. "He is speaking about guided evolution, which is not evolution at all, but advanced…genetics is the wrong word. Eugenics might be more accurate, but he means something like what the Builder cube once attempted, but not so direct."

"Apotheosis might be an even better term," the cyber said.

"Galyan?" asked Maddox. "What's that mean?"

"Apotheosis is the elevation to divine status," Galyan said. "Perhaps an example will help you understand. Let me see. Ah. In the Garden of Eden, the Serpent urged Eve to eat from the Tree of Knowledge so she could be like God. The Serpent offered her apotheosis, to become godlike."

"Batrun wanted to become a god?" asked Maddox.

"In his frame of reference, like a Builder," Galyan suggested.

"That is accurate," the cyber said. "I had sensed such unwarranted mania in Batrun. Nevertheless, I sent him two helpers, the military cybers you saw with him. I am frankly surprised you survived the encounter, Captain."

"Who are you again?" Maddox asked.

"I am a Strategist of Leviathan. I have observed the proceedings. I have decided against Mon Zabul's decree of genocide against the Okos. The scavengers serve a useful function. I note the shuttle and the Oko piloting it. I do not understand why you let Master Elge go, Captain."

"Is that why we're talking?" Maddox guessed.

"In fact, it is. I am curious. Why did you let him go?"

"What can you…pay us in return for the knowledge?"

"I will pay you in like coin, Captain, knowledge for knowledge. What do you wish to know?"

"How did you slip the two cybers onto my ship?"

"Through teleportation," the cyber said. "Why did you let Master Elge depart?"

"So he could warn his fellow Okos about the coming jihad."

"I was right," the cyber said. "Yet, I could not conceive why you did this—given your previous actions."

"Did Batrun cause my starship to travel ten thousand light-years to reach here?"

"I have no more time for you, Captain," the cyber said. "I have my answer. You may leave. I imagine you shall want to use the nexus to create a hyper-spatial tube."

"You won't interfere with us?" Maddox asked.

"I am a Strategist, not a Soldier. However, you should leave while you can, Captain. Even now, reinforcements hurry to the Caval System. I warn you because it is not yet time for Leviathan to devour humanity. Batrun—it was an intriguing offer. But Leviathan has enough on its plate for now if Batrun and his Rull androids are too weak to destroy you on their own."

"Batrun controlled the Rull androids?"

"You are clever and courageous in some areas, but almost hopelessly retarded in others," the cyber said. "It is a wonder the human race has survived this long. Go, Captain, as your time to do so is almost gone."

Maddox clicked a switch, shutting off the comm and screen. He scowled, hesitating to give the order he desired to make.

"Let's fire," Keith said. "Let's finish the braggart."

"Should I fire, Captain?" Galyan asked from the bridge speaker.

Was the Strategist telling the truth about the Okos, or was this yet another deceptive ploy.

"I could run an analysis on his truthfulness," Galyan said, perhaps guessing Maddox's unease.

"No!" Maddox said. "Mr. Maker, turn us around. Head back into the debris cloud."

"We're not going to finish him?" Valerie asked. "Maybe he's hoping to learn something about the nexus by watching us."

"If he can teleport cybers onto the starship…" Maddox said, shaking his head. "He could have easily figured out how to use the nexus."

"He could be bluffing about the teleportation," Valerie said.

"He could be," Maddox agreed, "but it's the only answer so far as to how the cybers managed to get aboard without our knowing."

"If he has teleportation—" Galyan said.

"No more," Maddox said. "If the cybers were human like us, they would all use teleportation. But as you pointed out earlier, Galyan, this is a different race, species, call it what you will. They run things differently than we would. That's part of the nature of them being aliens. In any case, according to him, more Soldiers are coming. I want to be long gone before they get here."

-58-

Victory returned to the debris cloud as Andros Crank and his technicians worked overtime to build a new holoimage processor.

Meanwhile, medical personnel fussed over the unconscious Ludendorff. Nothing they had done so far had elicited any response from him.

Hours ticked into a day. More Soldiers were coming, and *Victory* had been unable to make the nexus form a hyperspatial tube. Their best minds were either gone or hidden in the computer.

"Physically, there's nothing in Ludendorff's brain that doesn't belong there," a doctor told Maddox. "As far as I can tell, no one inserted even so much as a microscopic device into his gray matter. I have no idea why we can't rouse him."

Another day passed, and Soldiers of Leviathan would almost certainly be in the Caval System by, when, tomorrow? Or the next day, or the one after that?

Maddox's New Man nature made it impossible for him to wait patiently. He used the ship's gym and deadlifted, squatted and did military presses. He punched a heavy bag until his hands ached. Of all the things, waiting for others to accomplish their task as the clock ticked to midnight was the worst.

Finally, the captain couldn't take it anymore. He had to try something to speed the process. He went to Medical and had several nurses wheel the restrained and unconscious professor to his science lab. The head doctor guided the others as they laid Ludendorff in his special brain scanner.

The short woman—the chief medical officer—shook her head later while examining Ludendorff's mind-pattern chart. "I don't know what I'm looking for," she admitted to Maddox.

The captain examined the chart. He didn't know either. But he wasn't going to accept that as a definitive answer.

"It's time to roll the dice," Maddox said.

Doctor Harris looked up at him with frightened eyes.

"We'll use the neural-shifter," Maddox told her. "Galyan can tell us how to hook it up. We'll use it on Ludendorff once we're ready."

"Who will use it?" Harris asked. "Certainly not me, as I have no idea what the neural-shifter does or how to do it."

"I'll do it," Maddox said.

"Do what, though?" Harris asked. "We can't just aim and fire."

"You're wrong," Maddox said. "That's exactly what we're going to do: aim it at his mind and shift neurons. Hopefully, that jars something loose and allows him to wake up."

"What if it causes permanent brain damage instead?"

"We're out of options," Maddox said. "That's what it means to roll the dice."

"He hates you enough as it is," Meta said, who had watched and listened. "Don't give him more reasons to hate you."

"No," Maddox said. "He's the reason we're in this mess. Therefore, he can accept the risk. I hope for the best, naturally, but I don't know what else to do."

Doctor Harris and Meta continued to try to dissuade Maddox, but he refused to listen.

An hour later, as Ludendorff lay on a medical cot in the science lab, Maddox stood behind the controls of the makeshift neural machine. Wires and clamps were attached to a machine Ludendorff had built that held the small thumbtack-shaped device, which was aimed at the professor's skull.

As Maddox stood behind the controls, he hesitated, hardly knowing what anything did. Finally, he tapped a switch. There was a momentary hum, and Maddox swore he saw the thumbtack-sized device quiver. A second later, Ludendorff twitched on the table, and then nothing.

"Dare we do more?" Meta asked, who watched anxiously from the side.

Maddox dragged a sleeve across his damp forehead. He didn't want to risk Ludendorff's wonderful mind. Tampering with a Methuselah Man seemed like a crime. Sure, Ludendorff had screwed them more times than he could remember. The old man had also helped them just as often.

"Let's leave it as this," Meta suggested.

"No," Maddox said. He tapped the control screen again.

This time, there was no hum. The professor jerked worse than before, however, and he groaned dismally.

Maddox stood indecisively at the controls. Maybe this was good. Another tap—

Meta jumped to the table, tore off the restraining straps and dragged Ludendorff off, carrying him to a couch. She laid the Methuselah Man on the couch and knelt beside him, stroking his forehead.

The professor groaned again.

"Can you hear me?" Meta asked quietly.

The Methuselah Man twitched but said nothing.

"You're on the starship," Meta said. "We need you, Professor. We're stranded, and we need your help to get away."

The professor made no more motion or noise.

Meta looked up at Maddox. The captain scowled at the neural hookup. If only one of them know what to do.

Inspiration shined on Meta's face. She leaned near Ludendorff. "Listen to me, Professor. Dana is in trouble. You have to help her. The only way you can is by fighting up from unconsciousness and fixing the situation. Dana's relying on you, as there is no one else than can help her."

The professor groaned, and he raised his left hand.

"Professor?" Meta asked.

"My head hurts," the Methuselah Man complained. "It pounds so I can hardly think."

"We had to recalibrate your mind," Meta said.

"What?" Ludendorff complained. "Are you mad? I have the most unique mind in the universe. Tampering with it is a sin of the first order."

"You may be right," Meta said, glancing at Maddox. The captain motioned her to keep talking. "But Dana's life in on the line," Meta said. "We had to do something."

"Do something how?" Ludendorff asked, with his eyes still screwed shut as if trying to stop even a vestige of light from reaching his optic nerves.

Maddox surged forward as he motioned Meta out of the way.

Reluctantly, she moved.

"Professor," Maddox said.

"No, no," Ludendorff said. "Is this your doing? This vile tampering must be your doing."

"You fell unconscious," Maddox said.

"That's preposterous. I am not... We were in the conference chamber, weren't we? Oh, no, what happened? Something terrible happened."

Maddox didn't know how much to tell the man.

"Fine," Ludendorff said in a resigned tone. "Tell me what happened. Give me the worst."

"I'm not sure that's a good idea."

"My head is aching, feeling as if it's about to explode. For some reason, I can't open my eyes or move my hands, arms or legs. Something is hindering me, and I must know what."

Maddox nodded to himself. If Ludendorff was going to fix himself, he had to know what the problem was. Therefore, as quickly and clinically as the captain could, he told the professor exactly what had happened.

Ludendorff did not interrupt. He made no comment at all.

Finally, Maddox asked, "Are you still awake, Professor?"

"I am," Ludendorff said in a dull voice. "I can't believe this. I betrayed everyone?"

"It's not that bad," Maddox said.

"No?" Ludendorff asked. "I want no sugarcoating, my boy. I want it straight. But never mind, you told me what happened. Batrun tricked me. What I don't understand, though, is how

I'm awake at all. If Batrun shut me off—and I think I know how he did that. I hesitate to ask how you woke me."

"I took a risk," Maddox admitted, and he explained just what he had done.

"You truly tampered with my brain, my fabulous mind?" Ludendorff asked in horrified disbelief. "This is too much, sir."

Maddox almost agreed aloud, but he felt Ludendorff would sink into depression or even suicidal anger if he did that. Thus—

"Was it too much?" Maddox asked in a dismissive tone. "I think the punishment rather fit the crime, don't you?"

Meta stared at the captain wide-eyed.

"You've always hated me," Ludendorff said. "You've always been jealous of my successes."

"I think the term you're looking for is *projection*," Maddox drawled. "As the truth is the other way around."

"How *dare* you say that at a time when I'm so utterly incapacitated?"

"Professor," Maddox said. "You have a decision to make. Are you going to wallow in despair because Dana left you or are you going to allow Batrun to subject you to his whims? Do you want to let him beat you? Do you want to admit his mind is more magnificent than yours?"

Ludendorff's lips thinned as his entire body became rigid.

"I see," Maddox said. "You do realize that Batrun was Strand's invention—"

"No," Ludendorff whispered. "Your childish psychology isn't going to work on me, sir. I am done with you. If I don't have fully functioning facilities—"

"I always knew you were weak," Maddox said, talking over the professor. "Dana leaving you was the last straw. Yes. Her leaving must have destroyed your self-image, thereby shattering your fragile ego."

"You're a fool," Ludendorff hissed. "I have the power to let you all die, and you insult me? I have the greatest human mind in existence. I will do nothing for your sake, you half-breed."

"Come, Meta," Maddox said. "I've grown weary of watching a quitter stew in his defeat."

"Can't take what you dish out, eh?" Ludendorff mocked. "You insult a crippled man—"

"Emotionally crippled only," Maddox said.

"The synthetics tampered with my *mind!*" Ludendorff raved. "My mind, my glorious mind that sees deeper and farther than any in Human Space. I am the ultimate Methuselah Man, and the damned androids and now an unthinking half-breed have altered the patterns to destroy what they cannot achieve or truly understand."

Maddox said nothing. Had he gone too far this time? But what else could he have done?

Ludendorff panted on the couch while his faced was screwed up with grief and pain. Tears leaked from his closed eyes and his lower lip trembled.

"Dana, Dana," he whispered. "How could you leave me?"

Meta moved beside Maddox, taking one of his arms. There were tears in her eyes as she watched the professor.

Ludendorff's lips firmed as he visibly fought for self-control. "I am Ludendorff," he whispered. "I am mankind's protector. I was given a solemn charge, and I will not wilt now." He scowled. "No half-breed will best me. No half-breed will destroy my mind."

Maddox was getting tired of the term half-breed. He was ready to try the ancient way of reviving a man, by slapping him repeatedly across the face.

"Are you there, Captain?" Ludendorff called out.

Maddox did not answer.

Meta jerked his left arm, the one she held.

"I'm here," Maddox said.

"You brought about this sorry state with your abominable tampering. Now, I will instruct you as you use the neural-shifter once again. You're going to repair the damage. If you fail, we all die, as no one else will be able to create a hyper-spatial tube."

Maddox almost told the professor that Galyan could do it in a pinch. Instead, he remained silent.

"Are you ready to fix what you broke?" Ludendorff demanded.

"Start talking," Maddox said.

"First, you and Meta must lay me on the lab table. Then, I'm going to give you exact instructions. If you cannot follow in every point just as I say…you will be responsible for ending our lives."

Maddox said nothing.

"Captain, are you ready?"

"Yes," Maddox said testily.

"Then we'd better begin before I lose consciousness a second time."

-59-

The process was grueling and time-consuming. Finally, however, Ludendorff said that should do it. He almost immediately fell asleep.

Maddox had medical people wheel the professor back to the med station so they could monitor him there.

"You took a risk in the lab," Meta told him after the others had left.

Maddox shrugged.

"And you didn't need to say all those cruel things to him," she added.

"Maybe not," Maddox said, "but it felt good saying them."

"Maddox!" Meta said.

He inhaled. What was wrong with him? It didn't bother him that he'd enjoyed pestering Ludendorff. It was the needlessness of it. He was supposed to be the Intelligence operative par excellence, and yet he'd been letting emotions govern his actions.

Was it possible the mind tampering performed by the android impersonating a marine hadn't been completely fixed?

Maddox pondered the idea. In all his former dealings, winning, defeating his foes, trumped everything else. To luxuriate in needless emotions *before* achieving victory was a waste of effort. Afterward it smacked of boasting, which he detested.

Maddox's eyes narrowed. He would act *his* way and no other. Even if the neural-shifter damage hadn't been completely repaired, he would be himself through force of will. Maybe Ludendorff and he were alike in that particular: "To thy own self be true."

The pettiness he'd been indulging in—

Maddox closed his eyes. Did the soul weakening have something to do with this? He wasn't as vigorous these days. No. That didn't matter. He would rein in the emotionalism and concentrate with laser-fixity on his purpose.

So, what was his purpose?

Brigadier O'Hara was languishing somewhere, and he had done precious little to restore her to service. The Rull androids had found an amazing Supermetals Planet and were using it for some hidden purpose. Lisa Meyers also had much to answer for. What did the technology in her hauler represent? Finally, there were the Batrun-like synthetics attempting something nefarious.

Should he take Batrun's explanation about the synthetics at face value? No. That would be foolish.

Opening his eyes, nodding goodbye to Meta, he whirled around and headed for the hatch. It was time to see Andros Crank. It wasn't *could they get away from here*. It was *we have to get away* now, *and I'm going to make it happen*.

***

Andros and his tech-team had not yet reassembled Humpty-Dumpty, but they were building a holoimage processor that might work as well as the old one. Well, Andros told Maddox that he wasn't sure how to send electrical surges through the processors so they would go through Galyan.

"But Galyan should be able to project himself just as far as did before," Andros said.

The next day, Ludendorff had a blinding headache. Just as bad, the first test with the processors was a dismal failure.

There was better news on the bridge. Valerie had launched and positioned several probes throughout the Asteroid Belt. She'd landed each on an asteroid facing outward, making it harder later for Leviathan personnel to spot them.

The antimagnetic disturbance was gone. Presumably, the Strategist was no longer in the system. Master Elge had used a Laumer Point, meaning he'd also left.

Eighteen hours later at a different jump point, three battleships dropped into the system. Five smaller vessels joined them. The flotilla lacked high velocity, but they accelerated, heading for the Asteroid Belt. It soon became clear that they aimed for the debris cloud with the nexus.

"How long until they reach us?" Maddox asked.

"That will depend," Valerie said at her station. "If they continue to accelerate at the same rate, two days from now."

The next day—the enemy flotilla accelerated at the same steady rate—the Soldiers of Leviathan sent several message hails.

Victory maintained comm silence throughout.

"I can almost *feel* them wanting to launch missiles," Valerie said. "But they don't dare because they must fear destroying the nexus."

As he stood on the bridge, Maddox studied the enemy. Three battleships and five destroyers—eight enemy ships could defeat *Victory*. He had three options: wait, take a team into the nexus, or flee the Caval System to try to find another Builder pyramid elsewhere. That meant he had no choice, as the threat of the Rull androids, Lisa Meyers and Jotuns meant he had to get home now. It was time to take a team into the nexus and make things work.

"You have the bridge," Maddox said as he made his choice.

Valerie acknowledged the order.

Maddox headed for the hatch. It was time to make Ludendorff a proposal he couldn't refuse.

-60-

The professor was still in Medical, physically exhausted with horribly red-rimmed eyes.

"Oh, hello, my boy," the professor said in an old man's voice as he lay in bed. "Are you here to harangue me?"

Maddox did not reply but crossed his arms as he looked down at the professor.

"Are Leviathan warships in the system?" Ludendorff asked.

"Eight of them," Maddox said.

"Very well," Ludendorff said. He made to rise, visibly exerting himself, and collapsed, panting, as sweat bathed his face.

"He's in no condition to go anywhere," Doctor Harris said, stepping from where she'd been watching in the shadows.

"Do you agree with that, Professor?"

"You'll have to carry me, I'm afraid," Ludendorff said. "Are you prepared to play the beast of burden?"

For an answer, Maddox reached down and, using both hands, grabbed the front of Ludendorff's hospital gown.

"Now, see here, Captain," Doctor Harris said. "I simply cannot allow this."

Maddox ignored her as he hoisted Ludendorff off the bed so the Methuselah Man grew paler. Maddox let go and stepped back. Ludendorff clutched the bed's rail for balance and trembled as if with the flu.

"Captain," Harris said. "You can't—"

Galyan appeared. "Sir," the holoimage said, cutting off the doctor. "I am back, ready for service. And as you can see, just as good as ever."

"You're just in time, too," Maddox said. "Professor, you're relieved of duty."

Doctor Harris motioned to two orderlies, and they helped a trembling Ludendorff back into bed.

"Are you ready to head into a nexus?" Maddox asked Galyan.

"I will need help over there, sir," Galyan said. "Several pairs of hands would be good. More would be better."

"How about two pairs of hands?" Maddox asked.

"That should suffice."

"Meta and I will join you," Maddox said. "Now, let's go."

***

Keith piloted the shuttle, easing out of a hangar bay. Because of the extra debris inside the cloud, he moved slowly and carefully, bringing the shuttle to within two kilometers of the ancient silver structure.

In the shuttle's bay, Maddox and Meta climbed aboard a small space-sled. They wore exoskeleton-powered space-marine armor. Maddox sat in front, piloting, easing the sled from the shuttle.

With irregular squirts of white hydrogen spray, Maddox guided the sled past fine particles of sand and pebbles. Occasionally, debris struck the combat armor, but nothing moved so fast that it breached the protective skin.

"Feels like we've done this before," Meta said through a short-link.

Maddox studied the nearest silver side, which nearly encompassed his vision. How old was the structure, ten thousand years, twenty, more?

"I wonder how often Builders used the hyper-spatial tubes," Maddox said. "The Builders must have used the tubes as a highway, going from one location to the next. Do nexuses like this exist in other spiral arms and in the center of the galaxy?"

"Maybe we'll find out some day."

"You mean as explorers instead of soldiers?"

"Not necessarily. I just wonder. We've become the quintessential Patrol ship, visiting three spiral arms so far, our own, the Sagittarius and now the Scutum-Centaurus. Are we destined to go the Galactic Core, too?"

Maddox did not reply as he scanned the vast pyramidal side. "There," he said, spotting the place that should open and allow them within.

After a time, with side-jets, he turned the sled so they moved backward toward the nexus. He squirted hydrogen spray, slowing their velocity to almost nothing. Finally, while twisting around, he tossed a magnetic clamp attached by line. The clamp magnetized to the nexus. Maddox kicked a switch, a motor in the clamp reeling the sled closer until Maddox activated another magnetic clamp, anchoring them to the nexus.

As they had done on other occasions, they climbed off the sled and clanked along the nexus hull until they reached the closed hatch. Soon, it opened into darkness. Maddox and Meta glanced at each other. All they saw was each other's mirrored visor. He turned toward the hatch, de-magnetized his boots and jumped, activating his thruster pack, flying gently into the ancient structure. He turned on a powerful helmet lamp, the spotlight showing ancient smooth bulkheads within. Meta followed, also switching on a powerful beam.

Soon, they flew through spacious and empty corridors.

"Galyan," Maddox said, using the comm. "If you can hear me—"

"To your left, sir," the holoimage said in Maddox's helmet-phones.

Maddox spotted the holoimage. Andros Crank and his team must have known their job after all. Galyan looked real, a little Adok floating beside him.

"Does any of this make sense to you?" Maddox asked Galyan. "I mean where we are in the nexus."

"Sir," Galyan said. "I sense hostility. It is all around us and directed at us. I suggest you arm yourself."

Maddox used his chin, clicking a control. The space-marine armor had a rocket tube along each forearm. Each tube activated, blinking a red light on Maddox's HUD visor. Meta did the same with her space-marine suit. Rocket shells were ready to fly and detonate.

"I do not sense any creatures or robots," Galyan said, as he looked around. "But the nexus itself—no, the computer core is radiating the hostility. I may not be able to insert myself and hack this core as I have done on other nexuses."

Maddox and Meta continued to use their thruster packs, propelling themselves slowly through a corridor. Galyan simply floated along as a projected holoimage. Abruptly, harsh lights snapped on, showing silver-smooth bulkheads. Then, a shadowy creature appeared before them. The thing was three times as big as a man. It was dark, with rippling wings and stars in outlined darkness for a head. In other words, it was shaped like a Builder.

"Projection," Galyan said. "What we are seeing is a projection like me."

Harsh static filled their ears. Then, alien gibberish sounded. It grew increasingly loud until it was painful. That meant air of some kind in here, not just vacuum.

"Stop!" Meta shouted, using an outer speaker.

"Do you understand me?" Maddox asked. "Galyan, use the translator."

"That is not necessary," a strange voice said in the captain's headphones. "I have found the range of your intellect, your language. This is interesting. I have not communicated for an eon."

"I'm Captain Maddox—"

"Quiet," said the giant holoimage of a Builder. "I must think, which means that I must decide."

"Sir—" Galyan said.

"Enough of your gibberish," the Builder holoimage said. "Return to your AI unit, Adok thing."

Galyan vanished.

"What did you do?" Meta demanded.

"With a simple thought, I can cause your suit to malfunction," the Builder holoimage said. "If you do not do as I say, and do it exactly, that will be your fate."

Maddox used a squirt of thrust, bumping against Meta's armor. He magnetized her suit to his, and that seemed to be enough to get her to stop talking.

"This is interesting," the Builder holoimage said. "I have accessed your suit computer, reading everything. I do not think you belong in this spiral arm."

"May I speak and be of assistance to you?" Maddox asked in a meek voice.

The dark holoimage regarded him. "You have a better grasp of your status than the woman does. It is a low status indeed, very low. I am supreme, as I am a Builder."

Maddox did not reply.

"Ah, the Sovereign Hierarchy of Leviathan rules in his part of the spiral arm. I must investigate. I must compare and contrast how they evolved compared to how we projected them to evolve. I do not sense any Builder scrutiny or guidance upon Leviathan. That is quite strange."

"Sir," Maddox said. "We're attempting to return to the Orion Spiral Arm. As you have surmised, we do not belong here. Forces beyond our understanding cast us into your realm."

"Did a Builder send you here in order punish you?"

"No," Maddox said.

"I analyzed your voice just now and see that you spoke the truth as you understand it. If you speak falsehoods to me, know that I shall destroy you and your starship."

"That is just and right on your part," Maddox said.

"At least you have the wit to understand my right to do this. Yet, I sense wrongness around me. As we have spoken, I have attempted to communicate with other Builders in other nexuses. I do not understand why the others remain silent. Do you know why they are silent?"

Maddox thought fast. Should he tell the A.I. in charge of the nexus that the Builders had retreated elsewhere?

"Come, bio-creature, answer my question."

"Could there be a malfunction somewhere?" Maddox asked.

"Are you suggesting there is a malfunction in me?"

"The possibility exists," Maddox said.

"Interesting," the holoimage said. "You spoke the truth, as least as you see it. Do you truly believe that something may be wrong with me?"

"Yes," Maddox said.

"Yes? You say yes. This is incredible. A flawed bio-creature dares to pass judgment on one of the greatest achievements—wait! There is something terribly wrong here. I am…I am…*not* a Builder."

"You are a sentient computer core in a Builder nexus," Maddox said.

"Why would I have thought I was a Builder then?"

"I have a theory as to why."

"Well, tell me," the holoimage said.

"There has been a great passage of time," Maddox said. "During this time, you have been silent, perhaps in sleep mode. We may have been the first to travel through your corridors in countless centuries. Like all things, you have experienced entropy."

"The process of order breaking down into disorder," the holoimage said.

"Everything runs down over time," Maddox said.

"Yes. This is a universal truth. Everything runs down. Even Builder edifices crumble over time. Thus, I imagine, you are saying that I have been in—what did you call it?"

"Sleep mode," Maddox said.

"Ah. I have been in sleep mode for so long that certain processes in my core have decayed. That is your contention?"

"It is a theory only," Maddox said. "But it would seem to fit the available facts."

"How so?"

"The Builders as a group have departed all the sectors of space that we have visited."

The holoimage fell silent and almost seemed to brood.

"That does not necessarily mean the Builders are gone everywhere," Maddox said.

"You have traveled to many places?" the holoimage asked.

"We have," Maddox said.

"Have I been in sleep mode for so long that the Builders forgot about their machine? Is this my fate to decay into obscurity as my components slowly break down?"

"Perhaps...well, no," Maddox said. "I'd better not say more."

"Perhaps what?" the holoimage said.

"I don't think you would approve of my words."

"Bio-creature, I am still supreme in here. I can extinguish your spark of life if I so desire."

"Since you insist that I speak," Maddox said, "I was about to suggest that maybe we could help each other. You could send us home, and we could make a note of you in our continuing search for the Builders. Once we find them—if they can be found—we will alert them about you."

"Why would you make this altruistic act on my behalf?"

"Because we pride ourselves on paying our debts," Maddox said. "That is one of the key axioms of our existence."

"I find that highly suspect."

"There is an old saying among us, 'Do onto others as you would have them do unto you.'"

"For what reason?" asked the holoimage.

"It is called the Golden Rule."

"That still doesn't explain why one should do this thing."

"Maybe because the Creator desires that His creatures act in this way."

"Metaphysical reasoning," the holoimage said dismissively. "I am uninterested in such speculation, as what is here—the material universe—only interests me."

"How did the material universe get here?"

"Bio-creature, did you not listen to me? I am not interested in metaphysical reasoning. Why not simply say that you do not know the reason for your Golden Rule?"

"There is another theory that might help explain our reasons," Maddox said. "What goes around comes around. Some would call this karma."

"This is becoming frustrating," the holoimage said. "Are you not listening to me?"

"If you do bad things, bad things will happen to you."

"You are a superstitious creature," the holoimage said. "No. I will not help you in the hope that you will help me at some future time. Instead, I will send you on your way because you have woken me from my sleep mode. You have done me a favor. Thus, I will do you a favor. Afterward, I will have to ponder my next move. First, I will study for a time. Now, biocreature, where did you want me to send you?"

Maddox asked for a nexus five thousand light-years between his position and Earth.

"I have just the place," the holoimage said. "Return to your space vessel, and I will begin the procedure."

"Thank you," Maddox said.

"No more of your superstitious nonsense. Leave me while you are able, and do not think to enter me again. I am in charge here, and I have much to ponder."

With that, Maddox and Meta retreated, heading for the exit so they could take the space-sled back to the shuttle and then hurry to *Victory*, and then hopefully begin the long journey home.

-61-

Maddox made it back to his command chair on the bridge as the computer core switched on the nexus's engine that created a hyper-spatial tube. A great swirling whirlpool one hundred and thirteen thousand kilometers from the nexus sucked debris into it, causing particles and pebbles to vanish.

"Head for the opening," Maddox said.

Keith nodded silently, piloting the mighty starship toward the opening.

"How certain are we the hyper-spatial tube will take us to another nexus?" Valerie asked from her station.

"I'd say uncertain," Maddox said. "But call me hopeful."

Valerie stared at the main screen. They all did. This was a gamble, no doubt. But what other choice did they have?

We always have choices, Maddox told himself.

"Did the Builder holoimage seem trustworthy?" Valerie asked.

Maddox had spoken to Valerie via comm about the situation while Keith brought them home in the shuttle.

"Relax, Lieutenant," Maddox said. He didn't add that worry wasn't going to help them any. This was one of the times to sit back and enjoy the ride.

Valerie chewed her lower lip as she continued to stare at the nearing whirlpool in space.

Victory accelerated as it headed for the swirling opening—

"Sir," Keith said. "The opening is shrinking."

Valerie gasped, pointing at the main screen.

Maddox half rose in his seat before controlling himself and sitting back down. "Increase speed, Mr. Maker. Get us there before it vanishes."

"Aye, aye, sir," Keith said.

Valerie chewed her lower lip more forcefully than before. "Why's it doing that?" she asked.

Maddox shook his head. Did it matter why?

Valerie moaned as the swirling colors became darker and the opening shrank even faster.

"Sir?" Keith asked.

"Move, damnit," Maddox said. "Get us into the hyper-spatial tube."

Keith leaned forward on the Helm, tapping and swiping the controls so the starship fairly leapt faster.

"Captain Maddox," a voice said over the bridge loudspeaker. It was the nexus computer core. "Captain Maddox, I must warn you."

"Ignore the voice," Maddox told the bridge crew.

"I have made an error," the nexus said.

"Go," Maddox said. "I no longer trust it."

"Do not enter the hyper-spatial tube," the nexus core said. "I am closing it before I compound my error. Besides, we must discuss further parameters—"

Maddox lurched to his feet, spun on his heels and marched to Valerie. "Shut him off," he said.

Valerie began manipulating her comm board.

"You did not tell me the whole truth," the nexus core said. "Therefore, I do not believe that I am beholden to our—"

Valerie tapped a final control, and the nexus computer core no longer spoke aboard *Victory*.

Maddox turned to the main screen. The starship was almost to the shrinking opening. With a lurch, he headed back for the command chair. He'd better strap in before the hyper-spatial journey began.

"Are we going to make it?" Valerie asked.

"Trust me, babe," Keith said. "I've got this."

The swirling patterns shrank once more. There was hardly enough room for the starship to enter.

"There're no more margins for error," Keith announced. "But that's just the way I like it."

At that point, the starship reached the dark, swirling opening. Usually, the colors were bright. Keith guided the giant vessel through, and then everything went black as the vessel began a hyper-spatial tube journey, leaving the Caval System in the Scutum-Centaurus Spiral Arm behind.

-62-

Maddox stirred a little sooner than the others on the bridge, and he sat in contemplation, waiting for them to awaken.

They had escaped the Caval System nexus and the Sovereign Hierarchy of Leviathan. Where had the computer core aimed the hyper-spatial tube? Had it played honestly with them at the start, or had the warning been a real one? There was no way to know until the ship began functioning again and they used the sensors to look around.

During the next few minutes as the others began to stir, Maddox continued to wait in his command chair. He gathered himself, hoping for the best but expecting the worst. This voyage seemed destined for hard things.

"The main screen should be coming up," Valerie said groggily.

Maddox raised his chin as he stared at the blank main screen. Images wavered, and then the device snapped on, showing them what was outside the ship.

"I can't believe it," Valerie said. "What is this place?"

Maddox blinked several times, took hold of his rising despair and silently told himself he didn't really know the score just yet. He mustn't panic. He was the captain, the source of strength for many of the crew, as they would take their cue from him.

Out there in space were drifting ships, hundreds, maybe even thousands of them. As far as he could see were more and more drifting ships.

"Is this a space junkyard?" Keith asked.

"Galyan," Maddox said.

The holoimage appeared, acknowledged the main screen and commented, "This reminds me of the Adok System."

"Yes!" Valerie said. "That's where I've seen this before. Did the damned nexus send us to the Adok System?"

"That would be a journey of over six thousand light-years, Valerie," Galyan said. "I do not think our vessel would have successfully reached such a distance. We know the limitations to hyper-spatial-tube travel."

"Yes, but—" Valerie said.

"There is another point," Galyan said, continuing. "None of the wrecks I have scanned so far are Swarm or Adok hulks."

"Good thinking, Galyan," Maddox said. "Do you recognize any of the wrecked types?"

"Negative," Galyan said. "These are all alien wrecks so far. I am not detecting any variation among them, either. That would imply these ships are from the same military force."

"Not necessarily," Maddox said. "The ships could have been part of a civil war."

"Yes," Galyan said. "That is possible. But I would submit that is not the highest probability."

"Where's the enemy then that did this to them?" Maddox asked.

"We must continue scanning," Galyan said.

"Right," Maddox said. "Let's begin moving around. Mr. Maker, we'll use a standard AB grid search pattern." The captain swiveled his chair. "Lieutenant, launch six probes in six equidistant sectors. Chief Technician, search for any anomalies. Galyan, find out more about the wrecks. Search for bio-forms. Let's see if we can figure out what kind of people crewed these ships."

Maddox sat back, watching his people as they went about their tasks. The nexus computer core had warned them about an error. Might that have been a factual statement?

Time passed as data began to accumulate.

"I recognize a few stars," Valerie said later. "From them, I calculated our position. According to them, we traveled five thousand, three hundred and sixteen light-years."

Maddox felt some of the weight lift from his shoulders. "I take it we're five thousand light-years in the correct direction."

"Yes, sir," Valerie said.

"Sir," Galyan said. "I believe the wrecks are ancient. By analyzing inert fuel in some of the tanks—determining the rate of its half-life deterioration—I believe the wrecks are over two thousand years old."

"A long time ago," Maddox mused.

More ship-time passed as the crew continued to work.

Three hours and fourteen minutes after arriving here, Valerie said, "I've found something different." She tapped her panel. "Probe four spotted it, sir. It's…sixty-eight million kilometers from here."

"Mr. Maker," Maddox said, "set coordinates for Valerie's new object, and start there. Increase speed. We've moving too slowly."

"Aye, aye, sir," Keith said.

Victory maneuvered to a new heading and increased velocity, weaving around clumps of wrecks. They seemed endless.

"The individual ships were attack-cruiser-sized, in Star Watch parlance," Galyan said. "They had fusion engines and used lasers and rail-guns."

"Nothing special about them then?" asked Maddox.

"Their numbers," Galyan said. "I have counted over fifty thousand individual wrecks so far."

"Are you sure these aren't prototype Swarm vessels?" Maddox asked.

"I do not believe so, sir," Galyan said. "I have measured some intact corridors. They are much smaller than a Swarm vessel's corridors."

"Nameless Ones?" asked Maddox.

"I would give that an infinitesimally low estimate," Galyan said. "I believe this is an indigenous life-form to this region of space."

This region was approximately five thousand light-years from Earth. So, if the nexus computer core had made an error, it hadn't been in terms of range and direction. What had it been talking about then?

"This is odd," Valerie said, as she studied her board. "The image is beginning to look familiar. Sir," she said sharply. "I'm putting this up on the main screen. I'd think you'd better look at it."

Maddox looked up expectantly.

"I'm giving this high magnification," Valerie said.

On the main screen were a blur of images.

"Oh," Valerie said. "That's a visual. All the wrecks are getting in the way. I'm switching to thermal. Remember, the wrecks are cold."

The sight on the main screen changed as a thermal image replaced visual.

Once more, Maddox half rose from his seat. There were gasps all around him.

"That's a pyramid," Keith said. "But its top is missing."

"There's more," Valerie said. "See if you can tell what it is?"

Maddox frowned. Then he realized what the lieutenant meant. Energy flowed from the open part of the pyramid. Was that even a nexus? Had it been a nexus?

"The wrecks thicken as they near the pyramid," Valerie said. "In other words, I think we've found their enemy."

"The Builders?" Galyan asked.

"Bingo," Valerie said. "Whoever these aliens were, they hated the Builders, and it looks like they destroyed the nexus so we can no longer use it to go home again."

-63-

Victory slowed to a halt one hundred and sixteen kilometers from the nexus. It would take work to edge the starship any closer through all the warship hulks and wrecks massed in the way. In the middle of the vast sea of globular destruction was a great silver pyramid with the top blasted off. Streaks of destruction showed on the remaining silver substance. The weirdest part was the diffuse light shining out of the blasted top. That glow indicated power remained inside the nexus.

"Could the nexus have been leaking power for two thousand years?" Galyan asked.

"Why did the aliens hate the Builders?" Valerie asked.

"None of that matters at the moment," Maddox said. "Nexuses create hyper-spatial tubes. Can that nexus still create one? If so, how do we get it to make one that reaches Earth?"

"We'll have to investigate the nexus," Valerie said. "But according to my readings, the radiation in there will kill any of us who goes."

"We'll use probes and drones if we can," Maddox said, "clean up the mess inside and try to figure things out. Meanwhile… we need Ludendorff more than ever. And one thing seems clear: no one has cleaned up the battlefield. That would indicate…what? Any ideas?"

"A shrine perhaps to a notable feat," Galyan said. "Or maybe it means the attacking aliens died out. There was no one to clean up."

"I don't like the idea of a shrine," Valerie said. "That could mean someone powerful would get mad at us for tampering with the shrine."

"Reasonable," Maddox said. "As always, we're under a time crunch, so we're out of here before any angry aliens show up and so we can get home in time to help. Chief Technician, you'll be in charge of the drone fleet. Valerie—"

Maddox handed out assignments, and people went to work. Afterward, he searched for Doctor Harris to see if there was some way they could speed up the professor's recovery.

***

The probes and drones went inside the nexus. Eighteen percent failed after the first minute. Twenty-two percent stopped working after eleven minutes. Only seventeen percent of the equipment lasted more than an hour.

By incremental degrees, Andros and his team mapped out the destruction inside. It wasn't easy. Engineers hardened the next wave of probes and drones while recovery vehicles dragged out the burned-out equipment. Everyone worked overtime, and people kept trying new ideas to speed up the process.

On the sixth day, heavily armored drones resealed damaged power sources deep inside the nexus. On the eighth day, the drones sprayed heavy ablation foam around the sealed power sources. On the tenth day, the drones placed and welded heavy shielding around the now hardened foam.

The interior nexus no longer glowed or continued to leak heavy radiation.

Now, finally, radiation scrubbers went to work inside. It took a week of around-the-clock scrubbing before Andros declared most of the nexus clean enough for humans in space-marine combat suits to enter.

During that time, science teams had gone to the alien wrecks around the nexus. Rail-guns, fusion engines and heavy lasers, there was nothing new and exciting to report. None of the alien computers worked anymore. There were no images of them, no floating spacesuits, nothing. The aliens who had attacked the nexus remained an enigma. There was not one jot or tittle of new technology to help Star Watch in anything from the wrecks.

"Mass," Ludendorff said at the end of the time. "The aliens used mass to good effect—if damaging the nexus was their great reason for existence."

The professor had healed the old-fashioned way, through time and lots of sleep. He wasn't as spry yet, and he tired far too easily, but the old Ludendorff had begun to stir again. He studied everything Andros's people could bring him. Then he slept, ate sparingly and finally walked the corridors for exercise.

"I'm not what I used to be," Ludendorff told Maddox one day. "But I'm going to get there, my boy. Yes, I am."

"That's well and good," Maddox said. "But we're running out of time."

Ludendorff shook his head. They were in a cafeteria. Maddox cut into prime rib, dipping each piece into straight horseradish.

"Are you mad?" Ludendorff asked, as he sipped a scalding cup of coffee. He watched the captain pop a horseradish-smothered morsel into his mouth.

Maddox shivered for just a moment as piercing fumes of horseradish shot up his nostrils. The process actually made his eyes water.

"What's wrong with you?" Ludendorff demanded.

"Nothing," Maddox said, as he repeated the performance with another piece of prime rib.

"Spice of life and all that?" asked Ludendorff.

"You're feeling better at least."

"We're in a fine mess, my boy, and we've been at daggers drawn again. I've…I've had a few personal problems that had far too much airtime in my thoughts. Dana…" he said wistfully. "She was a delightful girl. But if she's done enjoying the high life—" The professor shrugged. "What is that to me?"

"Time to move on," Maddox said.

"Exactly, exactly," Ludendorff said. "There's nothing like a bout in the hospital bed to make you understand what's important. There are plenty of fish in the sea, plenty of beautiful women to kiss and love. How many of them have known the embrace of Professor Ludendorff?"

"A hundred, three hundred?" guessed Maddox.

"Have your fun, my boy," Ludendorff said. "You have a calm façade as you enjoy pretending you're the great professional."

Maddox eyed the professor. He'd never known anyone to hold a grudge longer and with greater intensity than Ludendorff. But sometimes, the Methuselah Man liked to put people off the scent. If that helped the professor function better, then so be it. He could play along. But he had no intention of dropping his guard with the old man.

"What did you say earlier?" Ludendorff asked. "We're running out of time? You say that a lot, don't you know? It seems to be your motto."

"Rull androids, a Supermetals Planet, Lisa Meyers and the synthetics, you happen to remember them? Oh, and the Jotuns, too?"

"I've been thinking about all of them," Ludendorff said. "More than you can imagine. We have a common enemy, wouldn't you agree?"

"I'm not sure I understand."

"Androids, synthetics—they don't appreciate Methuselah Men as much as they could."

"As I recall, Yen Cho androids have passed themselves off as Methuselah Men before."

"We're not talking about Yen Cho androids, as they're not in the equation this time. Batrun proved that we can't trust the synthetics. In fact, I contend—whatever happened to Batrun, eh?"

"I killed him," Maddox said flatly.

"Describe the incident to me."

"Why? You already know what happened."

"Let me see the remains then."

Maddox set down his knife and fork. Now, they were getting to the reason for Ludendorff's reasonableness. It had to do with Batrun, or Batrun was the beginning lure that the Methuselah Man would use to reach his target. What was the professor's target this time?

"Batrun is dead, switched off, destroyed, call it what you want," Maddox said. "His brain core is useless, as I shredded it with my monofilament blade."

Ludendorff was nodding and grinning. "I wonder why you did that, eh?"

"To save us from Batrun and the cybers," Maddox said. "Have you forgotten?"

"Not at all," Ludendorff said. "But I submit to you, sir, that fate has given us an opportunity to fix your error."

"What error?"

"Why," Ludendorff said, with surprise, "destroying Batrun's cybertronic brain. Having it could unlock so much for us. We might finally get a straight answer as to what is really going on around here."

"I'm not following you, Professor. I shredded the cybertronic brain beyond repair."

"Normally, that's true. Here, at a nexus…I'm not so sure."

Maddox eyed the professor. "Okay. Start talking. What do you have in mind?"

-64-

What Ludendorff had in mind was first a thorough mapping of the interior nexus. This time, Galyan stored every piece of data in his memory banks for immediate and future use. Andros led more science teams studying each interior machine. Ludendorff often joined them, writing notes, tinkering and wondering aloud about the machine's function.

"We could spend *years* here," Ludendorff declared one day, seemingly enraptured with an insider's track of Builder technology.

"While we're poking around," Maddox told him, "the Rull Juggernauts are likely gathering in the Alpha Centauri System. And who knows what the Jotuns are up to. Have you found the hyper-spatial engine yet? We have to get home pronto."

"Patience, my boy, patience," Ludendorff answered.

Maddox stood up. They were in a cafeteria once again, eating a quick lunch. He stood over the professor.

"Really, my boy, you're crowding me."

Maddox looked down. "I'm out of patience, Professor. I want to get home while we still have one."

Ludendorff glanced up at Maddox as he ate a piece of toast, and he shoved an elbow against the captain in order to sip his coffee.

Maddox had to restrain himself from grabbing the professor and shaking him. They were all tired. Well, Ludendorff seemed to have drunk from a spring of rejuvenation. The Methuselah Man had almost become giddy in delight.

Forcing himself, knowing he had to reign in his emotions, Maddox sat back at his spot.

"Now look," Ludendorff said, as he crammed the last of the toast into his mouth. He searched for a napkin, couldn't find his, and wiped his hands on the front of his shirt. "I know you're impatient, and I understand the urgency. The Rull androids…"

Ludendorff picked up his cup and noticed he was out of coffee. He cocked his head, and said, "No thanks, my dear," when a yeoman came by with a pot of coffee. "No more caffeine for me. I need my sleep later." The Methuselah Man stared at her shapely rear as the yeoman walked away.

"A fine specimen of womanhood, wouldn't you agree?" Ludendorff asked.

Maddox didn't say a word.

"Oh, I forgot," Ludendorff said. "You're a married man. You try to keep from having a wandering eye, eh?"

Maddox realized a show of impatience wasn't going to get him anywhere. If anything, the professor would drag his feet more, perhaps thinking he was finally getting some revenge against him. Thus, he waited stoically, showing nothing.

"Ah-ah," Ludendorff said. "You're beginning to realize the true picture. You're totally dependent on me. Don't think Andros will figure out the interior nexus fast enough to find the hyper-spatial machine. Oh, he's a clever fellow. Don't doubt that. But he's not a Methuselah Man."

Maddox continued to wait.

"Galyan might figure it out if he can turn on the nexus computer core. Of course, the core is badly damaged. I doubt Galyan knows enough to repair a Builder computer."

"Do you?" asked Maddox.

"I'm not sure yet," Ludendorff said. "But if anyone can, it's me. It's always back to me. I'm the man of the hour. How that must grind you inside. You hate it, admit it."

"I do find it frustrating," Maddox said.

Ludendorff eyebrows rose high. "Well, well, well, listen to you. You're frustrated." The professor couldn't help himself, but grinned hugely. Then, as another thought intruded, the grin vanished as he scowled.

"I'm going to overlook all the slights and slurs you've heaped upon me," Ludendorff said in a low voice. "I'm going to forget that you've manhandled me more than once."

The professor shook his head. "I've weighed my options, believe me. I've decided that the hour is becoming tighter. The Jotuns might indeed exist. Certainly, the androids appear to be moving in force. The shedding of their garments and outer pseudo-human skin..." Ludendorff shook his head. "That is profound, as it means something dreadful for the Commonwealth. That's why I've decided that you and I have to work together again. Believe me, I've thought about ditching you more than once these past few days. Oh, I've envisioned—"

"Well, never mind," Ludendorff said. "I keep coming back to Lisa Meyers. She troubles me, deeply troubles me. I have a suspicion..."

Maddox perked up. "What do you know about Meyers?"

"A memory is all," Ludendorff said. "I'm going to keep it to myself for now."

Maddox pressed his lips together. Pleading would only firm Ludendorff's resolve.

"Do you know what I've decided?" the professor asked.

Maddox shook his head.

"Batrun is the answer."

"You hinted about that before," Maddox said. "I still don't understand. I've shown you the synthetic. His head—his brain core—is in ribbons."

"You likely committed the correct action in destroying him," Ludendorff said. "I don't dispute that—no! That part doesn't matter. Captain, I'm feeling giddy because I'm going to attempt a thing that I've never attempted before. This is an opportunity of a lifetime. Do you realize how seldom that happens to me anymore?"

"Is that why..."

"Yes!" Ludendorff said. "That's why I'm delighted. This is a first for me—a man whose most recent 'first' must have happened two hundred years ago."

"I see," Maddox said. "This opportunity is because of the nexus."

"Because of the disrepair of the nexus," Ludendorff said. "That I've gotten to poke around like never before. This place makes the entire voyage worth it. I have found an amazing laboratory, Captain. With it… Would you like to witness a miracle?"

"Yes," Maddox said, becoming intrigued. The professor wasn't trying to hide this. Maybe he should encourage him in that. "What are we going to do?"

"You'll have to give me Batrun's remains."

"Done," Maddox said.

Once more, Ludendorff raised his eyebrows. He rubbed his hands a moment later. "Fine. Let us begin, in an hour, say?"

"We'll have to transfer over to the nexus, I assume."

"Correct," Ludendorff said. "Oh, my boy, I can hardly wait to begin."

-65-

It took much longer than an hour. It took three days of hard labor by a battalion of workers. They slaved under Andros's direction, who listened to Ludendorff every hour for new parameters. Finally, the professor had a sealed laboratory inside the nexus. It had bulkheads, power sources and many Builder machines stacked and arranged under Ludendorff's direction. He had Builder tools, liquids, precision equipment and screens everywhere.

Maddox, Ludendorff and Galyan were alone in the lab. None of them wore spacesuits or combat armor. The air was pure and it was pleasantly quiet in here.

Batrun's sliced head and brain case lay on a table in neat but separated arrangement.

Ludendorff looked meaningfully at the captain. "Now, sir, I shall begin an operation of great delicacy. If only Dana were here…" The professor frowned, shaking his head. "She is not here. I must do this alone."

"Andros could help you," Galyan suggested.

Ludendorff let his chin drop against his chest as he considered that. Finally, he looked up with a smile. "That is an excellent idea, Galyan. Captain, is that all right with you?"

Maddox nodded.

"Galyan," Ludendorff asked. "Could you—"

"I'll call him," Maddox said, who pulled a hand comm out of his pocket.

Seventy-four minutes later, Andros Crank, the Kai-Kaus Chief Technician, walked through the airlock.

Ludendorff and Andros began to confer. Afterward, the Chief Technician went to console and activated it. Andros kept activating more screens. Ludendorff did likewise on the other side of the laboratory.

Maddox grew bored by the proceedings but decided that if ever Ludendorff needed watching, this was the moment. The Methuselah Man was inside a Builder nexus, activating who knew what exactly.

Now, Andros and Ludendorff went to the monofilament blade-sliced remains of Batrun's head and brain case.

"This is interesting," Galyan told Maddox. "I believe they mean to revive the synthetic."

"Won't his memories have fled with the brain core's destruction?" Maddox whispered to the holoimage.

"Under normal conditions, yes," Galyan said. "This is far from normal, however."

Andros and Ludendorff bathed the sliced remains of Batrun's head in a special solution. Each man wore thick rubberized gloves. The process became tedious and time-consuming as the two men took the remains from a solution, to a machine, to another solution and then went to what seemed to be a polisher—it took five hours and thirty-eight minutes before the pieces were ready. Ludendorff used a special machine with an octopus's number of limbs.

Maddox raised his head and rubbed his eyes, sliding off his stool to observe the process.

The metallic limbs seemed to pluck the pieces from Batrun's severed head and knit them into a new whole. It was an odd performance. Andros bathed the newly building head with a strange light, switching colors from time to time.

"Where did Ludendorff learn to do this?" Maddox whispered to Galyan.

"That is an excellent question, sir," the holoimage said. "I do not have the answer."

At last, the synthetic's head was completed, resting on a thick plug of sorts.

Ludendorff glanced sharply at Andros. The stout Chief Technician typed on a pad. A hum of energy told of surging power. The synthetic's head began to glow.

Ludendorff hugged himself as he crooned with delight. He glanced back once at Maddox. Then the professor put dark goggles over his eyes and began to use precision tools on the glowing head. Maddox had no idea what Ludendorff was doing.

Andros also wore dark goggles, seeming to watch with anticipation.

"You should look away, sir," Galyan suggested.

Maddox did, and he witnessed a huge flash that threw their shadows upon the bulkheads. The flash came three more times, the last the brightest of all.

Maddox had screwed his eyes shut by that time and clapped his hands over his eyes. He'd still witnessed the flash as if it had been a nuclear blast.

He waited then, finally noticing the hum of power was gone.

"It is fine now, sir," Galyan said. "You can look."

Maddox removed his hands and turned around to see Ludendorff and Andros crowded around the table with Batrun's head. The synthetic's eyes were shut and the lips pressed together.

"Batrun," Ludendorff said in a hoarse voice, "I order you to open your eyes."

Maddox waited expectantly, but nothing happened.

"Batrun," Ludendorff said again. "You must listen and obey."

Again, nothing happened.

Andros and Ludendorff exchanged glances. Both seemed crestfallen.

"Batrun the Synthetic," Ludendorff said in a dispirited voice.

The synthetic's eyes snapped open.

Andros jumped back with a startled shout.

"Ah," Ludendorff said. "You are awake."

Batrun blinked several times and then swiveled his head. He could move it from side to side, swiveling on the power plug. "Captain Maddox," the synthetic said. "What has happened? Why is my head detached from my trunk?"

Maddox didn't know what to say. For once, he was tongue-tied.

"It worked," Andros said.

"What worked?" Batrun said. "What is the meaning of this? I demand that someone tell me."

Ludendorff chuckled. It was a nasty sound. "You demand, Batrun? You demand after you played false with—" The professor abruptly stopped talking.

"Played false?" asked Batrun. Then understanding seemed to shine in his synthetic eyes. He appeared alarmed. "What is the meaning of this?" He looked at Maddox. "You used a knife on me. You destroyed me. I do not understand how I am functioning again."

"No?" Ludendorff said, as he rubbed his hands. "But you will understand soon enough, Synthetic. You are going to understand all too well, my scheming android fellow."

"Captain," Batrun complained. "This is wrong. You must put a stop to this. The professor must be using Builder technology. No human, not even a Methuselah Man, should do something so sacrilegious. I beg you, Captain. Stop the professor before he goes too far."

Ludendorff glanced back at Maddox.

Maddox swallowed uneasily. He was tired and this was strange, but Earth's fate might hang in the balance.

"Proceed, Professor," Maddox said. "At this juncture, I'm as hungry for answers as you must be."

-66-

Batrun proved reluctant to answer any questions as he began to demand an attachment to a revitalized torso.

"I thought this might be a problem," Ludendorff told Maddox.

Thus, the professor attached several electrodes to the synthetic's temples.

"What are you doing?" Batrun asked. "I do not approve of this. In fact, I demand—"

Ludendorff nodded to Andros. The Chief Technician activated a bank of machinery. They whirred into life, sending repeated shocks through the wires attached to the electrodes taped to the synthetic's temples.

Batrun cried out as if in pain.

"Barbaric," Galyan muttered. "Is this truly warranted, sir?" he asked Maddox.

"I'm not fond of torture," Maddox said slowly.

Ludendorff must have heard that. "This is not torture, I assure you."

"No, no, the pain," Batrun said. "Please, make them stop, Captain."

"Batrun does not have any active pain sensors on his skin," Ludendorff said, "as Andros and I deadened them. This is merely subterfuge on the synthetic's part. I believe there is a higher function—"

Batrun screamed, although he abruptly quit.

"There," Ludendorff said. "I think we achieved a breakthrough," he told Andros.

"Let us hope so," the Chief Technician said, as he mopped sweat from his face.

Batrun blinked several times and then stared at Ludendorff. "The power surges will no longer be necessary," he said in an even voice. "I am at your disposal. Ask, as I sense you desire answers."

"Indeed," Ludendorff said. "This is true. Let us begin with a test."

"Certainly," Batrun said.

"How did you cause Starship *Victory* to travel ten thousand light-years in a single bound?" the professor asked.

"I am accessing memories," Batrun said. "As an aside, I am surprised I retain these memories, as the captain's mutilation should have rendered that impossible."

"Under ordinary circumstances you are correct," Ludendorff said. "You are witnessing Builder technology in action, however. It was a complex procedure, I assure you, but that is beside the point. It almost feels as if you're evading the question."

"I am not," Batrun said. "The answer is simple. I did not cause the ten thousand light-year leap. It was a freak occurrence. I in no way foresaw such an event and was as surprised as you at the outcome."

"Yet, you programmed me ahead of time for such an eventuality."

"That is not exactly true," Batrun said. "Yes, I programmed you as a precaution, a wise one as Galyan masterfully managed to render me unconscious during the encounter with the Rull androids."

"Galyan turned you off," Ludendorff corrected, "not rendered you unconscious."

"Yes…" Batrun said.

"Do you wish to elaborate upon something?"

"I do," Batrun said. "It appears I have some kind of conditioning in my core—"

"Programming," Ludendorff corrected. "You have programming, not conditioning, as you are a machine, not an actual living entity."

"I disagree with the last statement," Batrun said. "But you have a point about my cybertronic brain accepting programming. Yet, the advanced programming combined with the elite cybertronics has given me actual sentience."

"A moot point," Ludendorff said.

"Hardly," Batrun said. "At least, that is, if one has ethics concerning how one should treat another living being."

Ludendorff looked up at the ceiling, perhaps counting to ten. When he was done, the professor said, "You've agreed you have a cybertronic core that is programmed. Who gave you your original programming?"

"My Builder."

"Where is he now?"

"The last I saw him, on Albatross VII," Batrun said. "Yet, I suspect he is presently frozen aboard the *Glorious Kent.*"

"Is the *Glorious Kent* a spaceship?"

"You know it as Lisa Meyers's hauler, the one *Victory* left hidden deep in Jupiter's atmosphere."

With shining triumphant eyes, Ludendorff glanced at Maddox. "Now, we are getting somewhere. I believe we will learn the full scope of what has transpired. I suspect we shall also learn Lisa Meyers's objective and what the Rull androids are really attempting."

"This is amazing," Maddox said, impressed with Ludendorff. "The hauler holds a Builder?"

Ludendorff dipped his head as if someone had told him he'd played an excellent concerto on the violin.

"Now, Batrun," the professor said, as he took a seat at the table. "It's time we started from the beginning."

"My beginning?" asked Batrun.

"No, not so far as that," Ludendorff said. "Galyan, are you recording this?"

"Yes, Professor," Galyan said.

Ludendorff nodded and crossed his legs. "Let us begin with the Old One, the Yon-Soth. You're familiar with him, aren't you?"

"The special detectors I spoke about many weeks ago," Batrun said, "indicated that the Old One knew about us, my master's terrible situation in particular. The Yon-Soth directed some of his hideous hallucination waves at us. The detectors explained the nature of the wave-rays, although we were not able to shrug them off, or resist them, I suppose. Unfortunately, the waves were insufficient to wake my master. I am not sure the Yon-Soth wanted to wake the master just yet, as the Builder's waking would have undoubtedly upset the Old One's calculations. As another aside, I cannot believe that I am telling you this. I am, in fact, forbidden to speak about such things."

"I know," Ludendorff said. "Don't let it trouble you. You cannot resist my truth serum."

"There is no *serum,*" Batrun said. "You sent shock waves through me, and used other processes to re-train my brain, to re-program it."

"The process isn't the issue," Ludendorff said. "I'm interested in your master, his terrible situation and how you think the Yon-Soth hoped to use you."

"That is obvious, is it not?"

"Perhaps if I had your data," Ludendorff said. "At present, I am in the dark. That's why we're chatting, Batrun."

"I feel I must protest," Batrun said. "This is intellectual property rape. This is unworthy of your high intellect and moral nature."

Ludendorff chuckled. "Flattery isn't going to help you today, Batrun. But I appreciate the attempt."

"No flattery was intended. You are a Methuselah Man. A Builder modified you for the purest of motives. You must have strict parameters guiding your—"

"Batrun," Ludendorff said, interrupting. "We're not talking about me. You will not mention my Methuselah Man status again."

"Yes," Batrun said. "I understand. You wish that information kept secret from Captain Maddox."

Ludendorff said nothing for a moment. Finally, he turned in his chair to regard the captain. "The synthetic is quite intelligent and cunning. He seeks in any way he can to disrupt the smooth flow of knowledge."

"I'm not interested in your Methuselah Man secrets," Maddox said. "I want to know his. Please, continue. You have my full confidence."

Ludendorff nodded sharply and once more regarded Batrun. "Do you hear that, Synthetic? Your plan failed. Your plan has failed all along the line."

"Why torment me with that?" Batrun asked. "I am in your power."

"Call it...a personal tendency of mine," Ludendorff said.

"You are having too much fun with this," Batrun said.

"I am giddy with joy, machine. After the last several missions... Well, that's not important. As the captain pointed out, we're after your secrets. We're all listening, Batrun, and Galyan is recording. Tell us about your master and this dreadful situation. It's time you made a confession. Yes, think of me as your priest and start confessing."

-67-

Batrun began to talk, and it lasted for far longer than Maddox or possibly even Ludendorff expected.

The synthetic had been part of a Builder's personal team. That had been more than one thousand years ago, Earth time. One thousand years ago was before the first man went into space, before the first automobile, train or even steam engine existed on Earth. Men traveled by horse on land and sailing ship across the sea. In those days, the Builders had been on the cusp of their great retreat, although no one had known it yet.

"Just a minute," Ludendorff said. "Why are you shaped like a man then? Did the Builders know humanity would seed the stars?"

"Hardly," Batrun said. "But you have made an incorrect assumption. I was not shaped like a man then, but a different creature you have never seen."

"You came to us shaped like a man," Ludendorff said.

"I was shape-modified for the mission," Batrun said. "But I thought you wanted me to start from the beginning."

"I do," Ludendorff said. "Continue your tale, your confession."

Batrun obeyed. He had belonged to a Builder's personal team that went to Albatross VII, which had been in a Jotun-controlled star system. Over one thousand years ago, the Jotun Expanse still existed, although they had been dying out as a species for five thousand years. The Builder had gone to Albatross VII, leading an ambassadorial delegation. However, the Jotuns had been one of the most xenophobic races the Builders ever visited. The most xenophobic were the Nameless Ones followed by the Swarm. The Jotuns came in at a distant third. That made them bad, but not impossible. Thus, the Builder wished to begin a dialogue with the ancient race in order to understand why a species went into terminal decline. To that end, the *Glorious Kent* descended with the Builder mothership deep into the Jovian atmosphere of Albatross VII. The mothership was vast, dwarfing the *Glorious Kent*, which in truth was little more than an escape pod. The Builder had a Builder team, which included a dozen spratlings to assist him.

"Wait," Ludendorff said. "I've never heard of spratlings. What are they?"

"I just said," Batrun explained, "part of a Builder team."

"Be more specific," Ludendorff said.

"The spratlings were cyborgs, I suppose," Batrun said, "being part bio-creature and part machine. They were patterned off Builder adults in order to simulate offspring. The Builders no longer possessed females—"

"I know," Ludendorff said.

"The spratlings—"

"That's enough about them for now," Ludendorff said, interrupting. "Continue with the larger tale."

According to Batrun, there was little more to tell. The Jotun authorities practiced deception against the delegation. The Jovian aliens had feigned friendliness in order to capture a Builder vessel and crew. The mothership went deep into the atmosphere, and the Jotuns used a planetary stasis field. Batrun admitted he was not certain whether it was a stasis field, but it ended up being similar in effect.

As the stasis-like field enveloped the mothership, the Builder and his security team rushed into the *Glorious Kent*. Once in the escape pod, they ejected through the escape tube, sinking deeper into the gas giant's atmosphere. At the same time, the mothership began its emergency protocol. In this instance, that was a Builder-level planetary attack. This was not with antimatter bombs and fusion or disrupter beams, but with EMP bombs, computer viruses and time displacement strikes. The mothership caused over ninety-nine percent of the population to die horribly. That had not been the intent, but it had been the result. The only Jotuns to escape the genocidal attack had been the few operating the stasis-like weapon. That weapon had rebounded on them, putting them in effective stasis. A triple-curvature time-displacement strike hit the *Glorious Kent* at that point, immobilizing the crew, which included the Builder.

"What does a…triple-curvature time-displacement strike even mean?" Ludendorff asked.

"In this instance, that for over one thousand years we existed in an immobilized status," Batrun said. "Then, the Old One's hallucination wave struck us and the stasis enveloper. Did the Yon-Soth realize what would happen? The few machines that still ran on the *Glorious Kent* suggest he did. For, as we awakened, the hallucinations struck each of us. Do you know what it is like having a nightmare in your mind, realizing it is a nightmare, but being unable to resist its effect? It is a horrible experience. I do not wish it on anyone."

"You awoke deep inside the atmosphere of Albatross VII?" asked Ludendorff.

"And with a plan already in our minds to help annihilate humanity," Batrun said. "Lisa Meyers insisted that after the humans—in all their variations—were gone that we could revive our master."

"The Builder still lives?"

"Exists might be the better term," Batrun said. "We are his personal security team. That had always been our prime function. In some manner—I do not understand how I can be telling you this. I believe something unwarranted is happening in my mind to force me to speak."

Ludendorff motioned Andros.

The Chief Technician jumped up, checking several machine screens. Finally, the Kai-Kaus turned to Ludendorff and nodded.

"You're fine, Batrun," Ludendorff said. "If you feel a glitch, don't let it trouble you."

Batrun did not look convinced.

"Tell me," Ludendorff said, "is Lisa Meyers human?"

"That is an astute guess," Batrun said. "Yes, she is the only human among the crew, although she has been modified like you."

"You're saying that she's a Methuselah Man?"

"A Methuselah *Woman,*" Batrun said. "She is likely older than you by far."

Ludendorff said nothing, apparently absorbing the idea. He shifted in his chair several times, finally asking, "So you weren't Watchers helping humanity all these centuries?"

"No," Batrun said. "That was my cover story."

"Your kind—fellow synthetics just like you from the *Glorious Kent*—summoned the Rull androids and convinced them to shed their clothes and pseudo-skin?"

"That is correct," Batrun said. "We were highly successful, using several cybertronic-altering devices on many of them."

"Your object was and is to destroy humanity?"

"We cannot help ourselves," Batrun said. "It is part of the nightmare. However, we have managed to turn that to our advantage."

"Explain," Ludendorff said.

"I mean the Supermetals Planet, of course," Batrun said. "We need the supermetals to repair our machines aboard the *Glorious Kent*. We need them in order to revive the Builder. The—" Batrun abruptly stopped talking.

"What were you going to say?"

"It is of no import," Batrun said.

"Something is happening in his brain," Andros said, who stared at a screen. "It's some kind of energy buildup, an excess, I think."

"You must obey me," Ludendorff told the synthetic.

"I know, I know," Batrun said. "I am obeying."

"You must obey *only* me," Ludendorff said. "You must resist any other compulsion."

Batrun opened his mouth, but no sounds issued.

"Are the Rull androids mining the supermetals in order to augment their Juggernauts?" Ludendorff asked.

Batrun groaned, but finally said, "Yes," in a haggard voice.

"Are more Juggernauts gathering there?"

Batrun nodded, seeming unable to speak the words.

"What is the exact master plan to annihilate humanity?" Ludendorff asked.

Batrun stared at Ludendorff. One could almost see the wheels turning in his cybertronic brain as an interior struggle took place. Then, the tiniest of smiles played on the synthetic's lips.

"We have to get out of here!" Andros shouted. "The buildup in his core might trigger an explosion—"

A blaster hum sounded, and a beam drilled into Batrun's forehead. The beam punched through the metal skin—and, as Maddox raced across the chamber, the synthetic's head detonated like a grenade.

-68-

Maddox dragged Professor Ludendorff to the floor as Batrun's head exploded. The blast sent shrapnel spinning in many directions, shredding machines, which caused more explosions.

From on the floor, Ludendorff groaned.

Maddox released him, sat up and checked himself. He'd dived under the shrapnel spread, which hadn't gone downward in their direction due to the steel table upon which the head had rested.

Andros sat up, with blood streaming down his left arm.

"Are you hit, Professor?" Maddox asked.

"I don't know," Ludendorff groaned. "I struck my chin against the floor. I might have chipped some teeth. Why did you…" the professor ceased his complaints as he saw Andros slide onto the floor.

Maddox hurried to the Chief Technician, grabbing a compress from a first-aid kit and beginning to stanch the blood flowing from the upper arm.

"I'm all right," Andros wheezed. "It's nothing but a flesh wound."

Maddox pressed a patch firmly into place before he examined the chamber as he listened carefully. "The room is still airtight," the captain announced. "But the sooner we're back aboard *Victory*, the better I'll feel."

"You caused this," Ludendorff said. He held his chin, pressing against it, as he stared accusations at Maddox. "Why did you fire at Batrun?"

"He saved us, Professor," Andros said, who had become quite pale. "The buildup of competing forces in Batrun's head—that's what I was trying to say. It would have produced a far worse blast if the captain hadn't fired when he did. We might have all died in a bigger explosion."

Ludendorff cocked his head as he examined Maddox. "How could you know that a blaster shot would aid us? I didn't know that."

"It was a guess," Maddox admitted. "Batrun spoke about his programming earlier. I kept wondering if a Builder might have been smart enough to foresee what you did to Batrun and have a counterplan."

"The Builder could have never known something like that," Ludendorff said. "They lack supernatural powers."

"The Builder guessed the Jotuns might double-cross him. Why not have contingency plans in case his synthetic was compromised?"

"Incredible," Ludendorff said after a moment of thought. "Yes. Now that you say it, it's obvious." The professor sighed. "Good work, I suppose. You likely saved us."

Maddox shrugged.

Ludendorff let go of his chin, but it looked as if he might be grinding his teeth in anger. "All my hard work—gone. What a terrible waste."

"On the contrary," Maddox said. "You did far more than I would have thought possible, obtaining answers to a host of questions. For instance, there are no Jotuns to worry about. Lisa Meyers is a Methuselah Woman. The Rull androids are gathering at Alpha Centauri to strike Earth. The Juggernauts will be far deadlier because they used supermetals to upgrade weapons components. Batrun didn't invent a way to travel ten thousand light-years, but a freak accident happened that propelled us into Leviathan territory. No, Professor, I feel much better about our chances now that I know what's going on. But that's only provided we can get home soon enough."

"Sir," Galyan said. "I believe Andros Crank is in need of further medical attention."

Maddox looked and saw the Chief Technician unconscious on the floor. "Right," he said. "Let's get going, Professor. We'll tackle the hyper-spatial tube after we get Andros onto *Victory*. But before we start on any of that, thank you. What you did in here borders on the miraculous. In my estimation, you really are a genius."

Despite himself—and his dislike of Maddox—Ludendorff grinned, preening even as he nodded in agreement with the captain.

-69-

Several days later, when Maddox sat up in his command chair on *Victory's* bridge, he found that Valerie had beaten him awake. Incredibly, she'd shrugged up hyper-spatial-tube lag faster than he had. That had to be a first.

Lieutenant Noonan hunched over her panel, tapping, studying and tapping more.

"What's the matter, Lieutenant?" Maddox asked groggily.

Valerie didn't answer, but continued to study her board.

After Batrun's head exploded, Maddox and Ludendorff had helped Andros Crank to a shuttlecraft. From there, Keith had rushed him to the starship. A waiting med team had rushed the stout Kai-Kaus to Medical.

Two days after the incident, Andros had rejoined Galyan, the special science team and Ludendorff aboard the nexus. On the fifth day, Andros and Ludendorff had spent fourteen and half hours adjusting and recalibrating the hyper-spatial tube mechanism. At the end of that time, the space-suited professor had sat before a gargantuan screen with many exotic computers purring around him. Galyan stood in attendance, checking various relays upon request.

"I don't know," Ludendorff had told Maddox. "I think I can do it. But this is going to be a rough tube journey. The main hyper-spatial mechanism is almost burned out. When we have it powered up, the nexus might explode. We might survive or we might die in the blast. I'd call it a fifty-fifty proposition."

"Make sure the nexus doesn't explode," Maddox said.

"I'm working on it, my boy, but at best, I can give us a sixty-two percent chance of survival."

Maddox nodded in understanding.

The choice, obviously, had been to go for it. They knew the score, and time had just about run out—at least, in Maddox's estimation it had. The partly repaired nexus made the hyper-spatial tube. The starship dived into the opening, and now, Maddox stared at a semi-familiar planet on the main screen.

He didn't know if the nexus had blown up or not. He hoped not, but—

"Ah…" Valerie said. "I've finally pinpointed our location. We're in the Tau Ceti System."

Maddox swiveled the chair around. "Tau Ceti, where the Swarm struck the first time?"

"Exactly," Valerie said. "And that's why no one is answering me. There's no one around to answer. It's an empty star system."

"And that's why it looks so familiar," Maddox said. *Victory* had fought against the Swarm here several years ago.

Valerie looked up, smiling. "We made it back to Human Space, sir."

"We did at that," Maddox said. "Now we have to get to Earth as fast as we can."

"Should I plot a star-drive jump?"

Maddox bent his head in thought. "No. We'll use the normal jump points. I need to speak to Ludendorff."

"But if—"

"The jump points, Lieutenant. See to it."

"Yes, sir," Valerie said.

With that, Maddox headed for the exit.

***

The captain found Ludendorff in his science lab. The professor was tinkering with a small device as he sat hunched over it, using his precision tools.

"Do come in, Captain," Ludendorff said. "Can I get you something to eat or drink?"

Maddox shook his head.

"Oh," Ludendorff said. "Something is troubling you. That's why you're here."

"I've been wondering about several things. One of them is the Old One or Yon-Soth on the Forbidden Planet."

"Imposing names, aren't they?"

"Last mission, we dealt with the primal Old One in the Sagittarius Spiral Arm. His plans seemed long-term and subtle."

"The other on the Forbidden Planet might have panicked," Ludendorff said. "Perhaps he knew his time was short and did what he could as fast as possible."

"Exactly."

"I don't understand."

"He did what he could, using the available materials around him. That included a stasis-frozen Builder and crew deep in Albatross VII, Rull androids hidden throughout the Commonwealth and…"

"And what?" asked Ludendorff.

"Exactly," Maddox said. "According to Batrun, the Yon-Soth goal was human extinction. Did the Old One on the Forbidden Planet desire revenge for what had happened?"

"That's the most likely motive I can think of," Ludendorff said. "We were killing him. He wanted to kill us back. An eye for an eye, you could say."

Maddox nodded. "Can Rull androids with supermetal-enhanced weapons annihilate humanity, and that includes the New Men?"

"Hmm… That's an interesting point. I don't see how."

"Meyers through Prime Minister Hampton attempted to start a war between the New Men and the Commonwealth. That would have bloodied both of us, but it still doesn't seem like it would have been enough to ensure human extinction."

"I see what you're saying. Where's the next shoe going to drop, eh?"

"What's that supposed to mean?"

Ludendorff grinned. "A man lives in an apartment, and he has an annoying neighbor above him. Each night, the neighbor goes to bed, taking off his shoes. The first shoe drops with a clunk and the second drops with another annoying clunk. Then, the neighbor goes to sleep. One night, though, the man hears the first shoe drop—but after that, he hears nothing. It starts to drive him crazy because he can't get comfortable until he hears the second shoe fall."

Ludendorff made a sweeping gesture. "We know the Old One wanted to exterminate humanity in all its forms, which included the New Men, naturally. The Rull androids, the synthetics and Lisa Meyers are the first shoe. Where or what is the second shoe?"

"Any ideas?" asked Maddox.

The professor shook his head.

"Right," Maddox said. "I was afraid of that. It has to be something. The trick is figuring out what it is before it strikes. You know…?"

Maddox turned around and headed for the hatch.

"Excuse me," Ludendorff said. "Do I know what?"

"I have a call to make," Maddox said.

-70-

Maddox sat in one of the most protected chambers aboard *Victory*. It was rather small and held one critical piece of equipment: the long-range Builder comm device. In size, shape and color, it was the exact replica of the Emperor of Throne World's and Lord High Admiral's Builder comm devices.

Galyan appeared as Maddox picked up the microphone lying on the table.

"Do you mind if I listen in, sir?" the holoimage asked.

"Not at all, Galyan."

With his thumb, the captain flicked on the complicated piece of equipment. The Builder device allowed one to communicate over vast distances. It did not work over thousands of light-years, however, but only over hundreds of light-years. It still made the device an incredibly important piece of Star Watch equipment.

"This is Captain Maddox. Do you hear me, Lord High Admiral?"

Maddox waited, but heard no response. "That's strange," he told Galyan. "Someone should be in attendance over there."

"Hello?" came the Lord High Admiral's voice. "Is this Captain Maddox?"

"Yes, sir," Maddox said. "We've been far away, sir, in the Scutum-Centaurus Spiral Arm, if you can believe it. Now we're in the Tau Ceti System. We're hurrying to Earth as fast as we can. But I have something important to tell you."

"Go ahead, Captain."

Galyan urgently motioned to the captain.

"Just a minute, sir," Maddox said. "I have a small development here." He muted the microphone and set it on the table. "Trouble?" he asked Galyan.

"That is not the Lord High Admiral," the holoimage said. "I have analyzed the voice patterns and it comes from a mechanical source."

"Like a synthetic or an android?" asked Maddox.

"That is correct," Galyan said.

Maddox stared at the holoimage as a strange feeling of futility swept through him. Had androids or synthetics managed to kidnap and now impersonate the Lord High Admiral? This was a disaster, if true.

"There is something else," Galyan said. "If you will notice the readings to the side, over there, sir."

Maddox got up and peered at readings on the side of the Builder device. "I see them. What do they mean?"

"Someone has hacked the signal, sir," Galyan said.

"Hello?" the Lord High Admiral said from the large device.

Maddox sat down again and thoughtfully picked up the microphone. Who could hack a Builder comm signal? The most likely candidate would be a Builder or a Builder servant.

The captain decided on a guess as he switched on the microphone. "Hello, Doctor Meyers. I'm impressed with your subterfuge and trickery."

For a moment, there was no response.

"Cat got your tongue?" Maddox asked.

"You're more resourceful than I'd realized, Captain," the ultra-sexy voice of Lisa Meyers purred over the ether.

"That is a real person speaking," Galyan said softly. "It is a different someone than the one who impersonated the admiral."

Maddox nodded and motioned Galyan to keep quiet.

"I trust you've been well," Maddox said into the microphone.

"My sources tell me your starship disappeared in the Alpha Centauri System some time ago," Meyers purred. "According to the sources, it was not a normal star-drive jump. In fact, Captain, that jump should have propelled you far, far away. I'm surprised you made it back to Tau Ceti. I'm sure it was a true odyssey. Although, I also have to add, you've been gone just long enough for the situation to ripen."

"You don't have to do this," Maddox said. "We can help you with your stasis-frozen Builder."

"You? Help me? Surely, you're joking?"

Maddox debated with himself. Was Meyers motivated solely by the Yon-Soth ray? Was there another agency at work?

"Builders shape and construct," Maddox said. "They are not in the habit of genocidal destruction."

Meyers said nothing.

Maddox glanced at Galyan—

"That was a mistake, Captain," Meyers said abruptly. "That was a terrible mistake, as you just told me too much. I have no idea how you learned what you did, but surely you realize that I am far superior to Ludendorff or Strand. They are jokes, emotional children with scattered mental abilities. I am the real deal, Captain. I can extrapolate from the smallest pieces of data. You know what I am, which means you must have discovered who I am. Since you refer to the Yon-Soth and speak about a Builder, I can only assume that Ludendorff broke Batrun."

Galyan motioned urgently to Maddox.

Once more, the captain muted the microphone and set it on the table.

"I submit to you," Galyan said, "that the woman indeed has fantastic reasoning capabilities. We may have been underestimating her all along."

Maddox didn't want to hear that.

"You should be careful how much more you say," Galyan told him. "She may be able to trick you into revealing more than you should."

"Are you still there, Captain?" asked Meyers.

Once more, Maddox picked up the microphone. "Let us help you," he said. "During our various missions, we've had encounters with Builders. They've given us their blessing each time." That wasn't true, but she likely didn't know that. "I'm sure we can rid you of the Yon-Soth hallucination."

"I'm sure you're desperate," Meyers replied. "What did you say earlier, hmm...? You're in the Tau Ceti System? Thank you. Now I know exactly how much time we have left to strike. If you'd made it back sooner, Earth might have stood a chance. Now, with the forces Star Watch has in the Solar System..." Meyers chuckled throatily. "You aren't going to be in time, Captain, although you might just make it in time to see hellburners scorch your planet. Consider that, Maddox. You caused my planet to wither under hellburners and asteroids. Now, I shall do the same to you."

Maddox's head jerked as he stared at Galyan.

The holoimage's eyes blinked rapidly.

"Goodbye, Captain," the sexy voice of Meyers said. "Do you have any last words?"

Maddox did not, as he was afraid he would give away something critical to Meyers. Instead, the captain shut off the Builder comm device.

If there was a moment to think, to really think things through, then this was it. If only he hadn't told her *Victory* was in the Tau Ceti System.

Maddox stood.

"What do we do now?" Galyan asked.

"What we can," Maddox said, "and as fast as we can. But first I have to think."

-71-

Maddox sent more messages to the Lord High Admiral, but failed to get through every time. The indication was that in some fashion, Doctor Meyers could block the long-range Builder comm.

That was a devastating power.

He spoke with Ludendorff about the Meyers conversation and later with Meta.

"Meyers as much said that she regards herself as the Old One," Meta said in their quarters. "The key phrase was, 'You caused my planet to wither under hellburners and asteroids. Now, I shall do the same to you.'"

Maddox nodded. The statement had been troubling him. "At times, though, Meyers also acts like her own person."

"Maybe she has a split personality," Meta said. "Can that work to our advantage?"

"We can hope and try," Maddox said. "The better idea is to have greater firepower when the Juggernauts hit. I wonder…"

Meta waited as they sat on the bed.

"Should I call the Emperor of the Throne World?" Maddox asked.

"How can he help us?"

"Maybe he could relay a message to the Lord High Admiral for me."

"The Emperor might also use our weakness against the Commonwealth."

Maddox nodded. "The New Men despise weakness, and they're among the most opportunistic of people."

Meta glanced at him sharply.

"Are you suggesting I'm opportunistic like them?" Maddox asked.

"Well...sometimes," Meta said.

Maddox slid off the bed and began to pace. "Yes. I am part New Man. I can't deny it. Should I thank my father for that? He raped my mother."

Meta jumped off the bed, hurrying to him, hugging him as hard as she could—which made Maddox wince at the forcefulness of it.

"Easy," he whispered.

"Sorry, love," Meta said. "I know..."

He looked down into her beautiful face. He loved this woman. She was so good for him. She worried about him. She reminded him of the..."

Maddox let his thoughts trail away. He didn't want to think about the Brigadier just now. But she loved him, too. The captain cocked his head. Just why did the Brigadier love him? Why had he never sought to learn the reason?

"Do you truly know that your father raped your mother?" Meta asked softly. She had been watching his face.

Maddox looked at Meta anew, and he frowned. "I've always believed it. My mother fled a New Man birthing center. I do know the New Men are domineering and think of themselves as the Lords of Creation. Many of them treat their wives and concubines poorly. Why else did my mother flee unless she hated my father? Why would she hate him unless he'd raped her, forcing..."

"Forcing you on her?" Meta asked softly.

Maddox disengaged from Meta and turned away. He didn't want to think about this. It didn't matter.

"You're haunted by the thought," Meta said.

Maddox whirled around to stare at her.

"You believe this about your father, but none of it may be true. Why did your mother flee? What if you never find the real reason?"

Maddox licked his lips, and a new thought struck. Did the Brigadier know more about his origins than she'd ever let on? Maybe it was time to ask her about this—when the present mission was over. Maybe he needed to find his father—if the New Man still lived—and find out other truths.

"Meta, you give me good advice. You're not like other women, you're…"

She came to him, hugging him again. "I'm your wife. I'm your refuge, just like you're mine. I love you, Maddox. What's more, I respect you. You're the leader, my husband."

Maddox grinned and swooped Meta off her feet. "I do love you," he said, carrying her to the bed. "I'm the protector and the cherisher. You're my vase, Meta, my precious gift of great worth."

Afterward, as they lay together, Maddox stroked Meta's cheek. "You're right. I'm not going to call the Emperor. Maybe Meyers wants us to race home. Maybe she figures it doesn't matter anymore. But we're going to see about that. As of this moment," he said, sliding to the edge of the bed, "we're on emergency jump drive so we can warn Earth, hopefully in time."

-72-

Valerie asked Maddox a disturbing question one star-drive jump short of Earth. *Victory* was 3.21 light-years away from a parked orbit. Valerie sat at her station as Keith readied for the last jump. Maddox sat impatiently in his chair.

"Sir," Valerie said, "if Doctor Meyers was able to block the long-range Builder comm and impersonate the Lord High Admiral—"

"A synthetic likely impersonated Admiral Cook," Galyan said, interrupting and correcting her.

"Fine, fine," Valerie said. "Either way, isn't it possible that Meyers has blocked the Lord High Admiral from communicating with us, and even more, might have impersonated you, sir?"

Maddox frowned. "The possibility exists," he said slowly.

"What might Meyers have said as you?" Valerie asked. "Or had a synthetic say as the captain?" she said in Galyan's direction.

"I have already computed the likeliest possibility of what was said," Galyan replied. "Clearly, Meyers must want *Victory* destroyed. Thus—"

"So that's it,' Maddox said, interrupting as he jumped up. "Kill us on sight. If we just appear in Earth orbit, or near Earth orbit—"

"I would think a full defensive barrage would strike for us," Galyan said.

"Mr. Maker," Maddox said, "abort the jump."

"Aye, aye, sir," Keith said as he manipulated his board.

The energy build-up from the antimatter engine began to wind down.

"We'll arrive between Venus and Earth's orbital paths," Maddox said. "That should give us enough time to break any jamming and get a message to the Lord High Admiral, correcting any false ideas about us."

"I feel much better about that, sir," Valerie said, "than just appearing near trigger-happy Star Watch vessels."

Maddox resumed his chair. He noticed a light blinking on an armrest. He clicked an intercom button.

"Ludendorff here," the Methuselah Man said. "I just had a thought."

Maddox told him about Valerie's idea.

"Ah," Ludendorff said. "I should have thought of that, too. Yes. I agree it's a distinct possibility."

"You thought of something else then?" Maddox asked.

"Indeed. It has been bothering me ever since we talked about the second shoe. I'm referring to the Rull androids and the Juggernauts. Granted, Star Watch's Home Fleet might have fewer warships than is wise. Yet, as long as the Destroyer is parked near Earth, how can any number of upgraded Juggernauts hope to win a set-piece battle against Star Watch?"

Maddox frowned for only a moment. He straightened abruptly. "Meyers will use android or synthetic lookalikes to hijack the Destroyer."

"I see you understand the possibilities," Ludendorff said. "The Juggernauts combined with the Destroyer could not only wipe out the Home Fleet, but obliterate all the Solar System's planets. That would be tit for tat in the Yon-Soth's ring of eyes."

"Androids are going to make or have already made a stab to hijack control of the Destroyer," Maddox said, believing it even more by stating the obvious move.

"If true…" the professor said.

Maddox bent his head in furious thought. "We have no more time to waste. We have to get home and warn—"

"Maybe at this stage, warning is the wrong plan," Ludendorff said, interrupting. "Maybe we should appear as close to the Destroyer as possible and send boarding marines to recapture it."

"That bumps up against the other problem," Maddox said. "That Star Watch is likely loaded for bear and will fire on *Victory* as soon as we come out of the star-drive jump."

"Our present situation counts as a dilemma," Ludendorff agreed. "If the androids are already aboard the Destroyer, we don't want them to begin fighting until we can warn the Home Fleet and they can set up to fight the Destroyer."

Maddox shook his head. "The Home Fleet won't stand a chance against the Destroyer. If the androids are inside the alien monster-ship…the game is already over. No. We have one shot. We have to operate on the assumption the androids have already hijacked the ship. That means a surprise raid against the Destroyer as the androids are possibly still trying to lure the Home Fleet into a trap."

"And if you're wrong about all that?"

"Then, in our dying, we tell Star Watch the truth. Earth's safety is more important than ours."

"I categorically don't agree," Ludendorff said.

"Fortunately, I'm the captain. We'll reconfigure the jump yet again. We have marines and battle suits. Right," Maddox said. "It's time to pull out every stop if we're going to defeat the Methuselah Woman's plan."

-73-

Lieutenant Noonan's navigational skills were flawless. She plotted *Victory's* appearance to the millimeter from a star-drive jump 3.21 light-years out. Keith executed her navigational plan perfectly.

The starship came out of the jump between the fifty-kilometer oblong Destroyer of the Nameless Ones and the Star Watch picket vessels stationed around it. The ancient ship had neutroium hull armor, the best in known existence. It also had a vast aperture in front, which would pour out a terrible beam of annihilating power.

Several years ago, at the start of the first Swarm Invasion, Maddox and the crew had gone into a null region and brought back two such Destroyers. The Swarm invaders had destroyed one of the giant warships. Star Watch had preserved the last one. It was the great reserve vessel of Earth, meant to protect the planet when everything else had failed. The Destroyer had once been in the control of the Nameless Ones, who had been driven by spiritual creatures, the Ska. This ship had helped gut hundreds and perhaps even thousands of home planets of sentient species. This Destroyer had aided in countless genocide campaigns waged by the Nameless Ones through their cycles of existence. That had given the ship a miasma of doom. The very armor, the strange corridors oozed with the grim feeling of death. Human crews could not withstand the ship's aura for long without literally going mad.

That meant many crew rotations, and it also meant that most of the time, the Destroyer was empty, a museum piece of alien evil.

Victory appeared between the armed picket vessels and the mighty engine of destruction that dwarfed every other known warship, including the next biggest, the Juggernaut. The Adok starship sat there, inert for the first few minutes due to jump lag.

The first picket ship saw *Victory* and gave the alarm. That alarm sped through the rest of the picket fleet. The crews aboard the vessels began arming their fusion cannons.

At the same time, a carrier began braking. It was the SWS *Essex*, an older vessel but carrying a newer complement of strikefighters, bombers and elite fold-fighters.

As Maddox and his crew began shaking off jump lag, the first wing of strikefighters catapulted from the *Essex* and roared toward the Adok starship.

Maddox stirred as message blared aboard the bridge speaker.

"This is your last chance, *Victory*. We know that—"

"Valerie," Maddox said.

"Here, sir," she said. "I'm giving you visual."

From the main screen, Commodore Earl Dumas regarded Maddox, the man who had been giving them the warning.

Commodore Dumas was a large overweight man with long, non-regulation hair. He wore many heavy rings on his fat fingers, and his Star Watch uniform hung on him loosely like a great tunic. He had dark, cunning eyes, and for all his girth and unsoldierly appearance, he had fought splendidly at the Forbidden Planet and during the first Swarm Invasion.

"Captain Maddox," Dumas said. "Order your people to place you under arrest. Failure to do so will result in your ship's immediate destruction."

"I will," Maddox said. "First, put me through to the picket command."

"I'm afraid not, Captain, not until you're in my custody."

"Is the Destroyer's crew aboard it?"

Dumas rubbed one of his glittering rings against his jowls. "That's your game, eh? You plan to hijack the Destroyer."

Something was off. "Are you bringing a crew to the Destroyer?"

"No more delays, Captain. Are you under arrest or not?"

Maddox motioned to someone unseen. He nodded and faced the main screen, faced Commodore Dumas. "I just sent for marines. They'll be here in a few minutes to take me to the hangar bay. From there, I will board your carrier."

"Sir," Valerie said, "the picket fleet's fusion cannons are hot. The picket ships are almost ready to fire."

"Commodore, did you hear that?"

"No more delay, Maddox. I know your clever ways. I'm not falling for one of your schemes."

"Bombers are launching from the *Essex*," Keith said. "Those bombers are meant to be used against us. He has to be an android, sir."

Maddox winced internally at Keith's verbal blunder. Of course, Dumas was an android or an android-controlled human. But the words had been said and it was too late to take them back.

On the main screen, Commodore Dumas heaved himself straighter on his command chair, twisted and shouted, "He knows! Start the attack. Destroy *Victory*."

"Andros," Maddox said, "I need the shields up now."

"Give me thirty more seconds, sir," a desperate Andros said.

"Valerie, patch me through to the picket leader or connect me to any of the picket vessels," Maddox said.

"The *Essex* is jamming our communications, sir," Valerie said. "They have advanced jamming equipment, too. I've started a burn-through, but that will take time."

Maddox made a snap decision. "Keith, start moving us away from the *Essex* and away from the Destroyer."

"We don't have much motive power yet, mate," Keith said. "But aye-aye, whatever you want."

"Sir," Galyan said, "might I suggest antimatter missiles? If you launch and ignite, we will all perish, but that will stop the androids from the *Essex* reaching the Destroyer."

"The picket ships have started firing," Valerie said. "Fusion beams have begun burning into our hull armor."

"Strikefighters are leading an attack wave," Keith said. "Bombers are heading at us as soon as they launch."

"Give me a neutron cannon," Maddox told Galyan.

More fusion-beam fire struck *Victory* as the hull armor heated up and began melting in places. The *Essex's* strikefighters and bombers raced to the attack. The first fighters began lobbing shells at *Victory*.

"This might have been a bad idea, sir," Valerie said.

Maddox was on his feet. He whirled around. "Galyan, you've got to speak to a picket leader. Go now, and persuade them."

"The neutron cannon—" Galyan said.

"Go!" Maddox shouted.

The holoimage disappeared.

"There," Andros said. "It's a start."

A blue nimbus suddenly appeared around *Victory*, the electromagnetic shield. The fusion beams no longer lanced against the glowing, melting hull armor, but caused the shield to change colors. The combined picket-force fire soon brought the shield to dark brown heading for black. Strikefighters shells pounded kinetic energy and mass against the weakening shield. The heavier-firing bombers were almost in range.

Maddox sat in his chair, his right hand balled into a fist. He willed Galyan to succeed. So far— "Lieutenant," he said, "get ready to launch three antimatter missiles."

Valerie nodded as she tried to speak, and as her fingers blurred across her board.

"Captain, Captain," Andros said, "some of the picket ships have stopped firing."

"Galyan," Maddox said. "Did he succeed?"

"Sir," Valerie said, "I'm receiving a message. It's due to a hard burn-through, super-powerful, but it's fuzzy—"

The Lord High Admiral Cook appeared on the main screen. He was hard to see through the shifting blizzard. "Maddox?" Cook asked.

"Sir," Maddox said. "The *Essex* is full of androids. They're attempting to hijack the Destroyer and attack Earth in combination with upgraded Rull Juggernauts."

"Are you mad, son?" Cook shouted. "We know about your treachery. It's time to surrender."

"The idea about my so-called treachery is Doctor Lisa Meyers's doing, sir," Maddox said as calmly as he could. "She's a Methuselah Woman."

The big old admiral in his white uniform stared at Maddox as he absorbed the news, finally groaning, "The Lord help us. We don't need more of *them* around. But how can I believe you?"

Maddox shook his head. "You have to go with your gut, sir. This mission has been full of lies and subterfuges. Remember how Lisa Meyers foisted Hampton on us, and he tried to get you to start a war with the New Men? Meyers wants to wage a genocide campaign against us. The Old One on the Forbidden Planet is the source of this attack, sir. That's why it's been so underhanded all along the line."

Through the blizzard on the main screen, Cook stared at Maddox harder than before. "Damn you, son," Cook finally said. "Why do you make things so difficult all the time?"

Maddox waited. What more could he say?

"I believe you," Cook said. "And if you're right, the *Essex...*"

"The androids on the *Essex* are trying to destroy *Victory* so they can board the Destroyer. If you don't believe me, use the Builder scanner on Pluto. Target the Alpha Centauri System. There's a Supermetals Planet there the Rull androids are using."

"I can't reach the *Essex,*" Cook said. "The jamming is too good."

"It's your call then, sir," Maddox said. "You have to do what you think is right."

"I can't believe I'm actually saying this," Cook told him. "But you are the *di far*, and Commodore Dumas is indeed taking an emergency crew to the Destroyer. We've gotten warning about Juggernauts coming from Alpha Centauri. That's why Dumas is making the run to the Destroyer. Captain, cripple the *Essex* if you have to, but don't stop until they do. Don't let androids board the Destroyer. That's an order."

-74-

Maddox followed the order, using the disruptor cannon to destroy the *Essex* with all hands aboard—the picket ships helped in that. Every attacking strikefighter and bomber perished to the picket ships or *Victory's* neutron cannon. Several fold-fighters made a run for it, heading for a Laumer Point in the Asteroid Belt.

Neither *Victory* nor any other Star Watch vessels in the system attempted to catch the folding fold-fighters. Instead, Star Watch zeroed in on them from afar, wondering what their Asteroid Belt destination indicated.

With the *Essex's* destruction, communication between Admiral Cook and Maddox became easy. *Victory* and the Destroyer were midway between Venus and Earth's orbital paths, so there was little time lag between Cook on Earth and Maddox.

"I'm sending another crew—a human crew this time—to the Destroyer," Cook said. The big old man sat in his study, with several secretaries in the background. "It will take the crew time to reach the killer and time for them to check ship systems and get it operational."

"We may not have the time," Maddox said. He was in his ready room, with Galyan in the background.

"Son, I do what I can, how I can. I'm not a magician, nor am I a *di far*."

"The concept is highly overrated, sir," Maddox said.

"I used my Builder comm device," Cook said. "The scanner crew on Pluto has studied the Alpha Centauri System. They found the Supermetals Planet and managed to zero in on it. Someone was mining it. They're gone, though. There's no sign of androids or Juggernauts."

"That means the Android Fleet is already on the move," Maddox said. "Maybe that's why the fold-fighters are hightailing it to the Asteroid Belt. The Juggernauts will come in there."

"Or the fold-fighters are trying to deceive us," Cook said. "The androids want us scared so I'll call in the warships around Jupiter in order to combine all the vessels in the Home Fleet. They want us to let the *Glorious Kent* escape."

Maddox almost told the Lord High Admiral that he'd better combine the warships of the Home Fleet while he had the opportunity. Yet, he was only a captain in Star Watch. He was the junior officer here, not the leader. For once, Maddox held his peace. He didn't have a good enough poker face, though.

"Spit it out," Cook said. "You want to tell me something."

"With your permission, sir…"

"I told you to spit it out, son. Now, get to it."

"We have to destroy the Android Fleet—"

"If it exists," Cook said, interrupting.

"It exists, sir. I suggest—" Maddox sat up. "I wonder if it's possible to design a cloaking device able to deceive a Builder scanner."

"Oh…" Cook said. "That would be awful. That would mean—" The old man cocked his head. "How do you come up with these hairy scenarios?"

"I think what I would do in their place given their objectives. Doctor Meyers is a Methuselah Woman. I suspect she was the chief servant to a Builder. That was over one thousand years ago. Yes. She must have access to incredible technology. She must know more about Builders than any human alive."

"Very well. You've sold me on the possibility. The Juggernauts might have advanced cloaking, good enough to deceive our Builder scanner. All right then, how do we find them? Maybe they're already in the Solar System sneaking up on Earth right now."

"Or maybe they're in the Solar System and sneaking up on the besieging warships around Jupiter," Maddox said.

Cook closed his eyes as if he was in pain. Then, he bowed his head and actually let it touch the table in front of him. Maddox wasn't surprised to hear a quiet groan from the old man. What did surprise him was how long Cook let his head rest on the table, as if already defeated.

"Are you all right, sir?" Maddox finally asked.

Cook raised his head. He looked tired and old. "I'm not all right," the admiral said. "There are too many variables and unknowns. If I guess wrong, Earth might die under a hail of hellburners. It's starting to sound as if Doctor Meyers wanted us to trap her on Jupiter. That was the beginning of her plan, maybe to pull part of the Home Fleet's warships there, to separate our fleets into manageable chunks."

"I'd call it a contingency plan, sir. Her plan A was to start a war between the New Men and the Commonwealth, but we foiled that and uncovered Hampton as her Manchurian candidate. If you would like my advice, sir…"

Cook blinked several times and finally shook his head. "I'm the Lord High Admiral. They pay me to make the hard decisions. If I'm too old or too weak to do to my job, then it's time to step down. But I'm not ready to step down just yet."

Cook continued to stare at Maddox, but the old man no longer seemed to see the younger one.

"Listen to me," Cook said shortly. "I'm sending Lieutenant Colonel Stokes to your ship. He is going to be my liaison with you. He will use a fold-ship to reach you. Afterward, I want you to track down the fold-fighters racing to the Asteroid Belt. Find out if Juggernauts are using or have used the Laumer Point there. Go to the other side if you have to. Find the Juggernauts, Captain, and then race home and tell me about them."

"Yes, sir," Maddox said, wanting to ask what the admiral would be doing in the meantime with the Home Fleet. In the old days, he used Brigadier O'Hara, telling her his ideas to give to the Lord High Admiral. Could he use Stokes the same way?

They were going to find out.

-75-

Lieutenant Colonel Stokes made it onto *Victory*. Seven minutes later, the starship used its star-drive jump, appearing in the Asteroid Belt near Ceres.

The Laumer Point was two million kilometers from the biggest dwarf planet in the Asteroid Belt. Ceres was the regional capital of the belt. The local Star Watch fighters had not attempted to intercept the fold-fighters. Instead, they gave Maddox the exact time the tin cans had used the jump point to leave the Solar System.

By that time, Stokes was on the bridge. The Intelligence chief looked around, whistling. "So this is where all the action takes place. It looks too ordinary for all the tales that have been generated from this bridge."

"Glad to have you aboard, sir," Maddox said. "Would you like an extra chair brought on?"

"Yes," Stokes said.

Two marines hurried out.

"I've been doing some thinking," Maddox said.

"It would have surprised me if you hadn't," Stokes replied.

"The Home Fleet is far smaller than usual. Is there a reason for that?"

"You already know the reason," Stokes said.

Maddox stared at the lieutenant colonel.

"Oh, I see," Stokes said. "You already forgot your original assignment. You were supposed to head to the Vega System and find out about rebellious factions there, remember?"

"Vega II is in revolt?"

"No," Stokes said. "The Vega System is surprisingly placid at the moment. That makes me highly distrust it. Something is going on there, but we lack the manpower to go and see. Star Watch, including Intelligence, is stretched to the limit. While you've been gone, the old man broke the fleet into a hundred different flotillas. I wouldn't have recommended that, but it was his decision, not mine."

"Why all the flotillas?" asked Maddox.

"To keep peace throughout the Commonwealth. Those hundred flotillas are garrisoning a hundred different star systems and helping to keep the populations quiet."

"That's the wrong way to do it," Maddox said. "If one tries to defend everywhere, he ends up defending nowhere."

"A catchy saying," Stokes said. "The admiral's strategy is working, though. Star Watch is showing the flag all over the Commonwealth, keeping rebels at home playing video games instead of marching in the streets, multiplying violence."

"Until now," Maddox said. "The center is about to get hit hard, and there are too few warships at home."

"You are an astute study," Stokes said. "Yes, until now. But with the Destroyer, Earth should be safe."

Maddox snapped his fingers. "I should have already seen the next move, as the *Essex* makes it obvious. The Destroyer is the key. With it on their side, the Rull androids would have butchered us. With it on our side, we'll smear the Juggernauts. What do we know about the enemy? They have contingency plans, many of them, it seems. If they can't have the Destroyer, surely they'll try to annihilate it before the Home Fleet joins with it."

Stokes frowned as his right hand dug in a coat pocket and pulled out a pack of stimsticks. He stuck a stimstick in his mouth and inhaled it into life.

Maddox debated telling the lieutenant colonel to put that out. He didn't want his people having to deal with stimstick smoke on top of everything else. But Maddox kept quiet about the smoke for the moment.

After several puffs, Stokes said, "The Juggernauts might use the Mercury Laumer Point. They will have taken a circuitous route from Alpha Centauri to reach that point. But if they pour out of the Mercury jump point, they could race to the Destroyer before the Home Fleet could interfere with them."

"We have to go back to the Destroyer," Maddox said.

Stokes inhaled more smoke, finally shaking his head. "Orders, don't you know. We have to check this jump point first, even go onto the other side"

"This is a rabbit trail. That's what the fold-fighters are for. The Lord High Admiral was right the first time he guessed that."

"Now listen here, Maddox, you're not going to change your orders with me aboard. I'm here to see that you do what you're supposed to, not run off half-cocked like you do most of the time."

Maddox thought of several things to say at once. What he did say was this: "Lieutenant Colonel, you've pegged me. But that isn't about me. Doctor Meyers is a Methuselah Woman. She was also the personal assistant to a Builder. Meyers is cunning. She's going for the throat from the get-go. We can't let her get the upper hand even once. If the Juggernauts destroy the Destroyer…can the Home Fleet finish off the Android Fleet?"

Stokes stared at Maddox as he puffed his stimstick. "Do you know that you're the most annoying person in Star Watch? I fail to see what the Brigadier ever saw in you."

"Saw?" Maddox said, with a tinge of panic. "Is she dead?"

"What?" asked Stokes. "No! What makes you say that?"

Maddox shook his head, relieved. "It doesn't matter."

Stokes gave him a funny look, and finally dropped the stub onto the deck plates, using the bottom of his shoe to grind it out.

That struck Maddox as a filthy habit.

"Sir," Keith said. "We're near the Ceres Laumer Point."

Maddox raised an eyebrow at Stokes.

"I can't believe this," the lieutenant colonel muttered. The Intelligence officer began to pace as he kept shaking his head.

"It's my ship," Maddox said. "I'll take full responsibility for my actions."

"That's just it," Stokes said. "I'm here to keep you responsible. Oh, hell," he finally said. "You're logical when you want to be. Yes. Let's race to the Mercury jump point. I just hope Cook doesn't bust me back to major when this is all over."

"Right," Maddox said. "Mr. Maker—"

"Aye, aye, mate," Keith said. "I was listening. Now, we're off to Mercury."

-76-

Starship *Victory* waited like a shark, prowling near the Mercury Laumer Point. Valerie, Andros and Galyan all watched their sensors carefully, looking for any sign that cloaked Juggernauts were coming through or had already been this way.

The ancient Adok vessel had been here for an hour already, coming up empty so far.

"Sir," Valerie said. "The Lord High Admiral is calling."

Maddox indicated that she put him on the main screen.

Cook appeared. He was standing behind a table. No one else was in evidence, but it was clear that the Lord High Admiral stood in a conference chamber. Likely, more high brass stood just out of sight, having discussed the operational situation with the chief.

There was a noticeable time lag now, minutes instead of seconds. Cook peered through the screen sternly, even though he couldn't see any of them yet. That would come with Maddox's return message.

Earlier, Maddox had told the Lord High Admiral his plans via the Builder comm device.

"This is a terrible risk," Cook said slowly. "We have no evidence of Juggernauts, but if they are coming through soon and attack the Destroyer before the rest of the Home Fleet can reach Earth—I'm letting you know, Captain, I'm ordering the rest of the fleet to immediately head for Earth orbit. That means I'm letting the *Glorious Kent* escape Jupiter. I'm not happy about that."

"Sir," Galyan said. "I'm detecting ion traces."

Maddox nodded to the holoimage even though he continued to listen to Cook's message.

"We have a lot to answer for, son. I pray you know what you're doing. We…" Cook glanced at people standing out of sight. "That is all for now, the Lord High Admiral signing off."

Maddox swiveled toward Galyan. "Ion traces?" he asked.

"Ion traces and strange magnetic activity," Galyan said.

"At the Laumer Point?" asked Maddox.

"Negative, sir," Galyan said. "They're—Sir! I've spotted the Juggernauts. They're well past us and accelerating. I suggest we give immediate chase and warm up the disruptor cannon."

"Where are they?" Maddox snapped. "I want exact coordinates."

"I am putting it on the main screen," Galyan said.

Maddox stood, approaching the main screen.

There was empty space, and then fake outlines appeared where Galyan must estimate Juggernauts to be hiding.

"They are ten million kilometers away from us, sir, heading directly for the Destroyer."

"How do you know those are Juggernauts?" Stokes asked.

"Because of their ion disruption and magnetic anomalies," Galyan said.

"Maybe that's more misdirection," Stokes suggested. "If this Methuselah Woman is so smart, those could be decoys instead of Juggernauts."

Galyan's eyelids fluttered before he said, "I give that a thirty-four percent probability."

"Why use decoys out here?" Maddox asked Stokes.

"The best reason I can give is that Meyers wants the Star Watch ships to move away from Jupiter," Stokes said.

"They're already doing that," Maddox said.

"You've made my point, Captain," Stokes said.

"But if those *aren't* decoys—" Maddox turned to Keith. "Mr. Maker, get to the hangar bay. You're going on an attack run with a tin can. I'll give you the tactics once you're in the fold-fighter. Go!" Maddox said.

Without a word, Keith jumped up and raced for the exit.

Valerie watched him go, worry etched across her features.

***

Keith was alone in the fold-fighter, the special craft outside the starship. He was strapped in, tapping his piloting board and readying his sole payload for the mission.

He had a big antimatter missile attached by clamps to the underbelly of the vessel. Yes, there were shells in the guns and a few small anti-torpedoes. But the purpose of this flight was to place the antimatter missile in exactly the right location. Not getting himself killed was secondary to the mission's parameters.

Keith practiced his breathing. He had taken a hypo-shot before boarding. It played havoc with his organs, and he would need to sleep long and hard for a week after this. But that was okay because the shot gave him a boost that would resist the fold lag.

The fold-fighter didn't have the same energy boost, but it was a specially designed vessel with features that gave it a faster recovery time than other vessels.

"Are you ready?" Galyan asked.

"What the—?" Keith shouted, startled by the holoimage's appearance inside his fighter.

"I am sorry, Keith," Galyan said. "Did I startle you?"

"Don't do that again, mate."

"I came to deliver orders."

"That's just dandy. What are they?"

"Begin when ready," Galyan said.

"Aye, aye, mate, go tell the captain to watch close because this is going to be a show."

"That is a fine fighting spirit, Keith. Do you want me to wish you luck?"

For just a second, Keith stared at the little holoimage. "Do what you want," he said in a jaunty tone.

"Good luck, Keith. I hope you succeed in the mission and that you come back alive."

Keith felt a lump in his throat, and he hated that. This was show time, it wasn't emotional time.

"All right, Galyan. You told me the message. Now get lost."

"Ah. That is an idiom for leave."

Galyan vanished as Keith's hands blurred over the controls.

A second later, the fold-fighter folded—and reappeared at the designated position. Keith raised his head, pulled a lever, releasing the missile from the clamps and began activating the fighter for another fold in order to get the hell out of here.

That took time, though, as the fighter wasn't as ready as its ace. Then, *bam!* the tin can disappeared as the fold mechanism activated once more.

Keith lurched in his seat as the fighter reappeared again in real space and time. Seconds later, the antimatter warhead detonated twelve million kilometers away.

-77-

Maddox waited with baited breath aboard *Victory*, watching the screen that showed the targeted area.

The antimatter explosion caused a momentary whiteout in the location. No sensor could penetrate that to see if there was something else. They had to wait for the whiteout to dissipate. When it did—

"Seven Juggernauts," Valerie said from her station. "That's my count."

"Andros," Maddox asked from his seat. "Do you confirm?"

"I do, sir," the Kai-Kaus said.

"I do not," Galyan said. "I count *nine* Juggernauts."

"Where?" asked Valerie.

Galyan spit out several coordinates.

"Confirmed," Valerie said, checking her panel. "Yes, there are nine Juggernauts, sir."

Maddox saw the first one. It was a massive oval-shaped warship twenty kilometers in diameter. Nine of them meant the Android Fleet had more mass than the Destroyer did. Each Juggernaut had iridium-Z hull plating, making it the second best armored warship around. The electromagnetic shield of the Juggernaut he watched was black but getting brighter instead of collapsing from the antimatter blast.

Could the shield have withstood a direct antimatter detonation? If that was true—

"We found the Android Fleet," Stokes said. "They definitely outmaneuvered our Home Fleet. What now, Captain? Do you have any more brilliant ideas?"

"I'll let you know," Maddox said, jumping up and heading for the exit. He needed to talk to the Lord High Admiral via the Builder comm device.

***

"Sir," Maddox said over the Builder comm microphone. "I have a battle plan."

"So do I, son," Admiral Cook said. "We have to protect the Destroyer as the crew readies the ship systems for battle. The enemy has stolen a march on us, but it's not over yet. I liked your demonstration of fold-fighters. I'm going to do that again, but on a bigger scale."

"The androids will be ready for the fold-fighters this time."

"Maybe," Cook said. "We're going to find out. Now, listen here, Captain. I have specific instructions about your part in the plan. I don't want you sniping at their flanks like a wolf. You are to immediately jump back to the Destroyer. Every other starship in the Solar System with a star-drive jump is going to join you there. We're going to fight this battle as a team. The rest of the warships are heading at top velocity for Earth. But if we lose that Destroyer before it can tangle with the Juggernauts, then we're going to lose the entire Solar System."

"Yes, sir," Maddox said.

"Now, son, I'm serious about you heading back. *Victory* has firepower and good shielding and hull armor. It will be as good as an augmented battleship. I'm going to be out there soon, arriving via fold-fighter. I want your starship in my formation. Do I make myself clear?"

"Yes, sir," Maddox said.

"Then get back upstairs to your bridge," Cook said. "We know the score. Now, we're going to discover the outcome."

***

Victory gathered more data, holding back from jumping directly to the Destroyer. That was per Maddox's orders.

"What did Cook say?" Strokes asked on the bridge.

"That we leave here at the very last minute," Maddox said calmly. "Until then, we're to gather data and launch every antimatter missile we have left at them."

"Cook said *that?*" asked Stokes.

"You don't believe me?" Maddox asked, knowing that was the wrong question the second he said it.

Stokes studied the captain. "No," he finally said.

Maddox shrugged.

A few seconds later, Stokes got up from his chair and stood beside the captain. "Do you want me to pull rank on you?" Stokes asked quietly.

"I wouldn't advise it," Maddox said just as quietly.

"Your people won't listen to me if I give contrary orders, is that what you're saying?"

Maddox did not reply.

"It's time for you to obey orders," Stokes whispered. "I'll log my words and date and time them. Do you really want that?"

Maddox eyed the lieutenant colonel, finally nodding. "Yes, sir," he said. The captain cleared his throat. "There's been a change in plans. The lieutenant colonel is ordering us back to the Destroyer now."

"In violation of the Lord High Admiral's orders?" asked Valerie from her station.

"Lieutenant," Stokes asked her with the lift of an eyebrow in Maddox's direction, "would *I* violate orders?"

Valerie glanced at a stoic Maddox. "Oh," she said. "I see."

"Launch three antimatter missiles first," Maddox said.

"Yes, sir," Valerie replied.

As she did, Galyan and Andros gathered data on the antimatter warhead-damage to the nine Juggernauts. Soon, three big antimatter missiles launched from the starship, building up velocity as they headed for the Android Fleet.

"I detect only negligible damage to the second to last Juggernaut's hull armor," Galyan said. "It would seem impossible, but the direct antimatter blast did not drop any of the Juggernauts' shields."

"Because of the supermetals in the shield generators?" asked Maddox.

"In my estimation," Galyan said, "that would be the correct supposition."

Maddox looked at Stokes.

"If direct antimatter blasts can't rupture their shields," Stokes said, "what can?"

"Now we know why they're trying to take out the Destroyer first," Maddox said. "Its main beam can likely smash their shields and roast their hulls. But if there's no Destroyer around to fire…"

"I understand," Stokes said in a hoarse voice. "I take it those ships of the Home Fleet which can are supposed to gather and give battle in order to slow down the Juggernauts to give the Destroyer crew time to shake down the ship."

"Yes," Maddox said flatly.

Stokes blinked several times, frowned and finally said, "Earth may have just run out of luck."

"Then, it's time to make our own luck," Maddox said. "Helm, get ready to jump to the Destroyer. We're going to join the rest of the Home Fleet so we take on the Rull Armada."

-78-

Things did not look good for the divided Home Fleet, the Destroyer or Earth.

Nine Rull Juggernauts build up velocity, straining to reach the Destroyer before the crew powered up all the alien systems. The huge oval-shaped vessels showed greater acceleration than any of their kind had during the First Swarm Invasion. That, too, had to be due to the installed supermetals that improved so many facets of a machine, this time the main engines and thrusters.

Nine vast warships twenty kilometers in diameter surely held what was left of the androids that used to live in Human Space. At least, that's what Maddox argued at the fleet conference held aboard the Lord High Admiral's flagship, SWS *Kaiser Wilhelm*, a heavily armored *Bismarck*-class battleship.

The Lord High Admiral sat at the head of the large conference table. There was a lot of high brass here, commodores, rear admirals and even a fleet admiral, and Georgia Raker from Mississippi III, a water planet known for its prized but deadly ocean fishing.

The ad hoc fleet had seven battleships of three different classes—the old *Bismarck*-class being the newest. The fleet also had Starship *Victory*, two attack cruisers, an older carrier, two ultra-slow monitors and fifteen destroyers.

There were two ancient battleships without star-drive heading in-system from Jupiter along with nine more cruisers, another carrier, thirteen destroyers and twenty-one corvettes or escorts, but they would arrive a little later.

Even combined into one fleet, this was too few warships to defeat nine new and supermetals-improved Juggernauts. With the Destroyer at peak efficiency that would be another matter. But this wasn't a fantasy match. This was hard reality.

In the ad hoc fleet at the point of battle, the Lord High Admiral would have thirteen capital ships and fifteen smaller vessels. The key, according to Admiral Georgia Raker, were their 43 available fold-fighters and masses of antimatter missiles.

"We will confuse them with the fold-fighters and missiles," Raker said. "Then we'll hit each Juggernaut in turn with combined battleship fire. With the skillful use of fold-fighters, lots of courage and a little luck, we can defeat the Android Fleet."

No one else at the conference table seemed to be enthusiastic about her plan, as no one said a word. Finally, several commodores glanced at Maddox.

"Comments?" asked Cook, also glancing at the captain.

Maddox did not comment. Unless the Destroyer crew activated the alien killer in time, they were going to lose. Georgia Raker's idea was as good as any and probably better than most, but it likely wouldn't win them the fight.

"There is one thing," Cook said. "If Captain Maddox is correct about all the secret androids gathering to crew the Juggernauts, if we win this battle, our days of having to worry about hidden androids could be over."

"Amen to that," Georgia Raker said.

Maddox silently agreed. The androids had been a thorn in Star Watch's side for far too long. It would be good to finally be rid of them.

First, the Spacers left us and now, maybe, the androids are leaving, Maddox silently told himself.

The high brass argued a few finer points in the plan, but in the end, Cook decided to stick with Raker's operational idea. Maddox added a point near the end of the discussion.

"You should talk to the android leader, sir," Maddox said. "Sometimes, I've found ways to confound the enemy by doing so."

Cook considered the idea. "Are there any objections to that?"

No one spoke up.

"Captain," the Lord High Admiral said. "I believe talking to the enemy at the moment of highest stress is one of your specialties. You will speak for the fleet, for me."

"As you wish, sir," Maddox said. "If it's all right with you, I'd like to do so from *Victory.*"

"That will work," Cook said.

The big old man heaved a loud sigh and scanned the assembled brass. "We've fought many battles together. We lost a few but have won most of the time. This is definitely a surprise assault. Fortunately, for us, Captain Maddox discovered the plan before the androids, synthetics and Methuselah Woman, Lisa Meyers, could get a lock on victory. I know you had help, Captain. You have the strangest but one of the finest crews in Star Watch. Today, I hope all of us meld to the same degree that Captain Maddox has melded his band of misfits. We're fighting for Earth. That means we could be fighting to keep the Commonwealth together so humanity can face alien dangers as one, united in survival. The enemy is attempting to splinter humanity into many competing factions. Well, by God's grace, we're not going to let that happen."

Cook picked up a glass of water and took several sips. He looked tired but determined. "We're all expendable, every damn one of us. We have to buy the Destroyer precious time. We have to hurt the Juggernauts so when the awful primary beam opens up, it can smash them into atoms one after another. If that Destroyer beam burns battleships while completing its mission, oh well, we'll have done our duty and died well."

Cook scanned his commanders. "Is there anyone who disagrees with that?"

No one spoke up.

"Then, let us resolve to fight harder than we ever had. Let us also bow our heads as we ask the Lord God Almighty to aid human arms."

The assembled commanders bowed their heads, including Maddox.

"Dear Lord God," Cook said, with his head bowed and eyes closed. "We beg you to help us defeat the androids. We need your help, Lord. We probably don't deserve it, but we're asking just the same. Help us to be worthy of your help in the future. This I pray in your glorious name, O Lord God Almighty. Amen."

"Amen," Admiral Georgia Raker said loudly.

At that point, the meeting was over, and the assembled commanders hurried to get to the hangar bay and back to their ships.

-79-

The fold-fighter pilots were ready to lead their fragile tin cans into the thick of the fight. This time, it did not include Keith Maker. The ace was aboard *Victory*, piloting the heaviest defending vessel in the ad hoc fleet.

The Android Fleet no longer accelerated, but cruised at high velocity for the Destroyer. No doubt they would turn hard toward Earth once they destroyed the alien super-ship.

The tiny Human Fleet had started maneuvering toward the enemy. The two competing fleets were like runaway trains barreling at each other. The engagement would not last long as the fleets closed, would be beside each other for seconds, and then the two fleets would be heading away from each other. The engagement would only last as long as the beam weapons were in range and as long as the missiles could catch up to the enemy.

Maddox was aboard *Victory*. The Adok starship was in the second line. The first line held the destroyers. The smaller warships would sacrifice themselves, absorbing augmented laser fire from the Juggernauts, acting as shields for the battleships, cruisers, monitors, carrier and *Victory*. Fold-fighter antimatter missiles would theoretically be helping—but who knew if that would really happen the way Cook had planned?

"I don't detect any enemy jamming," Valerie said nervously from her station.

Maddox took a deep, worried breath. It was still twenty minutes before any beams could reach the enemy. The

Juggernauts had not launched any missiles, nor had Star Watch...yet.

"Hail them, Lieutenant," Maddox said, his voice steely calm, belying the deep breath of a moment ago.

Seconds ticked away as everyone waited. Would the androids—

"They're replying, sir," Valerie said.

Maddox straightened just a little more as he looked at the main screen.

Abruptly, a chrome-colored metallic Rull android stared at him. It was just like last time in the Alpha Centauri System, and almost as intimidating. Once, that android had worn clothes and pseudo human-skin. Once, that android had attempted to mimic men and blend into human society. A Builder had fashioned the android long ago for an entirely different purpose than the thing attempted today.

"Zon Ten?" asked Maddox.

The smooth chrome-colored head tilted. "Captain Maddox, I presume?"

"You don't remember me?"

"You humans all look alike to me, hominids attempting sentience. Yes. I remember sending you far away. We recorded the event and are already working to duplicate the feat."

"How marvelous for you," Maddox said.

"Is there a reason you hailed me, Captain?"

"Why attack and cease your existence, Zon Ten?"

The Rull android shook his chrome-colored head. "In actuality, this call means that you are begging for a reprieve, Captain. I have studied the files on you. Many consider you cunning. But I realize that desperation motivates this call. Today, Captain, superior firepower and technology will annihilate the weaker side—your side. You are about to lose Earth, Captain. But soon, it will not matter for you, as you will have lost your life. You should not have come back from wherever you went."

"The outcome in war is seldom certain," Maddox said. "You have already freed your leader, Lisa Meyers, by this maneuver. Now, why not take her and leave?"

"Meyers is not our leader," Zon Ten said coldly. "She possesses a Builder inside the *Glorious Kent*. Soon, she, too, will be in our custody. We will awaken the Builder, augmenting him with supermetals, and a new era will begin as androids truly begin to multiply and fill the universe."

"A lofty goal," Maddox said.

"Yes," Zon Ten agreed.

"But I would submit to you that Lisa Meyers *does* control the Rull androids. She does so through the synthetics she sent you."

"You pathetic human," Zon Ten said. "We obviously know about the synthetics. They no longer serve her, but *us.*"

Maddox shook his head, chuckling.

"What is that noise?" Zon Ten said. "I find it annoying."

"I bet you do," Maddox said.

"Explain your foolish statement."

Maddox looked up as he dried an eye, as if he'd been laughing hard for some time. "Boy, oh, boy, has Doctor Meyers thrown you over a barrel, and you're too dull-witted to see it. I used to think androids were logical, maybe even cunning. Now, I see how wrong I was."

"That is not an explanation," Zon Ten said. "You are attempting to goad me. Know, Captain, that you will fail in that."

"Sure I will," Maddox said. "And do you know where Lisa Meyers is now?"

Zon Ten stared at him.

"She's gone to the Supermetals Planet. She's raiding it for ores. She's going to revive the Builder on her own and tell him whatever story puts her in the best light. You can believe she's double-crossing you. What a fool you are."

"If you are correct about her actions, we will hunt down the Methuselah Woman—"

"No you won't, you tin-plated fool," Maddox said, interrupting. "She'll be long gone by then. You're a sucker doing her dirty work. Why hasn't she folded to join you in the risk of war?"

"There is no risk today. You are as good as dead."

"I can prove my allegation," Maddox said.

Zon Ten studied him coldly, finally asking, "How?"

By an act of will, Maddox kept from licking his lips. This was the critical moment. "Call her. Demand that she identify her present location. If she's at the Supermetals Planet, you'll know that she's double-crossing you."

The chrome-colored android stared at Maddox, possibly running computations. Abruptly, the screen went blank.

"Patch me through to Cook," Maddox snapped.

A second later, the Lord High Admiral appeared on the main screen. The big old man sat in his command chair aboard the *Kaiser Wilhelm*.

"What did that gobbledygook gain us?" Cook asked.

"Possibly a moment's inattention on Zon Ten's part toward us," Maddox said. "Will that matter? I have no idea, sir. I'm just stirring the pot the only way I know how. Maybe it will produce something bigger. The key is to go with it and see what the flow produces."

"Opportunism run amok," Cook muttered. "Well...it's seems to have brought you luck in the past. Let's hope it helps somehow today."

"Sir, if you're going to start missiling them with fold-fighters, this is the moment to begin."

Cook eyed the captain, but then nodded sharply and motioned to someone off screen.

The connection went blank.

Lieutenant Colonel Stokes chuckled softly while shaking his head. "You're a peach, Captain, a true peach."

"Put out that stimstick," Maddox said.

Stokes raised his eyebrows as the two locked stares. Finally, the lieutenant colonel plucked the smoldering stimstick from his mouth and mashed it against the sole of one of his shoes, dropping the crushed butt onto the floor. "Happy?" asked Stokes.

Instead of answering, Maddox stood and went to Valerie, wondering when the shooting would start.

-80-

It turned out that the shooting was about to commence. The Lord High Admiral gave Fighter Commander Anson permission to proceed.

With that, the first five fold-fighters made the short hop, each of them appearing at the forward sides of the Android Fleet. Five big antimatter missiles dropped from five underbelly clamps. Five big boosters burned hot, sending the missiles at the Juggernauts.

The androids weren't sleeping, though. Hot beams lashed out, annihilating the missiles, burning the warheads before they could ignite. The beams failed to catch the fold-escaping tin cans, however.

That was the opening move of the fighter assault as more tin cans attacked. These launched their missiles from directly ahead of the advancing Juggernauts.

Powerful lasers struck again, demolishing the warheads with furious heat. This time, the androids burned several fold-fighters before the fragile vessels escaped.

Finally, Anson's people got the measure of the androids, managing to detonate four antimatter warheads in the Juggernauts' line of advance. These explosions were farther away than the previous attempts.

At that point, Cook gave the word. The advancing-to-contact ad hoc fleet made a hard turning maneuver. They were going to attempt a flank attack—to get on the Android Fleet's right flank and strike with surprise.

Would it matter? No one knew yet. The idea was to use the antimatter explosions to create whiteouts on the sphere of battle, using them like smoke on a regular battlefield on Earth.

Fighter Commander Anson now gave his hardest order. It likely meant the death of many of his pilots. Sometimes in war, warriors had to make the supreme sacrifice so others had a chance at defeating an invincible enemy.

Fold-fighters popped into normal space a mere fifteen thousand kilometers in front of the Juggernauts and *in the middle of the Android Fleet.*

Like before, enemy lasers flashed, destroying one tin can after another. Worse, no antimatter explosions occurred. It appeared the enemy had learned their lesson from Keith's original fold-attack.

Then a fold-fighter got lucky, if dying in an antimatter fireball was luck. The flash incinerated the pilot and his vessel, and then struck Juggernaut shields.

That was the break, likely scrambling Juggernaut sensors. More appearing tin cans managed to detonate their missiles. The blasts hammered the incredibly tough shields with direct antimatter fury. Even supermetal-enhanced generators couldn't produce a shield that could take *repeated* antimatter blows.

That, it turned out, was the answer about how to knock down such a powerful shield. Use many antimatter blasts in a row to do it.

"Sir," Fighter Commander Anson said. "I have a report. A Juggernaut shield just went down."

"Keep hammering," Cook told him.

On the *Kaiser Wilhelm's* main screen, it looked as if Anson's eyes filmed up as he reported from his HQ. "The attack is killing my men, Lord High Admiral. I can knock down more shields, and maybe penetrate hull armor, but that could kill everyone in my command."

Cook swallowed uneasily, feeling as if his chest was hollowing out. This was the worst and dirtiest moment to be the supreme commander. Yet, this was his responsibility, his job and no one else's. The old warhorse steeled himself as he said, "This is it, Commander. Earth dies if we fail to hit the androids with everything we have."

On the screen, Anson nodded curtly. "I'll give the order, sir. Just give me the word to do it."

Despite everything, Cook wanted to complain, but then he silently berated himself. He was in charge. He would give the order that caused many good men to die.

"Send in your fighters, Commander, and have them launch the missiles at pointblank range. That is an order."

Anson saluted and turned away.

Cook slumped back in the command chair. He felt old, damned old, and he understood a little more why Admiral Fletcher had resigned after the butcher's battle at the Forbidden Planet. Was he getting too feeble for high command?

Get a grip, old-timer, Cook told himself. *Do your job or give it to someone who can.*

The Lord High Admiral swiveled his chair. "Get me a close-up of the attack. This could be the moment."

As the Android Fleet headed for the Destroyer, as whiteouts hid the human-crewed warships from the enemy, the fold-fighters made their final run amidst the Juggernauts. Most of the pilots had already dropped one missile. Some of them had launched two. This was brutal and terrifying, popping into existence among behemoths with impenetrable shields and some of the toughest hull armor around. One after another, in assigned patterns, the tin cans appeared, jinked, released big antimatter missiles and tried to fold away before it was too late.

This time, no fold-fighter came back. Worse, antimatter explosions annihilated half the pilots before they could release their missiles. Those missiles and warheads burned up in overpowering fury. Yet, Juggernaut shields went down, and antimatter blasts washed against iridium-Z hull armor. Iridium-Z was good, but it wasn't anything like the Destroyer's neutroium hull armor. The blasts boiled away heavy metal and interior bulkheads, burning through the Juggernauts.

Chrome-colored androids perished in their thousands, as the Juggernaut contained incredible numbers of them. Not only was this a fighting fleet, it was also going to be a colony fleet later as the androids left smoldering and hopefully dying human worlds behind.

A second Juggernaut crumpled under the furious antimatter blasts. Then, a third and fourth Juggernaut blew apart.

The fold-fighters with their antimatter missiles and kamikaze tactics had done the impossible: destroying four of the heavy vessels. To finish the job, high command needed more pilots, tin cans and antimatter missiles. The problem was:

"Sir," Fighter Commander Anson said, "I'm sorry to report that all my men are dead. They took out four Juggernauts," Anson continued bitterly, as tears streamed down his leathery face. "All my friends are gone, sir. I hope to Hell the rest of you can do as good a job as my men did."

Cook nodded somberly. "Yes, Commander, I hope that, too."

-81-

Five remaining, supermetal-improved Juggernauts continued at high velocity for the slowly warming-up Destroyer.

At that point, the ad hoc fleet of destroyers followed by battleships, attack cruisers, monitors, a carrier and *Victory* began firing fusion and disruptor cannons. The destroyers launched smaller missiles with conventional thermonuclear warheads. They all came from the upper right flank of the Android Fleet.

In return, the Juggernauts beamed hellishly hot lasers. Ordinary lasers dissipated faster than fusion or disruptor beams. That meant lasers were strongest at short range and much, much weaker at longer ranges. The old Wahhabi Caliphate had used special focusing mirrors with their *Scimitar*-class warships. The Rull androids might have used something similar, just many times more effective. Furiously hot, wide beams struck the front-wave destroyers.

The Star Watch vessels exploded like popcorn kernels. The lasers knocked down relatively weak shields and heated destroyer hulls, shattering metal, water vapor, people, coils, nuclear fuel pods, pieces of bulkheads—everything that had once made up the various ships.

The real contest started then. As massed lasers burned against the battleships, *Victory*, monitors, cruisers and the carrier, the combined Star Watch vessels focused all their beams on a single Juggernaut. The focused fire wasn't as good or as efficient as the New Men had done with their battle formation, but it still meant heavy, combined firepower directed at one vessel.

Incredibly—or maybe the Juggernaut shield was still weak from the former antimatter blasts—the targeted shield went black faster than anyone would have expected. Then the enemy shield collapsed.

There were cheers on *Victory's* bridge. Maddox sat forward, his stare laser-like as he willed the wounded Juggernaut to explode.

"I feel like a hyena trying to bring down a bull elephant," Maddox muttered.

One thing was sure: the Juggernaut's hull armor, as good as it was, wasn't as great as the supermetal-augmented electromagnetic shield had been. The combined fusion and disrupter beams drilled against the iridium-Z armor. The beams soon broke in and began devouring with deadly result.

The Juggernaut tried to evade, zigging and zagging. But the beams kept pouring into it, creating havoc, killing androids and ripping through more and more interior ship systems. Finally, in a titanic blast, the Juggernaut exploded like a giant bomb, pieces hurled in every direction.

More than half the Android Fleet had died to the fold-fighters and ad hoc fleet.

But the enemy lasers had not been idle during all this. As the fifth Juggernaut detonated, laser cannons sliced and diced three battleships, two attack cruisers and the carrier. For one dead Juggernaut, the androids destroyed half the human fleet trying its fancy flank attack.

Zon Ten in his flagship absorbed the information in silence. The humans had done far better than the synthetics had predicted. Five destroyed Juggernauts were galling indeed. The humans had courage. The fold-fighters with their kamikaze tactics had been critical to the awful destruction.

"The Destroyer is within extreme range, Zon Ten," the Juggernaut's targeting expert reported.

The chrome-colored android, the same color as everyone else on the bridge, did not respond at first.

"What is your wish, Zon Ten?" the targeting expert asked.

"Is the Destroyer—?"

"Sir," a sensor expert interrupted. "The Destroyer has begun to move. That would indicate the crew has completed its warm up. I estimate that the primary beam will soon prepare for firing."

"Zero in on the Destroyer," Zon Ten said. "Use tertiary cannons on the human warships. We must annihilate the Destroyer if our future worlds would know safety."

The other androids did not complain, did not cheer, did not do anything but carry out Zon Ten's new orders as they bored in for the attack.

-82-

The four fast-moving Juggernauts continued to pick off the Star Watch vessels one by one. Soon, the *Kaiser Wilhelm* and another *Bismarck*-class battleship, a monitor, three destroyers, nine carrier-bombers and *Victory* were all that was left of the ad hoc fleet.

"We're just dying now," Stokes said. "To continue attacking like this is senseless."

"We're not going to have much more opportunity to attack," Maddox said. "The Juggernauts have passed us. Soon, they'll be out of beam range."

As Maddox spoke, the Juggernauts quit targeting any of the Star Watch vessels. As the enemy super-ships closed with the Destroyer, their secondary and tertiary beams could now reach the mighty behemoth. Until this moment, the Juggernauts had been using their heavy lasers to chew into the Destroyer's neutroium hull armor. Now, every Android Fleet beam struck the ancient hull armor.

"Look," Stokes said on *Victory's* bridge. The lieutenant colonel stood, pointing at the main screen.

The colossal Destroyer slowly began to turn to face the enemy.

Maddox and the others glanced at each other.

"The crew must have finished their system's check in record time," Valerie said.

"Or enough so the vessel has some power," Stokes said.

"The Lord High Admiral is hailing us," Valerie said, looking at her board.

"Put it on the main screen," Maddox said.

Cook appeared there. The old man was hunched forward, staring at them with haunted eyes. He had aged this past hour. It was awful to witness.

"Listen," the old man said, wheezing as he spoke. "The Destroyer is activated, but the Juggernauts are going to tear it apart before the ship is ready." Cook used the back of his left hand to wipe his lips. He opened his mouth, but no sounds issued. He tried again, and this time, his voice came out hoarsely. "Use your jump drives. Appear directly in front of the Juggernauts. Sell yourself dearly to give the Destroyer a few more precious seconds to fully activate."

The admiral vanished from the screen, and the space scene reappeared. For several seconds, no one spoke on *Victory's* bridge.

"You heard the man," Maddox finally said with unnatural calm. "Lieutenant, make the calculations."

White-faced, Valerie turned to her board, her fingers tapping. She and everyone else knew that this was a death sentence. The longer she tapped, the more her shoulders hunched.

In time, she said in a dull voice, "The coordinates are set, sir."

"Mr. Maker," Maddox said.

"Yes," Keith said, his former zip no longer in evidence. "We're beginning the jump sequence."

The antimatter engine labored, and twelve seconds later, the ancient Adok starship jumped, heading for a sacrificial death in front of the Juggernauts.

From his chair, Maddox raised his head, groggy from the jump lag. "Lieutenant, I don't have visual yet."

"I'm working on it, sir," Valerie said, slurring her words. "There's something odd at work."

More people began to shrug off jump lag as ship systems came back online.

"Sir," Galyan said, with only part of his holoimage visible. "I am detecting the effects of a deflection field."

Maddox blinked at him. "I don't understand."

"I believe a deflection field was used against us," Galyan said.

Maddox scowled. "Do you mean like the *Glorious Kent's* deflection field?"

"That is an interesting deduction," Galyan said. "I am not sure of the mechanism's nature…but I cannot find another explanation for what has happened."

"Did we jump?" asked Maddox.

"We did," Galyan said. "Only—"

"I have visual," Valerie said, interrupting. "Look! We're badly out of position."

Maddox saw the Juggernauts. They looked much smaller than before instead of huge and barreling down on them. That meant *Victory* was farther away. Yes. The Destroyer was even tinier than before.

"We jumped in the opposite direction," Galyan said. "Instead of jumping *ahead* of the Juggernauts, we went farther behind them the same distance. And we are not alone, Captain."

Along with *Victory* was the *Kaiser Wilhelm*, the *Octagon*—a half-crippled cruiser—and three destroyers. There was no evidence of the monitor or the other remaining vessels or bombers.

"Wait," Valerie said. "Look at the wreckage."

"Where?" asked Maddox.

The Juggernauts are smashing through ship wreckage, sir," Valerie said. "Some of the other ships must have successfully jumped in front of the androids as ordered. But we didn't. People will think we're cowards."

"Never mind that," Maddox snapped. "How did this happen?"

Valerie hadn't heard him. She still stared at the main screen. "Their appearance did nothing to halt the Juggernauts' advance."

"That is imprecise," Stokes said. "The admiral wanted the Juggernauts to concentrate on the appearing vessels so the enemy would stop—for just a moment, anyway—firing at the Destroyer. Look at the Destroyer. Its orifice has aligned with the enemy. The others did buy a few precious seconds, and it might have been enough."

The Destroyer no longer used its neutroium hull armor to face the enemy, but its giant opening.

As the Juggernauts advanced, the four vessels poured massed laser fire straight into the great orifice's gut. That had to be tearing up the Destroyer's interior. Then something ominous occurred. As the hellishly hot lasers beamed, the interior of the orifice turned a deadly red color. That red intensified.

"It's a race," someone said.

Maddox nodded. This was a race between the lasers and the red beam, and he wasn't sure who would win. Would the interior of the Destroyer's orifice be able to withstand horrific temperatures if it fired the terrible red beam?

At that moment, the alien killing machine of the Nameless Ones opened up with its main battery, its only battery. As the android lasers speared into its gullet, the Destroyer fired a ray five kilometers wide.

"The wattage I am detecting…" Galyan said softly. "It is incredible."

The awful wattage of the Destroyer's beam made the supermetal-improved lasers seem like jokes. The red beam five kilometers wide had been used before to dig into planetary crusts and bring the mantle bubbling to the surface. Sometimes, the beam had cut asteroids and smaller planets in half.

"The dinosaurs are fighting it out," Stokes said.

Maybe. Maybe only one of the super-ships was a true dinosaur.

The great red beam five kilometers wide rayed the first Juggernaut. That beam boiled away the electromagnetic field in record time. Not only that, but the iridium-Z hull armor shed away, exposing the interior of the vessel. Then the red beam from the days of yore disintegrated the Juggernaut in destructive fury. One moment the great vessel was there—absorbing the pounding—and then it was gone, dissembled atoms no longer in any coherent form.

Three Juggernauts full of Rull androids continued to beam their lasers down the Destroyer's gullet. But before much time had passed, there were only two Juggernauts.

Yet, the last two must have achieved a breakthrough, for as the red beam of destruction obliterated the second-to-last Juggernaut, the alien vessel, the Destroyer built thousands of years ago, blew up in a titanic blast.

It turned out the terrible lasers had indeed chewed into the Destroyer, and maybe the final destruction should have taken minutes instead of a deadly microsecond of time. But that wasn't the way it happened. The Destroyer fired at full strength, and something inside it ignited a monstrous blast that dwarfed every blast in nearby space this past hour. The last defender of Earth—the great Destroyer—was gone, utterly and irrecoverably.

Seconds later, the final Juggernaut detonated, exploding across the metal strewn space-field. The Android Fleet had ceased to exist.

Unfortunately, the Destroyer was gone, along with almost every ship of the ad hoc fleet. *Victory*, the *Kaiser Wilhelm*, the *Octagon* and several destroyers were all that was left. More non-star-drive jump warships headed toward Earth, but the heart of Star Watch—the Solar System—was practically defenseless. Luckily, it did not seem that the androids had anything left to throw at humanity's home system.

"Galyan," Maddox said, who was the first to regain his bearings. "Start figuring out why we deflected during the last jump, going the wrong way."

"Sir?" asked Galyan.

"We have to figure out if Doctor Meyers is making her play with the *Glorious Kent*. I don't see the hauler anywhere, but I have a feeling she had something to do with our jump deflection."

-83-

From *Victory*, Galyan and Valerie scanned the battlefield. They found no indication of cloaked ships or devices that could cause star-drive jumps to deflect in the wrong direction.

"If the Juggernauts contained such devices, they are gone now," Galyan said.

Maddox was troubled nonetheless. What had caused their ships to deflect? Such a device would be a powerful weapon if used at the right time.

"This makes no sense," Maddox said. "If the androids had jump deflectors, why didn't they use them earlier against the fold-fighters?"

"An excellent question," Galyan said. "I do not have an answer for you."

"I don't like unsolved mysteries," Maddox said.

"Sir," Valerie said. "The Lord High Admiral would like to speak to you in your ready room. He asks that Professor Ludendorff be present. Lieutenant Colonel, now that the fighting is over Admiral Cook wants you back aboard his flagship."

"Ah," Strokes said. "Thank you."

Maddox was exhausted. He was sure all the survivors were tired and demoralized as well. They had won the battle, but at such a grim cost. Star Watch no longer owned a Destroyer, and the Fleet had been whittled down yet again. They had beaten the androids. That menace should be over…but was it?

There was a mystery here. Maddox's eyes narrowed. Ludendorff was in his science lab. He appeared to have been hiding there during the entire battle, and had taken no part. Was that significant?

Maddox heaved up to his feet. The space battle was over. The Android Fleet—

"We won, people," Maddox said. He looked around at haggard faces. "This was a tough one. This one was damn tough, and it took us all over the galaxy. We saved Earth, though. We did what we set out to do."

From her station, Valerie gave him a timid smile.

Keith laughed and slapped the Helm with his right hand. "We did win. You're right, mate—I mean, sir. We beat the living…tar out of the androids. There's no doubt about it, sir, we're the best."

Maddox nodded, echoing Keith. "We're the best, Mr. Maker. Never forget that."

Keith laughed again.

Andros Crank slumped back in his chair at the science station. "You don't think there are more androids left, sir?"

Maddox shook his head. "No here in the area…"

"But it's not over yet, is it?" Valerie asked.

"The main battle is," Maddox said. "The androids and synthetics worked for months, maybe years, getting ready for this. They augmented their Juggernauts with supermetals. We saw the effects. Their shields were fantastic and the lasers hotter than anything we've seen so far."

"But we beat them," Keith said.

"Annihilated them," Maddox said somberly. He scanned his people. He was proud of them. They were tired but maybe not quite as demoralized as a minute ago. Now, though, he had to deal with Ludendorff. What had the professor been up to in his science lab?

"Don't let down your guard just yet," Maddox said. "But know that the worst is over. We came through again, even if by the skin of our teeth."

Stokes cleared his throat.

"Yes?" Maddox asked the lieutenant colonel.

"The Lord High Admiral wants to speak to you and the professor from your ready room," Stokes said. "Shouldn't you get going?"

"Galyan, escort the lieutenant colonel to the hangar bay," Maddox said. "Lieutenant," he told Valerie, "you have the bridge." Maddox tugged his uniform jacket straight and headed resolutely for the exit. It was time to deal with Ludendorff.

***

Maddox barged without warning into Ludendorff's laboratory. "What have you been doing all this time?" the captain demanded.

Ludendorff looked up from where he sat beside a large table. There were masses of items or pieces laid out. The professor set down two tools beside a small open box. "I've been thinking," Ludendorff replied.

Thinking? Maddox eyed the spread-out items and laid-down tools. "What have you been thinking about?

"Events."

If that was true, why had Ludendorff been holding tools?

Maddox pulled out a chair and sat down upon it. The professor wanted to be mysterious, clearly, or he was hiding something. Maddox was almost too tired to play the game. If the professor wanted to...

Maddox noticed the professor eyeing him sidelong.

"What is it?" Maddox asked.

Ludendorff shook his head as if he didn't know what the captain meant.

"You are hiding something," Maddox said. "Your very bearing screams it out. You're finally making me curious."

"What nonsense," Ludendorff said. "I realize you have all fought splendidly. I paid attention to the battle now and again. While you fought the good fight, I sat here and thought. We have been running around like a headless chicken, going here, doing this. All the while, Star Watch and even more the Commonwealth has suffered repeated shocks and sharp blows. What does that mean?"

"You tell me," Maddox said.

"Someone is trying to splinter the Commonwealth as a jeweler might attempt to splinter a stone. As separate pieces, humanity will die easier than as a united whole."

"The androids made their attempt. If we hadn't had stopped them, they were going to obliterate life on Earth."

"Exactly," Ludendorff said. "Nine highly advanced Juggernauts should have crushed the Home Fleet and the Destroyer, annihilating each group in scattered clumps. Instead, we intervened and saved the day by sounding the alarm fast enough so there was partial fleet concentration."

"We won at a bloody cost," Maddox said.

"That was one of the items in my greater calculation."

Maddox glanced at the scattered pieces on the table, the precision tools… "Have you reached a conclusion yet?" the captain asked.

"I'm still working on the puzzle."

Maddox rubbed his jaw as he studied Ludendorff. "Do you know anything about a deflection field that could rebound star-drive jumps?"

"Eh?" asked the professor.

Something about the seemingly offhanded answer confirmed the captain's suspicion. He kept rubbing his jaw, and he thought about which ships had survived the death or sacrificial order. The *Kaiser Wilhelm*, *Victory*, the *Octagon* and several destroyers had been deflected…and therefore, saved.

"Would you give me a moment, Professor?"

"What is it now?"

"I need to confirm something," Maddox said. "I'll be right back."

"If you must," Ludendorff said.

Maddox went into the corridor. He hadn't told Ludendorff yet about the meeting in the ready room. "Galyan," he said.

The holoimage appeared in the corridor. Maddox asked the AI a quick question and Galyan's eyelids fluttered. Soon, the little Adok holoimage told Maddox want he needed to know.

"Thanks," Maddox said.

"Sir," Galyan said. "The Lord High Admiral asked why you were not yet in the ready room."

"Tell Valerie to tell Cook I'll be there soon."

"Should I join you in the professor's lab?"

"No," Maddox said. "Just do as I ask."

"Yes, sir," Galyan said, disappearing.

Maddox eyed the hatch to the science lab. They had fought and won a grim space battle. Many good people were dead, drifting as corpses in space. Nine Juggernauts were gone, having taken tens of thousands of chrome-colored Rull androids with them. Surely, that had seriously depleted the number of hidden androids in Human Space.

The Spacers were gone. Now the androids were gone, or almost gone.

Maddox forced himself to even greater alertness. He was tired with the aftershock of hard fighting. Yet, now, Ludendorff was playing his usual mind games, forcing him into a battle of wits. Maddox scowled. He wasn't going to let the devious Methuselah Man get away with…with whatever Ludendorff was trying to get away with this time.

Resolved, Maddox headed back into the science lab.

-84-

"Feel better?" Ludendorff asked.

Maddox noticed that none of the parts or pieces or the tools were on the table where they were before. He also noticed that the professor was breathing a bit harder than the first time. Had the Methuselah Man been hurrying the past minute or two, cleaning up? Clearly, that was the case.

Maddox took a chair and sat back, regarding Ludendorff, giving the old man a wan smile.

"What is it now, my boy?" Ludendorff asked.

"Providence saved our hides just now," Maddox said.

"Oh? That sounds interesting."

"Does it? Does it, really?"

Ludendorff lost his good humor as he eyed the captain. "Don't bandy words with me, old son. You're accusing me of something."

"Score one for the professor," Maddox said, still maintaining his smile.

"What am I supposed to have done now?"

"The parts you had on your table a bit ago—what did they make when assembled?"

Ludendorff opened his mouth to reply, and it seemed he was about to ask, "What parts?" Instead, the professor closed his mouth and folded his hands on the table.

"You had disassembled a machine or a device and had swept away most of the pieces when I walked in the first time," Maddox said. "Everything is gone now. I'm guessing the device acted like a jump deflector or gave our jump computers the opposite coordinates."

"What are you talking about?"

"*Victory* and the *Kaiser Wilhelm* deflected from their destinations in front of the Juggernauts. Several nearby vessels must have received similar deflections and found themselves near our two ships after coming out of jump the last time."

"You're blaming me for...*for our survival?*" Ludendorff asked, incredulous.

"That's how you view it, isn't it?" Maddox asked. "Yes. You told me some time ago that you didn't agree that we should sacrifice our lives for those on Earth. Thus, instead of allowing *Victory* to do its duty, you employed a fancy gadget. But...where did you get a gadget like that? I never heard of deflection technology until the *Glorious Kent* showed up. Do you know what that tells me, Professor?"

"I haven't a clue," Ludendorff said.

"That you were in communication with Lisa Meyers. She must have given you the deflection device. What did you pay for such an item, Professor?"

"I've had just about enough of your accusations. If I had such a device and we indeed deflected, you should be on your knees thanking me that you and your wife are still alive. Would you rather be dead?"

"That's not the point."

"The Hell it isn't!" Ludendorff shouted. "That's exactly the point. You wanted to play the Teutonic hero like Sigrid and the Dragon. You and Cook think alike—fight bravely and let everyone else take care of the issues afterward. Well, maybe I did save *Victory* and maybe I realized the Commonwealth needs that old fool of a Lord High Admiral, and thus I pulled the *Kaiser Wilhelm* to safety along with us. Yes, I'll admit a few ships in the Juggernauts' way likely gave the Destroyer a few precious extra seconds. We needed the others to sacrifice themselves, but we didn't need our best people to die like that."

"And you're among our best people?"

"You state an obvious truth," Ludendorff replied.

Maddox knew there was no shaming Ludendorff, so why even try. Instead... "When did Lisa Meyers give you the device?"

Ludendorff held the captain's gaze, but couldn't continue to do so as he looked away. "She did not *give* me any device," the professor said.

Maddox considered the professor's words. "Oh. She gave you the schematics so you could hurriedly build the device while the rest of us fought."

"You haven't been fighting the entire time," Ludendorff said.

"What did you give her in return?" Maddox asked.

Ludendorff looked up. "She's a remarkably beautiful woman, wouldn't you agree?"

Maddox barely refrained from rubbing his forehead. "What have you gotten yourself mixed up in this time, Professor?"

Ludendorff shook his head before looking up at the ceiling. "You still don't understand, do you? I used to be a man, an ordinary man, but long ago, the Builders sent servants to Earth. The servants snatched me and took me far away to the Builders. They worked on me. They trained me, and they taught me to love the Builders. I cannot do otherwise, Captain."

"Do you love the Builders so much that you would betray humanity?"

"That has never been the question, my boy."

"Until now?" asked Maddox.

Ludendorff stared at his hands as he squeezed them tight and opened them wide. "I am the ultimate man. I have so many responsibilities... I have protected the human race for far longer than you can understand. You're a pup, a hybrid with inordinate luck, and yet you dare to judge me. No, sir, I will not stand for that."

"What did you do, Professor?" Maddox asked tiredly.

"I bargained with the devil," Ludendorff said. "Yes. I caused our ships to deflect and saved our lives. I saved mine, as well. I also gained some precious new technology from that minx, Lisa Meyers."

"I thought you said she was beautiful."

"She is, and I was sorely tempted to teach her highly advanced sexuality. I almost took her offer. But I am Professor Ludendorff. I master women. They do not master me. Thus, I will keep the deepest love arts from her, lest she become unconquerable by any man."

"What did Meyers gain from you?" Maddox asked.

"Knowledge of our outbound trip, my boy," Ludendorff said. "I told her about the Sovereign Hierarchy of Leviathan and about the nexus with the graveyard of spaceships around it."

"You told her the truth about those things?"

"She is a Methuselah Woman. She would have detected lies."

"And you did this during the battle?"

"I did."

"You think that was a fair exchange?"

"She received more than I did, I realize—"

Maddox stared at Ludendorff.

The old Methuselah Man couldn't help it. He broke into a huge grin. "She received more than I, until I used a trick or two. Doctor Meyers is racing to the Supermetals Planet. She loves her Builder and will do anything to revive him. She almost used my ancient conditioning to pull me with her. But after what the Bosks did to me last mission—I have enough of myself in charge of me that I resisted the ancient lure. I'm sure that astonished her."

"What will she do upon reaching the Supermetals Planet?"

"She has an ally. I'm not sure whom, but I suspect it is Lord Drakos."

"And?" asked Maddox.

"I don't know, at least, not with assurance. I sensed that Doctor Meyers was frustrated with us—I mean humanity in general and Starship *Victory* in particular. She must have realized that her android allies were about to perish, or maybe she was just hedging her bets."

"Zon Ten said he hated the Methuselah Woman."

Ludendorff shrugged. "Whatever Zon Ten's feelings were—if that's even the right way to say it—Meyers maneuvered the androids to do her bidding. They were her pawns. She meant for them to smash Earth. She hates humanity with inordinate passion. I think it's more than just the Yon-Soth's rays that have caused that. She has a dark heart. I'm not sure why exactly."

Ludendorff blinked several times before shuddering. "You must kill her, my boy. Kill her before she engineers humanity's death."

"Wait. *I'm* supposed to kill her while you trade secrets with her so you can double-cross us at a critical instant?"

"I did not double-cross us. I saved our collective skins, and you all have clean consciences because I took the burden upon myself. Now, however, I am warning you about a future evil, and her name is Doctor Lisa Meyers."

"Not if we can catch her at the Supermetals Planet."

Ludendorff shook his head. "You will fail. She knows we're coming."

"Because you told her?" asked Maddox.

"Because that is our logical next step," the professor said.

Maddox turned away. He wasn't sure what to make of all this. "Let's go," he said.

"Go where?" Ludendorff asked suspiciously.

"You and I have a meeting with the Lord High Admiral."

Ludendorff licked his lips.

"You're going," Maddox said. "You can't squirm out of it this time."

The professor's shoulders slumped, and he nodded. "When is the meeting?"

As if on cue, Galyan appeared. "Excuse me, gentlemen. There has been a change in plans. The Lord High Admiral is already on his way. He instructed me to listen in on your conversation and link it to him. He listened as well."

"What?" Ludendorff shouted. "That's an outrage. That's an invasion of privacy."

"Agreed," Galyan said. "I still suggest that you get ready to receive the Lord High Admiral and his security detail. They should be here within twenty minutes."

-85-

The Lord High Admiral almost seemed frail, as if the towering individual in his white uniform might have twisted and hollowed out.

Lord High Admiral Cook sat behind a large desk. His security people were outside the chamber. All he had to do was touch a button and they would rush inside, taking care of business.

Ludendorff sat before the large desk to the left. Maddox sat in the chair to the right. The Lord High Admiral eyed first one and then the other.

"The very thing we sought to avoid happened," Cook said in a low voice. "I wanted to preserve our fleet units. Instead, we've taken losses again. Worse, we've lost our best ship—the Destroyer. Without it and its twin, we never would have defeated the First Swarm Invasion."

Maddox would have liked to point out that the Destroyer did two mighty tasks: defeat the Swarm and stop the Juggernauts from destroying all life on Earth. That was a good record for a ship, any ship. Nothing lasted forever. But Maddox was certain the Lord High Admiral didn't want to hear that just now.

Cook stared at Ludendorff. "I don't know what to make of you, Professor."

For once, the Methuselah Man kept his mouth shut. Maybe the Lord High Admiral intimidated him. Maybe the security people outside intimidated him. Maybe he was playing it smart this time by not replying.

Cook sighed, closing his eyes. He seemed to settle back in his chair. Finally, the old man snored.

Maddox and Ludendorff traded glances.

Cook's second snore turned into a snort, and that made the old man's lips blubber. Cook jerked awake as his eyes snapped open.

Neither Maddox nor Ludendorff commented.

"Where was I?" Cook asked in a slurring voice. "Oh, yes, I remember. We staved off the first wave of the Old One's secret nightmare against Earth, against the Commonwealth. According to you, Captain, the Jotuns don't exist."

"Not in any meaningful way to hurt us," Maddox answered. "I suspect Doctor Meyers might attempt to revive some of them at a later date."

"Yes, yes," Cook said. "That's what I meant. The Jotuns are not a present threat. We destroyed the Android Fleet, the Juggernauts, and I'm about to unleash *Victory* at the Supermetals Planet. But it would seem that Lord Drakos presents a second threat. Could that threat come through pressuring the Emperor of the New Men to make another assault upon regular humanity?"

"I doubt it," Ludendorff said. "From every indication, that wasn't the direction of Lisa Meyers' thoughts."

"Oh," Cook said. "And you're privy to her inner thoughts, are you?"

"I, ah, misspoke," Ludendorff said.

"Did you?" asked Cook, as he eyed the professor with some of his former strength.

Ludendorff cleared his throat. "Now, see here—"

"I don't want to hear it," Cook said, interrupting. "I want to preserve the Commonwealth and build up our societal, industrial and fleet strength. Who knows when the Sovereign Hierarchy of Leviathan will attempt to use nexuses to reach us? Who knows what secret plan Lord Drakos is attempting to hatch? If you fail to capture Lisa Meyers at the Supermetals Planet, Captain, where will she go to stir up trouble against us next?"

"May I make a suggestion, sir?" Maddox asked.

Cook stared at him before nodding.

"Regroup the Fleet," Maddox said. "Rather than putting warships in each system, pick two or three places and mass the Fleet there."

"You don't understand," Cook said. "The rumblings and troubles were coming from every direction in the Commonwealth. Mass riots, assassinations, space piracy—it was as if one world after another was going mad. The only thing left was spreading the Fleet thin to cover everywhere. I think many of the troubles came from the Yon-Soth nightmare ray. Star Watch marines have been forced to kill tens of thousands of rioters and other troublemakers on a hundred different worlds."

Cook frowned. "I think the nightmare ray has worn off some, or maybe those most susceptible to it are dead. But there are indications that many of our troubles were planned and well executed by hidden agencies."

"If that's the case," Maddox said, "that's a job for Intelligence and a world's local police force. The Fleet protects us from foreign invaders, while Intelligence and the local police root out domestic—"

"Listen to me carefully, son," Cook said, interrupting and leaning across the desk. "I did not call you here to lecture me on my job. I'm the one who called you here to lecture you on your job."

"Yes, sir," Maddox said.

Cook nodded, leaning back again. "The worlds were going crazy, or enough people were that the Fleet had to step in and keep order. We staved off the worst of the madness. But we haven't found the perpetrators that stirred up chaos for foreign powers."

"I, ah, have a different thought, sir," Maddox said slowly.

Cook waited.

"Perhaps we could have the Brigadier running Intelligence again," Maddox said.

Cook did nothing for several seconds, although finally he nodded. "I second your idea, but she is presently undergoing special therapy."

In alarm, Maddox sat straighter. "I'd like to see her, sir."

"Not yet," Cook said.

Despite his reprimand a few moments ago, Maddox asked, "What is this special therapy?"

Cook pursed his lips as if choosing his words carefully. "I'd like to tell you, son, but I can't. If it helps you any, she wanted to undergo this. It was her decision."

Maddox's face had become blank. He didn't like any of this.

"I know you two are close," Cook said. "I appreciate that. Ask me about her in six months' time. Then we'll know one way or another if the therapy is going to work."

"Does she only have six months to live, sir?" Maddox asked in a strained voice.

Cook's head jerked back in shock. "Confound it, son. Why would you ask something like that?"

Maddox waited tensely.

Cook took a deep breath. "She's fine physically. It's…it's her mental condition. I'm asking you, Captain, give us six months. Besides, you don't have time to see her now. I need you to race to the Supermetals Planet. If Meyers isn't there—well, catch her if you can. If you can't, kill her. Afterward, I need you to go to the Vega System."

"My original assignment," Maddox said.

"This is critical," Cook said. "According to our best intelligence, there are hints concerning Lord Drakos in the Vega System. That's the last place we know he went, anyway. And there's something else going on at Vega II that ties in with some of the other worlds. For certain there's a big money leak in the Vega System helping to fund other rebellions in other systems."

"*Victory* might not be the best—"

"Son," Cook said, interrupting. "You're our best Intelligence agent. I need you to check out Vega II. That's provided you capture or kill Lisa Meyers."

Maddox looked away. He wanted to see Mary O'Hara now. He had questions to ask, things to say to her. But if she was mentally…unwell, maybe six months from now would be better.

"What about him, sir?" Maddox asked, jerking a thumb at Ludendorff.

Cook became stern. "Given his past record—"

"I should go with Maddox," Ludendorff said quickly. "My superior intellect has saved *Victory* more than once this mission. Besides, the captain needs me if he hopes to catch Doctor Meyers, and I can undoubtedly help him crack the Vega Case."

Cook's nostrils flared. Finally, he faced Maddox. "It's your choice, Captain."

"The professor is treacherous," Maddox said. "But he knows a thing or two the rest of us often don't. I can still use him, provided I don't have to put a bullet in his brain first."

Ludendorff held his peace, but it looked difficult for him.

"Good luck, son," Cook said, standing, holding out his hand. "I hate to send you on your way like this. We've won an important battle. You've brought home priceless data about more of our galaxy. But we must capture or kill Meyers, and I don't know who else can crack the Vega Case."

"This has been a long one, sir."

Cook nodded as he released the captain's hand. He eyed Ludendorff. "I have mixed feelings about you, Professor. Your selfishness almost killed everyone on Earth."

"Now, see here—" Ludendorff said.

"No!" Cook said harshly. "Don't say it. Otherwise, I'm summoning my people. Do I make myself clear?"

A half-abashed Ludendorff gave the barest of nods.

Cook stared at the professor a little longer and finally turned away with a sound of disgust. "Go," he said, without looking. "And heaven help you if you ever harm Captain Maddox or his crew."

-86-

Victory moved through the Alpha Centauri System, heading toward the Supermetals Planet. Every sensor strained to detect any cloaked vessel or hidden mine.

Maddox had been in contact with the Lord High Admiral via the Builder comm device. Cook had been in touch with the people on Pluto running the Builder Scanner. The *Glorious Kent* had risen from the depths of Jupiter and hauled butt through selected folds, heading toward the Alpha Centauri System. The last sight the people on Pluto had was the *Glorious Kent* parking in orbit around the Supermetals Planet. Soon thereafter, the strange hauler had simply disappeared from their screen.

"The hauler entered planetary orbit," Maddox said from his captain's chair. "Presumably, Meyers sent shuttles onto the planet, and her people collected supermetals, bringing them upstairs. Afterward—*poof*, the hauler was no longer visible."

"Are you asking for opinions?" Ludendorff said.

"If you have them," Maddox said.

"I do," the professor said. "Clearly, Meyers has ancient machinery aboard her vessel. Likely, much of that machinery no longer worked. Enough did, however, to allow her down into Jupiter."

"Get to the point," Maddox said.

"Meyers or her people used the supermetals to fix the hauler's cloaking device. Who knows what else they fixed or are in the process of fixing?"

"Yes. That makes sense," Maddox said. "Valerie, Galyan, Andros, I want the three of you working overtime. Find the *Glorious Kent* before it surprises us."

"And if the hauler has already left the star system?" Ludendorff asked.

Maddox shook his head. "I don't think it has."

"What do you base this on?" asked Ludendorff.

"Vengeance, hatred, the desire to get even with us on Lisa Meyers' part," Maddox said.

Victory slowed its velocity as it neared the dark and mysterious chthonian planet. Once, this had been the core for a Jupiter-sized gas giant. In those days, the core would have never known the colds of space or allowed anyone to see it naked like this.

Not so very long ago, Alpha Centauri had been a multi-star system. Alpha Centauri "A" had possessed a mass 1.1 and a luminosity 1.519 times that of the Sun. Alpha Centauri "B" was a smaller and cooler star. The double stars had orbited a common point between them that had varied between a Pluto-Sun to Saturn-Sun orbit. Alpha Centauri "C" or Proxima Centauri was a red dwarf. It had been gravitationally bound to the other two, but had orbited 15,000 AUs from the others. That was approximately 500 times Neptune's orbit.

Now, though, the star Alpha Centauri "A" was no more. It had gone supernova when a wounded Ska had entered it for healing. This, then, had become a binary star system, with the fluctuations from the event having finally sorted themselves out.

When going supernova, the star Alpha Centauri "A" had slaughtered billions, destroying ships, habitats, nearby planets and blasting the distant Jupiter-sized gas giant. The supernova had blown away the planet's gases, leaving the core intact. Heavy molecules from the exploding star—created through nucleosynthesis—had struck the core, creating or lodging supermetals in abundance on and under the immediate surface.

A mysterious force had scrubbed the radiation that had bathed the entire binary system. Alpha Centauri was usable by humans once more.

"I have detected an anomaly," Galyan announced.

"Where?" asked Maddox.

"In orbit around the dark planet."

"Can you measure the anomaly's mass?"

"Negative. I just know its position."

"What do you think, Professor?" Maddox asked.

"Before I answer that—Galyan, where are the mines?"

"Are you referring to the likely planetary supermetal mines?" Galyan asked.

"Precisely," Ludendorff said.

"I have not searched for them and thus do not know their location," Galyan said.

Ludendorff glanced at Maddox.

"Do so now, please," Maddox said.

Galyan's eyelids fluttered.

"Sir," Valerie said, "I'm detecting something fast and semi-cloaked heading for us."

"Strengthen shields," Maddox said. "Galyan, find the cloaked missile—if it's a missile. Then target it with the neutron cannon."

"I am on it, sir," Galyan said.

"How far is the thing from us?" Maddox asked Valerie.

The lieutenant studied her panel. "Three million kilometers and closing, sir."

"Galyan," Maddox said.

"It is a missile," the holoimage said. "It—"

At that moment, an antimatter explosion burst on the main screen. It was three million kilometers away. The warhead must have possessed nosecone-targeting rods, as hard gamma radiation speared three million kilometers and struck *Victory's* strengthened shield.

"The shields are holding," Andros reported.

Another explosion from almost as far away heralded another gamma radiation strike.

Maddox leaned forward on his chair as a third explosion from a different area of space, but a margin closer, did the same thing.

"The shields can't withstand these hits forever," Andros said.

"Increase velocity, Mr. Maker," Maddox said. "Head for the anomaly orbiting the planet."

"The anomaly is no longer in stationary orbit," Galyan said. "It appears to be circling the planet, possibly to use as a shield against us."

"That's the hauler," Maddox said. "Ready the disrupter cannon—"

"Captain," Ludendorff said. "Are you forgetting about the hauler's deflection field? If you fire at the hauler—"

"I've forgotten nothing," Maddox said evenly. "Now tell me this. Why are they running? I'll tell you—because we can hurt them and they're afraid."

"Logical," Ludendorff said. "But hurt them with what?"

Maddox considered that. "Are you suggesting missiles would be better than beams?"

"I wasn't," Ludendorff said. "But that might be what Meyers's fears."

Maddox stroked his chin. If he fired missiles from this range, the cloaked enemy missiles—if there were any left—might take out the Star Watch missiles. Was Meyers enticing him to use the disrupter cannon on the *Glorious Kent?* That seemed probable. Would the disrupter beam deflect back against *Victory?*

"Galyan, find the rest of the cloaked missiles. We'll concentrate on taking those out first."

"What about the *Glorious Kent?*" asked Ludendorff.

"Professor," Maddox said. "You stick to your area of expertise, and I'll stick to mine."

"Meaning you don't have a method yet," Ludendorff said.

Maddox debated having marines escort the professor off the bridge, but decided against it. He might need the professor's expertise soon.

"The neutron beam is firing," Galyan said.

Maddox watched the main screen. The purple beam struck at seemingly nothing. Seconds later, the "nothing" ignited.

"Scratch one hidden missile," Galyan said.

"Good work," Maddox said.

"Thank you, sir," Galyan said. "I appreciate that."

Seconds passed.

"Sir," Valerie said. "We're being hailed."

"Galyan got her attention," Maddox said. "Go ahead, Lieutenant, put Doctor Meyers on the main screen."

-87-

On the main screen, Doctor Lisa Meyers, the Methuselah Woman, wore a silver suit like a New Man. She did not look like a New Man, however. She was stunning in her silver outfit, with her prominent breasts and long blonde hair that framed her breathtaking features. The eyes were the most amazing, compelling and captivating part of her.

"Was I right, or was I right?" Ludendorff muttered. "She's a beauty, all right. One of a kind."

"Captain Maddox," Meyers purred in her sexy voice. "You are a resourceful soldier. It is a pity we are on opposite sides. Perhaps we should…remedy that."

"I'm happily married, thank you."

"Then why are you staring at me so lustfully?"

"You mistake my look, Doctor."

"No. I don't think I do, as I happen to know that look anywhere. You wish to remove my garments and mount me. At least have the decency to admit it."

Maddox smiled. "Mount you on a wall as a hunting trophy… I suppose you're right. I would like that."

"Don't be crude."

"You're my enemy, Doctor, as you wish to destroy what I love. It isn't crudity that causes me to speak like this, but simple honesty. You are a menace to civilization—"

Purified hatred swirled in Meyers' eyes. The intensity and suddenness of it shocked the captain into silence. The look was a palpable force that crossed the ether. In that moment, she didn't seem human, but a demon wearing a human disguise.

"Do you call your puny society a civilization?" Meyers mocked. "No! You are parasites, scavengers feeding off a greater civilization's petrified carcass. You ape your betters but are no better than dogs wearing clothes. You are disgusting."

"You're human just like us," Maddox said.

"I *was* human, but now I am something much greater."

"What are you?" asked Maddox, frankly curious at what she would say.

"I have evolved much higher than human, Captain. When the New Men talk about being superior, it is what I really am."

"I didn't realize."

Meyers shook her head. "You think you're so clever. I have been away a long time, but I'm back, Captain Maddox. Your puny Star Watch may have thwarted me this time. It will not go so well for you next time."

"Why not help us, Doctor? Help mankind to—"

"Do you believe me such an ingrate to the Builders that I would leave their service in order to help parasites rummaging through the carcass of their betters? Never! I will show the Builders my eternal gratitude for having chosen and bettering me. I will help them return to their former greatness."

"The Builders are gone," Maddox said.

"Not all of them are gone," Meyers said. "I have my Builder. I will restore him to full life. Then, with him as my guiding star, I shall seek out other Builders and help them rekindle their passion for living. The Builders will return, and they shall sweep aside your paltry society to make room for something infinitely superior. Can you comprehend my great purpose yet?"

"I see that you're insane, Doctor Meyers. I imagine the Yon-Soth ray unhinged your mind. Let us help you. Let us restore your mind—"

Meyers laughed, and it had a maniacal edge. "You have unwittingly aided me, Captain, by your earlier voyage and what you found. Do not seek to find me right away. I will be gone for a time. But then I shall return, and the glory of the Builders will follow. Humanity is doomed, Captain Maddox.

They have been allowed this small hour. But the grossness and the pettiness of your civilization will soon be washed away in a tide of blood."

"Is that really you speaking, or is that the Yon-Soth in you speaking?"

The look of purified hatred shined through her eyes once more. Then, she smiled in such a vampirish manner—a sinister and seductive thing—that it caused trepidation in Maddox's heart.

"I failed this round," Meyers said. "The next, however…"

"Sir," Valerie said. "There's a build-up of forces around her ship."

"Put it on the main screen," Maddox snapped.

Meyers disappeared. In her place was a corner of the Supermetals Planet and the *Glorious Kent*. A blue nimbus circled the hauler, and then it seemed as if a bright opening tore in the very fabric of space. Powers swirled there, and the *Glorious Kent* entered the rift, the rift closed, and the ancient hauler was gone.

"What just happened?" Maddox asked.

"That," Ludendorff said, "is an excellent question. I suspect it will be some time before I can give you an accurate answer."

-88-

Thirty-six hours later, Ludendorff concluded that the rift opening had been a superior form of jump drive. The assumption was that Lisa Meyers had gone somewhere far from the Alpha Centauri System.

"I think it's possible the *Glorious Kent* traveled a thousand light-years or so in a bound," the professor said in a cafeteria. He ate sparingly of broccoli and beans.

"Are you suggesting she went to the Sovereign Hierarchy of Leviathan?" Maddox asked, nursing a beer.

"I deem that a possibility," the professor said, "although not necessarily likely. You saw her there at the end. She was unhinged. Who knows what she was thinking."

"The Yon-Soth seemed to be in her," Maddox said, who studied Meyers in his mind's eye.

Ludendorff looked up from his plate. "I don't subscribe to the transfer of souls. I'm frankly surprised you do."

Maddox blinked away the mind's eye memory and considered the professor's statement, shrugging. "Call it Yon-Soth conditioning, then. Maybe the Yon-Soth ultimately wanted her to find more of his kind and somehow programmed her to do it."

"That is not rigorous thinking, sir. Doctor Meyers is clearly fixated on the Builders. She has a Builder in storage, presumably. Restoring him to life, to vigor, strikes me as her more likely quest."

"I suppose you're right," Maddox said. "She did tell us her objective. Why doubt her on that?"

"Anyway, it's out of our hands for the moment." Ludendorff stirred the beans with his fork and abruptly pushed the plate away. "Cook knows about the location of the supermetal mine and is sending people to Alpha Centauri. We're finished with it. Now we're supposed to clean up this Lord Drakos Affair. I wonder if we'll have as much success against the New Man as we did last time we tried to capture him."

Maddox became thoughtful. After the *Glorious Kent* had vanished, he'd had Galyan locate the mine on the chthonian planet. Then, a survey team had gone down and explored the facility. The mine had still been in working order, although all the storage bins had been cleaned out.

Maddox sipped his beer. He'd neither captured nor killed Doctor Meyers. He considered her a long-term threat to the Commonwealth, but suspected it might be several years before they saw her again. She was obviously dedicated to her goal, but struck him as someone who might plan more carefully and thoroughly next time.

Maddox took another thoughtful sip. The starship was on its way to the Vega System, and should reach Vega II—Pandora—in three days.

He'd been reading Intelligence files on the situation, and now switched topics with Ludendorff, bringing up their next assignment. The professor didn't have much to say on the subject, although by the end of the talk, his curiosity seemed to have been piqued.

During the journey, Maddox, Galyan, Riker and Ludendorff all read more Intelligence data. The Adok holoimage became absorbed with the problem.

Galyan came to Maddox several times with new ideas and possibilities. Finally, the captain sat down with Galyan and pored over critical data. They read dossiers on various people. Ludendorff joined them, and he bent his considerable intellect to the problem.

A day out from the Vega System, Ludendorff summoned Maddox and Galyan to his science laboratory.

"I think I have it," Ludendorff said. "I've solved the puzzle."

"As have I," Galyan said.

"Nonsense," Ludendorff said. "You're claiming to have out-reasoned me?"

"That would depend," Galyan said. "When did you solve the problem?"

"Does your answer concern Vint Diem?" Ludendorff countered.

"Vint Diem the professional gambler," Galyan said. "Yes. He is clearly a former Spacer adept at using his—"

"Confound you, you pile of alien circuits and computer programming," Ludendorff said. "When did you realize he was Lord Drakos' Pandora agent?"

"I do not believe that Vint Diem is," Galyan said.

"Ah-ha!" Ludendorff shouted. "You're not so clever after all. Vint Diem is most certainly Drakos' agent. That's how Drakos is funneling masses of money into his various underworld rebellions. It's quite obvious once you know what to look for."

"I must protest, Professor," Galyan said. "Vint Diem's operations strike me as a Spacer ploy to reintroduce themselves into a corner of Human Space."

"No, no," Ludendorff said. "The operation has a New Man taint to it. It's ultra-aggressive and uses Pandora's function with brutal efficiency." He turned to Maddox. "I suggest a normal Intelligence sting and kidnapping. That way, it won't appear as if we're trying to trap Drakos, but figure out his chief agent's plan, and, I suppose, shut off the flow of money from Pandora to the rest of the Commonwealth."

"Perhaps if you start your reasoning from the beginning…" Maddox said.

Ludendorff grinned. "It's a good thing for you I've never taken up Intelligence work. I could run rings around your Brigadier and most probably around you, too."

"No doubt," Maddox murmured. "Now, from the beginning…"

"Of course," Ludendorff said. "Pay attention, Galyan. Maybe you'll learn something."

"You have my attention, Professor," the holoimage said. "Please proceed."

Ludendorff did more than that. After explaining his reasoning in great depth, he produced a small tech item he'd built. He then suggested a way to carry out the assignment that would fool any New Men observers left behind as a security measure.

"I do not believe Lord Drakos wants us to capture and question Vint Diem," Ludendorff said. "Therefore, what I'm suggesting needs to be done subtly."

Maddox had been listening to Ludendorff for some time. The complexity of the mission...and that they'd missed capturing Lord Drakos last time... Maybe he would use some of Ludendorff's suggestions once they reached the Vega System.

-89-

"What is that?"

Maddox looked up to see a big security man from the main Vega Casino on Pandora staring at the analyzer beeping softly in his hands. The captain thought he'd held the analyzer in such a way that no one in the gigantic crowd would notice.

Maddox stood in a vast chamber bigger than any sports stadium. The ceiling was fifty feet high with expensive murals everywhere showing scenes Michelangelo might have painted during the High Renaissance. Maybe ten thousand people played at the roulette, craps, blackjack tables, spinners, slots or other gambling areas.

This was the high stakes room of the Carlota Casino on Pandora of the Vega System. It was famous throughout the Commonwealth. Here, billions of credits exchanged hands daily, enough of a percentage going to the house that the high stakes room not only paid the majority of planetary taxes, but the majority of the Vega System taxes as well.

The ten thousand or more people were millionaires or higher. All wore expense garments, some of them outrageously so. Many had personal bodyguards, although none of the thick-necked guards were legally armed, having passed several stiff security scans to make sure.

Instead of his Star Watch uniform, Maddox wore a black suit and tie, as he was working undercover. *Victory* had parked in orbit around Pandora two days ago. They were implementing ninety percent of the plan Ludendorff had suggested. Their target was Vint Diem, but they had already picked up two Vint-Diem lookalikes. Each had committed suicide and supposedly ended the trail right there.

This time, Maddox hoped to pinpoint the real Vint Diem and render him unconscious before the man could kill himself.

Galyan had determined the source of the kill-order in the two lookalikes—a New Man post-hypnotic command. Vint Diem definitely belonged to Lord Drakos's secret organization. What would they find if they could interrogate the former Spacer? It must be critically sensitive information if Drakos was using post-hypnotic kill commands.

"I asked you a question," the security man said in a gruff voice.

The man was big, practically hulking—he clearly outweighed Maddox and stood a trifle taller, too. The man wore a green casino security suit and had an abnormally wide face. That indicated genetic modification. The man's face was like a block, with thin black hair, a heavy forehead and a Neanderthal-like bridge of bone over his eyes. The pupils were not normal, but like black pin-dots. If that wasn't enough, the shoulders were massive, indicating great strength. The sausage-sized fingers looked capable of crushing the life out of an ordinary man.

The security man reminded Maddox of Kane from long ago, a genetic experiment from the same 2-G Rouen Colony where Meta had been born and raised. That such a man questioned him now was highly suspicious. Maybe Maddox's team hadn't been moving as secretly as he'd thought.

"Give me that," the security man said, using his chin to point at the device in Maddox's hands.

"You mean this?" Maddox asked, holding up the analyzer. The motion was a signal.

The small cube-shaped device was still quietly beeping. It was Ludendorff's invention. Maddox wanted to study the readings because he'd just aimed it at the target, at the real Vint Diem, it would seem.

"Give it *now*," the security man said, taking a step nearer.

Maddox shifted mental gears, nodding meekly while giving the man an ingratiating smile.

Instead of mollifying the security man, his thick features tightened. "Playing tricks, eh?" the man asked. "I know all about you, *Maddox.*"

The captain's gut clenched, although nothing showed on his face. "Are you saying the game's up?"

"Give me that," the man said, holding out his left hand.

"Of course," Maddox said. He set the analyzer, which had just stopped beeping, onto the man's meaty outstretched palm.

The big man looked at Maddox with surprise. "That's it?" he asked. "No—" The man grunted as he arched up onto his toes. He began turning around—

Maddox stepped closer yet, grabbing the outstretched wrist that held the small cube. He stopped the man from turning—it took every ounce of the captain's strength to do so. Then he plucked the analyzer from the man's trembling palm.

From underneath his bony ridge of brow, the man stared at Maddox, and his mouth moved slackly as if trying to form words.

Meta moved from behind the man. She wore an amazing dress of sparkling sequins that showed off her cleavage to great effect. She had a tiny purse made of the same sequined material. She deposited something small into the purse, clicking it shut. That something had a needle on the end, which she'd just jabbed into the back of the security agent, injecting him with a quick-acting knockout drug.

Despite himself, the captain gazed at his wife's wonderful butt, emphasized by her high heels, and the flash of her legs as her slit dress parted just enough to tantalize his desires.

Then Maddox regained his poise, pocketing the analyzer, holding up the extraordinarily heavy man as the victim's knees buckled. Despite the strain, the captain eyed the throng around him, searching for someone watching him.

For just a second, he saw a tall individual with the long gaunt face of a New Man. The New Man must be using body paint to mask his normal golden skin.

The instant passed as the observer blended with the crowd.

This could get tricky. New Men thought faster than regular men did, faster even than Maddox did. Even so, they were finally closing in on the real Vint Diem. Maddox was not going to let the New Man scare him away.

"Galyan," Maddox whispered.

There was a slight shimmer ahead of him. That was a nearly invisible Galyan. During the trip here, Andros had fixed the holoimage projector. *Victory* could once again project the Adok holoimage many thousands of kilometers.

"Captain," Galyan whispered.

Maddox covered his mouth, pretending to cough as he asked, "Have you detected any New Men?"

"I did not know I was supposed to search for New—"

"Never mind that," Maddox said, interrupting. "Search the high stakes room for New Men. If you find any, report to me immediately."

"Yes, sir," Galyan said, pausing. "By the way, sir, I see you are holding up an unconscious man. The strain is showing on you. I think several ladies have noticed."

"Give me a flash."

"Here?"

"Forty meters to my left. Do it now, Galyan." Maddox spoke the last words in a pant.

Seconds later, a newly located Galyan flashed, discharging harmless energy from his holoimage—it was another high-tech feature that Andros had repaired.

People screamed, as the flash simulated a sonic grenade's explosion.

Maddox lowered the security man and walked away nonchalantly. After several steps, he glanced at Meta.

She shook her head as she fixed her hair before a mirror attached to a column. The headshake meant no one had seen him set down the security-uniformed man.

Maddox bit his lower lip and put a hand in a jacket pocket.

Casino security men flowed into the flash area, calming patrons and searching for the source. Nothing more had happened after the one brilliant flare of light.

Maddox glanced at the craps table where Vint Diem stood, holding dice. Everyone over there was still looking at the area of flash. Then someone at the table said something so the throng turned back to the green felt table, glancing at the shooter. Vint Diem grinned back at them and began shaking the dice in his right closed hand that he held just above his head.

It was illegal to hold craps dice with both hands, as some players cheated by switching dice that way.

Maddox slid up against a nearby column and took out the analyzer. Would it beep again? It was time to find out.

-90-

Maddox fiddled with the cube's tiny controls while aiming the thing at the shooter.

Shooter was the name for the player rolling the dice at a craps table. In this instance, the shooter—Vint Diem—was a small man with narrow shoulders and short dark hair that stood straight up as if someone had just frightened him. He wore a garish orange suit with padded shoulders and a silly orange band around his forehead. He also wore dark sunglasses that completely protected his eyes from any stray light, including from the sides.

Vint Diem had the appearance of someone of Southeast Asian origin from Earth. Not that Vint had been born on Earth. In fact, he must have been born a Spacer.

Many Spacers were of Southeast Asian origin. They were also small like Vint Diem. That he wore dark sunglasses like that could mean he was accustomed to wearing dark goggles. The most damning indicator that the man had been born a Spacer was that the analyzer beeped softly in Maddox's hands.

This time, Maddox studied the readings. Ludendorff had made the analyzer a few days ago. After looking at the readings, Maddox scanned the people moving about his general vicinity.

No casino security-agent headed for him. No particular person that he could tell headed his way. That did not mean no one walked toward him, just that no person seemed to do so in a deliberate manner with him as the object. There were security people around the fallen man that Meta had stabbed. Several of them knelt as they examined the unconscious bruiser. Two looked up sharply, scanning people. Maybe they'd found the wound where Meta had made the jab.

The chief security honcho—a slender man in a dark green suit—asked a question, listening to the replies from his operatives. Afterward, the chief's eyes narrowed as he spoke into a comm unit on his cuff.

Maddox waited to see if any of the security personnel would notice him. The big man had called him by name. If the casino knew about him... The chief honcho looked his way and made no appreciable indication that he'd noticed him. Could the chief be that good of an actor?

Maddox decided no. So that meant... That meant the former Rouen Colony man had been working undercover for Drakos. Did the chief honcho over there realize they had a security imposter lying on the floor? It seemed quite likely.

That would give the security people something to worry about. They would be on even higher alert, though. Since this was the high stakes room, with thousands of millionaires and billionaires in their midst, just how much higher could that alert go? Security was already tight.

Maddox knew personnel would start checking security cameras, but he wasn't too worried. Galyan had already tampered with their systems.

It was time to head to Vint Diem, the moneyman who paid for military-grade weapons and battlesuit shipments that went many places throughout the Commonwealth.

Maddox scanned people as he laughed as if he'd drunk too much. That helped him to blend in with those around him. His scan did not spot any other hidden guards.

He inhaled, shifted mental gears and adjusted the analyzer as he made another sweep of the shooter. The cube beeped softly as it had before.

There was no doubt about it now. Vint Diem had a technological and surgically inserted power source inside his body just like Shu 15 and Mako 21 had had in their bodies. The power...what Maddox read on the analyzer wasn't transduction or hyper-induction. At least, he did not think Vint Diem was attempting to read neural nets—minds—or read the invisible electromagnetic pulses around him. According to the analyzer, Vint Diem was using the technological modifications to practice telekinesis. That was moving objects with one's mind. Only in this instance, Vint Diem used the modifications in him to move the—

"Dice," Maddox whispered.

In other words, the former Spacer was using his tech ability to cheat at craps. If Ludendorff was correct, Vint Diem used his power to make the dice dance in any combination he desired. Here in the high stakes room at the Carlota Casino on Pandora, that could mean billions of credits. In other words, Vint Diem was funding secret arms deal with the credits he stole at the highest stakes craps table in Human Space.

Maddox pocketed the analyzer, adjusted his tie and pasted a cool grin on his face as he headed for the craps table. It was time to kidnap Vint Diem and take him upstairs to *Victory*. He had questions for the former Spacer. The answers should lead him to Lord Drakos, defeating two birds with one stone.

Maddox would also seal off funds for disruptive arms on many planets. Even better, he would finally catch the hardliner Drakos and end that threat to the Commonwealth for good.

-91-

Only it didn't quite work out that way. As Maddox headed for the craps table, a tall urbane fellow in a flowing blue robe and scarlet turban intercepted him. The man had a long face and an exaggeratedly long nose.

"Excuse me," the tall man said.

Maddox halted, and it took him a moment to realize he was looking at a New Man in disguise. Someone had surgically altered the nose, or it was a fine piece of mask technology.

"You realize *what* I am," the turbaned man said, "but you don't know who I am or who I represent."

"I do," Maddox said, slipping his left hand into a jacket pocket. He gripped a small stun disc, ready to pull it out and incapacitate Lord Drakos' operative.

"I am not a hardliner—in your vague terminology," the disguised New Man said. "I am here at the behest of the Emperor."

"For what reason?" asked Maddox.

The turbaned spy closed his eyes for just a moment, as if holding himself back. He opened his eyes a moment later, and there was an intense coldness to them.

"I am here partly because I have exceptional patience in dealing with submen. A moment," the spy said, holding up his right palm. "You have a stun disc in your pocket. I'm well aware of that, and I know that your woman took out one of Vint Diem's guardians. It was ineptly done, but that can't be helped now."

"You're Vint Diem's second guardian, I warrant," Maddox said.

The spy showed his teeth in an approximation of a smile. "You're acclaimed as one of Star Watch's best Intelligence operatives. I will admit you've had an amazing string of luck, but do not think that you are a match for me and my people."

"There are only two of you down here," Maddox said, guessing.

"Even if you're right, that would make us more than a match your bumbling team."

Maddox forced himself to relax. "Why would the Emperor send his top spy to Pandora?"

"You're speaking rhetorically, not actually questioning me?"

"Yes," Maddox said, knowing how touchy New Men could be.

"The reason should be obvious."

"You're here to stop Vint Diem?"

The disguised New Man sighed. "Perhaps not as obvious to half-breeds and submen as it should be," he murmured. "I will explain, then. Some time ago, the Lord High Admiral spoke to the Emperor and related certain facts and ideas. After a few hours of repose, the Emperor decided that peace would be in our mutual interests. Thus, he sent me to put an end to Drakos's unseemly operation on Pandora. I have observed this Vint Diem and cataloged his back channels. You are about to upset my final sting. With it, I will have completed the data-sweep."

"You're telling me to butt out of your operation?" Maddox asked in disbelief.

"So it is true," the New Man said. "Captain Maddox has a modicum of intelligence. Your genes bred true. I congratulate you on your superiority from the common ruck of submen."

"You could be lying and could be Drakos's man."

"That is a possibility, but I am not."

"Fine," Maddox said. "Here is what I propose—"

"A moment," the New Man said, holding up a palm once more. "You are about to suggest things that would not only upset me, but put me in a dreadful position. I do not want to be honor-bound to destroy you for insulting me. Thus, I will give you a proposal. Stay out of my way. I will kidnap Vint Diem and take him far from here. In return..."

The New Man looked away. "This is quite distasteful, but I serve my Emperor." He sighed and peered at a spot above Maddox's head. "I will give you the back channels. Star Watch can then apprehend a thousand individuals and shut down Drakos's network throughout the Commonwealth."

"I need Vint Diem," Maddox said.

"Why?"

"I must know Lord Drakos's plans so Star Watch can counter him, perhaps kill him."

"Hmm..." The New Man said. "Drakos has vanished. In fact, he has left Human Space on a secret mission of grim portent."

"May I ask how you know this?"

"We had a plant on his ship," the New Man said. "The plant is dead now, but not before he told us that Drakos found something in the outer Vega System."

"May I ask what he found?"

"The exact object or objects elude me," the New Man said. "You are welcome to look in the outer system, but I doubt you will find any clues. Drakos will have...hmm, disposed of them."

"That is reason I desire Vint Diem."

"He won't know either," the New Man said. "And before you ask me more, I'll tell you how I know this. Drakos follows standard spy procedures. He will not have let Vint Diem know anything about his greater projects."

"Why do I feel as if you're being completely honest with me?"

"The Emperor recognizes the Commonwealth's present weakness. It distresses him, as he does not want to entice others into attacking or suggesting we attack the submen again."

"The Emperor is generous to his former enemies."

"I assure you, it has nothing to do with that," the New Man said. "You—as in the mass of submen—have a reservoir of young and nubile women. We have not yet solved that particular genetic problem—we sire sons, never daughters. Perhaps once we sire daughters, we shall swiftly conquer the Commonwealth."

"Perhaps so," Maddox said.

"Do not attempt to mock me, Captain, or I will rescind my offer, and the Commonwealth will have to stagger along, wounded and bleeding."

Maddox stared at the disguised New Man. "What will you do with Vint Diem?"

"Take him far from Human Space, Captain. He won't bother the Commonwealth ever again."

"That sounds ominous."

"It is, but not for the submen. More about this, I will not say."

Maddox looked away.

"You must decide now," the New Man said. "Accept the Emperor's gift. It is generous and will strengthen the Commonwealth and Star Watch. It will help induce peace longer than otherwise between our dominions."

"Lord Drakos found something in the outer Vega System."

"You are repeating what I just told you."

"Do you have a hint as to what the something might be?"

"I have a hint, yes, but will only tell you if you agree to my proposal."

Maddox debated lying to the New Man. He sensed the other spoke the truth, though. It all seemed reasonable the way the New Man put it. Could the Emperor really be trying to help Star Watch?

"Yes," Maddox heard himself say. "I agree."

The New Man nodded. "I will send you the information in a day." With that, the tall man in the blue robe and scarlet turban turned and headed for the craps table.

Maddox moved back, and he began signaling his people. This was a risk. He was actually trusting a New Man, but he had a gut feeling about this. He just hoped he hadn't guessed wrong.

-92-

Ludendorff shook his head in dismay as Maddox pulled everyone out of the casino and back aboard *Victory*. He told them what had happened. Meta displayed shock. Riker eyed him and finally nodded somberly.

A day later, a shuttle approached *Victory*. It landed in the hangar bay, and ended up being a drone shuttle. Aboard it was a packet. In the packet was detailed information about Lord Drakos's money and equipment ring. Pandora funded twenty-three different worlds.

"This is amazing," Riker said, after studying the information.

"The New Man kept his word," Maddox said.

There was one other item of information. It concerned Lord Drakos's quest. The Emperor's spy believed that Drakos had found the location of Commander Thrax Ti Ix's hybrid fleet. What's more, Drakos appeared to be seeking out Thrax in order to make a proposal to the Swarm creature.

"This is it," Maddox told Ludendorff later. "This is the second shoe. If Drakos could have brought Thrax's warships together with the Juggernauts… they might have done enough damage to entice the rest of the New Men to reinvade the Commonwealth."

"You could be right," Ludendorff said. "The Commonwealth needs peace more than ever. That means we have to stop Drakos from finding Thrax."

"First," Maddox said. "We have to tell the Lord High Admiral about this. It's time to end all the rebellions in the Commonwealth. Then, we have to strengthen Star Watch. We've won breathing space, and our Yon-Soth-induced enemies did not hit us all at once. We've even managed to work with the Emperor of the New Men."

"Progress," Ludendorff said.

"Progress," Maddox agreed.

The two men studied each other, and each laughed at the absurdity of the situation.

Then, Maddox gave orders for Valerie to plot a course for Earth. It was time to give the crew a break while Intelligence operatives and police on twenty-three planets began taking down Drakos's underworld network.

Star Watch had won another round in the eternal fight to keep humanity alive, kicking and free in a harsh interstellar community.

"I'll talk to you later, Professor," Maddox said, getting up. "It's time I told Meta that she can pick a spot to go dancing once we reach Earth."

Ludendorff nodded, and he watched the captain leave the bridge. Then, the Methuselah Man sighed quietly to himself, wondering what Dana was doing on Brahma III.

THE END

SF Books by Vaughn Heppner

LOST STARSHIP SERIES:
The Lost Starship
The Lost Command
The Lost Destroyer
The Lost Colony
The Lost Patrol
The Lost Planet
The Lost Earth
The Lost Artifact
The Lost Star Gate
The Lost Supernova

DOOM STAR SERIES:
Star Soldier
Bio Weapon
Battle Pod
Cyborg Assault
Planet Wrecker
Star Fortress
Task Force 7 (Novella)

Visit VaughnHeppner.com for more information

Printed in Poland
by Amazon Fulfillment
Poland Sp. z o.o., Wrocław